S0-BBV-202

SOLDIER NO MORE

SOLDIER NO MORE

A NOVEL

by

ANTHONY PRICE

LONDON
VICTOR GOLLANCZ LTD
1990

First published in Great Britain 1981
by Victor Gollancz Ltd,
14 Henrietta Street, London WC2E 8QJ
This edition 1990

© Anthony Price 1981

ISBN 0 575 03028 3

Photoset in Great Britain by
Rowland Phototypesetting Ltd, Bury St Edmunds, Suffolk
and printed by St Edmundsbury Press Ltd,
Bury St Edmunds, Suffolk

*For Jeanne and
Elwyn Blacker*

CONTENTS

PROLOGUE

Pyrexia of Unknown Origin

STARING AT THE blank ceiling above him, Roche knew exactly how poor bloody Adam had felt in the garden, stark naked and scared out of his wits.

But finally God cleared his throat to indicate that he had reached a decision.

"All right, you can put on your clothes, Captain Roche. And don't look so worried. There's absolutely nothing to be alarmed about—I'm not going to invalide you out, or anything drastic like that, if that's what you've been afraid of."

Despair filled Roche. Ever since they'd decided to refer him to God he'd been buoyed up by the hope that there might be something rather seriously wrong with him, at least sufficiently for them to throw him out on the grounds of ill-health. To that end he had most scrupulously avoided taking the medication his French doctor had prescribed, and had done everything he had been told not to do. But he never did have any luck.

"Then what's wrong with me?" he said plaintively. "There is *something* wrong, damn it!"

"Oh yes . . . you've had a fever, but you're getting over that now, even if somewhat slowly . . . . What I meant is that there's nothing organically amiss. You're basically healthy." God reacted to his doubts by increasing his own air of reassurance. "You've had . . . and to some extent you still have . . . what my late distinguished predecessor in this job always diagnosed as 'a touch of the old PUO'."

"PUO?" Roche's spirits fell even lower. PUO sounded rather common, and not at all serious.

" 'Pyrexia of Unknown Origin'. But then he learnt most of his medicine in the Ypres salient in 1917 . . . whereas I learnt most of mine with the Americans in Italy in '44. And they called it variously 'battle fatigue' or 'combat fatigue' when it came to causes, as opposed to symptoms." The reassurance became even blander. "I've seen much worse than you, Captain—you've still got a lot of mileage in you, don't worry."

About a quarter of a mile, to the café-bar on the corner of the boulevard to be exact, thought Roche.

God smiled at him. "Are you due for any leave?"

"Not until October."

"We'll change that." God took a piece of paper and uncapped his fountain pen. "What precisely is it that you do?"

Roche frowned. "I'm afraid I can't tell you that."

11

God continued to smile at him, while reaching down into a drawer in his desk. "My dear Captain Roche . . . you wouldn't have been referred to me if I hadn't been cleared to ask that question. I look over all you fellows from SHAPE and NATO, and the Embassy . . . But to set your mind at rest—" he pushed what he'd taken from the drawer across the desk towards Roche "—will that suffice?"

Roche recognised the letter-head, and the rank on the identification folder positively overawed him.

"Yes, sir."

"Not 'sir'. I left the red tabs behind in Italy." God replaced the authorisation and identity card in his desk. "The only difference in our relationship from the purely civilian is that I'm obliged to report on your state of health to London. But, as I say, you don't need to worry. Your case is by no means unique in these dark days. In fact, the first thing you've got to do is to *stop* worrying, Captain."

Worrying was what Roche was doing, and the ex-Brigadier had already exacerbated his worries by moving towards the causes of his patient's PUO.

"Yes, sir." There was only one thing for it: he had to confirm God's initial snap-diagnosis for the origin of his anxiety, even if it was the reverse of the truth. "You're really not going to kick me out?"

"Perish the thought!" God regarded him benignly, then glanced down at the open folder at his elbow. "Sandhurst?"

"No, sir. National Service—regular commission after Korea."

"University?"

"Before National Service, sir."

"Just so . . ." The nod seemed to confirm the greater likelihood of PUO among graduates who had remained with the Colours than among Sandhurst career officers. "And now Military Intelligence here in Paris?"

"Yes, sir."

God looked up. "In the field?"

This was what Roche had feared, for it was easily checkable if it wasn't down there in front of him already. But fear had given him time to prepare for it.

"Not really, sir. Pretty damn desk-bound at the moment, actually. I'm a communications officer, mostly economic traffic related to military capabilities—that sort of stuff." He shrugged modestly. "There are specific additional assignments from time to time, naturally . . ." He left the implication of secret heroism unspoken between them.

"Such as?"

Roche thought of his latest report, on *French perceptions of the extent of direct Soviet involvement in the supply of arms to the FLN*. But the answer to that, as supplied by Jean-Paul and cleared by the Russian military attaché as being suitable for transmission to the British, was that French intelligence correctly perceived direct Soviet involvement as negligible.

But that wouldn't quite do. "I'm currently working on sources of arms for the Algerian rebels, sir."

God nodded. "An assignment not without risk, that would be?"

Another modest shrug would do there. If he'd been set to look into the private arms sources, which was worth doing, it might well have been dangerous. But with Jean-Paul and the attaché to help him, the Soviet inquiry had been less hazardous than crossing the road.

"And they're working you hard, of course?"

Roche's two highly efficient squadron sergeant-majors handled nine-tenths of the communications work, and the only difficulty in the *French Perceptions* report had been in finding respectable sources to account for what Jean-Paul and Ivanov had told him, with his former French contacts mostly hostile to him since Suez.

"The French are a bit awkward these days, sir." He advanced the only truth he could think of with proper diffidence.

"Very true." God smiled understandingly. "And that's half the trouble with you people just at the moment. It's a matter of stress, and it happens to all of you . . . . You have to understand that you're only ordinary men, but you have to do extraordinary things from time to time . . . and that exacts a correspondingly extraordinary price. That's what battle fatigue was: the overdrawing on men's emotional current accounts. You, Captain Roche . . . you are probably well-adjusted for normal withdrawals, but not for the contempt in which your French colleagues now hold the British, since the Suez business. In some people it manifests itself as boils—one of the embassy secretaries has a splendid one on his bottom at this very moment. The poor fellow can hardly sit down to eat his dinner—"

The only Frenchman who frightened Roche was Jean-Paul, and he wasn't at all sure that Jean-Paul was actually French; and he still got most of what he needed from dear old Philippe Roux, anyway. It was the Comrades who sickened him.

"—but with you it's PUO, Captain. But I'm not going to pack you back to England, that would only scar you permanently. If you run away now, you'll run away again." God picked up his fountain pen and wrote on his piece of paper. "Now . . . I'm going to give you a month's leave—go and find the sun in the south somewhere, and laze in it—" he looked up again quickly "—I see you're not married . . . but have you got a girl-friend? If so, take her . . . if not—get one. Right?"

Roche was speechless.

"I'll give you a tonic—and take that too. But go easy on the alcohol—I want you mended, not drugged. Do you understand?"

"Yes, sir." Roche needed a drink badly now.

"But stay in France. Your French is fluent, I take it?"

"Yes, sir." His fluent French, thought Roche, was probably why he was still here. "Why France?"

"Because most of your problem is here, and you've got to come to terms with it. Take the girl-friend—take the tonic . . . and take a month." God passed a month across the desk to him. "And come back and see me in five weeks—"

Five minutes later Roche had the shakes again, right on the street outside God's house and worse than before. And five minutes after that he was fortifying himself in the café-bar at the corner, in preparation before phoning in to Major Ballance.

He stared into the drink, trying not to drink it because he already needed another one.

A genuine illness, if not an actual disease, might have been enough to put Jean-Paul off. But what he'd got was the shakes, and a month to get rid of them, which was worse, because in a month they'd be worse too. And then, or very soon, Jean-Paul would see them; and then it wouldn't be a tonic and a month's leave, because it would be a matter of Jean-Paul's preservation.

He had drunk the drink, and the waiter, who knew his man, filled his glass without being asked.

God had been right about one thing: it was a sort of disease, even if it wasn't some bloody *pyrexia* of unknown origin—it was a *pyrexia* of known origin . . . *pyrexia*, whatever it was, sounded like the sort of disease a careless young soldier might have picked up out east, and that was really what it had been, he saw now.

A disease.

He had caught it on a beach in Japan, and it had been feeding on him for six years without his knowing about it, and then without his understanding the symptoms he had experienced—not until the first authentic reports had come out of Hungary had he begun to add the facts to those symptoms.

Or was that really it?

But causes hardly mattered now. All that mattered now was the progression of the shakes from his hands to his face, because when that happened Jean-Paul was bound to recognise the tell-tale signs, which he must be trained to spot.

With an effort, he left his second drink half-finished and found the phone.

"Roche here—Bill?"

"How are you, young David? What did the quack say?"

"He's given me a tonic, Bill."

Major Ballance started to laugh, but the laugh turned into a paroxysm of coughing before Roche could add his month's leave to the tonic.

Roche waited for the noise to subside. "Bill?"

"A tonic?" Major Ballance managed at last, still wheezing. "Then you will allow me to add a little gin to it—export gin."

"What?"

" 'Most Urgent from London for Captain Roche'—you've got a signal all of your very own, dear boy! Somebody up there loves you after all."

It was too early for Bill to start drinking. "What d'you mean, Bill?"

14

"I mean . . . you've got a posting—and a very good one too. It couldn't have happened to a nicer chap."

Roche leaned against the wall. "A posting?"

"That's what it amounts to. They want to see you there tomorrow morning at 1100 hours—a nice civilised time—FSMO 1100 hours, best bib and tucker."

Roche's hand started to shake again. "What's so good about that, Bill? Maybe they're going to bowler-hat me." That would be the day! But something worse was far more likely.

"Not *what* but *who*, David. And *where* . . . Sir Eustace Avery in Room 821, Eighth Floor, Abernathy House—that's the rest of it. So I'm booking you an afternoon flight to give you time to take a leisurely breakfast tomorrow. Congratulations."

"Sir Eustace Avery?" Roche dredged his memory. "Isn't he the one you said was a stuffed shirt?"

"Ah-ha! Stuffed shirt he may be. But he was plain Mr Avery then, on the RIP sub-committee last year—now he's been birthday-honoured into *Sir* Eustace, as a reward for his great and good services in the late catastrophe . . . So if he wants you, young David, you'll be hitching your waggon to a star, not vegetating in our communications room here . . . . The Eighth Floor of the Abernathy overlooks the river, too—on the Embankment, just past Cleopatra's Needle. Very 'igh class property for very 'igh class operations."

"What operations, Bill?"

"The new group, dear boy—don't you ever listen to the in-house gossip?"

Bill always knew everything. "What new group?"

"Ah . . . well, it is a bit secret, I suppose. Maybe I shouldn't gab about it on an open line." Major Ballance brightened. "But then the Frogs aren't really into wire-tapping, and everyone except you this side of the Kremlin already knows about it. So I don't suppose it matters much . . . *Sir* Eustace's new group—'Research and Development' is the euphemism in current use . . . He's been recruiting for the last month—everyone hand-picked, true-blue and never been a card-carrying CP member, even as a child . . . and with automatic promotion, so rumour has it. Big time stuff, in fact . . . . so congratulations, Major Roche."

Roche was horrified. This was worse than God's solution to his problems—far worse.

"But Bill . . . I've got a chit for a month's leave in my pocket—sick leave."

"Then tear it up. This is your great opportunity—you miss this one, and you'll be sucking on the hind tit for the rest of your life with the awkward squad, like me. Besides which, it's an order, so you don't have any choice." Bill's voice hardened, then softened again. "And it's what you really need for what ails you, young David. A cure is much better than a tonic for a sick man—"

15

He had to phone Jean-Paul next, but he needed the rest of his drink more than ever.

Room 821 sounded more like a kill than a cure for his sickness. In fact, the only person who'd be really pleased was Jean-Paul himself, who was always reproaching him with the slowness of his professional advancement and the low grade of his material.

He stared into the colourless liquid. There was no escaping from the truth that he'd always been a great disappointment to the Comrades, as well as to himself. If Bill was right—and Bill was usually right—it was the cruellest of ironies that he was now about to go *up* at last when he was at last resolved to get *out* at the first safe opportunity.

But they'd got him now, both of them: if he fluffed the interview, he'd be on borrowed time with Jean-Paul; but if he didn't fluff it he'd be exactly where the Comrades had always wanted him to be, and then they'd never let go.

There was only one option left, but it terrified him utterly.

He'd already thought about it, he'd even had nightmares about it, waking and sleeping.

PUO was a laugh: he hadn't got PUO and there was no cure for what he'd got.

The only treatment for gangrene was amputation.

RECONNAISSANCE:

Young Master David

I

"Mr Cox?" inquired a voice, disembodied and slightly metallic, but also recognizably female.

Roche looked round the lift for some evidence of a microphone, and found nothing. There weren't even any controls: Cox had simply ushered him into the blank box, and the doors had closed behind them, and the lift had shuddered and moved upwards. Or downwards, as the case might be, for all the directional feeling he had experienced—downwards would have been more appropriate. Not down to a particular floor, but down to a *level*, and some level in the Ninth Circle of Nether Hell, which Dante had reserved for the traitors.

"And Captain Roche," replied Cox, to no one in particular, unperturbed by the absence of anything into which the reply could be addressed. "Captain Roche's appointment is timed for eleven-hundred hours, madam."

The Ninth Circle was reserved respectively for traitors to their lords, their guests, their country and their kindred, but Roche couldn't remember in which order the levels were disposed, down to the great bottomless frozen lake far beneath the fires of Hell. But it did occur to him that—strictly speaking—he was now for the first time in a sort of limbo between all the circles and levels, since he was at last absolutely open-minded on the subject of betrayal: he was prepared to betray either side, as the occasion and the advantage offered.

The lift shuddered again, and the doors slid open abruptly. Roche was confronted by a sharp-faced woman of indeterminate age in prison-grey and pearls, against a backdrop of London roofscape.

"Captain Roche—I-am-*so*-sorry-you've-been-*delayed*-like-this," the woman greeted him insincerely. "Have you the documentation, Mr Cox?"

Cox, apparently struck dumb with awe at this apparition, offered her the blue card with Roche's photograph on it which he had collected, with Roche, from the porter in the entrance kiosk.

The woman compared Roche with his photograph, and clearly found the comparison unsatisfactory.

"This is supposed to be you, is it?" she admonished Roche, as though it was his fault that the photographer had failed.

Roche was at a loss to think of any other way that he could prove he was himself when she abruptly reversed the card for him to see. It certainly didn't look like him, this fresh-faced subaltern—not like the wary (if not shifty) Roche who faced him in the shaving-mirror each morning.

He took another look at the picture. This was undoubtedly the Tokyo picture of 2/Lt (T/Capt) Roche. And, true enough, this Roche had been just twenty-one years of age, while looking all of eighteen, and the shaving-mirror Roche of this morning, six years of treason on, didn't look a day under forty.

He grinned at her uncertainly. "I was a lot younger then—Korean War, and all that . . . 'A Roche by any other face', you might say, Miss—Mrs—?" He floundered deliberately, trying to take the war into her territory.

"Mrs Harlin, Captain Roche." She expelled the invader with a frown. "A Roche by any other face?"

He struggled to keep the grin in its trenches. "A joke, Mrs . . . Harlin. *Romeo and Juliet*."

Macbeth would have been more appropriate, with *false face must hide what the false heart doth know*. But false face wasn't doing very well at the moment.

"Indeed?" Mrs Harlin had met jokers before, and their bones were whitening on the wire of her forward defences. "This photograph needs updating, Captain Roche."

Cox, shamed at last by the massacre of the innocent, coughed politely by way of a diversion. "Do you wish me to remain, madam? Or will you ring for me?" he asked her humbly, without looking at Roche.

"Just do what the book says, Mr Cox."

"Thank you, madam," said Cox, taking two paces back smartly and thankfully into the lift, still without looking at Roche.

"Captain Roche, Sir Eustace," said Mrs Harlin.

Sir Eustace—Mr Avery that was, of the RIP sub-committee—*Sir* Eustace was standing behind a huge desk, half-framed by the great gilded frame of the portrait-of-a-naval-officer behind him.

Roche thought: *That must be the Sargent picture of 'Blinker' Hall and if Avery's got that picture for his room then Bill Ballance and Jean-Paul are both right about the new group.*

"David—"

Roche tore himself away from Admiral Hall's basilisk eye. It was Thain, the only man in Personnel Recruitment who had thought well of him after he'd fluffed half the tests in training.

"David—let me introduce you—Sir Eustace, this is David Roche, about whom you've been hearing so much these last few days."

Christ! Thain had come up in the world since PRT days, to be in this company, overlooked by Admiral Hall himself. But that at least accounted for his own presence, even if 'hearing so much' could hardly ring true. Since his PRT debacle he'd been little more than a hewer of wood and a drawer of water, in spite of Thain's approval. So there really wasn't so much to hear about.

"Sir Eustace," he mumbled. But he had to do better than that—here—now—by God! He had to *shine*—

"Colonel Clinton, David—"

Clinton was another new face, but the name rang faint warning bells: one glance at Colonel Clinton was two glances too many—the thought of Colonel Clinton hearing so much these last few days was blood-curdling.

Clinton smiled a terrible non-smile, far worse than Jean-Paul's bullet-in-the-back-of-the-neck grin. "Roche."

"Sir!" Roche did his best to make the word stand to attention for him.

"And St.John Latimer, of course," concluded Thain.

St.John—*Sin-jun*—Latimer was very young, and podgy with it; and languid, like an Oxford undergraduate who had strayed into the wrong party but was too idle to do anything about it.

"Latimer," said Roche.

"St.John Latimer," corrected St.John Latimer, swaying at Roche's *faux pas*.

Latimer—plain *Latimer*, damn it—was standing to the right and slightly behind Colonel Clinton, in the creature-to-the-Duke position, so that was what he might very well be since he was too young to be here by right of experience and seniority. But he might also be some sort of catalyst, introduced to sting a reaction from the provincial and dull Captain Roche.

"Is that so?" Well, if they wanted a reaction, at least let it be a controlled one. "Jolly good!"

Like all good catalysts, Latimer showed no sign of change at this controlled Roche-reaction, he didn't seem even to have heard it.

"Yes . . ." It was Thain who produced the reaction, and it was a decidedly uneasy one. "Yes—well, I must be off now—" he gave Roche a glance which was more charged with doubt than encouragement, like a gladiatorial trainer delivering a novice into the arena "—subject to confirmation and—ah—mutual agreement, David, you will be transferred from the Paris station to Sir Eustace's care . . . on a temporary basis, of course—"

Sale or return—as the liquor store off-licence would have put it. Or *suck-it-and-see*, as Roche's old squadron sergeant-major more accurately would have pronounced.

"—Colonel Clinton will fill you in on the details."

The figure of speech was unfortunate after the memory of SSM Lark had been conjured up in Roche's memory: to be filled in at Shaiba Barracks involved the scattering of blood and teeth in all directions.

"Sir Eustace—Colonel—" Thain looked at Latimer, who was examining the pattern on the carpet, and decided against including him in the general farewell. Perhaps he hadn't come up in the world, or not as far as the present company and venue had suggested; perhaps he had only been present to complete the formality of pushing the doomed Roche out on to the arena's sunlit ellipse of sand for the killing.

"Thank you, Malcolm. You've been a great help," said Sir Eustace with the easy insincerity of long experience. "I'm sorry you have to go . . ."

He wasn't sorry. And, what was worse, Thain wasn't sorry either.

"David—nice to see you again," Thain nodded.

He wasn't sorry because he expected Roche to fluff it again. And maybe that had also been what Jean-Paul expected, except the possible benefit of his *not* fluffing it outweighed the attendant risk. What was more, his—Roche's—very presence here, win or lose, increased his value as a bargaining counter on the board. After this, for Jean-Paul, he would be worth trading in for some other advantage as he had never been before. He was on the way to becoming a blue chip.

And that made his own betrayal of Jean-Paul even better sense, as a pre-emptive strike, to mix the very latest Israeli jargon with that of the Stock Exchange. More than ever, he had to do well now simply to keep ahead of them—both of *them*—until he could bargain on his own account.

The door closed behind Thain.

"Now then, David—sit down—" Sir Eustace indicated the central chair in front of his enormous desk.

Roche sat down.

There was a file on Sir Eustace's blotter, which he pushed forward into the sphere of influence within Roche's reach.

Roche made no attempt to pick up the file, let alone touch it, never mind open it. Instinct was in charge now, preventing him from breaking the taboos.

"We've got another David for you, in there," said Sir Eustace.

"Audley," said Colonel Clinton. "David Audley."

"David Longsdon Audley," said St.John Latimer.

"We want him," said Clinton.

Roche stared at him. "He's one of theirs?"

"He's one of nobody's," said Clinton. "But we want him to work for us. And you are going to get him for us, Roche."

II

"It'll take about an hour, maybe," said the mechanic.

Roche frowned. "An hour?"

"I'm on the pumps as well, see . . ." The mechanic sized him up. "And then I got to find the right parts."

"What parts?" Roche hadn't intended to argue the toss, but with what he'd most carefully done to the engine not an hour before, half an hour's work was a generous estimate, and no replacements were necessary. "What parts?"

"Ah . . . well . . ." The mechanic blinked uneasily. "There's this bracket, for a start—" he reached into the engine and wrenched fiercely at something out of sight "—you didn't ought to go round with it like that, it'll let you down when you're miles from anywhere." He shook his head. "An' it's a fiddling old job, too . . . maybe three-quarters of an hour, say?"

Roche realised that he had miscalculated. He had concentrated on the necessary time element, but had not allowed for time being someone else's profit.

"You've got the parts?" he capitulated.

"Oh yes, sir." The mechanic relaxed. "It's only I dunno where to put my hand on 'em right off. But I've got 'em, don't you worry."

"Hmm . . ." Roche looked at his watch. "It's simply that I've this important business engagement and I don't want to be too late. So if you can hurry it up as best you can . . ." He left the possibility of extra reward implicit in the plea.

"Half-hour, sir," said the mechanic cheerfully, recognising a sucker. "There ain't much traffic today, so it should be quiet on the pumps, with a bit of luck."

"Can I use your phone?"

" 'Elp yourself, sir. In the office—"

Roche dialled the number he'd been given, and a woman answered.

"Roche for Major Stocker . . ." Stocker was new to him too. They were all new to him, apart from Thain, who was unlikely to appear again. It was like making a fresh start, in a new job, as a new person . . . with a new personality which he could adjust according to need as he went along.

"Roche here, sir. The car they gave me has broken down—I'm phoning from a garage just outside Leatherhead—yes, sir, Leatherhead—" he didn't say which side, but even if the Major offered to come and collect him the distance was nicely calculated.

The Major didn't offer.

"The man says three-quarters of an hour, but I don't think it'll be as much, sir . . . Yes, sir, I'll ginger him up—I'll be with you as soon as I can, sir."

He didn't like the sound of the Major. But then he had never liked the sound of majors, who always seemed to exist in a limbo, either embittered with the failure of their hopes or hungry for the promotion almost within their grasp.

Still, that was a good job well done: he had his half-hour now, and a generous half-hour too, all correct and accounted for and accountable, and above all innocent. The rest depended on others, and on their correct observance of the routine.

He sauntered across the forecourt towards the workshop feeling re-assured, if not happy. It might all be routine, and the Comrades were always sticklers for routine. Yet the effort involved even in this routine, and the precautions they had taken in communicating with him, made him feel important, and more important than he had felt for years. And if the feeling was a secret one, like the rich man's pleasure in stolen masterpieces in his hidden gallery, then that was a small price to pay for the enjoyment of it.

The mechanic withdrew his head from the raised bonnet and bobbed encouragingly at him.

"Found the right bracket, sir—just the job!" He plunged his head back quickly, before Roche could question him or God could strike him down for bearing false witness against the British Motor Corporation.

Roche nodded uselessly at his back, and continued his aimless saunter, back on to the forecourt, slowly past the pumps, to the very edge of the highway.

He glanced down the road incuriously, and then looked at his watch, hunching himself momentarily against the chill wind of a failed English August. He wished that he hadn't given up smoking, but perhaps the new Roche would start smoking again. He had given up cigarettes because Julie didn't like them, and had started drinking instead; and it had been Jean-Paul who was always cautioning him to give up drinking, or almost, because he was drinking too much and too often. But the new Roche owed allegiance to neither Julie nor Jean-Paul, only to himself; and although the new Roche now also frowned on drink, which warped the judgement, cigarettes only sapped top physical performance . . . and the ability to run away was no longer an essential requirement, with what he had in mind for himself.

Meanwhile, he let himself seem to notice the church on the other side of the road for the first time. It was a very ordinary sort of church, old but not ancient, with a squat spire only a few feet above the roof and a lych-gate entrance to the churchyard. A dozen yards along from the lych-gate there was the opening of a narrow track which appeared to skirt the churchyard wall, leading to the rear of the church. In the opening of the track a dark-green Morris Minor van was parked, with an overhanging extending ladder fixed to its roof, from the end of which a scrap of red rag hung as a warning. A nondescript man in blue overalls, with a cigarette end in his mouth and a *Daily Sketch* in his hands, leaned against the van, the very model of a modern British workman as portrayed in the cinema and the Tory newspapers, reality imitating the art.

Or not, as the case may be, decided Roche, having already noted the man as he had coaxed the car into the garage and observing now that there was no one else in view—maybe art imitating reality imitating art. And it was time to find out.

He took a last look at the garage workshop, waited for a lorry to pass, and then strolled across the road to a point midway between the lych-gate and the track.

Somewhat to his disappointment the man gave no sign of interest in him beyond the briefest blank-eyed glance over the top of his paper.

Roche paused irresolutely for a moment, looking up and down the empty road again. Then his confidence reasserted itself, on the basis that he had nothing to fear.

If he was wrong about the man, it didn't matter. And if he was right, whether the man turned out to be his contact or a mere look-out, it had been foolish to expect anything else: if he was the look-out then he, Roche, was the one person on earth who wasn't worth a second glance; and if he was the contact then the empty roadside was the last place on earth for a comradely embrace and the exchange of confidences. It made him positively ashamed of the new Roche's naiveté; the old Roche, that veteran of a hundred successfully clandestine meetings, would never have let his imagination set him off so prematurely.

Nothing to fear. He had told *them* where he was going, and they had set up this meeting, deliberately within his time schedule; and if it was that important to *them*—or even if it wasn't—they could be relied on to oversee *their* security; so that if there was the least doubt about that security then there would simply be no contact, and he would have to soldier on until they were ready to try again.

He pushed through the gate and crossed the few yards to the porch with the unhurried step of a Roche with a clear conscience and half an unscheduled hour to kill. If they didn't make contact it would be annoying, because the more he knew about *Audley, David Longsdon*, the better; but at this stage of the proceedings it was no more than that—merely annoying. So then he would just look at the church, which might well be more interesting inside than out, because that was very much what he would have done if the delay had been genuine, because looking at churches was one of his hobbies.

Absolutely nothing to fear. It even occurred to him, and the thought was an added reassurance, that they had orchestrated this scene out of their knowledge of him, for that very reason.

The heavy latch cracked like a pistol shot in the stillness of the empty church beyond.

If they were here, then still *nothing to fear*. The time might come when he had everything to fear, but at this moment each side trusted him, and valued him, and it was "This is your big chance, David"—Jean-Paul the Comrade and Eustace Avery, Knight Commander of the British Empire, were in accord on that, if on nothing else.

And so it was, by God!

"Mr Roche."

At first sight, half-obscured by a great spray of roses, the fragrance of

25

which filled the church with the odour of sanctity, the speaker might have been the twin brother of the *Daily Sketch* reader outside.

"I am a friend of Jean-Paul. You can call me 'Johnnie', Mr Roche—and I shall call you David."

The flatness of the features and the height of the cheekbones mocked 'Johnnie' into 'Ivan'; or, if not Ivan, then some other East European equivalent, with a Mongol horseman riding through the man's ancestry at about the same time as this church had been built.

"Johnnie," Roche acknowledged the identification.

"How long do we have?" The voice didn't fit the face, it was too accentless, any more than the face fitted the name; but now, subjectively, the whole man—who wouldn't have merited a second glance in a crowded street—the whole man overawed him no less than Clinton had done.

"About half an hour."

"Where are you going?"

"To Guildford. I'm due to meet a man named Stocker."

"Major Stocker?"

"That's right. You know him?"

"Why?" Johnnie ignored the question. But he couldn't think of Johnnie as Johnnie: the face, and those dark brown pebble-eyes, neither dull nor bright but half-polished in an unnatural way, made him think of Genghis Khan.

"He's going to brief me on this man Audley."

"He's your controller—Stocker?"

"No—I don't know . . . I'm to report back to Colonel Clinton when—"

"Clinton?" The eyes and the face remained expressionless, but the voice moved. "Frederick Clinton?"

"Yes—?"

"He was there? At your meeting—on the Eighth Floor?"

"Yes. But—"

"And you are to report back to *him*—not Avery? Or Latimer?" Genghis Khan pressed the question at him like a spear. "Clinton?"

"Yes." It was disturbing to see his own fears reflected in Genghis Khan's evident concern. "Is that bad?"

"You . . . are to report back to . . . *Clinton* . . . about this man Audley?"

Audley, David Longsdon. Born, St. Elizabeth's Nursing Home, Guildford, 10.2.25. Only son of Major Nigel Alexander George Audley (deceased), and Kathleen Ann, née Longsdon (deceased), of The Old House, Steeple Horley, Sussex . . .

He didn't even bloody well seem interested in *Audley, David Longsdon*, damn it!

"Yes. What about Clinton?"

"This man Audley, then—" Genghis Khan ignored the question again, as though it hadn't been asked. But it was no good thinking of him as *Genghis Khan*, and letting him ride all over *David Roche* as though over a helpless

Muscovite peasant: he had to be *Johnnie*, and he had to be resisted.

"What about Clinton?"

The pebble-eyes bored into him. "He frightened you, did he?"

"If he did?"

"He should. He's good, is Clinton."

"He frightens *you*, does he?"

"No. But he does interest me." The Slav features failed to register the insult. "He is an interesting man, I think."

"He interests me even more. Because I have to report back to him, and you don't."

Genghis Khan, refusing to be Johnnie, inclined his head fractionally to accept the truth of that. "Maybe later. But not yet—not now. You tell me about Audley now, David."

That was probably as much as he could expect to get about Clinton, decided Roche, since Clinton was evidently a wild card in the pack. But Audley was another matter.

"I thought you would be able to tell me about him."

Genghis Khan almost looked disappointed, as near as he was able to indicate any emotion.

"I gave you his name," said Roche.

"So you did. But what do you expect us to do—to go asking questions?" The head moved again, this time interrogatively. "And we ask the wrong question in the right place—or the right question in the wrong place, which is no better—and then what? Someone asks questions about us—and then someone asks questions about you, maybe? And is that what you want, eh?"

"I didn't mean that. I mean . . . you must have something on him, damn it!"

"On Audley? But why should we have anything on Audley?"

Roche frowned. "But Sir Eustace said—"

Sir Eustace said—

"How long have you been in Paris then, David?" Sir Eustace Avery asked.

"Nearly three years, Sir Eustace. Two years and ten months, to be exact."

"To be exact? You sound as though you've been marking the calendar." Sir Eustace sat back, raising a cathedral spire with his fingers. "Don't you like it there?"

"It's . . . a lovely city." Roche decided to push his luck. "And the food's good."

Sir Eustace regarded him narrowly. "But the work's dull—is that it?"

Chin up, Roche. "Mine certainly is."

Dull, dull, dull!

"Even though liaison is an integral part of intelligence work?" The finger-tips at the point of the spire arched against each other. "And you're in charge of communications too—" Sir Eustace looked down at the open file in front of him "—and communications are your special skill, aren't they?"

My file, thought Roche despondently: aptitudes, test marks, assessments, with more bloody betas and gammas than alphas.

But that wasn't the point. The point was that the Eighth Floor didn't muck around with communications—or with communications experts.

"I mean, we got you from the Royal Signals, didn't we?" Sir Eustace continued, looking up at him again. "In Tokyo, wasn't it? During the Korean business?"

Since it was all down there in front of him, in black and white, the questions were superfluous to the point of being both irritating and patronising.

"I put down for the Education Corps, sir," said Roche. "I was posted to the Signals."

"Indeed?" Sir Eustace raised an eyebrow over the file. "Let's see . . . you'd already been to university . . . Manchester?" He made it sound like Fort Zinderneuf. "Where you read History—that was before you were called up for your National Service?"

"French history mostly, actually."

"French history?"

"It's a well-established qualification to the Royal Corps of Signals," said Roche, straight-faced.

"It is?" Sir Eustace gave him an old-fashioned look. "But you volunteered for the RAEC nevertheless—did you want to be a schoolmaster, then?"

"No, Sir Eustace." Roche cast around for a respectable reason for joining the RAEC while not intending to go into teaching after demobilisation. He certainly hadn't wanted to be a teacher *then*—that had been Julie's idea later. *Then* . . . he hadn't particularly wanted to be anything; and a degree in History, and more particularly a knowledge of French history, had equipped him with no useful qualification except for transmitting that otherwise useless interest to the next generation. And so on *ad infinitum*, from generation to generation—that bleak conclusion, as much as anything else, had turned him against teaching. The conviction that the later French kings had been not so much effete as unfortunate had somehow not seemed to him of great importance in the creation of a more egalitarian Britain, not to mention a better world.

"Why, then?" persisted Sir Eustace.

He met Sir Eustace's gaze and, to his surprise, truth beckoned him once more. And not just truth, but also a sudden deeper instinct: these were the top brass, not the middlemen he was accustomed to report to—their rank and demeanour said as much, Thain's obsequious departure said as much, and Admiral Hall's portrait confirmed the message. They hadn't summoned him here simply to give him his orders, they had other people to do that. He was here because they wanted to look at him for themselves, to see the whites of his eyes and—more likely—the yellow of his soul.

It was his chance, and he had to take it. And he wouldn't get it by answering 'Yes, Sir Eustace' and 'No, Sir Eustace' like the scared, time-serving nonentity he was.

"I thought, if I fluffed the selection board, or I didn't stay the course as an officer-cadet at Eaton Hall, then at least I'd end up as an Education Corps sergeant in a cushy billet somewhere," he said coolly.

"You like cushy billets?" Sir Eustace pounced on the admission. "Isn't Paris a cushy billet?"

"Yes, it is—"

"I don't know a cushier billet than Paris!" Sir Eustace looked around him for agreement.

"Or a duller one, either," snapped Roche, seizing his opportunity before anyone could answer. "And I'm not a poor bloody National Serviceman any more either—and that's also the difference. And I wasn't conscripted from the Signals to Intelligence—I volunteered."

Sir Eustace met his gaze steadily for a moment, and then nodded slowly, not smiling, but at least acknowledging the point.

"Yes . . . ." To Roche's disappointment it was Clinton who spoke now. "And just why, in your considered opinion, is Paris so dull these days?"

Roche transferred his attention to Clinton, and wished he knew something—anything—about the man beyond what the faint warning bells had whispered to him.

He licked his lips and decided to play for time. "I handle the liaison traffic," he began cautiously.

"I know that," said Clinton.

Roche's courage sank. Sir Eustace had digested the assessments in the file, yet was prepared to give him the benefit of the doubt. But Colonel Clinton had reached a different and hostile conclusion, and there wasn't any time to play for.

"They don't love us, the French." He had to find something to give Clinton, something which might impress him.

"Go on."

"They don't even like us . . . . Last year, for maybe six months—from the time Nasser seized the canal through to the landings—they tried to like us, but even then it was a bloody effort. But they tried." He paused.

"Go on."

"Now they don't even try." When he thought about it, the one thing he did know about Clinton was that he didn't know anything about him. Which meant that he hadn't been active in the Paris station. "They used to say that the Entente Cordiale was buried somewhere between Dunkirk and Mers-el-Kebir." The words were Bill Ballance's.

"Where?" St.John Latimer cupped his ear.

29

"Where we blew half their fleet out of the water in 1940, Oliver," said Sir Eustace.

"Oh—*there* . . ." St.John Latimer looked down his nose at Roche. "Oran, you mean."

Roche concentrated on Clinton. "Now they say the corpse has been re-interred beside the Suez Canal, somewhere between Port Said and Ismailia. And their next entente will be with the Germans, who are likely to be more reliable."

"So?" Clinton again packed *tell me something I don't know* into the question.

"So they don't give us anything. Or practically nothing—in effect, nothing . . . But that's fair enough really, because we give them the same in return—nothing, as near as damn it."

Clinton favoured him with a tiny nod. "So you've got nothing to trade—is that it?"

Nothing to trade in more ways than one, thought Roche bitterly. Nothing to give dear old Anglophile Philippe Roux, who made up for his embarrassment with marvellous lunches, and nothing to give—or very little to give—to Jean-Paul either.

"Is that it?" repeated Clinton. "Is that all?"

The difference between Philippe and Jean-Paul was that Jean-Paul didn't seem to mind. Indeed, not only was he neither disappointed nor worried by the lack of information, but he was rarely even much interested in what there was. It was as though he knew it all already.

And then suddenly, as he was about to admit that it was all—and enough to account for the dullness of Paris, if not to satisfy Colonel Clinton that Captain Roche was God's gift to Intelligence—more of Bill Ballance's ideas sprang into Roche's mind.

"No, sir."

Roche inspected the ideas first from the front and then from the back. They were fully armed and equipped, and their boots and buttons were shining.

Clinton was waiting.

"You asked me for my opinion, sir." Roche used the extra seconds to re-inspect the ideas. It didn't matter whether they were false or not—in fact, he himself was living proof that they weren't false, really. But now that he was no longer on Jean-Paul's side that didn't matter. "And this is only my opinion, sir—I'm not in a position to substantiate it." He allowed himself to glance uneasily at Sir Eustace for support.

"Go on, David," Sir Eustace encouraged him.

"Well, sir . . ." He came back to Clinton. "I think we're well-advised to restrict the traffic. Because I strongly suspect the Russians have got the French Special Services buttoned up from top to bottom. I think they already know what the French are giving us, for what it's worth—which isn't much. And I think most of what we give them goes straight back to

Moscow—" he let himself break off, as though afraid he had gone too far.

"Yes?" Sir Eustace leaned forward.

Roche shrugged. "Well . . . there's a lot of talk about their reorganising at the moment. But that isn't because they believe they've been penetrated, it's because the present set-up can't handle the Algerian war, and holding on to Algeria is their Number One priority at the moment. In fact, if anything, they think they're secure at the moment—"

This time the break was genuine, as it occurred to Roche that the next thing Sir Eustace—or more likely Clinton—would ask him was for the source of his suspicions, unsubstantiated or not, and since he could hardly admit he was parrotting Bill Ballance, that put poor old Philippe in the cart, than whom no one was more truly red-white-and-blue and the soul of honour.

"I rather think there's someone high up who's sold that as the official line, and they're sticking to it, anyway," he added belatedly.

"Where did you get this?" asked Clinton.

"It's pretty much rumour, sir." Roche felt himself slipping.

"But you believe it?" Sir Eustace prodded him. "Obviously—you do, eh?"

Obviously—he had to. "Yes, sir. I think they're blown."

"Have you talked about it with your contact?"

There was no escape. He had to have a source, and the source had to be Philippe. And, no matter with what regret, the choice between the careers of Commandant Roux and Captain Roche was no choice at all.

"In—in a roundabout sort of way, Sir Eustace." In a very roundabout way, actually. Because it had been British security, not French, that they had been talking roundabout, in effect.

"And what did he say?"

Au revoir, Philippe. "He said . . . he said that people in glass houses shouldn't throw stones. Or words to that effect."

"What words?"

Roche rocked on his chair. "He asked me if we knew yet who'd tipped off Guy Burgess and Donald Maclean, among other things." There was no denying Philippe had said that, even if the context had been subtly different.

"Who is your contact? Is he reliable?" Sir Eustace frowned down at the file, and finding nothing there, frowned up.

"I've no reason to think not." But he had to go, nevertheless. Because now that the possibility of a leak had been aired, then the possible unreliability of Philippe Roux not only demonstrated his own shrewdness but also accounted for any small leakages which might otherwise now be traceable back to David Roche. So—*adieu, Philippe!* "But . . ."

"Yes?"

"I don't know. I've just got a bad feeling about him. Nothing I could put my finger on—just a feeling." The feeling was guilt, but in his present scale of priorities Roche thought he could handle it.

"Who—" Sir Eustace broke off as he caught the expression on Colonel Clinton's face. "Yes, Fred? You think David has made his point?"

The corner of Colonel Clinton's mouth had twitched, but not with anything approaching amusement judging by the expression on the rest of his face.

"He's made his point right enough." Clinton nodded. "But I was thinking of Roux, as a matter of fact."

"Roux?"

"His contact—their liaison man. Philippe Roux."

"You know him?"

"Not personally. But he was in Berlin about three years back, before my time. And he was on Gehlen's Red List then as a probable KGB contact."

"That is good," said Genghis Khan. "He gave you Roux—and he gave you Gehlen."

"Damn it—I gave him Roux!" The thought of Philippe Roux being no better than David Roche—and not only no better, but also not so good professionally speaking, if the West Germans had penetrated his cover—had been somehow shocking as well as disturbing. He had had Philippe down as true blue.

"So you gave him only what he already knew, and in all innocence. And now you have told me, and I know—and that is good too," Genghis Khan nodded approvingly. "And, what is more, I will do nothing about it, I assure you. Roux must take his chances—you are more important than Roux, David."

That was highly reassuring, but he couldn't help looking at Genghis Khan interrogatively nevertheless.

"Clinton trusts you. He gave you Gehlen—and he has been with the Gehlen Organisation for the last two years, liaising with them." Genghis Khan nodded again. "So he gave you Roux, and he didn't need to—and that is even more pleasing."

Roche wished that Genghis Khan could show his pleasure more obviously, but the face was still as expressionless as a waxwork.

"I rather got the impression he didn't like me much."

"Liking is not necessary. In any case, it is not you he dislikes, it is Sir Eustace Avery—and the man Latimer, he will be disliked too. I would guess that you are their choice, and they are thrusting you on Clinton. But at least he is disposed to make the best of you."

The way Genghis Khan was talking, estimating the likes and dislikes of the British top brass, suggested that he himself was above half-way up the ladder. And it also suggested that Genghis Khan had decided to emulate Colonel Clinton in trusting the eminently trustworthy David Roche with his confidences. And that happy state of affairs had to be capitalised on while it lasted, to help him play both sides against the middle as required.

"I think you'd better explain that—'thrusting me on Clinton', Johnnie."

On second hearing it didn't sound so flattering, either. "Why do they dislike each other? Just what is happening?"

The pebble-eyes bored into him. "What is happening . . . what is happening is that they are each survivors of the great disaster which has befallen your service in recent years. Do you understand?"

"No. Not really. Tell me."

Genghis Khan looked at his watch. "There is not time, not now. It is enough that they are two of the survivors—Clinton has survived because he was absent at the right time, so he was lucky . . . or perhaps he was prudent, perhaps it would be safer to assume that—and Avery has survived because he was also lucky, but in a different way . . . and because he has the right connections—because he is a political animal and not a pure professional like Clinton—indeed, he is a great survivor . . . And that is also why they dislike each other."

It was going above Roche's head, but Genghis Khan was right: they were running hard on time.

"So now they must build again, with what they have—" Genghis Khan looked hard at him "—and what they can get."

And what they have is me, thought Roche, *and that's one measure of the disaster, by God!*

"You obviously have some special qualifications they need, I am thinking," said Genghis Khan speculatively, "to get them what they want."

What they want.

"So now I think you'd better tell me about this man Audley," said Genghis Khan.

III

"No, Roche, I cannot tell you anything about this fellow Audley that isn't in the file," said Major Stocker brusquely. "What I know is in the file."

Major Stocker wore a Royal Artillery tie beneath a face which was weathered like a block of Blenheim stone cruelly exposed to the elements over several centuries.

"What I know is in the file," repeated Major Stocker, as though to pre-empt any feeble Roche-protest, "because I compiled the file."

And Major Stocker also frightened Roche in the same way as Colonel Clinton had done; perhaps not quite so much, allowing for rank, but almost as much because—according to Genghis Khan's informed guess—he was Clinton's creature, and had therefore been quarried from the same hard strata.

33

Yet, nevertheless, he didn't frighten Roche quite as much as Genghis Khan had done, and that made all the difference.

"But there must be something—"

"Of course there's something, man!" They had had two minutes together, but already Stocker had no time for Roche, that was plain: Captain Roche in Major Stocker's battery would have led a dog's life. "That's why you're here, damn it!"

"I mean, something you know that isn't in the file—about what sort of man he is—damn it!" Fear hardened Roche into resistance.

What sort of man he is: David *Longsdon* Audley—

Oliver St.John Latimer didn't like David Longsdon Audley—had never met him, had never sat the same exams, had never packed down in the same scrum (the idea of Oliver St.John Latimer stripe-jerseyed for a game of rugger was beyond imagination), never eaten in the same mess (the idea of Oliver St.John Latimer crammed into the same tank was equally beyond imagination)—but Oliver St.John Latimer didn't like David Longsdon Audley, and that was a fact if not a fact in the file. Because he'd said so.

"He's a tricky blighter, if you ask me," said Oliver St.John Latimer, eyeing Sir Eustace Avery coolly, equal to equal, and then David Roche pityingly, superior to inferior.

("Latimer is one of the new recruits," said Genghis Khan. "Eton, then Merton College and All Souls at Oxford—a very gifted young man—we would like to know very much how they recruited him . . . perhaps also a very nasty young man . . .")

"A tricky blighter, then," said Latimer. "Arrogant, selfish, indisciplined, bloody-minded, ruthless, cunning—take your pick." He stared into space as he listed David Longsdon Audley's virtues, at a point above Roche's head.

"Brilliant," supplemented Sir Eustace. "Brave."

Roche achieved a surreptitious sidelong look at Colonel Clinton, and was rewarded with a fleeting vision of Clinton observing Oliver St.John Latimer in an unguarded moment.

"Clever—I'll grant you clever," begrudged Latimer.

"A First at Cambridge," murmured Sir Eustace. "An Open Scholarship when he was seventeen—the Hebden Prize—and a First after the war."

"Anyone can get a First at Cambridge," said Latimer disparagingly. "It isn't difficult."

"And a doctorate," said Sir Eustace.

Latimer sniffed. "On a singularly obscure aspect of Byzantine religious history. Which I also strongly suspect he cribbed from an even more obscure untranslated Arabic thesis on the subject . . . I know of a chap who did

34

exactly the same with a Ph.D on Richard Hooker—all out of an untranslated German book . . . But—clever, I'll grant you, yes!"

David Longsdon Audley . . .
   Educated: Miss Anthea Grant's Kindergarten, 1930–33; St. George's Preparatory School for Boys, Buckland, 1933–38; St. Martin's School, Immingham, Hampshire, 1938–42; War Service (see below); Rylands College, Cambridge, 1946–49 (Open Scholarship in History, 1942; Hebden Prizewinner, 1948; 1st Class Honours, 1949; Ph.D., 1953).

"And brave." Sir Eustace allowed the hint of a sharper edge into his voice, almost as though he was deliberately taking a cut at Latimer.

"Ah . . . well, I wouldn't like to set myself up as an authority there, Eustace," said Latimer off-handedly, as impervious to the cut as a rhinoceros to the brush of a thornbush. "They didn't give him any pretty ribbons, but that doesn't prove anything, I suppose—medals being no more than a lottery. But no doubt a gallant officer."

War Service (Immingham School OTC, 1938–42) Army, 1942–46 (conscripted); OCTU, Mons Barracks, Aldershot, 1943; 2/Lt, Royal West Sussex Dragoons, 1943; 15th Armoured Division, 2nd Army, Normandy, July–August 1944; Lt. September 1944, attached Intelligence Corps; T/Capt., February 1945; demobilised, Oct 1946.

"Wasn't it the Duke of Wellington who asked to be preserved from 'gallant officers'?" Latimer cast a lazy glance in Colonel Clinton's direction. "I suppose military bravery is in the nature of a communal activity—the urge to conform multiplied by the bloodlust of the hunting-field, would you say, Fred?"

Clinton shrugged. "I'm not an authority on it either, Latimer. I can't say I've ever thought about it."

"But he was a cavalryman of some sort, wasn't he?"

"He served in an armoured regiment, if that's what you mean," said Clinton evenly.

"The Royal . . . something Dragoons . . .?"

"West Sussex. He was with them in Normandy."

"But not for long, if I remember correctly?"

Was this being staged for his benefit, Roche wondered—or did they always spar like this?

"They didn't last long. They were practically wiped out in the bocage country, south of Caumont." Clinton paused. "If I remember correctly."

"In the best British cavalry tradition," agreed Latimer. "It was a smart regiment, I take it?"

"It was a good yeomanry regiment," said Clinton icily.

"That's what I mean—sons of the local squires in pretty uniforms—gold braid and magenta-coloured breeches, and all that."

"Magenta was their colour, yes."

"How ghastly! Doesn't go with anything, magenta—I should know, because it's my old college colour too," murmured Latimer. "And it was after that debacle you met him first, wasn't it, Fred?"

Suddenly Roche began to watch them both much more carefully.

"Briefly," said Clinton, equally briefly.

"Yes. And that's where the book of words starts to become rather sketchy," nodded Latimer.

So it wasn't for his benefit—they were fencing with unbuttoned foils, decided Roche.

Latimer had done his homework on Audley, no matter what he pretended—even down to knowing that the regimental colour of the Royal West Sussex Dragoons was magenta, which was a dead giveaway to the depth of his research. But, nevertheless, there was still a lot that he didn't know about Audley—and therefore a lot that wasn't in the file—for which, even for any unconsidered titbit an irritated Colonel Clinton might let slip, Latimer was now unashamedly fishing.

But, much more to the point, 2/Lt Audley had met Clinton in 1944, and although obviously still very young had been involved in intelligence work thereafter.

So . . . they didn't just want Audley as a recruit—they wanted him *back*.

"So then he went to work for you," confirmed Latimer obligingly.

"Not for me," Clinton shook his head.

"For us, then." Latimer waited for a moment or two. Then, when it became clear that Clinton wasn't going to elaborate on that piece of negative intelligence, he turned to Sir Eustace. "What exactly did he do? Beyond causing a lot of trouble to a lot of people, if I read between the lines correctly?"

Sir Eustace smiled almost genially, as though he didn't want to offend Latimer. "It isn't really grist to our mill any more, Oliver. It's all water under the bridge—'in another country, and besides the wench is dead', and all that."

"You mean—still classified?" Smiles didn't fool Latimer.

"If you like. But also unimportant now. You've seen his fitness reports."

"*Un*fitness reports, more like," amended Latimer. "Oh yes, I've seen them. And I've talked to Archie Forbes at Cambridge too, and he pretty much confirmed them. Arrogant, selfish, indisciplined, bloody-minded, ruthless and cunning."

"He's matured since then, Oliver."

"Or hardened."

"So much the better." Sir Eustace's voice roughened. "At all events, Oliver—and David—I want him. And I want him quickly."

Latimer gave Roche a quizzical look, almost as though he was seeing him for the first time. "Well, you're welcome to him. But I say he's a tricky blighter—"

"So he worked for them." Genghis Khan did not appear either particularly surprised by the news, or embarrassed by the fact that it was news. "And then left them."

"And you've got no record of him?" Roche made no effort to conceal his disappointment. "Nothing?"

"The inquiry into our records is in progress. But now I will inquire more urgently, since we know there is something to look for. Do not despair."

"I'm not despairing. I just expected more help, that's all—if it's so important."

"It is important." Genghis Khan's fractional nod was, by the standard of his immobility, a wild gesture of agreement on that, Roche supposed. "It is so important that it is all the more important for us not to rush in to help you, I think. We must help you with caution, is better."

That sounded very much like *all aid short of actual help*, thought Roche bleakly. Between Sir Eustace's *I want him quickly* and Genghis Khan's *we must help you with caution* and St.John Latimer's *he's a tricky blighter*, not to mention his private plans, he was already in over his head, and he hadn't even started.

"And above all you must be cautious," Genghis Khan compounded the situation. "At least until we know what they want, there must be no risk taken, no slightest risk."

"They want Audley, damn it—we know what they want," snapped Roche.

"Sir Eustace Avery wants Audley." Genghis Khan stared at him unblinkingly. "But Oliver Saint-John Latimer does not want Audley—"

"*Sinjun*. It's pronounced *Sinjun*, not 'Saint-John'," said Roche. "*Sinjun* Latimer."

Genghis Khan blinked just once, like a lizard. "He sees Audley as a rival. And it is also perhaps that Avery intends him to be a rival . . . But that is not enough, there must be more . . . And there is Clinton. There is always Clinton—he must be considered."

"More?"

Genghis Khan ignored him. "To go to such trouble for one man. There must be more—there *will* be more."

He was having difficulty adjusting his thought-processes to the limitations of a decadent fascist-capitalist society, that was it. Recalling Audley's Russian equivalent to the colours would not have presented such problems.

"I don't see why." Arguing back was risky, but if there was something else behind the man's certainty he needed to know it. "They think he'll maybe play hard to get, that's all. He worked for them during the war, and they approached him again a few years ago, but he turned them down flat. They think I can do better."

37

The lizard-blink was repeated. "Why you?"

Roche decided not to be insulted. "I have what they call 'a sympathetic profile' apparently. It seems we both read history at university." He could see that sympathetic profiles and history both left Genghis Khan unmoved. "And I have a high security clearance."

That did the trick: Genghis Khan smiled, or almost smiled, and Roche wished he hadn't. It was more like the corpse-grin out of an Asiatic burial mound in which the khan presided over his circle of slaughtered slaves and horses.

But mercifully it lasted only for a moment. "So you have been cleared to approach this man Audley . . . But that changes nothing. What matters is why they need him so urgently—that is what we want to know."

"It may be what you want to know. But if I don't find out a lot more about Audley than there is in the bloody file we'll never get that far," said Roche bitterly. "So I hope to God Major Stocker knows what he's about better than you do! Because if I fail—"

"If you fail?" Genghis Khan shook his head slowly at Roche. "If you fail Sir Eustace Avery will not retain your services?"

Roche's guts knotted. "It's possible."

"Then I think you would be well-advised not to fail, David Roche," said Genghis Khan.

"I mean, what sort of man he is—what makes him tick?" he pressed Major Stocker. "You must have some ideas about him, more than what's in the file?"

Major Stocker pursed his lips. "Not really, no—I haven't actually met him, you know. I've just assembled the facts."

Stocker was Clinton's man, so it seemed, and there was nothing very unnatural about that. In peacetime, you made the best with what you could get, and what soldiers could get usually consisted of other soldiers. He himself, although he was hardly a reassuring example of the process, was another instance of it, out of the additional factor of conscription and the accident of the Korean War. But he could have wished for the Audley file to have been assembled by someone more like Latimer.

"Seems a pretty ordinary enough chap on the face of it," Major Stocker struggled with his inclination to stay inside the safe defences of the facts in spite of Roche's appeal to him to crawl out into the no-man's-land of opinion.

"On the face of it?"

"Yes . . . That's to say, prep school, public school, then in the war— decent regiment until they pulled him out of the line—" Stocker made Audley's attachment to Intelligence sound like victimisation, with Audley more sinned against than sinning "—doesn't look as though he fitted in awfully well there, but he did his time."

"No remission for good behaviour?"

"What?"

"They kept him on right to the end—October '46. And the university term starts in October. I seem to recall chaps getting special release in my day," said Roche politely, to make up for his lapse into facetiousness.

"Nothing unusual about that, if he was on a job. His fitness assessments were pretty damning, certainly—looks like maybe someone had it in for him for something he'd done."

"You don't know what he'd done—what he'd been doing?"

"Yes . . . that is, no." Stocker shook his head. "I put in a request on a 'Need to Know' basis, but it was denied. I was told that it wasn't relevant."

"Is that unusual, in your experience?"

"Oh yes—quite usual. They hold on to that sort of thing as long as they can, as a matter of course. But in this case Colonel Clinton also turned down my request. He said there was no need for me to know."

"You went to Clinton after your request had been denied?"

"Naturally." Stocker regarded him candidly. "I never take the first no as the final answer . . . . But, at any rate, Audley made up for all that at university—he's bright, no doubt about that. Not popular, but very bright. Good at games . . . rugger mostly, almost first-class at that, but not quite. Club level—helped to found a local club on his home territory—funny name—"

"The Visigoths."

"That's right—it's in the file . . . they won the Wessex League in '54 . . . and the usual squash and fives, at college level, nothing special."

"Clubbable, in fact?" Audley did seem a depressingly normal public school product—school, regiment, university, work-and-games, *mens sana in corpore sano*. Apart, that was, from St.John Latimer's assessment.

Stocker was looking at him, and Stocker hadn't answered. Perhaps he hadn't heard?

"Clubbable?" Perhaps Stocker was unacquainted with the word. "Joins in, plays the game, and all that?"

"Yes." Stocker continued to look at him. "Yes and no."

"What d'you mean—'yes and no'?"

Stocker considered his contradictory answer. "I rather think I mean 'no', actually."

Roche waited for the Major to elaborate the contradiction.

"You know . . . we don't know where his money comes from?" Stocker went off at a surprising tangent.

"The file said 'private means'," said Roche, deciding not to press the Major on that 'yes-and-no-meaning-no' on the assumption that he would come back to it in his own good time.

"Yes—that's what they are—*private*." Stocker nodded. "They're so damn private we don't know what they are, or where they are, or where they come from."

Audley was living in France at the moment, in the south near Cahors. But before that he had been on the move constantly, through Spain, Italy, Greece and Turkey, and even in the Middle East, only returning to England at carefully spaced tax-evasive intervals. And while it wasn't the sort of life-style that necessarily needed vast resources, its funding could be made very difficult to check, and with only a little ingenuity too.

"He's officially domiciled in Switzerland," continued Stocker. "But I've half an idea the money is in Lebanon. The difficulty is that Colonel Clinton doesn't want him alerted that anyone is sniffing around, so we're having to move very slowly. So slowly as to be practically stationary."

Roche frowned. "But I thought his money was inherited? Wasn't his father well off?"

Stocker shook his head. "Just a façade. Or . . . there must have been money there at some time, but by the time the father was killed early in the war it had nearly all gone. The flat in London went in '39, and most of the land had already been sold by then. There was the house . . . it isn't so big actually, but it's very old and it is rather nice . . . but even that was in a very poor state of repair, and the father was dickering to sell that too. He was posted to France just as he was about to sign on the dotted line."

"That was in 1940?"

"That's right. He was killed just before Dunkirk."

"And the mother died before that."

"Yes. She died when Audley was very small. But fortunately for him she'd taken out an education insurance policy for him, otherwise the house would have had to go. It was that tight." Stocker paused. "But since then he's had the house repaired, and he's even bought back some of the land. So he's picked up quite a lot of hard cash from somewhere, that's for sure."

"He writes books though, doesn't he? And articles for magazines?"

"History books—and learned magazines." Stocker wrinkled up his nose at culture. "And I doubt there's much profit in the early Middle Ages. You've seen the list of his works?"

Roche nodded. "Hardly best-sellers, I agree."

"Best-sellers? You couldn't rent a council allotment with *The Influence of Islamic Doctrines on Iconoclasm in 8th Century Byzantium*. He bought two hundred acres of Sussex farmland last year."

"So he makes his money some other way." The more Roche thought about Audley's finances, the less he liked leaving such loose ends untied behind him. Stocker's facts had merely whetted his appetite for opinions the Major seemed incapable of giving. "There are still ways of making quick money if you're clever. And he's clever."

"Meaning dishonest?" Stocker regarded him dispassionately. "Very well, I'll go on digging. But I can't promise quick results there."

Roche sighed. "So what are you promising me . . . sir?"

Stocker nodded out of the bar towards the dining room. "Lunch first."

"And then?"

"Half-an-hour's drive. We should reach Immingham just after the pub closes."

"Immingham?"

St. Martin's School, Immingham, 1938–42 . . .

"That's right. You want to know what sort of man Audley is. Wasn't it Wordsworth who said 'the child is father of the man', eh?" Stocker looked at his watch. "If that's true, then I think there's someone at Immingham who may be able to help you, Captain Roche."

IV

THE RUGGER POSTS of the St. Martin's School, Immingham, 1st XV pitch stood tall and very white against their backcloth of Sussex landscape, on a vivid green field of late summer grass, dwarfing the two figures beside them.

Roche rounded the corner of the pitch and turned towards them at last, along the goal-line. But although he knew that they had seen him the moment he had appeared from behind the pavilion, they still took not the least bit of notice of him.

". . . ah, well you may have it your way, Major Willis, sir—"

God! Another major!

"—but I say it's in good heart, and if we leave it alone it'll be right enough with no more fussing, if we get a drop of rain."

"But will we get that, Mr Badger? You want to put your trust in God, and I say that God helps those who help themselves." Major Willis bent down and examined the grass at his feet. "I don't know . . . I don't think it's as vigorous as it ought to be for the time of year—" he straightened up abruptly "—so let's have a third opinion, eh?"

"Eh?" The groundsman frowned at him, and then at Roche, since there was no other possible opinion in sight.

The schoolmaster also turned towards Roche. He was a slightly-built man, with a ferrety look which reminded Roche of Field Marshal Montgomery.

"Captain Roche, is it?" he inquired peremptorily.

"Major . . . Willis?" And also the Field Marshal's rather nasal voice. But not, judging by the smell of Scotch whisky, the Field Marshal's celebrated abstinence, thereby confirming Stocker's intelligence work. "My—ah—my colleague, Major Stocker, phoned you, I believe, sir."

"So he did—jolly good! Now then—" Willis gestured to the great open expanse of playing field "—are you a sportsman? Of course you are, I don't need to ask, do I!"

41

Roche felt that he had been warned, yet insufficiently forewarned nevertheless.

"So what d'you think of it, then? Am I right—or is Badger here right?"

It was all just grass to Roche, and rather lush, if anything.

"My game was hockey, actually." It might be a risk, admitting that, but it was less risky than remaining on the subject of grass.

"Hockey?" Willis frowned at him. "What club d'you play for?"

"None, at the moment. I haven't played for some years—the last time I played was in Malaya, actually."

Willis nodded. "For the Army?"

"Yes." That was stretching the truth, but if sporting prowess was the way to Major Willis's heart then so be it.

Willis nodded again. "They're rather good, aren't they—the Malays?"

"Damn good," said Roche heartily. "But it was a scratch game—we were on the way to Korea at the time. That was the main fixture just then."

Willis stared at him for a second. "Ah . . . yes, I see what you mean—the main fixture, what!" He nodded once more, and then turned to the groundsman. "Well, Mr Badger, we'll let it wait until the weekend—right?"

"If you say so, Major Willis, sir," the groundsman nodded lugubriously, and stumped away down the goal line.

"He knows he's in the wrong—and he just doesn't want to do the work—he knows damn well that I know it, too!" Willis shook his head at Mr Badger's departing figure. "The trouble is, it's no good knowing better than other people these days—I've been suffering from that all my life, and I ought to be used to it by now, I suppose . . ." He swung back to Roche in another of his abrupt Montgomeryesque movements. "Now then, Captain—what's this 'matter of national interest' with which it is alleged I can help you, eh? Let's have it straight, with no frills—identity card first— right?"

Roche watched him scrutinise the identity card.

"Seems okay. 'David Roche'? Can I call you David?"

"Yes, Major—"

"And we'll put a stop to that, for a start. Badger calls me 'Major' because he served in the same battalion with me for most of the war, and he knows it annoys me. He was an idle sergeant and I was an unpopular major, so we made a good pair, both civilians at heart . . . But you don't have to 'major' me. The boys call me 'Wimpy' now, so you can do the same—right?"

"Right . . ." Or it would be right if he could get a word in edgeways.

"Right, then! Suppose you tell me about this national interest of yours? But I should warn you—you'll have to make a damn good case if you want me to help you. I'm not in a giving frame of mind these days, you know."

Roche looked at him questioningly. "I beg your pardon?"

"And so you should. Since Suez, my lad—when I was of a mind to go to the Canadian Embassy, or whatever they call it, and ask them if I could emigrate, except they would probably have told me they didn't want old buffers like me. . . And then we came a cropper—*et penitus toto divisos orbe Britannos*, as Virgil put it. So where was 'the national interest' when we invaded Egypt, then—eh?"

"I didn't have anything to do with Suez—"

"Naturally. Like when Field Marshal Haig said to the poor squaddie 'Where did you start the war, my man?' and the poor fellow replied 'Christ, sir—I didn't start it!' But is that a sufficient answer, I ask you? So where is the national interest now, Captain Roche?"

The plain white envelope in Roche's breast-pocket began to make its weight felt.

"Only in the last resort," Stocker had advised him. *"Use it if he positively won't talk. Fred Clinton doesn't want it used, but you'll have to exercise your best judgement there."*

"Well—spit it out, man! Don't just stand there," Willis exhorted him.

"Yes, sir—" Roche floundered.

" 'Wimpy'. You call a man 'sir'—or 'Major Willis', for that matter—and you're halfway to making an issue of it. But if you call him 'Jack', or 'Harry', or 'Wimpy', then you can get away with insulting him to his face," said Willis, of a sudden half-conciliatory, almost friendly. "Don't be put off by my bark—it's only a concealment for a total lack of bite, dear boy. I talk too much, that's my trouble. It's part natural—the way I'm put together—and part guilt-complex that there are still young fellows like you, having to look to the 'national interest' a dozen years after we won the war, which we'd never have had to fight in the first place if we'd stood up for what was right and in the national interest—*audiet pugnas vitio parentum, rara iuventus* . . . but I don't suppose you've had time to study the Classics—'how they fought shall be passed on to a younger generation smaller because of their parents' crimes'—the context was different, but the sense is there, I'm sorry to have to admit . . ."

Stocker had described him as being 'mildly eccentric', especially on the subjects of sport and the classics, and therefore unpredictable; but reputedly benevolent after his lunchtime sessions—out of term, naturally—with his cronies in the local pub; and a formidably good teacher, and a ladies' man, but a bachelor—and, for God's sake, what did all that add up to?

"Well, David?" said Willis. "The national interest, then?"

It added up at the moment to the reduction of David Roche almost to a tongue-tied Sixth Former with doubtful prospects in Higher Cert.

"Yes . . . Well, I'm told you were one of the executors of the will of Major Nigel Alexander George Audley, Mr Willis—"

Note i. *Father, ed. Eton and Balliol College, Oxford; major, Prince Regent's Own South Downs Fusiliers (T.A.), killed in action, France, May 1940.*

"—and Legal Guardian of David Longsdon Audley—"

43

Willis looked at him blankly for a moment. "What?"

"You're David Audley's legal guardian?" repeated Roche.

"I *was*, yes." The schoolmaster emphasised the past tense.

"You were a friend of his father's?"

Willis nodded. "Yes."

"And you taught the son—at his prep school?"

Another nod. "Yes."

"And here at Immingham?"

"Yes."

Roche waited in vain for something more than that third successive 'yes', until it became obvious that in spite of being self-confessedly talkative Willis was now determined to be monosyllabic.

"So you knew him quite well?"

Willis bent down to examine the grass, probing it with his fingers as though he was looking for something. And so he was, of course, thought Roche. But it wasn't in the grass.

"Who?" Willis didn't look up, though.

"The son."

Willis straightened up slowly. "Why do you want to know?"

"The national interest, Major."

Willis faced him. "I told you, I don't like being called 'Major'—and particularly at this precise moment, I think."

"Why not—at this precise moment particularly?"

"Because I suspect it's to remind me that I once held the King's Commission—'Right trusty and well-beloved', and all the rest, *Captain.*"

The envelope would be required. Stocker had known that all along.

"Don't think that I've forgotten that allegiance," said Willis. "It's simply that there are other allegiances—like that of a legal guardian, for example. And a teacher's too . . . 'in loco parentis' covers both—'in the place of a parent', if you have no Latin, Captain." Willis paused. "How would you say 'in the national interest' relates to 'in loco parentis', morally speaking?"

Roche waited. The briefly monosyllabic Willis had been a little unnerving, but now that the man had started to talk again he could afford to wait.

"I concede the classical precedents. It would have presented no problem to a Roman father, and certainly not to a Spartan one . . . But nowadays they encourage children to inform on their parents behind the Iron Curtain, and we regard that as an attribute of barbarism. And I don't see why the boot shouldn't be on the other foot as well, in all honesty."

The whole drift of Willis's soliloquy was fascinating, in that he'd taken it for granted Audley was the subject of a security investigation of some kind. But what was surprising was that Willis himself didn't seem in the least surprised.

"What makes you think I want you to 'inform' on him, as you put it?" he inquired innocently.

Now Willis did seem a touch surprised. "My dear fellow, I can't imagine you want me to 'inform' on his father! Apart from the fact that Nigel's been dead these sixteen—seventeen—years, I hardly think his . . . gentlemanly activities, such as they were—his gathering of rosebuds—were ever likely to be of the slightest national interest, or of any other sort of interest, except perhaps sociological, as a footnote to the 1930s. So that only leaves young David, and you clearly wish me to 'inform' on him—even so unworldly a person as myself can see that!"

"But—"

Willis raised a hand. "And I must tell you that on mature consideration I don't think I will, and for two reasons . . . Of which the first is that I doubt that I have anything of the slightest importance to impart, since I haven't clapped eyes on him for several years, and we correspond but rarely with each other . . . And the second, and to my mind much stronger reason, is that . . . as his former guardian and teacher, not to mention the friend and brother-officer of his father . . . I'm not prepared to sneak on him—certainly not without a very much better reason than anything so vague as 'the national interest'. Indeed—whose 'national interest'? Not that of those who conceived the Suez landings of last year as also being 'in the national interest', I can tell you!"

Roche nodded deprecatingly. "I do take your point, sir—" he could no more bring himself to call the man 'Wimpy' than he could have called the terrifying Johnnie 'Genghis Khan' to his face "—but I don't think you quite understand why I'm here . . . why we need your help, that is . . ."

"Indeed?" Willis regarded him with an expression of polite but absolute disbelief.

"We want David Audley to help us," said Roche.

" 'With your inquiries'?" murmured Willis. "Isn't that the phrase: 'A man is helping the police with their inquiries'? But I do understand that, my dear fellow. I understand it perfectly. And nothing you say is going to stop me understanding it."

Roche took the envelope out of his inside breast-pocket and handed it to Willis.

"What's this, then?" Willis looked at the blank envelope suspiciously.

"It's for you, sir."

"It's not addressed to me. It's not addressed to anyone!"

"It's for you, sir, nevertheless," insisted Roche, aware that he was quite as curious about the contents as Willis must be.

He watched the schoolmaster take a spectacle-case from his pocket and perch a pair of gold-rimmed half-glasses on his nose, and then make a nervous hash of splitting the stiff white paper, which was definitely not Government-issue.

The single sheet of paper inside matched the thickness of the envelope: it was slightly curved from its carriage inside Roche's breast-pocket, but not crumpled, and it gave a dry parchment-like crackle as Willis opened it.

Handwriting, that was all Roche could make out.

"Good God!" exclaimed Willis. "Good *God!*"

It was going to work, whatever it was, thought Roche. Everyone had a key to them somewhere, and Clinton had obtained Willis's somehow.

"Well I never!" murmured Willis. "Good God!"

It was a pity that Audley's key wasn't so readily available. But, for a guess, Audley didn't have a simple key, but more likely a combination of numbers; and one or more of those numbers was apparently locked up in Willis's head—and some more numbers might be locked up in some numbered account in Zurich or Beirut as well. But this was a start, and he ought to be grateful for that. Because only in opening up Audley could he gain access to sufficient funds with which to bargain for his own freedom, and be shot of the lot of them.

But Willis had read his letter, and was now looking at him with a new expression in his eyes. "You work for him—that foxy beggar?"

Clinton's features broke through the mists in Roche's mind—the high colour, which had nothing to do with blood pressure but only with blood, and the sharp features, sharper even than Willis's ferrety-Montgomery look—*foxy* would do very well for them, even though the hairline had receded back and down to reveal the freckled skin stretched tight over the skull, leaving only a tide-mark of that once-red hair above the ears. No beauty now, Clinton . . . and the foxy look was inside now, radiated rather than apparent.

But Clinton, for sure—

"I'm very much inclined to agree with you, Oliver. Audley *is* a tricky blighter. And, what is more germane to our present problem, there was an attempt made to recruit him again shortly after he came down from Cambridge. And it failed abysmally—it was bungled, wouldn't you say, Fred?"

"It was none of my doing." Clinton pointed his muzzle at Roche. "This time we must know what we are about, Roche—"

"The hair's all gone now," said Roche carefully.

"It has?" Willis flicked a glance at him, and then returned to the far distance. "That'll be the effect of the sweat, I shouldn't wonder . . . I've seen the same thing with some of our old boys, coming back for Reunion Night—crowning glories smooth as billiard balls—yes! And what is he now—a full general? He was just Major Clinton then—'Freddie' to his betters . . . or his elders, anyway, if not his betters . . ."

Another major. The whole world was full of majors today: majors gone up, like Clinton; majors in the balance, like Stocker; majors long dead, like Nigel Audley, cheated of his destiny; and majors ossified in wartime memories, like this little schoolmaster before him. And even one other potential major too!

And yet . . . once upon a time this garrulous schoolmaster had crossed Clinton's path, which neither he nor Clinton had forgotten; though there was nothing remarkable in that, any of it, for Clinton must have made a lot of men sweat over the years, and he hadn't finished yet.

"He's not a general . . ." He left the end of the statement open, as though there was more to come.

"Doesn't matter. I'll bet he tells the generals what to do! He wasn't above telling 'em a thing or two when—" Willis stopped suddenly, cocking his head knowingly at Roche "—but that's another story . . . It's a small world, though—a small world . . . All those years ago, and now *this*—out of the blue—a damn small world!"

He lifted the paper, but didn't offer it to Roche. Instead he fumbled in his pocket, producing first a pipe, which he stuck between his teeth, and then a gunmetal lighter.

"And he's still foxy, too," he muttered, snapping the lighter and applying the flame to the edge of the letter. When it was well alight he looked up at Roche, the twist of a smile lifting the opposite corner of his mouth to that which held the pipe. "Instructions!"

Roche watched the flames consume the paper right down to the last finger-hold, which the schoolmaster abandoned just in time. The charred remains floated to the ground, where they lay for a moment still in two complete and almost recognisable pieces; then the breeze shivered them, and lifted them, and finally broke them up, drifting them away across the field.

Willis put his pipe back in his pocket. "Maybe I should be a little bit frightened, instead of merely obedient—and very grateful he didn't order me to chew it up and swallow it instead. It would have been most uncommonly indigestible."

Whatever there had been between them, it was wind-blown ashes now, and all that could be recovered from it was whether or not it had served its purpose, decided Roche philosophically. It would have been nice to know more, but it didn't really matter apart from that.

Willis looked at him again. "Very well, then—I think your last meaningful question was 'Did I know David Audley quite well?' And the answer to that is 'Yes, as well as anyone did, and probably better than most'—and certainly a lot better than Nigel Audley ever did, although that's not saying much, in all conscience—so, *yes* is the answer to that one, David Roche."

So the paper had been the right key, and doubly the right key, if they were right about Audley—

"This time we must know what we are about, Roche," said Clinton. "Because some fool, whoever it was, went at it bald-headed last time, in '49—you're right . . ." He nodded at Sir Eustace.

47

"Yes . . ." Sir Eustace accepted the nod and passed it on to Roche. "Bad psychology . . . and probably bad timing too—too soon after the war. Too many scars not properly healed, most likely."

"I don't know about that," St.John Latimer demurred. "He didn't have a bad war."

Clinton looked at Latimer without speaking, and for a moment his eloquent silence monopolised the debate.

"What I mean is, by the time he got into it, we were winning—" Latimer plunged forward again "—and in any case that's not quite the received wisdom, according to Forbes at Cambridge—the war-weary hero explanation. What Archie Forbes seems to think is that he had other fish to fry at the time, that's all."

"His academic work, of course," agreed Sir Eustace, whose attitude towards the Clinton–Latimer cold war appeared to be one of indifference, if not ignorance. "He had a research fellowship of some sort, didn't he?"

"He did, yes—a minor one." Latimer sniffed.

"And that was the fish, Oliver, was it?"

Latimer scowled. "Forbes wasn't too sure about that. The truth is, so far as I can make out, they regarded Audley himself as a bit of a queer fish."

"Queer?" Sir Eustace raised an eyebrow.

"I don't mean *queer*—" Latimer waved a pudgy hand irritably "—the one thing you can't accuse the fellow of is being queer. I mean *odd*—"

"Eccentric?"

"Not that either . . ." Latimer's scowl deepened as he searched in vain for the word he wanted.

Sir Eustace examined the file in front of him. "Well, there's nothing out of the ordinary here . . . certainly not down to '49 . . . nothing at all."

Latimer nodded. "That's right. There's nothing strange at all. And maybe that's what's so strange, I don't know . . . But they didn't like him, anyway. Or they didn't trust him, might be more accurate. And no one seems to know why, not even Archie Forbes, who was his tutor and supervisor."

"And our talent scout," murmured Sir Eustace. "Which is why they didn't elect him to a fellowship after the research grant ran out, I take it, Oliver?"

"That's the way it seems to have been." Latimer's face wrinkled with distaste. "But the precise reason why . . . eludes me still, I'm afraid."

Evidently, the fact that Audley was arrogant, selfish, indisciplined, bloody-minded, ruthless and cunning—not to mention generally *tricky*, in summation—did not count in St.John Latimer's estimation of the reckoning of any collection of Cambridge dons, as debarring Audley from election to a college fellowship. There was some other bar, but he did not know what it was.

"You don't happen to have a nice fellowship in your gift by any chance,

Eustace?'' The distaste was still etched into Latimer's face, if anything even deeper.

"For Audley?"

"Uh-huh." And that of course was the reason for the Latimer expression—soliciting a plum for a man he detested. Or maybe *envied* would be more accurate? "I suppose Oxford would do as well. He'd probably turn his nose up at a redbrick place." Latimer flicked a glance at Roche.

"You think that might interest him?"

Latimer scratched his head. "It might. But after having been turned down once . . . I don't know, I just don't know . . but with this fellow I can't believe it'll be as easy as that." He looked directly at Roche. "And I wish I knew why."

Colonel Clinton grunted. "Which is why—*this time*—we must know exactly what we are about, Roche—"

"—so, *yes*, I knew him, David Roche," said Willis, nodding at Roche, but then looking away from him towards the distant rugger posts at the far end of the pitch. "And yet, the answer could just as well be *no* for all the good it'll do you."

Yes—and no—had said Major Stocker.

Roche looked up at the rugger posts towering above him, and began to suspect even more strongly from his own inadequate knowledge of the game that Willis was kicking for touch, not so much to gain ground as to win time in which to let the defenders get in position.

"David Audley was in the war, wasn't he?" As of now, if the dialogue was going to go off at a tangent, it would be David Roche's tangent.

"The last half, yes," agreed Willis coolly, taking the change in his stride, his defenders ready. "He was in Normandy about the same time as I was, actually."

"In an armoured regiment?"

"Yes. Yeomanry lot, dashing about the place in Cromwells, to the west of us—we were poor bloody infantry."

"He did quite well, I gather?"

"He didn't let the side down, no," agreed Willis. "And they did have a pretty rugged time in that neck of the woods, the tank chaps—bad country for them, that bocage. Good anti-tank country—we'd have loved it. Badger had a bloody field day in it, with his PIAT! But of course *they* were on the receiving end, trying to push south, past Caumont towards Flers and Condé, to take the heat off the Yanks at the time of the break-out." He smiled at Roche. "Lovely place for a holiday—marvellous food—but a rotten place from which to winkle hard-bitten Jerries with the Fuehrer's stand-fast order in their pockets." He paused, and nodded to emphasise his military judgement. "He did all right, did young David, even if he was a bit over-sized for his tank—he performed satisfactorily, anyway . . . And,

49

more to the point, he survived, which in itself indicates a certain skill. Mere longevity is a considerable virtue, in peace as well as war, don't you think?''

Stripped of all its verbiage, and allowing for the fact that the schoolmaster had a tongue like a cow-bell, there was more there than old soldierly memories. Willis had known exactly where his ward had gone into battle, and the long odds against his survival unscathed; and if it was all a gentle joke now, casually thrown off, it wouldn't have been a joke then—no joke at all.

"There's a lot to say for surviving, I agree." He returned Willis's smile. "But his father didn't do so well there, did he!"

"Ah . . ." For one fraction of a second the change in direction caught Willis unprepared. "Yes . . . that is to say, no—he didn't—" the eyes clouded as the defences were adjusted "—though, again, perhaps it wasn't altogether ill-timed, in so far as being killed can ever be considered well-timed—but Tacitus did say it of Agricola, after all—*felix opportunitate mortis*, and all that, eh?''

"What?'' exclaimed Roche, totally outflanked.

"A charming fellow, Nigel Audley—quite delightful . . . manners, breeding, grace—and guts . . . everyone liked him, everyone admired him. Good-looking, and clever with it—*the expectancy and rose of the fair state*—he had that rare quality of perfection which prevented lesser mortals envying him his silver spoon, he was too far above the rest of us for that, we were simply grateful for knowing him—that's the simple fact of it, David Roche.''

Roche was struck speechless by this panegyric: David Audley's father was too impossibly good to be true.

Willis regarded him tolerantly. "Ah—I know what you're thinking: *de mortuis nil nisi bonum*, and all that. But it's not true, you can ask anyone who knew him, and every man-jack of them—and every woman too—will bear me out.''

Roche waited for him to continue, but he seemed to have run out of steam with surprising suddenness.

"He was killed in 1940, wasn't he?''

"What?'' Willis turned towards him, frowning. "Why do you persist in asking me questions to which you already know the answers?'' he asked sharply.

And that was uncharacteristic too, thought Roche, taken aback by the sharpness. If the defences around David Audley were well-sited, those protecting his father were in even greater depth, and suspiciously so for such a paragon.

"Do you always ask your pupils questions they're not sure of—or do you lead them from what they know to the more difficult ones?'' he countered as gently as he could.

Willis stared at him, at first vaguely then focussing exactly. "*Touché* . . .'' he nodded, accepting the rebuke. "You made me remember things I'd

forgotten—I'm sorry—you're quite right, and you have your job to do . . .
Yes, in 1940, when the skies were falling in on us—in 1940, in France."

And he hadn't told everything, either: because in one particular respect,
and the most important one, he had already indicated that the paragon
wasn't a paragon.

But that could wait for the right moment.

"How did you come to meet him in the first place?"

Willis looked at him questioningly. "I taught him—when he was at St.
George's, Buckland—but you know that—"

"I meant the father." Was that a simple misunderstanding, or was it
deliberate?

"Oh, I'm sorry—I thought we were back with David . . . I knew the
family. And I got to know Nigel pretty well at Oxford, of course. I was at
Univ—University College—he was at Balliol—Eton and Balliol, like *his*
father—" Willis caught himself "—but you hardly want to know about
that."

"I think I want everything you can tell me."

Willis shrugged. "Oh . . . he was killed in '17, on the Scarpe, commanding our old territorial battalion—the Prince Regent's Own. And Nigel was
killed in '40, in the same battalion, not far away . . . that's all—history more
or less repeating itself, don't you know."

So David Audley must have felt a bit queasy, landing in Normandy in '44;
or certainly after the break-out had commenced, which might have taken
him back over the same ill-omened ground. With such a family tradition
survival did indeed have great virtue.

"Why didn't David join his father's unit?" The question was hardly
important, but there was something niggling in the back of Roche's mind.

"He couldn't have, even if he'd wanted to—it didn't exist any more. After
it was massacred in '40 it was never reconstituted. The nearest equivalent
was the West Sussexes—that's where they put me afterwards . . . But I
suppose the armoured corps was more fashionable than the poor bloody
infantry—blitzkrieg and Rommel and all that—more likely to take a young
man's fancy." Another shrug. "I don't know—what made you join whatever you joined, David?"

That was no joke—or no joke meriting the truth, anyway. "I was too
young to know any better."

Willis nodded understandingly. "Well, there's your answer. And just as
well, too, because war's a young man's sport, and it relies on a high degree
of stupidity—like volunteering for air crew. He was prime cannon-fodder,
young David—he didn't know any better . . . Whereas Nigel and I—we
were almost too old, we were a different sort of fool altogether: a 'no fool
like an old fool' variety, trapped by foolish patriotism in the 1930s." The
corner of Willis's lip drooped. "But there we were in '39 and '40—in the
front line, and far too old to be there. And after that, the ones who
survived—like me—we were the veterans, we were." He grinned at Roche.

51

"I even commanded a battalion for one brief, utterly unmemorable spell in '45—not for long, because they're not *that* stupid, the brass-hats—not for long . . . but I remember in '42 and '43, some of my young fellows were quite apologetic about my being there—and even more in '44, as though I'd arrived on the battlefield by some ghastly administrative accident."

How old was he, then? With a little bouncy fellow like this—plenty of healthy sport divided by a substantial intake of alcohol at the local pub made it hard to judge, and the Audley file had had nothing to say on his legal guardian's *curriculum vitae*.

"Yes . . . but, of course, the truth was, we *were* too old—and Nigel was even older than I was when he copped it—far too old for playing dangerous games like that! Fair enough if you're on the jolly old touchline, urging the team on and shouting instructions—'tackle him low, you stupid boy'. But to be actually on the field, getting wet and cold and muddy—and not only that, to have people shoot real bullets at you into the bargain—that's really monstrously unpleasant, you know."

Roche cursed his inability to stem the flow, aware at the same time that there was something the schoolmaster had said that he wanted to pull him back to—what had it been, though?

"He must have married very young—Nigel Audley?" he cut in quickly, as Willis opened his mouth to expatiate further on the horrors of war.

"Eh?" Willis stared at him vaguely for a moment, as though he found it difficult to withdraw from his memories. "Oh . . . I suppose so. Does it matter?"

"David Audley must have been a honeymoon baby, practically."

"Must he?" The vague look was tinged with irritation. "I can't say I've ever bothered to work it out, you know." Willis shrugged dismissively. "But I hardly see what that's got to do with you. Or me."

"What was she like? The mother?"

"She died when he was a baby."

"Yes, I know. But what was she like?" Roche didn't know why he was pressing the question, only that it was there in his mind.

"Oh . . . she was . . . very young." Willis fished in his pocket again, for his pipe.

"Yes?"

Willis jammed the pipe between his teeth. "Yes what?"

"What was she like?" repeated Roche obstinately.

Willis removed the pipe and commenced filling it from an ancient leather pouch. "What was she like?"

"Yes," said Roche.

"What . . . was she like?" Now it was the lighter's turn. *Puff.* "Didn't really know her that well." *Puff, puff.* The wind scattered the smoke. "Nice enough girl." *Puff, puff, puff.* "So I believe."

"They met at Oxford, did they?"

"Mmm—think so." Willis took the pipe from his mouth suddenly and pointed the stem at Roche. "What's all this in aid of, David Roche?"

Roche met the question innocently. "Didn't Colonel Clinton make that clear in his letter, Major?"

"Not *Major—Wimpy*. You keep forgetting, don't you!" The schoolmaster's voice was mildly chiding on the surface, but Roche sensed the anger swimming beneath.

"Sorry!" he apologised quickly. This wasn't the moment to antagonise the schoolmaster—and, for a guess, that was a warning signal his pupils wouldn't have missed, too.

"All right, then . . ." Willis—*Wimpy*—accepted the amends with a nod. "Your lord and master made it very clear, even abundantly clear, one might say, that Our Sovereign Lady, Queen Elizabeth, requires the services of her father's former right trusty and well-beloved lieutenant of dragoons, my erstwhile pupil . . . yes, he did make *that* very clear, I grant you . . . and quickly too, she wants him. And that has a familiar ring about it also, I must say—meaning that owing to the vast stupidity and incompetence of some others among her right trusty and well-beloved servants she has her royal knickers in a twist."

Well, that was one way of putting it. And it was quite characteristically Willis's—Wimpy's, damn it!—way, lacking only a Latin tag.

"But what he did *not* make clear—" Wimpy cocked a sudden sharp eye at Roche "—always supposing it's not mere vulgar curiosity on your part, David Roche . . . is the reason for all this inquiry into *my* David's remote antecedents. You must have his family history to hand, with his military record—and no doubt you've got more than that . . . So why the rest, eh?"

Obviously Clinton's letter had not spelt out the past in detail, but that left Roche in a quandary as to how far he ought to go to rectify the omission.

"And please don't tell me that you're just obeying orders," continued Wimpy, still watching him closely. "It wasn't good enough for our late enemies in '45, so it isn't good enough for you now."

And yet in a way that was the answer, thought Roche. He was here asking these questions of this man because he had been directed to do so, not for any reason of his own.

"Come on. Or I shall begin to suspect you're busy putting lies together for me," said Wimpy silkily. "And I might find that . . . discouraging."

There was no more time. "It isn't that. I'm not sure how far I can trust you, that's all." Damn it! It was gone now.

Wimpy smiled again, a winner's smile. "I don't think you've a lot of choice—do you? As the Good Book says, you just have to cast your bread on the waters."

"All right." It was time to cut his losses. "You could say 'the child is father of the man', for a start."

"*You* could say it." Wimpy's face closed up. "*I* would say . . . that a child has many fathers." He paused for a moment, then gestured towards the rugger pitch. "There's one father, if you like. Certainly one of David Audley's fathers, I'd say."

Roche looked at him questioningly.

"Yes . . ." Wimpy nodded. "'Audley spent a cold and quiet afternoon at full-back'—I believe that was his first appearance in print at his prep school, in the school mag at St. George's, the first time he played for the school, in the under-twelves."

"And you taught him rugger there?"

"I had a hand in his education. But at St. George's the essence was not so much the games master as the headmaster, to whom certain forms of play in rugby football were a form of Christianity, or otherwise ethical behaviour— it was unChristian to tackle high . . . not because it was dangerous, but because it was ineffective . . . running straight was the same—you were in trouble with the Head if you didn't tackle low, or run straight, or fall on the ball when the other forwards were advancing, or do these various things, because that was the moral, decent, ethical thing to do."

"You taught David Audley at St. George's and here at Immingham?" Roche rallied.

"So I did. David Audley came up from his prep school with a scholarship . . . in the same year, the same term. We were new boys together, yes." He grinned at Roche, as though the memory had mellowed him.

"Okay, then." Roche grinned back. "But what I'm going to tell you is classified. I wouldn't want my boss to hear about it."

Wimpy acknowledged the confidence with a single nod. "Understood. And I wouldn't want you to think that anything I may say to you as a result is because Fred Clinton has twisted my arm—far from it! Whatever I tell you now is for my young David's sake. Because it's time he did a proper job of work—time he matched his racket to balls worthy of him . . . time he did something difficult, instead of wasting himself on mere scholarship—which is for him quite ridiculous . . . And all of which, of course, the egregious Clinton is relying on—with me as well as David. And that's the whole difference between us, between the goats and the poor bloody sheep: we both know how people tick, but he knows how to make them jump as well. So . . . what is this that's so frightfully classified, then?"

The man was no fool. Through all the verbiage and side-tracking he held to his primary objectives, one after another.

Roche watched him narrowly. "You know David Audley worked for intelligence at the end of the war?"

"For Clinton?"

"Or someone like him—yes."

Wimpy nodded. "I didn't know. But it doesn't surprise me one bit. Not one bit."

No fool, and perhaps more than that, thought Roche, observing the little schoolmaster's deadpan reaction. Viewed from the spectators' stand, the connection between Clinton and the once-upon-a-time Major Willis had

54

seemed a remarkable slice of luck in the process of gathering information about David Audley. But from the players' point of view such happy coincidences could never be accepted on their face value until every suspicious element of cause-and-effect had been eliminated.

"Yes?" inquired Wimpy innocently.

Too innocently. Because all a player had to do to eliminate this coincidence was to rearrange the facts to make better sense of them.

"He mustered out when he went up to Cambridge in '46, I take it?" urged Wimpy, offering his intelligent guess as any innocent seeker-after-knowledge might have done.

Much too innocent. Because, in spite of his repeated allusions to the purely regimental nature of his military service as a 'poor bloody infantryman', Wimpy had known Clinton well long before David Audley had put on his dragoon's uniform; and Clinton had never been a 'poor bloody infantryman' in his life—he had been Genghis Khan's 'professional from way back', a career intelligence officer.

"That's right—"

Yes, and doubly right: if this little schoolmaster hadn't been a full-time intelligence player, he had done his time on the substitutes' bench, in Clinton's team. And that answered that nagging little question, hitherto unanswered: *how did a callow dragoon subaltern, however bright, get pulled out of the battle into intelligence work at the age of nineteen or twenty?*

"—it seems he caused a certain amount of . . . hassle in the work he was doing, as a matter of fact, actually . . ." Roche trailed off deliberately, passing the ball back to Wimpy.

The schoolmaster smiled. "He made waves? Yes . . . that doesn't surprise me either. When he was young he was . . . he appeared to be, I should say . . . malleable—biddable, you might say. But there was always a well-concealed streak of obstinacy in him—it was as though he seemed to be doing what you wanted, but in the end it turned out to be what *he* wanted, don't you know!" He shook his head, still smiling. "When he grew up, as he got older, the streak became more obvious. But back in '44 he was worth saving, and he still is, by God!"

The last piece of the Clinton–Willis connection slotted into place with jig-saw accuracy. That smile was made of more than pride in a bright pupil and affection for a dead brother-officer's only son: for a guess it had been Wimpy himself who had recommended Audley to Clinton back in 1944, to get him out of the front line.

"Bloody awkward, is the way I've heard it." He smiled back at Wimpy.

Wimpy managed to adjust his smile at last to something more properly neutral. "But they like him now, enough to want him back, nevertheless?"

"I don't think they ever stopped liking him, actually." A little soft soap wouldn't go amiss, especially when there had to be an element of truth in it, whatever Latimer might maintain.

"They . . . meaning you?" inquired Wimpy politely.

Roche shook his head. "They meaning they." It would do no harm to differentiate the decent Roche, just doing his duty, from the foxy Clinton. And there was a bit of truth in that too, anyway. "They parted when he went up to Cambridge in '46, when he was demobbed. But they tried to re-enlist him again after he graduated, you see—before my time—"

"Ah!" Wimpy raised his hand. "*Now* I see what you've been driving at—why you're here, asking all these damnfool questions! Why didn't you tell me straight off?"

Roche stared at him questioningly. "I beg your pardon?"

"My dear man—Glendower in Henry IV—'*I can call spirits from the vasty deep*'—I sent David tickets to see that at Stratford in '52, and bloody marvellous it was too! *He'd* understand—and Hotspur replies: '*Why, so can I, or so can any man—but will they come when you do call on them?*'—that's the question!" Wimpy beamed at him. "Not under military discipline any more, like in '44—so when they called on him he wouldn't come, naturally . . . once bitten, twice shy!" And then suddenly the smile vanished, as though it had been switched off from within. "But now it's different, isn't it!"

The switch to seriousness was somewhat disconcerting. "How d'you mean different?" said Roche cautiously.

"Because they *wanted* him in '49, or whenever it was, after Cambridge. But now they *need* him, that's the real difference." Wimpy nodded again. "Because something's happened, and they've damn well got to have him, one way or another—isn't that the strength of it?"

And that was even more disconcerting: by whatever reasoning, the little schoolmaster had reached the same conclusion as Genghis Khan, that Audley's recruitment was not an end in itself, but a means to some other end.

"You could be right," Roche admitted.

"I usually am, though it's never done me much good." The smile came back as suddenly as it had disappeared. "But don't worry! On this occasion it's at least to your advantage. It's high time *my* David was gainfully employed, as I've already said." Wimpy gestured down the goal line. "So come on, then . . . and 'you shall come and go and look and know where I shall show'. Though I can't guarantee that you shall know neither doubt nor fear in the end, as Puck promised."

"Puck?"

"Kipling—*Puck of Pook's Hill*." Wimpy began to move down the line. "*Puck* and *Stalky & Co* are your two set books for this examination, my dear fellow. My young David was brought up on those two books, when the world was also young . . . Kipling and the rugger field . . . and then the battlefield—so which was illusion and which was reality, eh? And then the cold war after the hot war to add disillusion, maybe?"

"I'm not sure I understand you," said Roche.

"I'm not sure I understand myself. But he's there somewhere, in the middle of it. And if you want to understand him you've got to go there yourself first, I think."

"Where?"

"Where indeed!" Wimpy thought for a moment. "A place first, yes. And a person too, I think—yes!"

"Where?" Roche abandoned the idea of *why*. "And who?"

"Someone who makes the best fruit cakes in Sussex," said Wimpy.

V

"WILL YOU HAVE another piece, sir?"

Roche studied the last third of the fruit cake, rearguards of guilt offering token resistance against greed. It *was* the best fruit cake in Sussex, beyond doubt; and very probably the best fruit cake in England, and consequently the best one in the whole world, almost certainly . . . and *was* would be the operative word for it if she carved them two more of her gargantuan slices, like those they had already consumed. But the opportunity was far too good to be missed.

He looked up from the fruit cake to meet Ada Clarke's gaze, trying to feign a moment's indecision for conscience's sake.

"But . . . what about your husband's tea, Mrs Clarke?"

Wimpy emitted a short, unsympathetic chuckle. "To hell with Charlie! Speaking for myself, Clarkie—"

"And you always do, sir, Mr William—" she cut back at him, quick as a flash, but smiling "—if I may make so bold as to say, sir—"

"You may, Clarkie—you may! And I always do—I admit it, I admit it frankly and unashamedly . . . for if I do not speak for myself, then who will speak for me?" Wimpy accepted the state of affectionate war between them with evident delight. "Not you, Clarkie, not you . . . *therefore* . . . speaking for myself, I will quote first that fine old French saying—which covers any claim Charlie may or may not have on that cake—'he who is absent is always in the wrong', Clarkie. In which case—"

"But I wasn't offering it to you, sir. I was offering it to—to—" Mrs Clarke blinked at Roche uncertainly: she had forgotten his name.

"To Captain Roche—of course! Who guards us ceaselessly, so that we may sleep safely in our beds—a thoroughly deserving case, Clarkie. Hardly less deserving than myself, a poor bachelor schoolmaster . . . . Cut the cake, Clarkie—bisect it into equal portions, and stop arguing!"

Mrs Clarke shook her head at him in despair, and turned back to Roche.

"You mustn't mind him, sir, Captain Roche—you must take no notice of him. Now . . ."

But she was already dividing the cake. She had known from the start that he would succumb to temptation, that her cake would reduce them both to greedy schoolboys.

"And don't worry about Charlie, sir. I always make two cakes at a time . . . it's habit, really: one for Charlie and one for Mr David, like in the old days. Only now Charlie eats both of them, that's all."

"Well . . . thank you, Mrs Clarke." Roche accepted his half-of-one-third. Poor old absent Charlie—half-witted, shell-shocked Charlie—was on to a damn good thing, whatever his handicaps.

A *damn* good thing: the little cottage smelt bewitchingly of cake and cooking and cleanliness, scrubbed and polished and apple-pie-ordered. The black kitchen range, out of which the paradisal cake had come, glistened with use and elbow grease; above it, on the mantelpiece, a line of cheap commemorative mugs caught his eye—the Queen's Coronation cup from five years back, then King George VI's, and Edward VIII's premature celebration, and so on through other coronations and jubilees to Queen Victoria herself.

"Interesting, aren't they?" murmured Wimpy. "You had the end ones from your mother, didn't you, Clarkie?"

"That's right, sir. Mine begin with the coronation of King George that was King Edward's brother—King Edward that married that American lady, or the Prince of Wales as he'll always be to me. He was a lovely boy, the Prince. I saw him once, at the races, when Charlie and me went to attend to a party the Master, Mr Nigel, was putting on—he gave me a lovely smile, like he knew me, as I took round the tray with the champagne on it, the Prince did . . . 'Course, I was younger then, only a slip of a girl." She nodded knowingly at Roche. "And he had an eye for the girls, he did, did the Prince of Wales."

Roche glanced covertly at her. She was little and dumpy, with cheeks reddened by all weathers and the heat of that black kitchen range. But those tight pepper-and-salt curls had once been blonde, and the sparkle in the blue eyes was still bright.

"So he did," agreed Wimpy. "And that, you might say, was his undoing in the end, eh?"

"And that Prince Philip—he's a lad!" Mrs Clarke warmed to what was clearly one of her favourite subjects. "Of course, he gets that from having been a sailor, like his Uncle, that was Lord Louis when I was a girl—I met him too. *And* Lady Louis—" she nodded proudly at Roche "—Edwina Ashley, she was, and beautiful like in those magazines, you should have seen her!"

Wimpy caught Roche's eye for a fraction of a second. "But that mug from the Silver Jubilee in 1935 ought to be yours too, Clarkie, surely? You were in service then?"

"So I was, sir. But so was Mother—and I broke mine, so that's hers, that one." She grinned at Roche. "To tell the truth, sir, Captain Roche, I got tiddly that night—all because of the Master, Mr Nigel, and his champagne . . ."

"A tradition of the house," agreed Wimpy, shifting his attention from Mrs Clarke to Roche as he spoke. "On great occasions the wine flows in the Old House—in the appropriate receptacle, naturally." He nodded at the line of mugs on the mantelpiece.

"That's right, sir," said Mrs Clarke, nodding at Wimpy and Roche as she spoke. "Filled to the brim with champagne, that was the rule. No wonder we all got tiddly!"

Roche reached up towards the nearest mug, fascinated.

"You look at it, sir," Ada Clarke encouraged him, "and see for yourself how much it takes. That was Master David's favourite, that one, he liked it because of all the writing on it."

Wimpy gave a derisive snort. "Absolute rubbish, Clarkie! He liked it because it was bigger than the others—it held more champagne, that's why. And he was drunk as a lord on both occasions as a result."

"He was sick both times, more like," conceded Mrs Clarke defensively. "But it could have been what he ate just as easily."

"He was beastly drunk—"

They were oblivious of him, duelling with twenty-year memories.

"It was too much rich food. All that smoked salmon, sir—and the caviare from Fortnum and Mason's . . . and I made him that Black Forest cherry cake specially—"

"Full of kirsch—precisely! He was tight as a tick, Clarkie dear. Kirsch plus champagne—no wonder!"

Or maybe Wimpy was very far from forgetting him—maybe quite the opposite . . . maybe this, very deliberately, was the beginning of Wimpy's special tuition on David Audley.

Mrs Clarke drew a deep breath. "Well . . . if he was . . . a bit tiddly—"

"Aha!" Wimpy seized her admission instantly. In any argument with Wimpy the loser would never be allowed to retreat in good order, pursuit would always be close and merciless. Indeed, he was already turning triumphantly to Roche. "Now the truth comes out, old boy!"

"Huh!" exclaimed Ada Clarke, also turning towards Roche. "And if he was, then who was to blame, I ask you!" She nodded significantly at Wimpy. "You don't need far to look, sir, Captain Roche—indeed you don't."

Wimpy spread his hands. "I'm not denying anything, Clarkie dear."

"Nor can you—I should think not!" She gave him a mock-disapproving sniff. "*No*, sir—" she caught Roche with his mouth full of cake "—you should have seen what he brought down here, for Mr David—I saw him slip out of the House with the tray . . . I was waiting on the guests of course—piled high with everything, like he was feeding a regiment . . . and a *whole*

59

bottle of champagne, and Master David hardly ten years old . . . and the Master sees him too, what's more—"

"I never knew that, Clarkie!" Wimpy leant forward. "You never told me that before."

"You never asked me. But *I* saw—and *he* sees you—" back to Roche again "—the Master, Mr Nigel, that is . . . And he says to me 'Aye-aye! Now where's he off to then, Mrs Clarke, eh?' with that look in his eye, like he half knew already—like he always did when it was you and Mr David up to your tricks, goin' up to London, and that—"

"Good God!" whispered Wimpy, a muscle twitching in his cheek. "He knew about—London?"

"When you took Master David to see the illuminations, for the jubilee—and the coronation?" She shook the grey-blonde curls with a quick, almost convulsive movement. "He didn't *know*—but he *knew* all the same—like, he couldn't know, because he wasn't here those nights, when you went off, but he knew somehow, I don't know how . . . You know Mr Nigel, sir—he always knew everything somehow—"

"Except which horse was going to win—"

"I mean about people, sir, Mr William, not horses." She stared at Wimpy in silence for a moment.

Wimpy nodded into the silence. Now, this time, and for the first time, they were both oblivious of him, thought Roche: now they were both wrapped and enveloped in a secret play in which they had acted independently, here in this sweet-smelling room and also up the drive, in the house which he hadn't yet seen, where the Master, Mr Nigel, had lavished entertainment on his smart friends—

"So . . . what on earth did you *do*, Clarkie?" Wimpy watched her intently.

"I told a lie, sir—a black lie." She half-smiled, the recollection of the black lie warming her memory. "You remember that Mrs Templeton, that went off in the end with Captain Wallace-White, and there was all that scandal?"

Wimpy's eyes widened. "Phew! Do I not! Lottie Templeton—*phew*! She was there—I remember that too, by golly!"

"That's right. And she fancied you, what's more, sir."

"Lottie Templeton? She never did, Clarkie!"

"No, sir. She fancied you."

"I fancied *her*. She just talked to me, that's all."

"You made her laugh. And she said you were clever, I heard her say so. She fancied you, and that's a fact."

Wimpy shook his head. "Oh . . . come on, Clarkie! Mere schoolmasters weren't Lottie's style."

"Begging your pardon, sir, anything in trousers was Mrs Templeton's style."

The servants knew, thought Roche. The servants always knew. And, judging by Wimpy's failure to reply this time, the same thing was occurring to him.

Ada Clarke nodded. "Yes, sir . . . So it came to me, right on the spur of the moment, and I says to him—or I whispers to him, more like—'I think Mr William is looking after Mrs Templeton in the summerhouse, sir'." She paused. "And she *was* in the summerhouse too."

"But not with me—" Wimpy blinked at her.

"No, sir. You weren't quick enough off the mark! But *he* didn't know that—or . . . he couldn't be sure, not without going after you, which he couldn't do, and wouldn't do—"

"You're wrong, Clarkie." He shook his head again. "He'd know better than that, whatever you say."

He always knew everything about people . . .

She looked at him silently for a second or two, curiously without any expression on her face. "Maybe he did, sir. But you know what he was like, about Master David—like he didn't want to know if he could help it? He was the same with those times the two of you went off—knowing, and not knowing at the same time . . . All he wanted was an excuse *not* to know, and that's what I gave him—an excuse. Because he said, 'Oh well, then that's all right then', and went off back to the party, to—" she caught Roche's eye "—back to the party he went, sir, Captain Roche . . . But it was *him* that gave Master David all that to drink, anyway, is what I'm saying." She nodded accusingly at Wimpy.

The schoolmaster sat back as though released from a spell. "I don't think poor Captain Roche understands a word we're saying, Clarkie. He can hardly be expected to fathom our ancient and exceedingly byzantine history."

There was an irony in that, though whether it was accidental or deliberate it was hard to estimate, thought Roche: it had been out of that byzantine family history and into genuine Byzantine history that 'Master' David had eventually plunged himself, as to the manner born.

But meanwhile his role was to draw Ada Clarke out in whatever direction Wimpy indicated.

He looked at her expectantly, as one desiring enlightenment. "Mr— Major Willis . . . brought the champagne down here . . . ?"

Mrs Clarke sighed. "The Master was always very strict with Master David when there was a party up at the house, you see, sir—"

"Strict?" Wimpy cut in. "He banished the boy at the drop of a hat, more like."

"No, sir. That's not quite fair. Some of those parties, they were . . ." Mrs Clarke searched for a word descriptive of Major Nigel Audley's entertainments, ". . . not suitable."

" 'Adults only'," supplied Wimpy. "There is an element of truth in what Clarkie says—or doesn't say . . . This was the thirties, you have to remember, dear boy—gangsters in America, and Herr Hitler's little experiment in Germany, and Uncle Joe in Russia, killing off everyone in sight . . . and Mussolini in Italy, and Kim Philby reporting the war in Spain for *The Times*—and for Uncle Joe, of course . . ."

"And unemployment in England," said Roche.

"And unemployment—for the unemployed," agreed Wimpy. "And for Nigel Audley and William Willis MA there was 'gather ye rosebuds while ye may'—and for dear Lottie Templeton too, for that matter . . . no one could say her nymphomaniacal instincts weren't well-advised in the circumstances—the jolly old wingèd chariot collected her in the Blitz in 1940, didn't it, Clarkie? I rather lost touch with her after Jack Wallace-White succumbed to her charms . . .?"

"No, sir. It was a V-1 in 1944," said Mrs Clarke. "She was driving a mobile canteen for the Church of Scotland, down in Camberwell it was."

"For the Church of Scotland?" Wimpy echoed her incredulously.

"That's what Colonel Deacon told me, sir. He said it was on account of her husband—him that was killed in the desert, I think . . . or was it that one, or the other one?"

Wimpy nodded. "Jack was certainly killed in the desert—Sidi Rezegh in '41. But the Church of Scotland . . . well, I suppose that was because all Jack's money was tied up in whisky distilling . . . and if Laurie Deacon said so, then it's not to be contested." He grinned at Roche. "That's *Mr* Laurie Deacon MP, QC *et cetera* now—he was one of the gang then, a smart young barrister who'd just taken silk . . . in fact, it was probably him in that summer house with Lottie, the blighter—Clarkie?"

Ada Clarke pursed her lips. "That's not for me to say, sir, Mr William."

"Or was it Georgie MacGibbon? He was killed at Kohima, Clarkie, so he won't mind if you tell me!"

Ada Clarke shook her head. "All I'll say, sir, is . . . it wasn't you."

Wimpy stared at her, and then nodded again, slowly. "Fair enough . . . 'It is knightly to keep faith—even after a thousand years'." His eyes came back to Roche. "*Puck of Pook's Hill*—Kipling's your set author for this exam, old boy, and don't ever forget it. We all knew it backwards—I read it to young David in this very room, by God! And the last party we ever had—do you remember that, Clarkie?—September the second, 1939—do you remember that—?"

"It was a Saturday, sir. I remember that because my Charlie was in uniform, and you brought him along with you—you and the Master, Mr Nigel, you were all in uniform—and I pressed three uniforms that night . . . those blooming battle-dresses with the pleats down the back—I had to put soap along the inside of them, to set the creases right—like knife-edges, they were, when I'd finished with them . . . and you all got horrid drunk that night—and my Charlie too, with you, what never got drunk normally—*I remember!*"

Wimpy's eyes glittered. "That's right. And young David was banished—as usual—and I came down here . . . I came down here while I could still walk, that is . . . and I found him sitting in front of the window, and he was reading *Puck*—the chapter where the Saxon chieftains come to the young Roman officers under flag of truce and invite them to plunder Britain together instead of fighting each other on the Great Wall—I remember too!'' The eyes came back to Roche, but this time they no longer saw him. ''And I went back to the house full of whisky and Kipling—they turned the Saxons down, of course, the young Romans did . . . 'The Wall must be won at a price' . . . and I looked at Nigel and Georgie and the rest of them, and I said, like the Saxon said, 'We be a goodly company; I wonder what the ravens and the dogfish will make of us before the snow melts'. *I remember.*''

The little room was silent for a moment, full of memories in which Roche had no part to play, except as an archaeologist. Then the schoolmaster blinked and focussed on him again.

''Pure melodrama, old boy! Because when the snows melted we were all still there, large as life and useless as a box of lead soldiers. The war didn't start off at all the way we expected—we'd readied ourselves up for battle and sudden death, and all we did was parade-ground drill and route marches for nine months.'' He grinned. ''My first war wounds were two dislocated thumbs falling off a motor-bike and a broken collar-bone playing rugger!''

''Ah—but it made up for lost time after that, the war did,'' said Mrs Clarke grimly.

''Very true, Clarkie,'' Wimpy nodded, no longer grinning. ''And the ravens and dogfish did get most of us in that party by '45, sure enough—only Laurie Deacon and I came back, in fact . . . and Laurie hardly counts, because he went straight into Intelligence—or straight in via the Judge Advocate's Department, anyway, and after that he knew too much to be allowed to risk his skin.'' He paused. ''And Charlie, of course.''

Ada Clarke sighed. ''Only half of my Charlie came back, sir. He left half of hisself back in Dunkirk . . . and I sometimes think it was the half I knew best—'' she caught herself quickly, with a half-glance at Roche, the stranger ''—but you're right, sir—you and Mr Deacon and Charlie . . . *and* Master David, of course—we mustn't forget him!''

''We certainly mustn't,'' agreed Wimpy, not looking at Roche.

''I never thought to see him go, that the war would go on so long, to take him as well as Mr Nigel—and I was sure that he was going to get killed too, he was that keen and pleased to go, being just a boy and not knowing any better . . . You know—'' she embraced them both with a proud look ''—I pressed his battle-dress just the same as I did for you, sir . . . and Mr Nigel . . . except Master David had a better one, what he'd got from a Canadian friend of his, he said . . . that last leave he had, before the old Wesdragons went off to France—'' she nodded at Roche to emphasise the occasion ''—that was just right after the Normandy landings they went—he was in the tanks, Master David was.''

''The 'Wesdragons' being the West Sussex Dragoons,'' explained Wimpy, almost as proprietorial as Mrs Clarke.

"That's right, sir. It's the cap badge, you see—Master David explained it to me. It's supposed to be a horse, because they used to be on horses in the old days, but it doesn't look like no sort of horse that ever lived, it's that badly done. So they reckon it's part horse and part dragon—the dragon being the proper badge of Wessex. It's all part of tradition, and tradition's very important, to my way of thinking—like doing a thing the old way, like it's always been done, which is the way it ought to be done—the proper way . . . And, of course, he said, a dragon's just right for them in their tanks, because it's all covered with scales—like in the window in the church, of St. George and the dragon—and they'd got all these iron plates to keep the bullets and suchlike out, you see."

"Huh!" murmured Wimpy. "All except 88-millimetres, and the odd *Panzerfaust*, anyway . . . and suchlike."

She frowned to him. "What's that, sir?"

"Nothing, Clarkie, nothing—just a thought, that's all."

Not so much a thought as a memory: *they were practically wiped out in the bocage, south of Caumont* . . . . Roche observed the two very different faces, the sharp ferrety features of the schoolmaster and the red-cheeked middle-aged countrywoman, as they watched each other, sharing overlapping recollections of past fears—fears they had shared for very different reasons, the one because he knew the perils lying in wait for young tank commanders, the other because she had seen so many of them march away, never to return.

And there was a third face, the one in the file, to be superimposed on those unrealised fears, hard and young and arrogant, quite unlike either of these—quite unlike the young 'Master David' he might otherwise have imagined from their evident affection, and yet the face which united them nevertheless: a broken-nosed, rugger-playing face.

"Ah . . . well, he did come back, sir, Mr William." Ada Clarke might not know a *Panzerfaust* from a hole in the road, but she had understood Wimpy's meaning in the end.

"He was invulnerable, certainly." The schoolmaster's agreement was strangely grudging. "But it was also a post-war version of him, Clarkie."

"Well, you wouldn't expect him to be the same, would you, sir?" Ada Clarke chided him sympathetically. "Growing up in the war . . . just waiting to take part—watching the other boys go before him, like young Mr Selwyn in the RAF, that was killed . . . and then seeing all those terrible things in those camps, that they showed on the films on VE-Day—" she turned to Roche suddenly "—I remember going to the Odeon Cinema in town that day, with Jim's wife Mavis, my sister-in-law . . . my Charlie didn't want to go, 'cause that was after he'd been invalided out, and he never wanted to see war films after that, only films with Betty Grable, and it was a war film that was on that day—I can't remember what it was—it was an American one, though . . . but I went with Mavis, anyway." She nodded at Roche, as though it was necessary to quote Mavis as corroborative evidence. "And in the interval the lights went up, and the manager—the cinema manager—comes on the stage and says 'Will all mothers with young children under the age of fourteen take their children outside—and all children, and anyone of a nervous disposition please go outside with them—because we're going to show these newsreel films that it's better they shouldn't see. And then they can come back afterwards when it's over.' And so Mavis had to go out of course, because she had young Jimmie with her—"

"Young Jimmie who's in the army now, is that?" inquired Wimpy politely, with only the merest hint of irony.

"Not in the army sir—a Royal Marine Commando, he is."

"That's right—of course! He was the one who went in at Suez last year?"

"Port Said, sir. And that mad he was when he came back—wouldn't stop talking about it, even though my Charlie didn't like it, and went off and wouldn't listen! But he says to me, young Jimmie does, 'We were winning, Auntie—going through them like a dose of salts—and they wouldn't let us go on!'—that mad he was! You should have heard him, sir!"

Wimpy nodded. "Yes. Perhaps I should have."

"Doing very well, he is. A sergeant now, and he's thinking of putting in for a commission and making a career of it."

"In spite of Suez?" Wimpy caught himself. "Sorry, Clarkie—you were in the cinema on VE-Day—?"

"Yes, sir . . . Well, of course, young Jimmie was only a nipper then—he was eleven years old, or thereabouts, must have been—so Mavis has to take him out. And she wasn't very pleased, either! 'You tell me what happens, Ada', she says . . . And . . . then they showed these films of the camps, where all the people were dead, poor souls—with arms and legs like matchsticks, and the bones showing through . . . just skin and bone, they were—I never saw anything like it in my life. Great piles of them, with the legs and arms hanging out—you couldn't hardly credit it, not unless you'd seen it—like scarecrows, poor souls." Ada Clarke shook her head, still only half-believing the evidence of her own eyes after a dozen years.

"Yes, Clarkie?" Wimpy jogged her gently.

"Yes, sir. Well . . . I thought—I can still remember what I thought, like it was yesterday—" she looked at Roche. "I thought 'he hadn't any right to do that, did Hitler'. I mean . . . killing people, that's bad enough, when they haven't done you any harm—but doing *that* to them . . . that's not *right*."

Roche waited.

"And then I thought—it's funny, but we had this German couple to stay at the house, friends of the Master, Mr Nigel—before the war . . . and they couldn't have been nicer . . . and I thought, they couldn't have known about this, not Herr Manfred and Frau Clara—they wouldn't have stood for it—they would have put a stop to that if they'd known about it, they would."

Out of nowhere, unsought and unbidden, the memory of the report on the Siberian camps and the recent Hungarian deportations came to Roche. It wasn't true to say that he hadn't believed the report; rather, he had accepted it on a level which had somehow rendered belief irrelevant to his own personal existence, his own reality.

But he had stood for it. Or . . . he had not stood against it: he had felt as anonymous, as removed from cause and effect, as guiltless as a bomb-aimer far above a darkened city, Hamburg or Dresden or Coventry or Moscow, just doing the duty which had fallen to him—which had to be done by someone—and armoured by the belief that the end must sanctify such means.

Yet now . . . even now he didn't know how he had argued himself into that original dishonesty, except that it had somehow been inextricably mixed up with Julie, and that her doubts had become his certainties . . . even, he didn't know how those certainties had become doubts again; or even if they were doubts—or that it was simply the accumulation of his own fears which was finally shooting him down, forcing him to descend into the fires of his own making.

"And then I thought—I can still remember thinking it, seeing our boys there in the film, in that awful place, with all the dead people—I thought 'Lord, I hope Master David isn't there, seeing such things right there in front of him . . .' " Mrs Clarke trailed off, blinking at Roche for a moment, then taking hold of herself. "It'd be enough to turn anyone's mind, that."

So that was the other fear Ada Clarke had slept with, night after night, while her adored Master David had galloped off to the war—and a fear she'd literally slept with, in the person of her Charlie, who had taken his wounds in the mind, on the Dunkirk beaches—that her Master David would also come back unrecognisable, handicapped in the same way.

He smiled at Mrs Clarke. "But he did come back all right?" he encouraged her. One thing at least: the excavation of Master David now seemed the most natural thing in the world.

"Oh yes, sir—"

"But different," cut in Wimpy.

"Not much different, sir. The big difference was before that—after the Master was killed, and right through until he went off to the war, he was difficult then. But that's not to be wondered at . . . And he was never an easy boy—"

"Which is not to be wondered at, either," said Wimpy drily.

"He was too much on his own, that's what. A boy ought to have friends. And being away at school so much—and even during the holidays too sometimes, when the Master was away, when he stayed on at school—he didn't have any friends, not of his own age." Mrs Clarke sniffed. "And that Mrs Templeton—"

Wimpy sat up. "Oh—come on, Clarkie!"

Mrs Clarke shook her head. "No, sir! I could tell a tale there—if I chose to . . . which I don't . . . But I could." Her lips thinned to a hard-compressed line. "She was a man-eater, she was."

"But not a boy-eater, Clarkie."

"Hmmm!" Her jaw hardened. "More like what they put in the local paper, sir: 'Pedigree bitch—house-trained, eats anything, very fond of children'."

"Clarkie!" Wimpy sounded genuinely shocked.

"I didn't say it, sir. It was Mr Deacon that said it—and it was Mr Deacon that put a stop to it too, in the end. You ask him if you think I tell a lie, sir, Mr William."

"Well . . ." As near as he had ever come to being at a loss, Wimpy was so. "Well, he never told me, Clarkie."

"Mr Deacon, sir?"

"David, I mean."

She shook her head. "Well, he wouldn't, sir, now would he? What Master David wants to forget, he forgets, and it's like it never happened to him. But what he wants to remember, he never forgets."

If Audley had that peculiar ability, it was a blessed gift, thought Roche. But, nevertheless, the boy and the man must still be the sum of this strangely twisted past in which so many influences had combined to tarnish the silver spoon he'd been born with.

"Hah—hmm . . ." Wimpy eyed Roche uneasily, as though the dialogue had outrun his intention. "And how's the house getting on, then, Clarkie?"

"Ah—" she shook herself out of the past gratefully "—that's getting on a treat, sir. They've finished the main roof, with all the timbers replaced that had the death-watch beetle. And they've done temporary repairs on the barn—only temporary, because Master David's coming home in the autumn to have a look at it himself before they do the job properly . . . But they've bought the tiles for that, from an old place up Guildford way that's falling down—he won't have anything new, won't Master David, it's got to be just right, no matter what the cost . . . thousands, he's spent on it, my Charlie reckons . . . Old Billy and Cecil have been on it three years nearly now, and not done a day's work anywhere else since they started—they're away today with the lorry, getting the oak beams for the barn that Master David ordered in the spring when he was here last."

"He was here in the spring, was he?"

"Two weeks, sir. And three games of rugger, that's what he did. And all the bills paid—and wages for me and Charlie, and Old Billy and Cecil, in advance right until the end of October, cash money—" she shook her head disbelievingly "—not like with Mr Nigel, nothing on tick, all cash money . . . It's got so if they want credit, Old Billy says, he could get anything he wants, the builders' merchants are so pleased to see him now—*not* like Mr Nigel . . . Except Mr Nigel never spent anything on the house, if he could help it, even with the rain coming in through the end gable so I had to put the old tin bath to catch it, to stop it coming through into the dining room! But not a drop comes in now, with the roof done good as new—"

Stocker's reservations on Audley's finances echoed inside Roche's head. There had been some money, and then there had been very little of it. But here was Audley satisfied with nothing but the best, even down to restorations in original materials plundered from old houses by his own private staff of restorers!

"And the bathrooms are done, like with things you never saw before—except Charlie remembers them, that he's seen in France when he was there—"

"Bidets, you mean, Clarkie?"

"If you say so, sir." Mrs Clarke sniffed her disapproval of all things French. "The plumbing's all done, anyway. And the electric wiring, that the insurance man wanted."

"And central heating?"

"No, sir—he won't have that done."

Wimpy nodded at Roche. "The lingering legacy of a public school education."

"But he doesn't come home much in the winter," said Mrs Clarke loyally. "He's like Mr Nigel there . . . So Charlie lights all the fires twice a week to keep the old place aired . . . and that roof's made a heap of difference, I can tell you." She nodded. "You wouldn't hardly recognise it."

Wimpy smiled. "I should like to see it . . . remembering the discomforts of the past." He flicked a glance at Roche. "Would you like to have a look, David? Would that be okay, Clarkie?"

"Of course, sir." She turned to Roche. "It's a beautiful old place, sir—it was a crime to let it go to wrack and ruin. But Master David's put that right." She gave Wimpy a sly look. "All it needs now is a woman's touch, to my way of thinking, sir, Mr William."

Wimpy shook his head. "No sign of that on the horizon, I'm afraid, Clarkie. And it'd need an exceptionally resilient young woman to handle our David—let alone capture him."

"Hmm . . ." Ada Clarke pursed her lips, but didn't deny the assessment. "A mistress it needs, I still say."

"It's had one or two of those, by golly!" Wimpy chuckled.

"I didn't mean *that*, sir—and well you know it! There were too many of *them* up to the war . . . But there's never been a real lady since—since—" she broke off suddenly, staring at Wimpy blankly for an instant, then seeming to notice Roche again as a stranger just in time. "There now! You want to go up to the house, and I've got my Charlie's tea to think about—if you should see him you tell him to come on back now, he's up there somewhere—" she rose from her chair and began fussing over the plates and teacups "—and there's some parcels for Master David you can take up for me while you're about it, and save me the bother—"

VI

THEY MADE THEIR way up the long, curving gravel drive between great banks of hawthorn and briar and elder interlaced with blackberry branches.

"Going to be a good year for blackberries." Wimpy nodded at the cascades of unripe greeny-red fruit. "Charlie never cuts the hedges back until after the jam-making and bottling—always wonderful picking along here."

Roche balanced the parcels with which he was loaded, and attempted to sort out his thoughts. He was aware that he had been fed with a great deal of information about David Audley, which might be priceless because it was of a kind that money and conventional interrogations would never have bought, except that he still didn't know why it should be so valuable.

"I used to pick them along here with Charlie when we were both boys," continued Wimpy. " 'Pick one—eat one' was our motto, as I recall."

Wimpy, as well as Ada Clarke and Charlie, was an old retainer of the Audley family, Roche decided. But there must be a class difference in the relationship which he hadn't yet worked out.

"You knew him—Nigel Audley—before Oxford?"

"Oh yes. My father was up there with *his* father—the one that was killed in 1917 . . . They were both at Balliol at the same time. Only Dad was clever and poor and Audley *grand-père* was clever and rich . . . But they rowed in the same eight, and they became friends. And they stayed friends even after Dad metamorphosed into a poor schoolmaster, like me after him—it's in the blood, I'm sorry to say, dear boy!" He bobbed his head at Roche. "Only I didn't really get to know Nigel until Oxford—I knew Charlie better until then, as a matter of fact. Poor old Charlie!"

Poor old Charlie . . . . This had been—and still was—a strange intertwining of people and families, across the boundaries of class and money, here and in Oxford, and through two world wars, which had turned the schoolmaster into Audley's guardian and the housemaid into something more than his nurse.

"She brought him up, in effect—Mrs Clarke?" The question followed the thought.

"David?" Wimpy nodded. "In effect—I suppose she did. In association with St. George's and Immingham and Rudyard Kipling, you might say—they brought him up too, just as much, no matter how much he resisted them."

"He . . . resisted them?"

Wimpy twisted a smile at him. "Not on the surface. One thing a boarding-school teaches you . . . is to conform or go under. And yet the saving grace of the British system is that it always manages to throw up a percentage of eccentrics and rebels nevertheless, to leaven the lump. So they have the great potential for good or evil . . ."

Bloody-minded, remembered Roche. That had been Latimer's assessment, and since Latimer was a product of the same system he should know a fellow spirit.

"I'm not sure that David has decided which horse to back," continued Wimpy. "Perhaps you'll be the catalyst—you're the man he could be waiting for. Freddie Clinton could be right."

Roche frowned. "What d'you mean? Right about what?"

Wimpy walked in silence for a time. "What do I mean? I think I mean . . . if you could recruit David—if he came to you of his own free will this time, not as a conscript, like in the war—"

"They don't conscript people into Intelligence."

"Wrong word? It was Intelligence or back to regimental duty, but after what he'd seen in Normandy that wasn't a choice . . . No, what I mean is, if you *can* get him to give you his loyalty freely just once, then that'll be it. 'Whether she be good or bad, one gives one's best once, to one only. That given, there remains no second worth giving or taking'—Pertinax in *Puck*, once again. I don't think he's given his best yet, to anyone or anything. That's all."

It was more than enough to Roche: it was dust and ashes bitter in his mouth. No one was a greater authority on the second best than he: he had spent years giving it, ever since Julie. Whoever Pertinax was, he was right.

"We're getting close to the house. It's just round the curve ahead, through the trees," said Wimpy. "It really is a fascinating old place—"

"What was wrong between Audley and his father?" asked Roche.

"Nigel?" Wimpy half-stumbled, tipping the topmost of his share of the parcels into the trackway ahead of him. "Damn! Mustn't damage the merchandise. Can you rescue that book for me, old boy? You're not so heavily laden as I am."

The division of the parcels had appeared equal to Roche, but it seemed churlish to refuse the request. He set down his own burden—of books also; all the parcels contained books by the shape and feel of them—and set about recovering the fallen volume, which had half emerged from its torn wrapping.

He couldn't resist the temptation to examine it—it would be a history book, something to do with Visigoths or Islamic doctrines, for a bet—

But it wasn't. Or rather, it wasn't quite: the garish dustcover illustrated the head of a warrior as though picked out in stained-glass, one-eyed and bearded and helmeted—*The Twelve Pictures*, by Edith Simon. Letting the remnants of the wrapping drop, he opened the book.

70

'The Twelve Pictures' is a novel as rich and wonderful as a medieval tapestry—a tapestry of beauty and terror . . .

"Interesting?" inquired Wimpy politely.

Roche looked up at him. "It's an historical novel—about Attila and the Huns." He couldn't keep the surprise out of his voice.

"Is it, indeed?" Wimpy reflected the surprise back at him. "I wouldn't have thought that would be quite his style of light reading—not *these* days . . ."

That was it exactly. Oxford and Cambridge were notoriously addicted to whodunits and mysteries—they were even given to writing the things. But historians (and although Audley wasn't an academic he was certainly an historian) were surely the last people to indulge in third-class relaxation in their own chosen subject.

"Let's have a look at the others," exclaimed Wimpy, his eyes alight with mischief and curiosity. "We shouldn't . . . but I can never resist temptation, old boy!"

It was hardly the place to start tearing open parcels, in the middle of a leafy lane, but the little schoolmaster had set down his parcels and was ripping at them before Roche could suggest as much.

"Here's another one—*The Restless Flame*, by Louis de Wohl . . . about St. Augustine of Hippo. And it's second-hand, so he must have ordered it—yes, it's from old Evan White in Guildford, of course! A damn good bookseller—he doesn't overcharge for the Loebs I've been extracting from him . . . And here's another one—Jack Lindsay's *The Barriers Are Down* . . . let's see . . . 'Gaul during the break-up of the Roman Empire'. And a new Penguin—Graves' *Count Belisarius*. I read that in hardcover before the war, I bought it for the school library in fact—"

They were all historical novels, new and second-hand; there wasn't a serious history book among them.

"Alfred Duggan—*Winter Quarters*," concluded Wimpy. "I must get that for the school library, I didn't know he'd got a new one out—a damn fine writer. I was arguing with Steve Bates, our sixth form History man, just not long ago that his hopefuls could learn more about the First Crusade from Duggan's *Knight with Armour*—aye, and more about the 5th century from Palfrey's *Princess in the Sunset*—than from anything he could offer them." He gave Roche a knowing leer. "He conceded Duggan, but Palfrey's purple passages about delicate over-bred Roman maidens having to submit to the sweaty embraces of hairy Goths were a bit too much for him." He sighed. "But we can't squat here all day, maundering over David's extraordinary taste in literature—and it is very odd, I grant you . . ." Wimpy gazed at the book in his hand.

Odd, certainly; though perhaps not altogether extraordinary if Audley had been raised on a diet of Kipling; and maybe not extraordinary at all on second thoughts, if the eccentric Wimpy's hand had been in that raising. And yet the little schoolmaster himself had magnified his own surprise, thought Roche: he had wondered at these books, even though they were undoubtedly Audley's books—apart from the carefully-typed addresses . . . *Dr D. L. Audley (to await arrival), c/o Mrs C. Clarke, The Lodge, Steeple Horley, Sussex.*

"Come on, then." Wimpy straightened up, balancing his armful of historical fiction but leaving their wrappers at his feet. "I'll ask Charlie to clear up this mess on his way home. The house is just ahead, round those trees—"

At first glimpse, through a scatter of silver birches, The Old House was disappointing—almost another Audley contradiction.

After Major Stocker's casual description—'not so big, but very old and rather nice'—Roche hadn't expected a minor stately home. But from the way Wimpy and Mrs Clarke had spoken, almost reverently, of the care lavished on the restoration and of the high days and nights of Nigel Audley's smart parties in the thirties, he had mentally prepared himself for a substantial manor, of the sort with which so many English villages were still blessed and which complemented the glorious little parish churches, his own special interest—medieval church, Stuart or Georgian manor, and Victorian school, plus ghastly twentieth-century village hall, that was the progression he had most often observed.

But The Old House was something different: a mixture of stone and weathered brick and half-timber, with windows and gables of different sizes apparently inserted at random—long and low . . . lower, indeed, than the windowless, ivy-covered barn beside it—the ivy at odds with a wisteria on the house—which had been tacked on to it at right angles, to form an L-shaped courtyard.

"Magic, isn't it!" murmured Wimpy, at his shoulder. "It always takes my breath away—I envy you the first sight of it, old boy. 'Earth has not anything to show more fair', and stout Cortez and Chapman's 'Homer', and all that, eh?"

The scales fell from Roche's eyes.

"Or 'Merlin's Isle of Gramarye', even," continued Wimpy softly, almost to himself. "The kitchen garden's full of bits of Roman tile, and we found coloured *tesserae* from a pavement when they dug the drain at the corner—I swear there's a villa underneath it somewhere . . . 'Merlin's Isle', that's what we used to say, David and I—there's a track that runs behind the house, just below the rise of the downland up above—

> *O that was where they hauled the guns*
> *That smote King Philip's fleet!*

"—remember Puck's song? Or maybe you don't . . ."

Roche's mouth was dry. "It's . . ." he swallowed awkwardly ". . . it must be very old," he said.

"Older than old. God knows how old!" Wimpy paused. "It's the servants' quarters, actually—the kitchen wing of the original house, the 15th century house that was burnt down in 1603—the very day Queen Elizabeth died, the

72

records say. But there was a fortified manor here before *that* house, and a Saxon hall before that . . . and, for my money, a Roman villa before *that*. And God only knows what before that, as I say . . . But the barn was built in the 1570s—the family was Catholic then, and there's a local legend that there's a 'Priest's hole' in the house somewhere, but no one's ever found it . . . It's certainly a fact that Elizabeth's officers raided the house regularly. But they never caught anyone, so it's either just a legend, or the hiding-place is too damned well hidden. You pays your money and you takes your choice . . . But David and I have spent hours tapping and poking and prying, when Nigel was away, and we haven't found anything yet . . . But we live in hopes, because—if you ask me—because it'll be a useful thing to have, a secret hiding place in one's house, in this country one day."

Roche looked at Wimpy questioningly. "What?"

"Oh, it'll be all right under Hugh Gaitskell—he may be a damned intellectual, but he's in the Attlee–Bevin tradition, the old Labour Party I voted for in '45. It'll be okay when he gets in after Macmillan—which he will next time . . . But there are some damned dodgy bastards in the wings after that, if you ask me—chaps who've never either done an honest day's work or smelt gunpowder properly . . . the way Ernie Bevin and Clem Attlee did, old boy . . . I tell you, we're in for a bad fifty years now—a bad twenty-five years, anyway, even if the bloody Russians don't shit on us from a great height! So a prudent Englishman would do well to have a numbered account in Switzerland—always supposing it was legal!—and a secret hiding place in his house—" he pointed at The Old House "—if only he can damn well find it!"

Roche blinked at him, and then stared at the house to hide his confusion. If David Audley didn't yet have the hiding place, it did look as though he had acquired the numbered account; and if this was what his legal guardian had taught him that was not to be wondered at, either. And just at this precise moment, he—David Roche, as ever was—wished that he had the same, only more so, and with better and more urgent reason.

"Hah—sorry!" Wimpy coughed apologetically. "Got on my jolly old soap-box in a moment of weakness—bad form—and particularly bad form with you, eh, old boy? And that isn't the object of this exercise anyway." He nodded towards the house. "*That* is the object which I wanted you to study, David Roche."

Roche studied The Old House obediently, though the act of obedience required no effort: he couldn't keep his eyes off it—off its detail, of which nothing appeared to have been planned and everything was irregular; and yet the whole, the sum of the detail, fitted together like a perfect jigsaw in its frame of trees, with the soaring curve of the downland behind it. The mystery of his first disappointment niggled him; had it been that he simply wanted something about Audley to be simple and predictable and ordinary?

"I'll say one thing for Cecil and Old Billy," murmured Wimpy. "They're a damned cantankerous pair of old rogues, but they've done a bloody marvellous job on that roof. If they can do as well with the barn, they may get into heaven yet . . ."

Roche shifted his gaze unwillingly from the ancient mulberry tree at the corner of the house, its sagging branches crutched with rusty iron supports as befitted the oldest living inhabitant of the picture, to the dilapidated roof of the barn, with its chaos of moss-covered tiles. In one place the ridge was sagging like the mulberry's branches.

"Well?" inquired Wimpy. "What d'you think of it?"

Roche estimated the artfully restored roof of the house against that of the barn. It would cost a pretty penny—that roof would have to be stripped, and the rotten timbers replaced . . . but Wimpy had said they'd found the oak for that—

"It's got you, hasn't it?" said Wimpy. "Good!"

Roche turned towards him, and found that he was smiling. "What d'you mean—it's got me?" He frowned. "Good?"

"It's in your face. It doesn't take everyone that way. But you're one of the lucky ones—or unlucky, maybe." Wimpy's own face was animated by mischief, almost malice. "I was hoping you would be, because it could help you."

It could help you?

"Let's say . . . you need to see this place, I think, if you're to have a chance of understanding *my* David—which frankly I don't any more, to be honest—" Wimpy seemed to have overheard that last unspoken question "—because this is David's obsession, so far as I can make out. And I don't wonder, even if he is hardly ever here—I don't wonder—"

Roche didn't wonder either.

"Yes . . . a bit of the old Matthew, chapter four, verse nine, eh?" said Wimpy softly. " 'All these things will I give thee, if only thou wilt fall down and worship me'—if I whispered that in your ear, supposing I had horns and a forked tail and oakum in my boots, how would you reply, young Roche?"

Had that been what the schoolmaster had seen in his face, thought Roche: had the envy been so naked?

He stared all the harder at the house to hide his annoyance with himself. To possess such a place—to hold such a piece of Old England—any sensible man would lie and cheat and steal, and do any dishonourable thing, certainly. And fight, of course, as no doubt those old Romans and Saxons and Normans had done—and scheme too, as no doubt those Elizabethan Catholics had done, with the Virgin Queen's Gestapo breathing down *their* necks—

He found a false smile to give Wimpy. "I don't think I could afford to run it on my pay, not even with the expenses thrown in, let alone employ Cecil and Old Billy, and Mr and Mrs Clarke."

Wimpy nodded. "Good point. I'd have to throw in gold as well, of course. But the Devil always does that, doesn't he!"

And yet there was a mystery here, to add to all the others, now that he'd seen the house: if this was David Audley's obsession, the restoration of the family home to its past glory, his father's intention seemed to have been the exact opposite—to use it, and mortgage it to finance its use, and to let it decay all the while . . . and even at the last to try to sell it over his son's head, which only a German bullet in 1940 had prevented?

"You think we might get at him—at David Audley—through the house, somehow?" Roche faced the little man squarely, frowning sincerity at him. After all, the virtue of this diversion was that if it paid off it would cease to be a diversion. Not Mr Nigel, but Master David, was the objective.

"Hmmm . . . not if 'get at' means 'threaten', certainly." Wimpy shook his head slowly. "Threatening my David could be . . . unproductive, let's say. It isn't something I'd undertake lightly—he has a streak of obstinacy a mile wide."

At least Wimpy and Oliver St.John Latimer agreed on something, then!

Roche nodded at the house. "Where does the money come from?" It was rather a straight question, but it followed naturally.

"Blessed if I know!" Wimpy's shoulders lifted. "I suppose you could look into that—he could be up to some fiddle, I shouldn't wonder . . . the way we're taxed these days, it can hardly be honest money, and that's a fact!" He turned his gaze to Roche, still with the ghost of the smile on his face. Then the eyelids shuttered like a camera, and the next expression on the reel was cool and calculating. "But I'd do that carefully if I were you, if it's a volunteer you're after . . . I think . . . if it's a fiddle it'll be fool-proof—income-tax-inspector-proof, rather."

Roche felt his own eye drawn again towards the house. He had never owned anything like it—he had never even imagined owning anything like it. All that he possessed could be packed into a tin trunk and two large suitcases, plus a couple of tea-chests for his books. Up until recently his heaviest piece of baggage had been an idea, an article of faith which he had pretended to himself was an unshakeable political conviction, which Julie had bequeathed to him as the sole beneficiary of her will. But he hadn't really owned the idea for a long time now, and perhaps it had never really been his.

"You take my point? I rather think you do, eh?" Wimpy was observing him narrowly, but was evidently misinterpreting his face this time.

Roche felt his back muscles shiver. How could the man have come so close, after having been so wide of the mark? "But his father didn't take the point, did he!"

"His father? Whose father?" Wimpy frowned.

"Audley's—David Audley's. 'Mr Nigel'—*the expectancy and rose of the fair state,*" quoted Roche brutally. "Wasn't 'Mr Nigel' about to sell the house?" He threw the truth down like a gauntlet between them, challenging Wimpy to choose where his loyalty lay, with the father, his old comrade-in-arms, or with The Old House and his David.

The schoolmaster's face clouded. "Ah . . . well . . . Nigel . . . was Nigel." He looked up and around nervously, as though he'd only just realised where he was, and Nigel-was-Nigel might be eavesdropping on them. "Clarkie said we ought to look out for her Charlie, because it's time for his tea—half of which we've already eaten . . . And she also said, *sotto voce*, as we were leaving—as I was leaving—that old Charlie's having one of his turns . . . in his downhill phase, as the headshrinkers say . . . which means, the sooner he's back home, the better. You just wait here, old boy, and I'll go look for him—he's in the garden somewhere." Wimpy started to turn away before Roche could open his mouth to protest. "Talk about Nigel later, maybe." The turn went through a full circle so that Wimpy was facing him again while retreating backwards towards the wrought-iron gate into the walled garden. "Just look after the books till I get back." Wimpy pointed to the pile of historical novels he had deposited on the gravel. "Or, better still, take 'em into the house and stack 'em on the table by the door, and then have a scout round for yourself—right?"

Roche shut his mouth. If Wimpy was transparently set on ducking the question, solving his loyalty-dilemma simply by quitting the field, at least he was offering something attractive in exchange: to enter The Old House without a running commentary was a chance not to be missed.

"Right." Wimpy waved vaguely, half at Roche, half at the house, and swivelled back towards the gate.

Roche watched him disappear through the trailing cascade of magenta-flowered clematis which covered the stone archway above the gate. Then he dumped his own armful of books alongside Wimpy's and stamped across the gravel forecourt to the porch.

As the door swung open a burst of sunlight edged with rainbow colours caught him full in the face.

He shifted his head, shielding his eyes from the light with his hand, and stared up the beam of light through an arch full of dancing dust-motes into a stained-glass window—a high window blazoned with a rich coat-of-arms, yellow and red and blue, set at the top of a carved oak staircase—beyond which the afternoon sun blazed.

Directly ahead of him was an immense refectory table, dark with age like the panelling all around it, with a great bowl of roses on it. Some of the roses had shed their petals in different-coloured piles around the bowl, on a fine coating of dust which the sunlight betrayed. He sniffed, and the scent of the roses, mixed with a damp cellar-smell from somewhere under his feet, combined with the stained-glass to carry him back to this morning's church and Genghis Khan. He wrinkled his nose, uncertain whether it was the cloying rose-scent-plus-church-smell which made him think of funerals, or the memory of Genghis Khan which also made him think of death, that disturbed him more.

His eyes were becoming accustomed to the strange mixture of brightness from the searchlight-beam of the sun and shadow accentuated by the dark panelling, with its ghost-marks of pictures which had once hung on the walls.

Family portraits, maybe? And no prizes for guessing what had happened to them, one by one, as Mr Nigel's horses let him down in the last furlong before the winning post, also one by one; the pictures were always the first thing to go, the easiest things to pack off to Sotheby's and Christie's. All that was left on the walls was a line of old photographs up the staircase, school and college groups of cricketers and oarsmen sun-bleached to pale sepia-brown; and the refectory table, which was too big to sell, and the grand-father clock in the furthest corner, silent at ten minutes to noon or midnight—had that also been too big, or not worth the trouble of selling? Or had Adolf Hitler saved the last furniture with the house by his own pre-emptive bid for Europe and all its contents in 1939?

In spite of the sunlight, the house was cool, almost chilly, he could feel its cold breath against his cheeks. It wouldn't do to let his imagination stray too far here: reason advised him that thick walls and stone-flagged floors could hold winter all the year round when the owner was mostly absent, and fires were only lit occasionally, and that this house had been trapped in the vicious circle of such absences for a generation, so it was no wonder that its atmosphere was unwelcoming; but beneath reason he could sense an older instinct of unreason, which whispered very different rumours inside his head, of the enmity of old things to the flesh and blood of intruders like himself, and to would-be destroyers, like Mr Nigel, who had not lived to come safe home to the house he had neglected.

Of course, it was foolish to let such thoughts unnerve him; and they were only the combined product of his own disturbed emotions, and his own fascination with old buildings, and maybe too much of Ada Clarke's rich fruit cake unsettling his digestion.

It was only an old empty house, and the afternoon sun was shining outside, and Wimpy wasn't far away—Genghis Khan was far away, and Audley was even further, and Mr Nigel was bones in a war grave long-forgotten, and none of *them* could touch him at this moment, any more than the house itself could reach out at him.

There were doors, panelled in the panelling, ahead of him—to the right, and to the left, under the staircase—that door would lead to the cellars . . . to the wine-cellar, at a guess; which would be full of racks emptied, but not renewed, by Mr Nigel, for another guess . . . cellars full of cobwebs and the damp smell which was in his nostrils, and he certainly wasn't about to scout around in *them* unless Wimpy was cheerfully leading the way, by God!

The door on the right didn't look much more inviting, but there were those arched passages on each side of him which he'd half-glimpsed in the first moment after he'd ducked the sunlight, before his whole attention had been drawn up to the stained-glass coat-of-arms . . . one way would lead to the day rooms, most likely—the sitting room, and the library, and maybe a study; the other way to a dining room, and a breakfast room, and then the kitchen and the pantries, and the servants' quarters; though with an old hodge-podged place like this, which already seemed vastly bigger inside than it had from the outside, full of unsuspected space, such regularity might well be a bad guess. He could only tell by looking for himself.

Left or right? Roche peered down the left-hand passage, undecided, his eye lifting to the flaking white-washed vaulting above the panelling. For sure this part of the house, which had survived the great fire on the day of Elizabeth Tudor's death, had in any case been the older wing. Wimpy had said—

The recollection of what Wimpy had said died unthought as he turned towards the right-hand passage, which was identical with the left-hand one, except that the door at the end of it was open, and that there was someone standing in it staring at him.

Christ! He hadn't heard that door open—there hadn't been a sound after his own footfalls on the flagstones which had carried him through the porch and the archway of the original door into the hallway—

Christ! He hadn't heard that door open because it hadn't opened: the man had been standing there, staring at him, ever since he had entered the house, watching him silently, as soundless as the house itself!

An insect crawled back up Roche's spine as he returned the stare. This right-hand passage wasn't exactly identical . . . or . . . or it was, but the wisteria overhung the low window recessed into the thickness of the wall on this side, deepening the shadow with a green cast.

It had to be Ada Clarke's Charlie—it was either Ada Clarke's Charlie or it would vanish in the instant he addressed it—

"Hullo there?" Somewhere between the intention and the final articulation the words lost their planned heartiness, and echoed hollowly down the passage instead. "Good afternoon—Mr Clarke, is it?"

That was better. The figure moved, shifting its feet so that the sound of hobnails scraping on stone released Roche from fear. Ghosts didn't wear hobnailed boots; or, if they did, the phantom hobnails wouldn't scrape like that; and ghosts weren't so substantial, and Charlie Clarke was nothing if not substantial: he filled the doorway, all of six-foot-three, with long arms and huge hands in proportion.

Also, the collarless striped shirt, the Fair Isle knitted pull-over and the shapeless corduroy trousers was no uniform for any self-respecting spectre in this setting. Doublet-and-hose, or satin breeches, or even Mr Nigel's well-pressed battle-dress—any of those might not be out of place in The Old House, but not a Fair Isle pullover. Not even the faintly green-tinged light which filtered into the passage through a window half-obscured by wisteria could make a convincing ghost of Charlie Clarke on second glance.

But if second glance stripped the supernatural from Charlie it did nothing to lessen the hostile vibrations which eddied round Roche as they stared at each other—the same sensation his sixth sense had picked up moments before, but had ascribed to the house itself. And there was something no less creepy about the sensation now that its source had become tangible: the way both Wimpy and Mrs Clarke had spoken of Charlie, the man was at best a simpleton, but at worst—*in his downhill phase*—perhaps something more dangerous. And the confirmation of that lay not only in the gorilla-length arms and meat-plate hands, but also in the way those addled brains had been able to transmit a signal before Roche had set eyes on the signaller. Which, by any standards, was strong magic to beware of, not to ignore.

"It's 'Charlie', isn't it?" said Roche tentatively. "Charlie, my name's Roche—David Roche." The giving of names freely was an old ritual of peaceful intentions.

The words unlocked Charlie's legs, but not his tongue. He took two slow steps out of the doorway, and then stopped. But that short advance carried his face out of deep shadow into enough light for Roche to make out the little pig-eyes and heavy chin separated by a button nose and tiny mouth in a brick-red expanse of face. The sum total was so close to being classically oafish, if not actually brutish, with no spark of anything in the eyes, that the contrast between Charlie and his wife was not so much surprising as painful.

Roche licked his lips. "I was . . . I was hoping to meet Mr . . . *Master* . . . David—your Master David, Charlie," he lied nervously. "Is he home?"

The mention of Audley appeared to take Charlie by surprise, his eyes almost disappearing into the frown which descended on them.

Charlie took a deep breath. "Not 'ere—" the words came from deep down, through layers of gravel "—what are you doin' 'ere?"

It was a good question, but altogether unanswerable. More than ever, Roche wished that Wimpy was at his side.

"I came here with Mr Willis, Charlie." However dim and downhill Charlie might be, he couldn't forget Wimpy. No one could forget Wimpy, he was supremely memorable.

"You know Mr Willis, Charlie." Whatever the Germans had done to Charlie at Dunkirk seventeen years before, they had done thoroughly. "*Major* Willis—Master David's guardian."

Charlie's baffled expression cleared magically. "*Captain* Willis, you mean," he growled.

"Captain Willis," he agreed hastily. *Captain* Willis?

"Arrragh!" The gravel rattled in Charlie's throat. "Captain Willis is 'D' Company, an' Mr Nigel, that's Major Audley—he's 'B' Company. An' Captain Johnson, that was Mr Johnson until just recently—'e's 'A' Company now, of course . . ." he nodded slowly at Roche ". . . an' 'C' Company is . . . is . . ." the nod faded away as Charlie cast around in the lost property room of his memory, and failed to find the name of 'C' Company's commanding officer, who had let him down by being unmemorable after seventeen years. " 'C' Company is . . ." he rocked slowly from side to side "—'A' Company is Captain Johnson, that was Mr Johnson as was . . ."

Roche watched the Caliban-face twitch with the effort of putting the names of men who had most of them been dead and buried for years to formations which had long been disbanded. Someone—some irate sergeant-major or despairing corporal—had once hammered those names into Charlie's memory so firmly that they were still there in the present tense.

"Captain Willis is out in the garden," he nodded at Charlie.

" 'D' Company—I just told you," said Charlie irritably. Then his incongruous little mouth twisted into some sort of grin. "Get hisself killed on that motor-bike of his one of these days, 'e will—Captain Willis, that was schoolmastering before the war broke out." He nodded back in Roche's direction. "That's 'im what learns young Master David his letters, an' thinks the world of 'im, like my Ada does—'D' Company, 'e is." He focussed on Roche, and frowned as though he was seeing him for the first time, but could supply no 1940 name for what he saw. "Who are you, then?"

"I'm—" Roche stopped abruptly as the macabre reality of Charlie's 'downhill phase' registered fully with him. The man was in his own private time-warp, so it seemed from all those present tenses and 'Captain' Willis and 'young' Master David.

"I'm Captain Roche, Royal Signals," he snapped.

Whatever it might mean, there was one sure way of finding out, albeit a cruel and risky one.

"Is Master David not home, Clarke?" he snapped in Captain Roche's military voice, long disused.

Charlie's features twitched with the effort of thinking.

"Well, Clarke?" Roche jogged him mercilessly. "Speak up!"

Charlie stiffened out of his stoop. "No, sir."

Roche braced himself. "Is Major Audley home, then?"

This time he hardly dared to watch Charlie's face, the thoughts behind it were unguessable and didn't bear thinking about.

"No, sir," said Charlie. "Haven't seen him today, sir."

God, it was true! One end of this interrogation stood in 1957, but the other was trapped in 1940, with no years in-between! And, what was worse—Roche's flesh crawled at the possibility—was *Haven't seen him today, sir* . . . . How many times did Charlie catch sight of his Mr Nigel, and the other ghosts of Mr Nigel's time, drifting round The Old House?

But he had work to do now, in 1957.

"Hmmmm . . ." Captain Roche's simulated annoyance almost choked him. "I was hoping to catch one of them, damn it!" He frowned at Charlie, whose face had settled into blank immobility. What business Captain Roche had with Mr Nigel and Master David was none of Fusilier Clarke's business.

And yet it was in that private area that the work had to be done.

"*Hmmm* . . . Seems to me, Clarke, that the Major doesn't hit it off very well with his son—am I right?" he said briskly.

Charlie started twitching again. "Sir?" The gravel reduced the word to a croak.

"Mr Nigel and Master David—why don't they get on? Speak up, man! Don't pretend you don't know!"

Charlie's mouth opened and shut, and his head jerked from side to side, and his eyes rolled and ended up staring past Roche, over Roche's shoulder to the line of ancestral photographs running up the staircase as though he was pleading with them to come to his assistance.

"Come on, Clarke—you can tell me. I'm a friend of the family, you know."

"And so you are!" The voice came from the doorway on Roche's right, just out of his vision, and it was Wimpy's.

"So you are, my dear fellow—a good friend of the family!" said Wimpy genially. "Afternoon, Fusilier Clarke." The geniality remained, but there was iron beneath the velvet. "You cut along back to your billet now and have your tea, and I'll talk to you later—right? Oh . . . and there's a bit of a mess on the road, you'd better clear that up smartly or sar-major will see it, and then there'll be hell to pay, I shouldn't wonder. Right?"

"Sir!" Charlie's hobnails cracked to attention on the flagstones. "Sir!"

Wimpy nodded. "Off you go then, Clarke."

Only after Charlie had departed did Wimpy move again, and then he circled Roche, ignoring him and breathing in The Old House's damp smell half-critically and half as though it was doing him a power of good.

"Well, old boy . . ." Wimpy didn't look at him ". . . you took a bit of a risk there, didn't you!"

"I did?" Ignorance was never an excuse, but it was all he had to offer.

Wimpy nodded at the line of photographs. "Big chap, Charlie Clarke . . . Seen him lift a five-hundredweight truck to save his mates popping the jack under the rear wheel, to change it—Charlie's only party trick, you might say . . . We had two like him in the battalion, with too few brains and too much brawn—never should have been recruited, except maybe into the Pioneers . . . I had one of them in my company, 'Batty' they called him, because of the way he'd run amok. But he was killed in France in '40."

Roche watched Wimpy sigh, and was grateful for the past tense: at least both of them were together in 1957 now, however uncomfortable the next few minutes might be!

"The other one was Charlie, in Jerry Johnson's company—General Sir Gerald Johnson as he is now—and Fusilier Charlie Clarke as *he* is still . . . they were both lucky, after a fashion, anyway." He looked at Roche at last, but bleakly. "They both survived, that is—Jerry to prosper in his chosen profession, and Charlie . . . after Dunkirk . . . to be Charlie, only less so at intervals—to be Charlie in 1940, *before* Dunkirk, as you have discovered, Captain Roche, eh?"

Oddly enough he didn't seem angry now. He seemed almost relieved by Captain Roche's abortive discovery.

"And you have been lucky too, I suppose one might say, Captain Roche," said Wimpy.

Ignorance and silence were still safest, especially when the latter might purge the former.

"Charlie was the gentle one, you see." Wimpy nodded. "Batty actually liked killing things—rabbits, Germans . . . fortunately he never had a proper chance with regimental policemen, but it was all the same to him. Charlie was different, he was always gentle . . . or almost always gentle—he meant to be as gentle as he could be, if people let him alone. That was all they had to do—just let him alone." He gazed at Roche almost sorrowfully. "But you didn't let him alone . . . and in this house too—he's very protective about this house. God help the burglar he ever catches here!"

Roche felt the air cold against his cheeks: he could testify to the truth of that, the memory of Charlie's protectiveness was in that air still.

"But you were lucky, as I say. I turned up just in time, before he took you apart," said Wimpy simply. "Very lucky for all concerned . . . Though, of course, I blame myself too, old boy."

There, at last, was the opening he had been waiting for, thought Roche, hot inside against the cold on his face from the memory of Charlie.

"So you damn well should!" he exclaimed. "You wouldn't answer the question. Every time I asked it, damn it!"

Wimpy shook his head. "Not 'wouldn't', old boy. I promised, but there's a time and place for the right answer, that's all." He pointed towards the staircase. "David put them up himself, but . . . typical David, putting them up . . . he did it when he came back from Normandy, the first time, on the last day of his leave . . . but Charlie carried the hammer and the nails . . . *typical* David—" he shook his head at Roche, as blank-faced as Charlie had been "—took them all out of the study, plus the extra one Nigel had buried in his bottom drawer . . . and that was typical Nigel too—putting it away, when he could have torn it up, and burnt it, and it would have been dead and buried . . . But *no*—he just put it in the bottom drawer for David to find; and he knew David would find it, because David finds everything sooner or later—just put it in the bottom drawer for David to find, and David found it *of course*. . . . So out they all come from the study, *plus the extra one*—with never a word to Clarkie and me—and Charlie holds the nails—and *bang, bang, bang*, there they are in public, for everyone to see on the stairs—the one place everyone *has* to see, with never a word to me, not ever . . . not even now—not *now*, not *ever* . . ."

Roche looked at the photographic gallery on the stairway, and then at Wimpy, and then at the gallery again. There were more bloody pictures there than was comfortable, if there was one *extra* picture which he was expected to home in on at first glance, to tell him what he ought to know.

"Go and see for yourself, my dear man—don't let me stand in your way, just go and see for yourself, eh?"

Roche went quickly, before the schoolmaster could confuse him further, either deliberately or accidentally.

The line was not so much a line, as a double zig-zag over half a century—more than half a century—of the history of Oxford-and-Cambridge and photography both.

Indeed . . . it went back to Great-Grandfather Audley, looking faintly like Prince Albert, in the smartly-cut but unpressed suiting of the time, blotched and faded by age, at the bottom of the staircase, gracing the Hoplites Society of Balliol College, to David Audley himself, vintage 1949, scowling from his college rugger XV, which had been added at the very top as a Cambridge afterthought—almost an act of defiance amongst a collection of otherwise exclusively Balliol College, Oxford: pictures of Father Nigel, Grandfather and Great-Grandfather, who had all been oarsmen in their college VIIIs, or ornaments of that same Hoplites Society . . . which, at a guess, from its name, and the stylish fashion of their evening dress, and the nonchalant don't-give-a-damn slightly drunken expressions they affected, must be an exclusive club for the young Classical gentlemen of their time.

God! What would Genghis Khan make of this collection? Here, to the life, were the young bloods of the Tsar's Imperial Guard, lazing it at ease among the empty Champagne bottles through the 1905 revolt, past the 1914 armageddon to the 1917 reckoning!

Roche concentrated his wits and his memory. Wimpy had said (or was it Sir Eustace, or Colonel Clinton, or Stocker? Or had it been in the records, merely?) that Mr Nigel's father had been killed in 1917—

It had been Wimpy: *My father was at Oxford with his father—the one that was killed in 1917*—take away the right number of years and that was where to look—was it?

But why should that be worth looking at?

All the same, he looked—frowned, rather—at the Hoplites of the generation before Passchendaele: a double row of languid young men, none of whom could have imagined himself as a rotting corpse in thick mud, and none of whom he recognised . . . although the list of names underneath indicated that there was a *D. N. D. Audley (hon. secretary)* in it somewhere, next to *The Hon. W. de V. Pownell-Lloyd (president)* . . .

Wimpy's own father ought to be here somewhere, though hardly among the rich young Hoplites, because he had been *clever but poor*, and that ruled him out of their company.

Maybe he would be among the oarsmen in the next picture—a crew comic not only for their close-fitting but elongated rowing uniforms, but also for their deadly-serious expressions, as though it had been the battle of Salamis in which they'd distinguished themselves, not Oxford in eighteen-ninety-something. But at least he could instantly identify the Audley in this crew—the familiar face stared at him out of the photograph—the Audley face, minus the broken nose, plus the rowing cap and the frail under-graduate moustache!

And there was a *Willis* in this crew, too—another plain plebeian *W. Willis* (another Wimpy?), but *Captain of Boats* no less, and in a victorious Eights Week, judging by the list of defeated colleges beneath the names of the oarsmen. So both families had something to be proud of in this particular photograph, clearly—

He studied the picture for a moment, and then shifted to the Hoplites Society group just below it, and then returned to the oarsmen. They bore the same date, and the same photographer's name, but the oarsmen were clearer—much clearer, much less faded—

Buried in the bottom drawer!

It was here, in this picture, on the wall for everyone to see—it was here, somewhere among *J. R. Selwyn (No.4)* and *D. N. L. Audley (stroke)* and *N. B-R. Poole (cox)* . . . and *W. Willis (bow, Captain of Boats)*, but he couldn't see it.

He looked at Wimpy again, and knew for certain that it was there in front of him—it was in Wimpy's face, by God!

He stared at the oarsmen again, and then at the Hoplites, and then at the oarsmen.

And saw at last, what had been there all the time—what had been there half the afternoon, but not in Wimpy's face.

Literally, not in *Wimpy's* face.

He checked the names underneath to make doubly sure.

The chickens had come home to roost, and *W. Willis (bow, Captain of Boats)* had rowed them all the way from the eighteen-nineties: he was the spit-and-image twin, minus the broken nose, of David Audley.

ADVANCE TO CONTACT:

Madame Peyrony's young ladies

VII

THE FRENCHMAN HAD been swimming strongly in the river current in the same place for all of ten minutes.

Molières, Beaumont, Roquépine, Monpazier . . . they had all belonged to the English . . .

The sight of the man battling to no purpose, together with the hot sun not long past its zenith and the warm stones under the rug, and the truffle omelette and the trout, all conspired to undermine Roche's concentration.

Villeréal, Montflanquin, Villeneuve, Neuville, Villefranche-du-Périgord . . . they were the French ones . . . but there were other Villeneuves and Neuvilles and Villefranches to be distinguished from them, which had been just as *new* and *free*, but also English, on this embattled frontier seven hundred years ago.

And *Domme*—French—high and golden above the river, which had betrayed him into over-eating when he needed a clear head—

Maybe that was how it had happened—*God! How I love this fat, fertile, self-indulgent country, so ripe for plundering but also so cruel and dangerous and ready to betray its enemies*—had that been the last Anglo-Saxon insight, the last clear English thought old John Talbot had had as the French cannon opened up on his archers at Castillon down the river five hundred years before—that it had always been too good to be true, the English Empire in France, from Bordeaux to Calais—too rich and too tempting and too strong for cold-blooded islanders?

He mustn't go to sleep! He wasn't even tired, he had slept five dreamless hours in the couchette from Paris–Austerlitz, lulled by the train sounds even through dawn halts at Limoges and Perigueux to be woken gently by the well-tipped attendant in time for Les Eyzies (*expense no object*—that was heady and frightening at the same time, and it had already been his undoing in the restaurant at Domme), and with Raymond Galles meeting him at the station in his own battered old Volkswagen, which had been driven down from Paris yesterday by some poor nameless bastard.

God! He mustn't go to sleep: he must think of his *bastides*, Beaumont and Monpazir, Villeréal and sun-baked Domme, and the rest of them on the list—all that Anglo-French history he had sweated and frozen over during his Manchester days, in those ghastly wind-swept, bomb-swept open spaces around the University and the History Faculty, which were dismal even when it was dry, like a piece of East Berlin authentically reproduced in England, no expense spared—

Roche shivered at the memory, coldly wakened by it, and twisted side-ways on to one elbow, blinking against the glare, the better to observe the lunatic swimming Frenchman.

He was still there, breasting the current in the same yard of river, hauling himself forward and instantly being carried back by the force of the water, and then hauling himself forward again, only to be carried back again in a perfect display of useless determination.

All that history . . .

The afternoon sun rippled on the broken water rushing by the swimmer. Perhaps it wasn't a useless exercise: maybe the man was stretching his sinews in preparation for some Marathon swim, across the Channel or the Hellespont, where tides and currents were hostile; and this way he could take his punishment at full stretch without ever losing sight of his little pile of clothes and belongings on the stony strand ten yards from him?

All that history had seemed just as useless, just as much mental energy equally pointlessly expended on the past when it was the present which had lain waiting in ambush for him in Korea and Japan, and if he'd understood more about that then perhaps he wouldn't be lying here now, not knowing any more whose side he was on.

And yet now *all that history* had become a qualification for something at last, at least in part, though in a way neither he nor his teachers had ever envisaged—

"That's everything then, I think," said Clinton, pushing the buff-coloured envelope across the table. "Ticket to Paris, a little spending money . . . Raymond Galles will have more for you when he meets you at Les Eyzies on Thursday morning. And Galles will have fixed your transport too—he's a good man, a born and bred Périgourdin, knows the country, knows the people. Been on our books since '41—would have been since '40, only it took him eight months to extricate himself from a PoW camp . . . Not used him much since '44, but you can trust him right down the line. A good man, he'll look after you . . . Thompson'll meet you in Paris, of course, with the cover material all written up—most of it you'll know, some of it you must re-write in your own fist, to make it look authentic, just in case anyone gets nosey—and your train ticket. Gare Austerlitz, 2150, all the way, arrive just before breakfast—time to refresh your memory and get some kip. Very convenient. Any last questions?"

"What historical material, sir?" He hadn't expected to be finally briefed by Clinton himself.

Shrug. "I honestly don't know, Roche. Thompson's choosing something appropriate to the area, naturally—something worth being there for. But he won't give you any of Audley's specialities, they're too damn esoteric, so I gather." Smile. "According to Master Oliver St.John Latimer, anyway."

A singularly obscure aspect of Byzantine religious history certainly rated as esoteric, thought Roche uneasily.

"Don't worry, man!" Clinton picked up the unease. "You'll be able to hold your own."

"I didn't get a First at Cambridge."

"Balls to Cambridge—and to Oxford." Clinton's jaw tightened. "There's too much Oxbridge in the service. That's one of its troubles."

So much for Oliver St.John Latimer—and Sir Eustace Avery!

"But you want me to recruit Audley nevertheless, and he's Cambridge, sir."

"Audley's a maverick." Clinton shrugged off the inconsistency. "And there's nothing wrong with the Manchester School of History."

"In which I got a shaky Second."

"Which should have been a First, according to your professor." Clinton leaned forward, frowning. "And your flat in Paris is full of books—"

"Yes, but—"

"*We chose you for this*, Roche," Clinton overbore him. "I told you before—we chose you very carefully—we chose you *particularly*—get that into your head, and don't ever forget it. You, and no one else, Roche."

Roche opened his mouth, and then closed it quickly. After The Old House and its secret he was consumed with curiosity about Audley, so that he almost wanted the assignment for its own sake.

"Because you can do the job, that's why." Clinton sat back. "When you learn more about David Audley—you may understand . . . but you ought to know one thing already, from what you heard in the Admiral's Room—"

Sir Eustace's room, under the Sargent portrait, where the Admiral's eyes had screwed into his soul, seeking out its innermost treachery: how could Clinton miss what the long-dead Admiral saw so clearly?

"—if we sent Master Latimer, with his Oxford First in P.P.E.—whatever that is—do you think Audley would change his mind for *him*? Not in a hundred years! Or Malcolm Thain—not in a thousand years! That man couldn't recruit a drunkard for a piss-up in a brewery, I don't think—not if we really needed him." Clinton wrinkled his nose in contempt. "But you, Roche . . . you just might manage it."

The train was in the station, but it was still moving, and it still might not stop.

"You're a bit of a dreamer, Roche. But you're also a soldier, and that's important, if you have to deal with David Audley, because whatever he may say about his military service—however he may denigrate it, he's proud of it."

Clinton was a strange man, thought Roche warily: not Oxbridge, even contemptuous of Oxbridge. But not unintellectual.

"And you're a scholar too—and that's also important for Audley. He values scholarship."

"Hardly a scholar, Colonel." The devil was still talking. "Not since Manchester. And not even then, not really."

"But still close enough. And you left to become a soldier." Clinton smiled evilly. "It should have happened to him—and you'll see that he knows how it happened."

"How it happened? I was called up, that's how it happened!"

"I mean, how you got into Intelligence—a volunteer, not a pressed man."

God! If they knew the truth about that!

"A scholar—but not Oxbridge . . . and *he* has his reasons for not loving Oxbridge . . . and a soldier," continued Clinton smoothly. "So you have the right profile of the pen and the sword . . . And you have one final attribute which neither Master Oliver nor Master Malcolm possess, more's the pity, I'm sorry to have to admit. Can you think what it is?"

The recollection of how he had really come to volunteer for that transfer from Signals to Intelligence was still unbalancing Roche: what the hell did he have that Latimer and Thain didn't, except that guilty secret?

"You'll send me back to Paris if I fail?" Clinton and Genghis Khan were brothers under the skin.

"Not to Paris. An ambitious young man can still be unhappy in comfort there. If you fail with Audley we'll bury you somewhere uncomfortable, Roche."

If he failed with Audley, and was relegated to counting paperclips in some backwater, then he'd never get away from either of them—until the Comrades decided to trade him for some minor advantage.

"But I don't think you'll fail. I think you can do the job," said Clinton, almost amiably. "And then you'll be Major Roche in London, I shouldn't wonder. 'And there is in London all that life can afford', as Dr Johnson said." He nodded at Roche. "So the incentive is a two-way one—"

Molières, Beaumont, Roquépine, Monpazier, Lalinde—

All the same, that clever-stupid bastard Thompson had still got it wrong, thought Roche morosely. The study of the medieval *bastides* of Aquitaine might be outside Audley's special historical period, and even a perfectly reasonable subject for a student of French history to study in this particular area of all others, the more so as it was also an uncommonly congenial region as yet unspoiled by *le tourisme*.

Nevertheless, if bloody Thompson had only taken the trouble to ask, instead of using his initiative, he would have learnt that student-Captain Roche, the *soi-disant* soldier–scholar, was far better informed on the 16th and 17th centuries than the 13th and 14th, and on the French Wars of Religion than on their endless dynastic blood-lettings with the English in the Middle Ages.

Roche rolled on his back and day-dreamed of the good old 16th century, when a chap could happily betray one side to the other, and change sides two or three times as commonsense dictated, and still be reckoned a man of honour if he timed his actions prudently.

That was *his* century, which he had studied most and enjoyed most; when there were two rival faiths, just like now, but with just enough elbow-room for the same man to make honest mistakes and learn from them without being damned, unlike now . . .

And his favourite century would have done well enough here, which had been debatable territory for the Catholics and Protestants just as it had been for the French and English in medieval days . . . well enough, or even better, remembering the Domme *bastide* where he'd lunched well, but not too wisely, only a few hours ago, which had been ingeniously seized from the Catholics by a famous Protestant commander who had then promptly changed sides and sold it back to its proper owners at a handsome profit to himself.

Those were the days! He could have prospered then, in those days. He could have served his own interest, and saved his own skin, and kept his self-respect as well. Whereas now . . .

Whereas now he was suspended between Clinton and Genghis Khan, and tied more tightly to each of them so that he could no longer even be sure where his best interest lay—or even where his best chance of survival might be.

But he didn't want to think about them, because more immediately there was *Audley*—

Only, before Audley, thanks to bloody Thompson, there was *Villeréal* and *Castillonès* and *Montflanquin* and *Villefranche-du-Périgord* and *Domme* and *Beaumont* and *Monpazir* and . . .

"Good heavens! Isn't it David Roche?"

The sun switched on and off and on, in blinding flashes between red-black, and his tongue was half as big again as it ought to be, and tasted of armpits.

"It *is* David! I thought I recognised the car back there—the Volkswagen—your *passion*wagen! Wake up, David!"

A shadow blotted out the sun above him as he fumbled for his dark glasses, which had slipped off his nose somehow while he had been dozing.

"David who-did-you-say?" Another shadow took the place of the first one, a bigger shadow with a fluffy aureole of hair. "Do I know him?"

"How on earth do I know? But I shouldn't think so—David's an army-type, commuting between the OEECD and NATO, doing frightfully important things . . . I met him at Fontainebleau—wake up, David!"

Roche managed to get his sunglasses back in position at last, to filter out the glare.

"What are you doing here, David?"

One thing was for sure—or two things, counting the fact that he had never done anything important between the OEECD and NATO as the first one of them: he had never seen this girl before in his life.

He blinked at her, the glasses sliding on the sweat which had accumulated on his nose. "Gillian Baker—Jilly!"

There was another girl coming into view, alongside the big one with the fluffy golden hair, a small, dark-haired one; three of them . . . but the one who was due to recognise him was doing the talking, and she had to be Gillian Baker—

Thompson on Gillian Baker: *Foreign Office assistant principal, Cheltenham Ladies' College and Oxford—plain as a pikestaff but super-bright—she'll get you on to the inside . . . not one of ours, but they're doing us a favour for once—someone high up must have twisted their arm, they've never done as much for us before . . . but they've got her in, and she'll get you in—you met her at a NATO reception and took her out to dinner afterwards . . . 'Jilly', you call her, and take it from there—*

"I adore soldiers!" exclaimed the big girl. "And isn't he gorgeous—what a tan!"

Roche didn't feel gorgeous as he staggered to his feet.

"And tall, too!" The big girl seemed set on demoralising him.

"What are you doing here, David? Are you on leave?" Jilly persisted. "Take no notice of my predatory friend."

"I was trying to sleep." It was hard to take no notice of the big girl: Jilly wasn't really as plain as a pikestaff, she had a beautiful slender body, just sufficiently rounded, to go with her snub nose and freckles; but the big girl would have stopped any merely casual conversation, not only with her splendid proportions but also with her slightly glazed expression, which contrived to be eager at the same time.

"We were just going for a swim," said the big girl encouragingly. "We always swim here—isn't that lucky!"

Roche couldn't help smiling at her, even though whatever it had been, this encounter hadn't been a matter of luck.

"Come on, Jilly—introduce us!" said the big girl. "Don't be mean."

"Do shut up, Lexy," said the dark-haired girl. "How can anyone introduce anyone when you're burbling all the time?"

"Oh—sorry! Sorry everyone—" The glazed-eager look embraced them all, settling finally on Roche "—I mean, if he's *yours*, Jilly darling, I mean double-plus sorry—"

"Oh God!" murmured the dark girl.

"He's not mine, Lexy," said Jilly. "He's not anyone's."

Lexy's mouth—a big generous mouth, revealing very white teeth with gaps in the centre—opened wide.

"Don't say anything, Lexy," said Jilly. "David—Lady Alexandra Perowne—David Roche—Meriel Stephanides—David Roche. End of introduction."

"Lexy for short. Pleestameecha, David." Lady Alexandra Perowne began to unbutton her dress.

"Hello, David," said Meriel Stephanides, offering a cool, long-fingered hand to Roche. The dark hair and the pale olive skin were as Mediterranean as the surname, but the voice was English home counties, refined in some exclusive boarding school. Also, now that he looked at her properly, he realised that she was the most arrestingly beautiful of all, so much so that he wanted to go on staring at her with pure platonic admiration, even while trying to take in Lady Alexandra's unbuttoning with entirely different thoughts in mind. For if Lady Alexandra was a splendid English rose in full bloom—or maybe more like a great big prize chrysanthemum—Miss Stephanides was some rarer and more exotic flower, delicate and subtly perfumed.

"Do you hunt?" Lady Alexandra's fingers stopped midway down.

Roche swallowed. "I beg your pardon, Lady Alexandra?"

"Are you cavalry? And 'Lexy', not 'Lady'. Are you cavalry? You look like a hussar. I met an absolutely smashing one at Christmas, at our hunt ball—Jerry Somebody-or-Other. He wore these marvellous tight trousers which looked like they'd been painted on him—Jerry Somebody—" she waved a rather grubby hand vaguely "—if you're a hussar then you'll know him. He has this birthmark . . ."

Roche tried desperately to concentrate on what she was saying, rather than what she was showing: there was already a generous portion of Lady Alexandra on view, but there was a lot more where that came from—and it was coming, what was more.

"No, I—I'm afraid I'm not a hussar," he said quickly, before she could render Jerry Somebody's identification easier by locating the birthmark for him.

"What a shame!" The grubby paw toyed with the next button. "But you don't look like a guardsman—"

He had to put a stop to this somehow: that button was going to give way any second now, and then even his sunglasses would be no protection.

"—you look too intelligent for a guardee—almost *haggard*, like Daddy's accountant—"

"Lexy—" interposed Jilly.

"No! Don't interrupt me when I've almost got it." The paw waved Jilly off, but then came back to the button, tugging at it distractedly. " 'Doing frightfully important things', Jilly said—something fearfully hush-hush, I'll bet—"

"*Lexy!*"

"I've got it!" The button gave way. "*You're in the Secret Service!*"

The moment of truth elongated as she pointed at him in triumph and the dress gaped open.

"You're bursting out all over, Lexy," said Jilly sharply.

"So what? We came here to bathe, didn't we?" Lexy paused. "I'm wearing my—" she looked down suddenly "—oh! I'm not, am I!"

"No, you're not, Lexy dear," said Meriel Stephanides. "You're definitely not in the Secret Service, like David."

"Oh—*damn*!" exclaimed Lexy, snatching clumsily at the edges of the dress. "You made me come away so quickly—you're always rushing me, both of you!" As she captured the dress the towel under her arm escaped, liberating two scraps of bright scarlet material at Roche's feet. He bent to retrieve them, half instinctively and half to give himself something to do other than goggling helplessly at a situation which had passed beyond his control.

Lexy's reflexes were one disastrous second slower than his: as he started to straighten up, she bent over him, and his head collided with soft breasts which momentarily enveloped him with expensive perfume, perspiration and embarrassment.

"Oh—ffffff—sorry!" She looked into his eyes at close quarters, but he was too overwhelmed to register her expression. "Thanks—" Pause—"—oh *bugger!*"

Roche croaked incoherently. What made things worse was that Jilly and Meriel Stephanides, the brains and the beauty of this incongruous trio, were laughing at him.

"Not at all like Tiffany Case," said Meriel.

"Or Vesper—or Gala Brand," said Jilly.

"Or James Bond, come to that," said Meriel.

"Who?" said Lexy, frowning at them.

"We told you—we gave you *From Russia With Love* to read, Lexy dear," said Meriel sweetly.

"But she doesn't read thrillers—remember?" said Jilly to her confederate. "She only reads historical novels—she's too busy swotting up on Galla Placidia, to keep up with David Audley tonight—remember?"

Meriel nodded. "Of course! To keep up with David! Sweet chance she's got—of keeping up with David!"

"Always supposing that she still wants to keep up with that David . . ." Jilly nodded meaningfully at Meriel. "With *that* David?"

"With that David?" Meriel glanced at Roche calculatingly. "Of course—*with that David!*"

"Tactics," said Jilly.

"Tactics!" agreed Meriel. "Conjure up the green-eyed monster as an ally: pit David of the Secret Service against David the Dragoon!"

"Of course! That's why she wanted to know whether he'd been a hussar!" Jilly bobbed agreement in turn. "Horse to horse—sword to sword! Or should it be 'sabre'?"

"We'll have to ask him." Meriel continued to consider Roche appraisingly. "But d'you think it'd be a fair match?"

Jilly eyed Roche like a horse-dealer at an auction. "Don't see why not. He's a damn sight better-looking, haggard or not. And he's younger."

"Always back a good young 'un against a good old 'un? But he's not much younger. And maybe he won't bite?"

Jilly looked at Meriel, and shrugged. "We can only try."

"Well then—you try. You know him, after all, Jilly."

"But it was your idea, Steffy."

"No, it wasn't—it was yours!"

Looking from one to the other, Roche decided that it was time the horse had its say in the auction.

"Could someone please tell me what's going on?" He tried not to sound plaintive.

For a moment none of the three girls spoke. Then Lady Alexandra rallied, drawing her dress together as much as its inadequacy allowed.

"Yes. As my Mum always says, 'bitches are women, and vice-versa'. And these two particularly, David," she said icily. "Whatever they say, you say 'no' to them."

"Nonsense!" snapped Jilly. "And it's your interests we're thinking of. Are you on leave, David? Or are you just passing through?"

Jilly was running the show. Whatever the 'idea' was, it hadn't been Steffy's—it was Jilly who was making the running—

Getting him in!

"I'm on leave. I've three weeks due to me." He smiled innocently, playing back to her. "As a matter of fact, I'm gathering material for my somewhat delayed doctorate."

"Doctor—what?" Lexy shook her blonde head at him.

"Doctorate. Not the Royal Army Medical Corps, Lexy dear—Ph.D–D.Phil, that sort of thing," said Jilly dismissively. "What's your thesis on, David?"

"The development of the *bastides* in the 12th and 13th centuries." It sounded as stupid as it really was when he said it out loud. Damn Thompson!

Lexy's mouth contracted involuntarily, the generous lips puckering into an interrogative *b* for *bastides*—

Suddenly, Roche had her pinned down in his memory, from yesterday in the plane and from last night in the train, before sleep had claimed him—from Kipling's *Stalky*, which Wimpy had given him in that farewell parcel beside the Lodge at Immingham: not an overblown English rose, and not a prize chrysanthemum either, but Mary Yeo, the tall daughter of Devon, the county of easy kisses, *fair haired, blue-eyed, apple-cheeked, with a bowl of cream in her hands—*

> *Pretty lips—sweeter than—cherry or plum,*
> *Seem to say—Come away, Kissy!—come, come!*

"No, Lexy." Jilly shook her page-boy curls wearily. "Not 'bast*ards*'— 'bast*ides*'. Remember when Mike and David took us to that place at Monpazier, under the arcades? That was a bastide—the whole village."

Roche's heart went out to the big girl, so confident and aristocratic—Do you hunt? Are you a hussar?—and yet so vulnerable and amiable and utterly inoffensive at the same time. He wanted to get her down on her back and make love to her, but failing that just to cuddle her protectively and not take advantage of her.

95

"They're the fortified towns—or mostly villages now—built round here by the English and the French in the old days, Lady Alexandra," he hastened to explain before Jilly could put her down again. "Sort of custom-built places to mark the frontier, where the inhabitants could trade and farm by day, and sleep safely at night behind their walls, do you see?"

"She knows," said Jilly. "She's been told all about it by David Audley—she knows . . . She's not stupid, she only pretends to be, to get the edge on the rest of us. Don't be deceived by her—she knows perfectly well. And her old Mum was talking about *her*, what's more—not *us*, David. You'd better remember that from now on." She put out her tongue at Lady Alexandra. "So just you watch it, Lexy—if you want us to help you."

Lady Alexandra answered with an even longer tongue. "And the same to you, Miss Clever-Baker—"

"Ladies! Ladies!" Meriel Stephanides interposed pacifically. "David—where are you staying tonight? And afterwards?"

Duty recalled Roche to the colours. "Well . . . not anywhere exactly, at the moment. I've got a tent in the car, with my things—I was going to look around, sort of . . ."

Lexy perked up. "Well—you can pitch your tent in our garden—"

"No he can't!" snapped Jilly. "Don't be an idiot, Lexy—Madame would kill us if she discovered another man walking around the premises at dawn, and well you know it—you of all people." She turned back to Roche apologetically. "Sorry, David, but much as we'd like you to . . . there's this Madame Peyrony who rents us this cottage, and she lives right next door."

"And she conceives it her duty to keep her eye on her jeunes demoiselles anglaises—Jilly's quite right. She's a bit of a dragon, is Madame Peyrony," agreed Meriel.

"She's an old bag!" growled Lexy.

"Old bag she may be. Nevertheless, she's got my boss's address—he's the only one who got us the place, David," explained Jilly. "And he believes that emancipation has already gone too far . . . and she's already threatened to write to him, after having chanced upon Lexy's *inamorato*—one of the many—swanning around in his underpants—"

"That's a slander!" said Lexy.

"Sue me any time you like, Lexy dear."

"It wasn't fair, anyway."

"It certainly wasn't fair! He was one of yours—and it's my address she's got! So *I* had to beg for mercy."

"I gave her Father's address too, darn it!"

" 'House of Lords, Palace of Westminster, London W1'," murmured Meriel. "And he'd probably be overjoyed to hear that you were courting a fate worse than death, getting yourself into trouble, with those little sisters of yours still on his hands."

"I haven't got myself into trouble!" protested Lexy.

"No—only Jilly, very nearly," said Meriel.

"Mind you . . ." began Jilly thoughtfully, her eye flicking for a fraction of a second at Roche before settling on Lexy again ". . . mind you—you could do a lot worse than get yourself into trouble with David Audley, you know."

"I wouldn't have David if he was the last man on earth!" exclaimed Lexy hotly. "And he wouldn't have me, either."

"Oh, he'd do the decent thing if he had to. And you shouldn't judge him by the bachelor squalor he lives in with those friends of his, Lexy dear. There's no shortage of the ready there—he could certainly support you at the standard of living God and your father have accustomed you," Jilly nodded wisely.

"*That's it!*" burst out Meriel. "Why didn't we think of it before?"

"Think of what, Steffy?" inquired Jilly.

"The Tower—David Audley!" Meriel pointed at Roche. "If Lexy asks him nicely, he'll put up *this* David for as long as he likes. There's room in the Tower, because they don't sleep there—they sleep in the cottage alongside, and only use that for their orgies."

"Good thinking, Steffy!" Jilly beamed at her friend.

"Of course I'll ask him," said Lexy. "He's bound to say yes, David." She grinned at Roche. "David is, I mean—the other David."

"Of course he's bound to," said Meriel. "It's one historian doing a good turn for another."

Roche decided that it was again time for him to show some interest in his fate. "David who?"

"David Audley. He lives just up the road from us," said Jilly. "He's a historian, like you. Only he's more or less a full-time one, sort of. He's got money, we think."

So did other people. Roche wondered how Major Stocker was progressing on the track of it.

"He's also Lexy's boyfriend—"

"—sort of, also," cut in Meriel-Steffy. "David the Dragoon—ex-dragoon, actually. He was in the tanks during the war, with Lexy's father. That's how we got to know him—it wasn't a casual pick-up."

"He wasn't actually *with* Daddy. I mean . . . he's not *old*," said Lexy loyally. "But he was *sort of* with Daddy, just after D-Day, you know . . ." she trailed off vaguely again.

"What she means, David, is that her daddy was a sort-of general in command of a brigade or something, and David Audley was a sort-of second lieutenant inside a tank," said Steffy. "But he was in her daddy's old regiment, so he counts as family."

"Anyway, he's frightfully nice, and you'll like him," said Lexy defiantly.

" 'Nice' is absolutely the last word that would come into my mind to describe David Audley," said Steffy. " 'Frightfully' might be applicable—like 'frightfully clever', or even 'frightfully drunk' on occasion."

"He was frightfully brave, Daddy said," Lexy regarded Steffy with disapproval. "They could never get him to shut the lid of his tank, he was always poking his head out of it, Daddy said."

" 'Frightfully inquisitive', that sounds like," said Steffy.

It sounded more like frightfully stupid, thought Roche. But in the meantime, Steffy either didn't approve of Audley—or envied Lexy's *inamorata* role?

"Anyway—we were thinking of introducing you to him before—it was your idea, Steffy," said Jilly. "Remember?"

Steffy frowned. "I thought it was yours?"

"No—yours. But now we've got a proper reason . . . And we're already invited up to the Tower for an orgy tonight, so we can combine business and pleasure."

"And it's David's turn to buy the drinks and hold the floor, too," said Steffy. "That'll put him in a good mood for a start."

Roche looked from one to the other, and to Lexy, trying not to goggle at them. In spite of the tough talk, they were still only three grown-up English schoolgirls; indeed, *because* of the tough talk, which was at least partially designed to impress him that they were women of the world, they couldn't really mean *orgy* when they said it. So he was a bystander to some sort of in-joke of theirs.

"Well, as long as *I* don't have to hold the floor," said Lexy fretfully. "I don't mind buying the booze, but I draw the line at having to spout."

"Your turn will come, Lexy. You're bound to draw the short straw sooner or later," said Steffy.

"It's all right for you—and Jilly. You're both too bloody clever for words, with your scholarships and your degrees. But all I've got is five School Cert passes and a bit of shorthand-and-typing—I'm no blue-stocking!" Lexy protested. "What am I going to talk about, for God's sake?"

The dress had begun to gape again: Lexy was certainly no blue-stocking.

Steffy spread her hands. "Sex, darling—what else?"

Lexy opened her mouth, searching for words but not finding any. So this was the moment, thought Roche, when David of the Secret Service must sing for his orgy, if not his supper.

"If you draw the short straw, Lady Alexandra, then I'll take it," he said gallantly. "It's the least I can do, whatever it is, in return for your speaking up for me, to find me a place to lay my head."

They all looked at him in silence for a moment. Then, before he could think of retreating, Lady Alexandra threw her arms round his neck and kissed his cheek.

"Put the man down, Lexy!" said Jilly. "At once!"

"Mmm . . ." Steffy pursed her lips. "I don't whether that's permissible under the rules."

"What rules?" said Lexy. "There aren't any rules! Let's go to the Tower at once and find a bed for this super chap, Jilly!"

"No!" said Jilly, in command as always. "David's not there yet. He's in

Cahors, talking with his French rugger boozers—you don't play rugger, by any chance, do you, David?"

It was like not being a hussar. "No, I'm afraid not. Hockey is my game."

"Thank God! Don't be sorry—I couldn't bear to go through the Lions' match against the Springboks at Ellis Park again, blow by blow! And we've been through it twice in French too . . . Anyway, he won't be back until nightfall—always supposing he doesn't drive into a ditch somewhere on the way back, that is." She gave Roche a grin, wrinkling her snub-nose. "Besides which, we came here to bathe, and I need cooling down."

Cooling down had its attractions, not least after that collision with Lady Alexandra's unrestrained curves.

"Me too!" He grinned back at her. It wasn't really a snub-nose, it was delightfully *retroussé*, and the grin beneath it was infectious.

"I shouldn't wonder, with what you've just been through!" And there was no maliciousness in that knowing look, either. In the catalogue of their very different virtues, Jilly Baker's might strike a higher total than either Lady Alexandra's and Meriel-Steffy's, when they were all added up.

"Right then!" Jilly's command never slipped for a moment. "David and I will bathe forthwith. Steffy will hold up a towel so that Lexy can attire herself in those inadequate red bandages of hers without causing offence to the local voyeurs, and then both join us in the Dordogne."

They didn't seem to mind being pushed around as peremptorily as Lexy's sort-of general father had once pushed his Audley subalterns to their deaths, they seemed happily accustomed to it.

Roche, less accustomed, found himself looking to the river to see if the Marathon-swimming, long distance-no distance Frenchman was still breasting the current—if this was their accustomed swimming place, to which Raymond Galles had so accurately directed him, was he one of the local voyeurs? Was all that effort in aid of them?

But there was no one there, the river was empty now. Had the sight of Lady Alexandra's charms, briefly glimpsed, been too much for him, spoiling his concentration for one fatal moment, so that the river had swept him away?

At any rate, he wasn't there, and they were alone.

"Right!" Jilly's voice turned him back towards her just in time to see her strip off her dress over her head with one continuous serpentine movement, to reveal a slender body in a white bathing dress.

He kicked off his sandals at the water's edge, and then the discomfort of the slippery stones under his feet brought him down to earth painfully.

"Come on—you have to do this bit as quickly as you can!" Jilly Baker took his hand, pulling him forward. "Once the current starts to lift you off your feet it's not so bad—"

The water swirled about his knees, and then frothed about his thighs, surprising him with its solid force even though he had watched the

Frenchman battle against it. He had never stepped into a river like this, which dragged at him as though it was alive.

"There's a flat piece there—see?" Jilly pulled at him, pointing to a rippling white shape beneath the surface just ahead of them. "There now! That's right—just hold me—make them jealous!"

Roche anchored his feet, one on bearable gravel, one on the smoothness of bed-rock stone which had been sandpapered by ten thousand years of shifting pebbles.

He looked back at the charade on the dry strand from which they had come. The rush of the river was loud all around him.

"Don't worry! They can't hear us. And Lexy'll take hours stuffing herself into her bikini," Jilly said conversationally, her cheek against his shoulder.

She was wet and slippery as an eel, and he didn't know quite where to put his hands, although he knew where he wanted to put them.

"I'm sorry about that, Captain Roche—David—can I call you 'David'? I shall have to, anyway—so . . . David?"

"Jilly." Her waist was the only safe place.

"I don't know what you're doing . . . and I don't think I want to know . . . But they said it had to be natural, after I picked you up, so it had to be Steffy who thought of it, if not Lexy—inviting you to Audley's . . . Only she was so slow to catch on."

"I thought you did it beautifully." He couldn't help kneading her stomach under water. "What's this chap Audley like?"

"He's okay—big, tough man . . . likes his own way too much for my taste. But he also likes it if you stand up to him. And he doesn't suffer fools gladly . . . So don't let him push you around just for good manners' sake . . . In fact, the best thing you can do is make a straight play for Lexy—it shouldn't be too difficult now."

"Not for you? I'd prefer that, if there's a choice."

She moved against him. "Thanks for the compliment."

"It wasn't a compliment, Jilly."

"Well . . . thanks for the insult. But, the way it was put to me, there isn't any choice. Play for Lexy, and put the rest down to might-have-been, David."

All the world was might-have-been. Julie was might-have-been.

"Won't Audley take exception to that?"

"Audley doesn't give a damn for anything, least of all competition. I think he really fancies Steffy more than anyone, only he's afraid she's up to something . . . Lexy isn't up to anything—but she's not nearly as stupid as she pretends, she just doesn't want a tough guy like Audley for a husband. She wants someone she can mother. Audley's just for kicks—and vice-versa . . . The point is, Steffy also fancies Audley. So you go for Lexy, and Steffy'll be on your side, and so will Audley."

Roche glanced quickly towards the riverbank, and had to tear his eyes away from Lexy, magnificently bikinied. Steffy was still undressing.

"Audley has two friends staying with him?" That was what Raymond Galles had said, he remembered belatedly.

"Yes, two of them. David Stein's ex-Cambridge—ex-RAF too. Photographic reconnaissance . . . I'm not sure whether he's an archaeologist, or an art historian—he's here for the cave paintings, the prehistoric stuff, anyway. But he's an Israeli now—"

"An Israeli?"

"Dyed-in-the-wool. Got three wars under his belt now—one world war and two Arab–Israeli wars. He was back flying with them last year, at Suez, though he won't talk about it. A bit hush-hush, as Lexy would put it."

"And the second one?"

"American. Mike Bradford. Also ex-Cambridge—no, Oxford—Rhodes Scholar . . . I don't know where Audley picked him up, or he picked Audley up, as the case may be—"

"They're coming, Jilly. Rhodes Scholar?"

"I think. Now he writes novels. Got a modest hit in the States last year—war novel. Another very bright fellow—like Davey Stein . . . In fact, they're all bloody clever, as Lexy would say—she's nice, is Lexy. The man who gets Lexy won't have time to live to regret it." She twisted to smile up at him. "He'll be too busy supporting a litter of huge, voracious children."

Roche watched Lady Alexandra and Meriel Stephanides pick their way across the stones of the dry margin of the river bed to the water's edge just upstream of them. Alongside the Anglo–Greek girl, and inadequately covered by what looked like two medium-sized scarlet pocket handkerchiefs, Lexy looked even bigger and pinker and blonder than before.

"She's got three brothers as well as three sisters," murmured Jilly. "And positively hordes of cousins. The Perownes come up like mushrooms, it's quite hard to keep track of them all. We've got one of them with us in Fontainebleau—one of the cousins. And I think it was through a cousin of some sort that David Audley got to know the family actually, rather than the General . . . Dragoons and Cambridge, and all that . . ."

That figured better than Lexy's account, thought Roche: second-lieutenants didn't usually strike up battlefield social acquaintances with generals. And, come to that, maybe the Fontainebleau cousin had been used to link up Jilly with Lexy.

"She's all yours now, anyway," said Jilly.

Go where glory waits, Roche, as Kipling would say, recalled Roche from his recent reading.

Well—a little cover was better than none at all . . . in this job anyway, if not in the case of Lady Alexandra's bikini: with Lexy introducing him to Audley, apparently at Steffy's suggestion, his own Jilly-link might pass as a mere accident, at least for the time being.

Having waded gingerly into the water until it reached to the lower handkerchief, Lexy hurled herself into the current with a mighty splash.

And the bonus she offered, apart from the cover she could give him, was that if he could get her to talk about Audley, who better than she to—

"Time to unhand me," whispered Jilly.

Roche started to obey, searching for another foothold beneath him, when Lexy surfaced alongside them, blowing water like a whale. The river had carried her down with astonishing speed.

"Put—" she spluttered more of the river"—*ouch!*—put the poor man down, Jilly—*ouch!* damn and blast these bloody stones! *At once!*"

Steffy surfaced on the other side of him, sleek as an otter.

"Jilly is our dark horse." She gave Roche a shrewd look.

"Jilly is not to be trusted," echoed Lexy. "What sweet nothings has she been feeding you about us, David?"

"Or what devious plans has she been hatching?" said Steffy.

The thought came to Roche that both Clinton and Genghis Khan might have put watchers on him. For once, since leaving England, he hadn't bothered to look over his shoulder, so there could be half-a-dozen of them by now, falling over each other. He looked around, scanning the banks on each side. There was enough cover to hide two rival regiments among the trees and tall reeds. If there were, then at least neither regiment would be hostile to him—not yet—but after this little play they'd be dipping their pens in envy for the composition of their reports.

"You're not married by any chance, are you, David?" said Steffy sweetly. "He's not married, is he, Jilly?"

"Not as far as I know," said Jilly.

"And not as far as I know, either," said Roche. "Why do you ask?"

"Oh . . . just, I've seen that worried look before—the one you've been casting about." Her smile was undiluted mischief. "Just shy? Well, don't worry about the Frog with the binoculars down by the bridge—he's always there. He's got a pash on Lexy."

Roche kicked himself mentally, once for missing the observer and again for betraying his thoughts.

"What I want to know," continued Steffy, "is what Jilly's been saying to you. She's not usually so gabby."

"How d'you know it's me he's got a pash on?" Lexy's mental reflexes appeared to be sure, but slow.

"Because he's never seen anything like you before, Lexy dear." Steffy looked at Roche. "You have to tell us, David."

"I was telling him about tonight, that's all," said Jilly.

"About the orgy? I bet he didn't believe it!"

Roche blinked unhappily. Nothing in his previous experience had prepared him for handling a situation like this.

"I don't wonder!" said Lexy. "I don't believe it either—and I take part in it! And if I told Daddy about it, *he* wouldn't believe it . . . but I shall never get the hang of it."

"That's because you don't prepare yourself properly. But you ought to be able to do better tonight, with a bit of last minute cramming—and your new David to cheer you on—"

"Don't bet on it. I'm just not cut out for that sort of thing, darling."

Roche felt the current drag at his knees. Even if he wasn't imagining all this, how could he possibly report the gist of it to Genghis Khan in less than an hour's time?

"Darling—it's easy!" chuckled Jilly. "You've just been reading all about Galla Placidia and her Visigoths—just lie back and imagine you're her, being *possessed* by a great big hairy barbarian!"

Roche let the river take him away.

VIII

EVEN WITHOUT BENEFIT of Thompson, Roche could see at a glance that Neuville belied its name: it was a lovely little honey-coloured *bastide* which hadn't been a 'new town' since the 13th century judging by the look of medieval gateway and surviving walls.

But Lady Alexandra allowed him no time to admire Alphonse de Poitiers' original defences.

"Do you really do something hush-hush, David?" It was a question she'd been working up to for ten kilometres.

So he was ready for it. "Frightfully hush-hush, Lady Alexandra. And also frightfully dull." And he also had his own question waiting for this opportunity. "Do you really take part in orgies in the Tower, Lady Alexandra?" he inquired politely.

"Oh—phooey!"

"Is that yes—or no?" He manoeuvred the Volkswagen through the gateway. "Where do I go from here?"

"Straight ahead to the square. You can park there, and it's quite near La Goutard's shop."

He drove on slowly. "Was that yes . . . or no?"

Lady Alexandra sniffed. "It was yes. But I bet your job isn't as dull as our orgies."

"Sounds a funny sort of orgy."

"You can say that again! You just wait and see—park over there, under the trees." She pointed. "And now you can help me do my shopping."

The prospect of the orgy certainly didn't seem to inspire her in the way he would have expected, and from the sound of her voice the shopping wasn't very popular with her either.

He looked at his watch. "Sorry, but I've got to make a phone-call. Where's the public call-box?"

"A phone-call?"

He shrugged and smiled at her. "One of the penalties of being hush-hush, Lady Alexandra. I have to let them know where I am each night." He put his finger to his lips. "Top secret."

"Oh—*you*! I suppose you're calling your girl-friend, more like!"

That had done the trick. "No. But they pass the information on to her, as a matter of courtesy."

"Okay! I asked for it!" Her vague smile returned. "The phone's somewhere down there, beyond the war memorial, by the Post Office place . . . and La Goutard's shop is back *that* way—come and bail me out of there when you've finished being top secret—"

Roche felt the accumulated warmth of the day rising off the cobbles under foot as he made his way past the heroic bronze Poilu of 1914, whom some fool had placed on the spot where the revolting peasants of 1637 had been broken on the wheel, according to Thompson, and with fine disregard for the way the monument spoilt the view of the medieval arcade nearby.

If he put his foot wrong now, he would be broken on some other wheel, but less publicly.

Yet he had no choice, he had to give Genghis Khan Lady Alexandra and the Misses Baker and Stephanides, not to mention the Israeli and the American, because he needed all he could get about them, and quickly.

The Comrades were obviously the best bet for all of them; their records were better and much more extensive than anything the British were likely to have. Indeed, the very fact that the British had supplied him with so little information, which they bloody-well ought to have known in advance with Galles down here, was proof of their incompetence.

Indeed . . . maybe the Comrades already had useful messages for him, which would help him to put the right questions to the British, to make *them* think all the better of him, as well as helping him forward.

The thought brightened him: that, after all, was the way he had planned it all—

He didn't recognise the voice on the other end of the line, but he hadn't expected to. All he had hoped for was the correct recognition sign and the 'clear' word to go with it, to indicate that it was safe to go ahead.

Any messages?

No, there were no messages. Had he made contact with the client yet?

Roche decided to hold that one back for the moment. Instead he inquired rather brusquely whether anyone was watching over him.

Why did he want to know that?

Because the other side was probably watching him too—he deliberately didn't elaborate on that possibility; it covered Raymond Galles if they knew about him, but if they didn't then there was no percentage in mentioning him at this stage—and he didn't want heavy-footed Comrades falling over them, or leaving their pug-marks for all to see.

There was a pause while the voice consulted higher authority at its elbow, and then an assurance that he had nothing to worry about on that score, he was on his own until he called for back-up, or until higher authority decided he needed it. But had he made contact yet?

No—but things were going according to plan. There was this woman—

"Baker—Gillian Baker . . . she's with the Foreign Office, a straight civil servant, just doing what she's told—"

The way he felt about Jilly, with the memory of the slender feel of her and the smell of her hair, he wasn't going to suggest otherwise. They would check up on her anyway—they would assume she wasn't straight, and if she wasn't, and if her cover wasn't good enough, then it was hard luck on her and better that he should know about it—but that was the least and the most he could do for her in return for that memory.

And Lexy—Lady Alexandra Perowne . . . P–E–R–O–W–N–E . . . the General's daughter, and the daughter of the Regiment, Audley's old regiment, no problem there—

And Steffy—Meriel Stephanides . . . S–T–E–P–H–A–N–I–D–E–S . . . they liked names because names were facts, and easy to check—Steffy, friend of Lexy, no problem there either—

"The names I want checked as quickly as possible are Stein—S–T–E–I–N . . . David . . . and Bradford—"

He repeated what little Jilly had told him in the river, but also Genghis Khan's own words about the dangers of asking too many questions in the wrong places.

"—I don't want anyone alerted that we're interested in these people, remember. I think it's very unlikely that they're not what they seem. It's just . . . if we've got anything on record about them already, I'd like to know. Then I can get the British working on them for me. Right?"

Again the voice paused for consultation, and Roche wondered idly whether it was Jean-Paul making the decisions, because he had been his controller in France, or whether Genghis Khan had taken over regardless of station boundaries. On balance he decided that it would be Genghis Khan, because the penetration of Sir Eustace Avery's new group was his baby, and also because this was an important operation and he was the senior of the two, at a guess.

Then the voice came back, deferring to him as before. They would check at their end, here in France, and that would be only a matter of minutes. The checks in Tel Aviv and Washington would take longer, but if he would call back in an hour they would be able to tell him when that information should be available.

Roche felt positively euphoric, almost Napoleonic then: he had never been treated like this before, with this whole huge communications apparatus at his beck and call. It hadn't occurred to him that they would go as far as Israel and the United States at the drop of a couple of names, falling over themselves to be helpful without his asking. And that . . . that could mean only one thing—his knowledge of how slow and bureaucratic they were normally, British and Russians alike, to clear such decisions, and how grudging they were in general with communications time for such inquiries, and how much more grudging in particular with small fry like himself . . . all that triangulated his position exactly, beyond reasonable doubt.

Jean-Paul had told him, and Genghis Khan had told him, and he had told himself over and over again, and yet had never quite believed it in his heart-of-hearts—and Sir Eustace Avery had also told him, and so had Colonel Clinton, and he still hadn't quite believed them, either. But here at last was the practical proof of it, demonstrated dramatically in a form he could appreciate—in man-hours of communication time at the peak period of routine transmissions when all the day's general material was scheduled, *they were clearing the way for his slightest whim, unasked!*

He glanced at his watch, trying to calculate how long Lexy would be. Not that it mattered, he could stall her with any cock-and-bull story and she would probably be slow anyway, and they had plenty of time, and the longer he had to pick her brains (what there were of them) the better.

He could spare them an hour, no sweat—

"Not an hour, I can't hold on that long here." Roche smiled into the mouthpiece. Let the bastards sweat a bit for past slights, and more recent ones too—Jean-Paul and Genghis Khan, it didn't matter whom, in conceding the importance of this assignment they had still treated him with the identical thinly-veiled contempt, like aristocrats with a pools winner. So let the bastards sweat! "Half an hour at the outside, that's all I can spare without compromising my position. So I'll call back in thirty minutes—right?"

Another pause, and this time he savoured every petty second of it, while they sweated out his ultimatum.

"Very well—half an hour." *Click.*

He returned to Lexy happily then, basking in his new self-importance.

Contrary to his expectations, she had almost finished her shopping expedition. But one earful of her atrocious dog-French, which she delivered unselfconsciously to the little swarthy Frenchman who bobbed attendance on her, confirmed Roche's guess that her success was due more to French gallantry than to any proficiency she might have with the language after umpteen years of expensive private education.

"Can I be of assistance?" Roche hastened to offer his own expertise, to impress her.

"Dear David—thank you—but no, I'm doing fine. They don't understand *a word* I say, but they're so sweet and helpful . . ." Lexy flashed a dazzling smile at the little Frenchman, who glowed appreciation back up at her from shoulder level, oblivious of the sour expression on the face of Madame, his wife, in the background.

"I've just got to buy the wine—" Lexy transferred a piece of the smile to

Roche, exerting the same sexual force in his direction unconsciously "—you can advise me there. It's all just red or white, sweet or dry, to me. Father's tried to teach me what's what, but ever since I opened a bottle of his Château Something-Somewhere for an old boyfriend of Mother's when we were having bangers-and-mash he gets all tight-lipped and upstream and troutish when we talk about wine. All I've managed to grasp is the shape of the bottles—like that's claret, and the tall brown ones are hock and the green ones are Moselle—or the other way round, maybe—and I can tell a shampers bottle of course . . . we've had a bottle of *that* before, and I quite liked it—" she pointed at the most expensive champagne on the shelf "—and this *dear* little man recommended it, too."

Roche shot a quick jaundiced glance at the dear little man, whose gallantry was evidently firmly based in avarice, and the dear little man managed an infinitesimal man-to-man shrug, not without difficulty, but also with a nuance of frank man-to-man envy, transmitting the encoded message *if all this gorgeous jeune milady anglaise is yours, m'sieur, and I have a living to make and a cold, hard bed in which to sleep, is there not room to make a small sacrifice to your good fortune, eh?*

"What are we eating tonight?" he compromised.

"Darling—it's my turn to cook . . . so we're having bacon and eggs and mushrooms and bags of *pommes frites*, and bread and oodles of butter—the famous 'Lexy Special', though it isn't really a Lexy Special without sausages, but I can't get proper sausages here, not *English* sausages—so what ought we to drink with that, David?"

The question threw Roche utterly. The Lexy Special sounded more like a cross between breakfast and high tea, in the life-style of the lower middle-class Mr and Mrs Douglas Roche, deceased, than that of Lady Alexandra Perowne, daughter of—if she was a 'Lady' it had to be the Earl of Some-where, at the least; and the proper beverage at those Roche meals was tea, as supplied by the Co-operative Wholesale Society, not vintage Moët et Chandon.

"Father always says you can drink shampers with anything," said Lexy helpfully, pointing to the champagne again, "even with breakfast."

Well, that was close to the mark in this case, thought Roche. And who was he to go against the advice of the Earl of Somewhere? And especially when Her Majesty was going to pay?

"Let's have that, then," he nodded quickly at her. "But only if you let me buy it for you."

"No, David!" She waved negatively at him. "Besides, I've got to stock up for several days, and—" her eyes left him momentarily, returning with a different expression in them "—oh golly!"

"Bonjour, m'sieur-dame?"

From the way the dear little man quailed and strove to de-materialise himself, Roche knew who was speaking before he turned towards the speaker.

"Qu'est-ce que vous désirez?" Madame embraced them both with her disapproval, even while directing her question like a spear-thrust at Lexy.

"Madame . . ." Lexy didn't quail, but she did swallow nervously. "Yes . . . well now . . ."

Roche saw instinctively where both honour and duty lay, and self-interest too. Up to now he had hardly distinguished himself, but here was a chance of demonstrating a bit of the old cavalry *élan* which Lexy apparently admired so much.

"Bonjour, madame," he said, drawing her attention deliberately.

For a moment, as she appraised him frankly, he felt more like an infantry-man who had unwisely left the safety of his trench than a dashing cavalry-man answering the trumpet-call to glory. But the euphoria of his victory over the Voice on the Telephone encouraged him to single combat.

She was all of six inches taller than her husband, almost to his own eye-level, and once upon a time she'd been a beauty, with Meriel Stephanides' colouring in Lexy's measurements. Imagining away the lines and the wrinkles, and the sag of sallow skin which had once been firm and creamy, Roche wondered what had yoked her to the dried-up shrimp at his back—had it been simple peasant avarice, her beauty in exchange for his money? Or had her boy marched away to Verdun and the Chemin des Dames forty years ago, with all the other likely lads, to Mort Homme and Fort Douaumont, and when he didn't come back, it didn't matter?

Well, it didn't matter. All that mattered was that she wasn't giving him her sour look now, that she was thawing under *his* appraisal, even that they were exchanging thoughts out of time—might-have-beens in which memory and imagination out-voted the years.

"M'sieur?" She cracked an almost-smile, showing yellow teeth, and not too many of them.

"Madame—" he plunged into his best idiomatic French, the words coming easily, and then more easily still, to sketch what he surmised were Lexy's requirements, only omitting that it was for bacon-and-eggs that the champagne was needed.

"Ah . . ." she nodded, her eyes ranging over the bottles, then coming back to him, caressing him.

The dried-up shrimp, emboldened by the change in her, made a sugges-tion, indicating Lexy's choice, and was instantly silenced with a frozen glance.

—That wine was not good, not of the best. *That* wine (at two-thirds of the price) was better . . .

Roche ordered a dozen bottles. Madame was kind to advise him—perhaps she could recommend a claret? And (a wine for Lexy—a seducer's vintage?) a white wine, even a sweet wine?

—M'sieur speaks French like a Frenchman! And, by the accent, from Paris . . . But M'sieur is an Englishman? And *en vacances*?

Roche warmed to his task. M'sieur was not on holiday, but on leave.

M'sieur was of the British Army, with the honour of serving with the French Army—serving in Paris, Madame's ear did not deceive her—but also a student of French history, of which there was so much hereabouts, in the most beautiful region of France—

(M'sieur was also aware of Lexy, wide-eyed beside him, and that Madame was also aware of Lexy.)

—and, as an old comrade of M'sieur Le Duc, Milady Alexandra's father, as he was passing through, it had been his pleasure to call on Milady Alexandra, of course . . .

(Bandying words with a shopkeeper's wife, such words, was hardly necessary. But it was all good practice, and it was clearly impressing Milady Alexandra mightily.)

(And, when Madame had digested it, and had acknowledged Milady with a little nod, it impressed Milady even more; because, if the nod was not yet quite approving, it was no longer altogether *dis*approving, and that was undeniably impressive.)

(It never failed, thought Roche with a mixture of cynicism and bleak self-knowledge, and satisfaction: the French were so accustomed to their contempt of the average Englishman for his halting use of their wonderful language that they were disarmed and flattered into helpfulness by any stray *anglais* who could distinguish a subjunctive from a hole in the road—the women no less than the men, and perhaps even more so.)

—So! And now . . . there were clarets and Sauternes (Madame swept a glance over her wines, and dismissed them all, and came back to Roche fondly) . . . but here in the south-west there were other wines of character, delicate and fine, of Bergerac and Cahors, of Rodez and Conques—pressed from the pineau grape—for M'sieur . . . and for Milady, the Monbazillac, sweet and perfumed—

"God, David—I've never seen anything like it!" Lexy surveyed the loaded Volkswagen with disbelief after the dried-up shrimp, sweating and terrified at his wife's command, had transported the cases to the little car under the trees. "What did you say to her? What did you *do* to her?"

Roche shrugged modestly. "I didn't do anything. I just smiled at her."

"Smiled at her! Wait until I tell Jilly and Steffy—she positively *drooled* over you, darling! Do you know what you've done—do you?" Lexy brushed ineffectually at the blonde tangle which had fallen over her eyes. "That was Madame Goutard—La Goutard in person! No one's *ever* unfrozen her—not even David Audley, le Grand David."

"Madame Goutard?"

"La Goutard—Madame Peyrony's bosom friend. They get together three times a week at the château, allegedly for tea . . . I think they swop spells and work out who's next for the evil eye and the ague. But you charmed her . . . I swear she even almost smiled at me! And she'll be on the phone to La Peyrony, with a bit of luck, telling her that at last we've rustled up a decent and respectable young gentleman to look after us, and that'll put us in good with La Peyrony—she thinks the sun rises and sets by what La Goutard says . . . What *did* you say to her?"

Roche spread his hands. This was evidently one of those days when he could do no wrong. "I just talked to her . . ."

"Well, you said the magic word." Lexy brushed at the tangle again, with a hand only a little less grubby for its immersion in the Dordogne river. "And like a native too—perhaps that's what did it. The Great David knows all the words, but half the time no one seems to understand what he's saying . . . and one look from La Goutard and I just dry up completely. But you were absolutely *super!*" She gave Roche a huge, dazzling smile. "*And* you paid for everything—" She plunged the paw into her handbag, which was the size of a haversack, and rummaged among its contents until she had gathered a fistful of creased and equally dirty banknotes.

Roche shook his head. "That's my contribution to the housekeeping, Lady Alexandra. I insist."

She blinked at him. "Please don't call me *Lady*. My umpteenth great grandmother—great times ten, but not good—was one of Charles II's innumerable mistresses, that's the origin of Father's title, and every time anyone calls me *Lady* it only reminds me that I'm a lady neither by merit nor inclination—especially as Father says I'm a throwback to the founding mistress of our line . . . At least I can pay for the wine, yes?"

She was gorgeous, dirty hands and tangled hair and every other button still undone, thought Roche protectively. Cleaned up and well-dressed . . . if she was a ringer for one of the Black Boy's playmates then no wonder the King had succumbed to her ancestor. As she was, she was no less irresistible, dirt and tangle and all.

But he had work to do. And dirtier and more tangled work too.

He waved away the banknotes. "I thought I might take a few bottles to—what's his name?—David Audley and his friends, if they're giving me room to pitch my tent among them—"

"A few bottles?" Lexy laughed. "Darling, that'd be coals to Newcastle— they're permanently *awash* in booze at the Tower, they live in an absolute haze of alcohol and intellectual conversation. But you don't need to worry, because they can be jolly—and when I tell them about La Goutard *letching* over you they'll welcome you with open arms . . . and open bottles." She grasped the door handle of the Volkswagen. "Did you make your rules-and-regulations phone call okay? Because I can't wait to tell Jilly and Steffy the great news of your conquest."

Roche looked at his watch. "Ah . . . I had a bit of trouble there—the lines all engaged, or something—so if I could try again in a few minutes . . . You can show me the sights of the town in the meantime, maybe?"

Lexy shrugged. "A few minutes is about right, darling . . . because there isn't anything worth seeing, except the church, so they say . . . but I've seen it, and it isn't worth seeing either—it's more like a castle than a church—"

Roche kept a straight face. That, of course, was why the church of Saint-Maur was worth seeing, precisely: it was a perfect *bastide* church, with its four flanking towers and parapet walks, and the downward-slanted loopholes with their stirrup-shaped bases giving the defending archers wider fields of fire—an innovation (according to the Thompson notes he had studied on the train) which a *bastide*-expert like Captain Roche would unerringly identify as a legacy of 12th century crusading experience.

But all that would be lost on Lexy, whose historical knowledge most likely ended in King Charles II's 17th century bed . . . and who was now reaching half-proprietorially, half-shyly, for his hand with one of those grubby paws of hers.

But at the last moment she thought better of it. Instead she raised both the paws for his inspection.

"Oh God—just look at me! Father always says that I attract grime . . . but this is thanks to David, damn him!"

Roche couldn't avoid examining the hands of Lady Alexandra Perowne, which at close quarters resembled those of a garage mechanic, black-stained and calloused, and broken-nailed.

"That's bloody David's bloody engine oil!" exclaimed Lady Alexandra hotly. "He thinks bloody cars run on petrol, faith and hope, and never a drop of oil or water, that's what he thinks! He's the cleverest man I've ever met—and he's an absolute bloody *idiot* with cars."

So here was another curious and unexpected insight into David Longsdon Audley, then.

In itself it was hardly important—that the man didn't have the skills one might have expected of an ex-tank commander. But—what was important—it warned him of how little he really knew about the man even though he knew so much that others didn't know.

He looked up for a moment, away from Lexy's oil-stained hands which the river had failed to clean, and caught a glimpse of one of Saint-Maur's towers through a gap in the roof-line. Then he forced his eyes and his mind back to the hands.

"You do his car maintenance for him?"

"Well, *he* can't do it. And the others *won't*—not even Davey Stein, who's supposed to know all about aeroplane engines . . . and Mike's even worse—he was in the engineers during the war, he's always telling us, too—but he won't even hold a bloody spanner for me. I tell you, darling—they'll have me sweeping the chimney and rodding their drains for them before they've finished . . . Not that I couldn't do both those things—the trick is to keep turning the rods clockwise." She frowned at him suddenly. "Or is it anti-clockwise?"

Roche couldn't help smiling at her. The three men had quite obviously got her hog-tied into doing their dirty work, but an informed guess suggested that she had held the ropes while they tied the knots—that what Lady Alexandra needed most was to be needed in some role other than in bed;

111

and if that involved crawling under a car, rather than into the back seat of it, then she'd require even less encouragement for the former than the latter. Protests notwithstanding, Lexy was doing what came naturally, and was happy with it.

And David Roche still had work to do, natural or unnatural.

"Davey?"

Lexy snorted. "Yes—I can see life's going to get rather complicated, with all these different Davids . . . Davey Stein, I mean—Colonel David Stein— every time the Israelis have a war, they put him up a rank, so he'll be a general next time, David says—oops! I meant David *Audley* that time— sorry!"

"He's in the Israeli air force?" Roche judged that a little intelligent interpretation of Lexy's stream-of-consciousness monologues would not go amiss.

"Well—no. I mean . . . he's not a regular, like you. What David—David *Audley*, darn it!—what David says is, every time Davey hears gunfire in the Middle East he just grabs the nearest plane and takes off . . . But he was in the RAF during the war, taking pictures—he flew Spitfires and things, you know . . ."

"He was in photographic reconnaissance?"

"Uh-huh, something like that. Shooting pictures, not people, is how David puts it, anyway."

What David Audley said, and how he put things, appeared to dominate Lexy's views.

"He smokes a perfectly foul pipe, but apart from that he's rather a poppet," continued Lexy. "You'll like him—he's frightfully clever, of course. But then they're all bloody clever—Mike too, in his own quiet way. I'm the only dumb one—the mechanic—" she exhibited her hands to prove it.

"Mike Bradford—the engineer?"

"During the war he was an engineer. With the American Army—he's an American, did I tell you?"

Roche shook his head.

"Well, he is. And he was an engineer, though I rather think he was more a blower-up of things than a builder-up, from what he says, if you know what I mean. But he's a writer now—novels about the war with rude words in them which make a lot of money for him—the novels, I mean, not the rude words . . . Or maybe it's the rude words that make the money—David says they're authentic, anyway. Or almost authentic, because in fact it seems every other word they said in the war was a rude one, and Mike hasn't gone quite that far." She frowned at him. "Although I can't imagine Father effing and blinding all the time . . . But I suppose it was all different then . . . *Anyway* . . . Mike writes his books and Davey digs up old bones, and then photographs them."

Roche nodded. The logical thing was to ask her about Audley now, but a more oblique approach would be preferable there. "I see. And they all first met during the war then, did they?"

"Did they?" She brushed at the tangle again with that characteristic gesture of hers. "I don't know . . . Were you in the war, David?"

"Do I look old enough?"

She examined him carefully. "Mmm . . . the question is, are you young-old or old-young? But probably not—not quite."

Roche half-smiled. "Not their war. Mine was the Korean War."

"Oh . . ." She sounded almost disappointed. "That was all that negotiating at Pan-mun-something, wasn't it?"

Could memories really be so short? thought Roche bitterly.

"I mean, it was a little sort of war," said Lexy.

"Not so little." The dark past rose inside Roche. "Not for all the people who died in it. It was a very big war for them."

"Oh—yes, of course!" Her face fell, and it was like the sun going behind a cloud. "I'm sorry, David—that was silly of me. Forgive me."

With an effort, Roche pasted the half-smile back on his face. "There's nothing to be sorry about. Compared with theirs it was a little war. And a long way away."

And besides, the wench is dead! The same words always came back to him when he was with another woman, sooner or later.

She looked at him uncertainly, still contrite.

"Mind you, it could have been a big war." He couldn't quite bring himself to change the subject, but he could drive it forward, like a barbed arrow in his flesh which could only be extracted by pushing it clear through him. "It could have been the biggest of all—if MacArthur had dropped the Bomb on the Chinese."

"The bomb?"

"The atomic bomb. He wanted to, you know. But fortunately he got the push instead."

Lexy brightened. "Instead of dropping the Bomb, he got dropped!" she exclaimed.

The half-smile wasn't so difficult now. "Who says you're dumb? That's good."

She grinned at him ruefully. "It may be good, but it isn't me—it's David. And the trouble is, I ought to be an authority on your Korean War. We had a whole orgy on it a few days ago—it was Jilly's orgy, because she was mixed up in all those endless talks at Geneva or somewhere, not long after she joined the Foreign Office or whatever, and she knows all about it . . . Only . . . only, the minute she started talking I went straight to sleep, and I didn't wake up until the end almost, when David was on about General MacArthur getting dropped instead of the atomic bomb." She shook her blonde tangle at Roche. "You've got to face it, David—I'm *hopeless*, absolutely *hopeless*!"

Roche was feeling helpless, rather than hopeless. The idea of a *whole orgy* on the Korean War, as observed by a very junior Foreign Office clerk just down from Oxford University, boggled his mind. Clearly, whatever activities transpired at the Orgies in the Tower, they were far removed from those of Nero and Caligula.

He looked at his watch, and discovered that he was late for his second contact.

The second contact was a different one, and it was quite unmistakable, even allowing for the distortions of distance and technology.

Accentless, passionless, almost sexless.

Genghis Khan.

"This is Johnnie—you understand?"

Absurdly, Roche smelt a faint fragrance of roses—a foully-cloying memory-smell of the spray of blooms under the lancet window of the little Sussex church, from behind which Genghis Khan had stepped. And it was the wrong church—it was too little and respectably Victorian, and altogether too far from the Genghis Khan reality: the *bastide* fortress-church of Saint-Maur de Neuville was Genghis Khan's church—not where he would have worshipped, but which he would have stormed and desecrated and burnt in the midst of dead children and screaming women, better dead—

"Are you there? Do you hear me?" Still no passion, no anger, even though the questions should have contained some emotion, urgency at the least.

"Yes." Even with nothing to signpost it, this was a very different voice from the obsequious and deferential voice of the first contact.

"Then listen. Once only I will say. First, there is a man to beware—Raymond Galles—G–A–L–L–E–S—garage proprietor of Les Mustiques, near Les Ezyies. He was a British agent, he may still be one."

Oh—shit!

"Yes?"

"Very well! *Subject*—Stein, David Aaron, reserve colonel, Heil Avir Le Israel—"

Genghis Khan wasn't wasting any time.

"—formerly flight-lieutenant, Royal Air Force Volunteer Reserve, DFC 1944; at present Fellow of Rylands College, Cambridge, university lecturer in Paleolithic Art; nothing known—"

"Nothing known?"

"—I say once—"

"But, damn it—he was flying last year—he was with the Israelis at Suez!" protested Roche.

"And I say *nothing known*. Ends," snapped Genghis Khan. "*Subject*, Bradford, Michael LeRoy; United States Army, 1942–46, captain 758th Combat Engineers, European theatre; visiting lecturer in English Literature and Language, Hawkins College, California; novelist; occasional script-writer, various Hollywood studios; extensive travel, Europe, Middle East, 1951 to date; known contacts CIA London, Paris, Beirut, Cairo, unconfirmed Rome, Bordeaux, Lyons. Category 'C' 1952, updated 'B' 1955. Ends."

That was better. Or not exactly better, but more predictable. Or, not better *at all*, even if Category 'B' was no more than the sum of those contacts, which could well be accidental and innocent with all the CIA agents that were in the field at any moment, which any travelled American might make through sheer chance. In short, Bradford had been observed in doubtful company four times, and maybe seven times, over five years, but had never been known actually to *do* anything; but the Comrades always assumed the worst until the subject proved the opposite, which was almost impossible, short of his actually offering them his services.

But that made Colonel David Aaron Stein's *nothing known* all the more surprising, because *nothing known* meant just that. As near as dammit, Colonel David Aaron Stein must be a-political, that meant; and, for an Israeli, that sounded near impossible—

"*Subject*, Baker, Gillian Agnes, only daughter of Archdeacon and Mrs Wilfrid Baker, Old Sarum, Wiltshire; scholar of Lady Margaret Hall, Oxford; Assistant-Principal, Foreign Office. Ends."

Nothing known didn't apply to poor Jilly—didn't and couldn't, even though they obviously didn't know anything much about her. Because with Jilly the established Soviet diplomatic analogy already applied: if she worked for the British Foreign Office she would already be guilty as charged, even if she hadn't turned up on Audley's doorstep as ordered to help Roche establish himself. He had been foolish to think they'd accept his word for her innocence.

"*Subject*, Champeney-Perowne, Alexandra Mary Henrietta, eldest daughter of Denzil Arthur Fitzroy Champeney-Perowne—" Genghis Khan managed the whole mouthful of names with his accustomed lack of passion "—Tenth Earl of Cotswold, MVO, DSO, MC, MA (Cantab.); brigadier-general, retired; colonel-in-chief, Royal South Wessex Dragoons; nothing known—"

Roche grinned into the mouthpiece. *Nothing known* in the case of Denzil Arthur Fitzroy *et cetera* meant that everything was known about him, and his father, and his father's father, all the way back to the moment when the bed-springs had creaked to receive His Gracious Majesty King Charles II alongside their resourceful Champeney-Perowne ancestress, and that it was all there to see in Debrett's and Burke's *Peerage* and *Who's Who*. And the idea of Genghis Khan quoting from those seminal works was captivating.

"—and Cornelia Ashley, née Vanderhorn, American citizen—"

Lexy's mum was a Yankee!

"—nothing known—"

Vanderhorn sounded like dollars—oil, banking, meat packing, peanuts?—dollars in exchange for the coronet of a marchioness!

"—born New Hampshire, American citizen—"

And that applied to Lexy herself: *Lexy* was an American citizen, by God!

"—known contact CIA London, New York, 1956. Category 'C' 1956—"

"You're joking!" exclaimed Roche.

"What?"

"I said 'You're joking'," said Roche.

"I am not joking," said Genghis Khan unjocularly. "Are you requesting repetition?"

"No. I'm requesting a little bloody common-sense. Are you telling me Lex—Lady Alexandra . . . is a CIA contact?"

There was a pause. "I am saying she is Category 'C' 1956." Another pause. "What are you saying?"

Roche thought for a moment, and came to the conclusion that a doormat was what people wiped their feet on. "I'm saying . . . I'm saying that I'm just about to make myself agreeable to Lady Alexandra Champeney-Perowne—if possible, *very* agreeable . . . and I suppose I'm also saying . . . I know the CIA are good, but surely they're not that good? So what the hell are you saying, then?"

There was another pause. Then "Wait," said Genghis Khan.

Roche waited. Category 'C' didn't mean anything, as he had already told himself. But in this instance he wanted to be sure.

The pause elongated. Obviously Genghis Khan was making further inquiries, even further afield on another phone. And the idea of Genghis Khan jumping for him fed Roche's courage and self-esteem at compound interest rates.

The phone crackled in his ear. "We are still inquiring. Are you able to wait?"

Another nought appeared on Roche's deposit of courage. "For a few minutes more, maybe . . . One thing, though: do you have any idea where Audley's money comes from? He seems to be 'of independent means', as they say, but his father . . . his father . . . was up to his ears in debt. So he's acquired ready cash from somewhere—and quite a lot of it. Have you anything on that?"

This time the delay was only to be expected, since this hadn't been one of the questions on the list, and sub-stations weren't geared for this type of uncleared traffic. But if Genghis Khan was as top-brass as Roche guessed he must be, then he just might bend the rules.

"We have nothing on that." He betrayed nothing in his voice, either. The bending was still in the balance. "I would prefer to talk to you face-to-face on the matter."

The idea of Genghis Khan swanning around in Raymond Galles's neck of the woods was not to Roche's taste at all. "That might be difficult. I'm going to be pretty tied-up the next day or two. I'm not sure I can get away."

"You will get away if I require you to do so."

116

Roche dug into his capital. "I'll get away if it's safe to do so. I don't promise anything—not if you want results."

He wished he could see Genghis Khan's face, even though there'd be no expression on it. Face-to-face was better, and in the end safer too, in spite of all the complications.

But not just now.

"Information has been received on Audley," said Genghis Khan out of the silence, apropos of nothing. "Rather curious information. He's a strange man."

You can say that again, thought Roche. "How d'you mean?"

Sniff. And *sniff*, in the context of Genghis Khan, was a manifestation of extreme emotion.

"He worked for British Intelligence, from maybe 1944 to 1946. In Germany, perhaps in France, perhaps in Spain . . . perhaps also in Greece—we are not sure. He was very young."

"And that's strange?"

"We are being circumspect, and that makes investigation difficult, and more so with the passage of time." Genghis Khan ignored the question. "He left them . . . it appears that he left them in anger in '46—mutual anger. We believe that he disobeyed orders. Or possibly he misinterpreted orders— again we are not sure. We are not sure about anything."

And they didn't like being unsure, that was for sure.

"But they surely want him back now," Roche goaded him. "And they tried to get him back once before, too."

"That is correct. It was at Cambridge, in '49. We have that authenticated beyond doubt."

There was more to it than that—and that offered a very obvious hypothesis. "Did *we* approach him at Cambridge—after he turned *them* down?" Roche chanced his arm. "What happened?"

Genghis Khan chewed on the questions in silence for a time. "It was . . . a very gentle contact. Very circumspect, you understand."

'Circumspect' was the in-word of the moment. But there was the minutest suggestion in that passionless voice that the very gentle circumspection of 1949 hadn't fooled David Longsdon Audley for one minute.

"Yes?" inquired Roche innocently.

"It was not successful."

"How not successful?"

Pause. "It was rejected."

"He went to the police, you mean? Or the Special Branch?"

Pause. "He threw our contact into the river, from a flat-bottomed boat."

The 'flat-bottomed boat' added a vivid realism to Audley's rejection of the chance to join the destined conquerors of the world. Recruitment— would-be recruitment—on a punt on the Cam was an unusually imaginative touch, nevertheless!

Roche smiled. "Well, he's a big fellow, so they say. I expect he caught our man at a disadvantage, anyway."

Sniff. "Our man was a woman."

Well! Well . . . maybe Oliver St.John Latimer did have it right, at that! And add *unchivalrous* and *eccentric* to all those other attributes into the bargain!

"I see what you mean by 'strange'," agreed Roche carefully. It was also rather strange that Genghis Khan should have told all this in such detail, unless he'd calculated that nothing but the truth would serve to warn Roche himself of the perils that lay ahead. "I'll make a point of not going boating with him."

"When he travelled in the Middle East—he has travelled extensively in the course of . . . historical research—" Genghis Khan brushed aside Roche's levity "—he made it a practice to visit the ministries of police to explain that he had served with British Intelligence during the war in Europe, but was no longer a serving officer. He did this in Egypt and Syria and Jordan and the Lebanon."

Well again! Now . . . *that* was what Genghis Khan had really meant by 'strange', not the Cam punting episode at all! And it was strange, by God! (It was not in the least strange that Genghis Khan knew about it: the Comrades had all those police ministries sewn up tightly, for sure, and it wouldn't have needed any circumspection to throw up that information, for even surer!)

But, of course, neither those ministries nor the Comrades would have taken such a disclaimer on its face value; rather, it would have put them on their mettle.

And yet, obviously, all consequent investigations had proved negative— obviously, not only because if it hadn't been so he wouldn't be here now, trying to recall this strange man to the colours, but also because if there had been anything to unearth, the combined efforts of half a dozen middle eastern security departments and those of the Comrades would have done it by now.

And yet it was still *strange* . . . or, it would be still so if everything about the man wasn't of a piece with it. In fact, with everything going against him, Audley appeared to have achieved classic *nothing known* status.

"So he's clean, then?"

"Until now," agreed Genghis Khan.

"Of course. As soon as I meet him he goes into Category 'A', naturally."

"I don't mean that—wait!" Genghis Khan abruptly cut off further inquiry.

Roche squinted down the sunlit street. He could see his Volkswagen, but there was still no Lady Alexandra beside it to force him to break contact before he had discovered what sort of relationship she had had with the CIA.

"Very well." The phone reclaimed him. "The woman Champeney-

Perowne is confirmed Category 'C'. But you are right—it is a bureaucratic nonsense nevertheless."

Roche's morale went down and up in quick succession. "What the hell does that mean?"

"She had a close contact. A known agent in their trade delegation in London, and then in New York. It is of no significance whatsoever—you can discount it."

"A close contact?"

"The contact was in bed. He has since left their service." Genghis Khan sounded as though he would have sounded angry if he had ever allowed himself the luxury of sounding anything recognisable. "We have wasted too much time on her. *Subject*, Stephanides, Meriel Aspasia, British passport; daughter of Nikos Stephanides, of Cypriot–Jewish extraction, hotel-keeper, London, known agent Sherut Yediot 1945–48, Mossad 1948 onwards; daughter known agent Mossad 1953 onwards, operating Cambridge and London Metropolitan area, present cover literary agent, Liddell Carver Associates—"

Christ!

"—active, inform Central Records movements priority urgent, ends."

Christ! thought Roche again numbly. Not Greek or Anglo–Greek, but Greek–Cypriot Jewish. And not just Greek–Cypriot Jewish, but Mossad. And not merely Mossad, but second-generation Mossad, the daughter of a man who'd been an Israeli agent even before Israel had existed. And not just second generation Mossad, but *active, inform Central Records movements priority urgent*—which meant a top-flight agent whose every movement had to be reported double quick to Central Records so that the Comrades in the field could be warned of trouble before it enveloped them.

He swallowed as much of that as he could. "Well, she's here."

"Where—exactly?"

"I don't know, exactly. She's staying with Miss Baker and Lady Alexandra . . . in a cottage owned by a Madame Peyrony, a few kilometres outside Neuville, where I'm phoning from. But I haven't been there yet." It was occurring to Roche belatedly that he was the Comrade in this particular field, and nobody had warned him that Meriel Stephanides was already busy ploughing the field up.

"But you're going there now?"

"Yes." His telephone-holding hand was sweating.

"Excellent!"

"What's excellent about it?" It also occurred to him that Genghis Khan had deliberately kept the good news about Meriel Stephanides to last, either in order not to demoralise him, or (more likely) just for the sheer pleasure of it.

"Her presence confirms the importance of whatever it is they want Audley to do—that is obvious." Genghis Khan paused in order to let the obvious sink deep into Roche's stomach. "Do you require assistance?"

Yes—

"No. I haven't even recruited Audley yet."

"Well, I advise you to do that as quickly as possible—for your own sake. Then we'll see about Mademoiselle Stephanides. Meanwhile, I will make contact with you tomorrow at 0900, by the south gate of Neuville. I will have further information for you by then."

Outside, in the sunlight, there was nowhere to go, nowhere to hide.

The heat which bounced up around him off the cobbles of the little square didn't warm him at all, it was repelled by the great block of ice inside him.

The more he thought about his situation, the worse it became. Because if Meriel Stephanides was . . . what she was . . . then it would be prudent to assume that the American, Michael Bradford, wasn't what he seemed to be, but something much more dangerous.

He didn't want to think about it. He wanted to run away, but there was nowhere to run away to.

Lady Alexandra was standing beside his Volkswagen, waiting for him. She saw him, and waved energetically. He waved back automatically, glad that she couldn't see his face from that distance. He had all of a hundred yards in which to rebuild a happy holiday smile on it.

IX

"Oh—*bugger*! Now Jilly's bloody egg's broken!" Lexy stabbed at the frying pan, as though it had let her down deliberately. "And of course I've got everything wrong—I should have done her bacon first, shouldn't I! Oh well, not to worry—she's probably still in the bath—go and see if she's still in the bath, David darling, and if she is then tell her to stay there—"

Roche blinked at Lady Alexandra, and tried to reconcile what he knew with what he was seeing, and opened his mouth and shut it again without speaking.

"And has Steffy come back yet? I think I'll throw this egg away and start again—I think I'll throw the bloody lot away and start again! I hope to God the chips are still hot . . . or at least warm—is she still in the bath?"

Roche swallowed. From the way she moved . . . or rather, from the way different parts of her moved under the dress, he could swear that she wasn't wearing anything under it.

"—I don't mean go *literally* and see whether she's still in the bath—I mean, you *can* . . . because there isn't any lock on the door, I broke it yesterday—but all you have to do is listen through the wall by your ear, that's all—don't lean too hard, or it'll fall down—"

Roche felt the wall tremble against his ear. It was paper-thin, and he could hear Jilly-washing-sounds distinctly through it. He nodded speechlessly at Lady Alexandra.

"Well, that's all right! Just tell her to go on soaking—tell her there's no hurry—right?"

Roche observed also that Lady Alexandra's face was dirty again, with a black mark down the side of her nose on to her cheek which was presumably a legacy from when she had stoked the boiler for Jilly's bath, after emerging from her own.

She had stoked the boiler, and she had cooked his supper and her own, and she was cooking Jilly's supper—the Lexy Special—in that exquisite dress, which must surely smell more of bacon fat and chips than Chanel by now—

(And the Lexy Special was a horrific greasy memory of hunger stemmed, but not satisfied: broken eggs, frazzled bacon and fried bread exploding into fragments, and limp chips congealed into inseparable lumps—*ugh!*)

He turned to the partition wall. "Jilly?"

"I can hear you. *I* heard." Jilly shouted. "Tell her just egg-and-bacon, no chips . . . And tell her not to incinerate the bacon."

Lexy was already smiling cheerfully at him when he turned back to her. "I heard too! They're all just unappreciative of my culinary efforts—all except David Audley, he never complains—he's a gentleman, like you, David!"

"He never complains—" Jilly's voice, deadpan as Genghis Khan's, came through the wall beside Roche's ear, faint but clear "—because his taste has been . . . institutionalised . . . by public school . . . and the Army . . . and Cambridge . . . so he doesn't know any better." Splash, splash. "His stomach . . . is permanently . . . disadvantaged."

"*Jealousy*—" shouted Lexy "—will get you nowhere!" She grinned her great wide-mouthed happy smile at Roche. "Would you like some more chips? Steffy'll never finish this lot now."

"Steffy . . . knows . . . better!" Splash, splash.

"*Shut-up!*" Lexy scraped the frying pan into the bucket beside her. "Would you like seconds, David darling?"

God! Perish the thought!

"No, I'm fine," said Roche hastily. "But . . . where's Steffy?"

Lexy waved the kitchen spatula, scattering fat over the top of the stove. "Oh, God only knows! She's always going off on her own somewhere or other. We think she's got a boyfriend tucked away—or one of her poor bloody authors she's galvanising into a masterpiece, maybe . . . but she won't say, she just swans off into the blue and that's that . . . *Not* to be trusted, our Steffy—*definitely* not to be trusted! And that's Mike's opinion too. He says she's a *femme fatale.*"

That was very true, thought Roche; it was even so true that it hurt. And it wasn't surprising that Bradford, the American, thought so, either; because in this operation, whatever it involved, there was no reason why the Americans and the Israelis should be on the same side.

"Darling—why don't you go out and see if you can spot her *en route*? If you walk up to the corner you can see for miles—but get yourself another drink first, we've still got bags of duty-free gin in those huge bottles we bought on the boat . . ."

Roche retired gratefully up the drive from the cottage, ginless but glad to be out of the kitchen, where the air was blue with burnt fat and treachery.

Because in this operation . . .

Ever since Suez the Americans had been bad friends with the Israelis, even though more in pique and sorrow than anger . . . and the way things had been going since Suez last year, they'd soon be co-operating again—at least so long as the Russians called the tune in Egypt.

Yet the key to everything was still Audley: and if he could find that key before the Americans and the Israelis did—

But in his case it wasn't a case of *if*: he had to find it, or else—

He stared out over the blue-hazed landscape, across the rolling hills and forests and enclaves of cultivated land, and saw none of it.

The stakes weren't any higher, because for him they had been at the limit from the beginning, from the moment he had decided to defect again if he could see a way to do so.

But now they were inescapable, because the bets were on the table—if he failed, then the Comrades would never forgive him this time. Only now the game was more complicated, with the Americans and the Israelites in it, with stakes of their own, and as yet he didn't even know why they were playing. And not to know *that* was very frightening. And the CIA, with all its unlimited resources, was even more frightening. And Mossad, with its limited resources but unlimited ruthlessness, was even more frightening still.

It made him feel sick to his stomach, and he couldn't control the sickness, so that before he knew what he was doing he was throwing up the Lexy Special into the stubble of the field at his feet.

For a moment he was bent double, swaying dizzily, his vision blurred with tears. Then he managed to steady himself, his hands on his knees, as he vomited again helplessly—he had lost his supper, and now his lunch was coming up.

He focussed on the stubble again, and found that he had instinctively lurched a few yards away from the disgusting mess, to an unfouled piece of ground. Among the dead stalks at his feet there was a fresh green plant growing, its tendrils snaking out from a fissure in the dry earth. He frowned at it, unable to identify the plant—there was another similar one a few yards away, and another beyond that, and another . . . they were in a line stretching down the hillside towards the road, and there were others dotted over the field, apparently growing haphazardly, but actually in other lines like this one.

They were young vines, of course. This cornfield had once been a vineyard, a little irregularly-shaped vineyard high on the ridge, penned in by woodland on three sides and by the road up from which he had climbed on the fourth; yet although the vines had been grubbed up, their deepest roots had escaped the plough and had endured the temporary conquest of the land by the corn to sprout again, unconquerable.

Well . . . Roche bent down to take the tender shoot at his feet into his hand . . . well, *he would beat the bastards yet, somehow; he would use them, and he would play them against each other—Genghis Khan against Clinton, and Clinton against Genghis Khan, and both against the Americans and the Israelis . . . and in the end he would go over to whichever of them looked like winning, whichever of them could best offer him safety and amnesty and oblivion, it didn't matter which—only survival mattered!*

"David!"

Lexy was striding up the hillside towards him.

"Any sign of her yet?" She paused for a moment, turning to survey the landscape below her, hands on hips, a splendid Amazon of a girl, Hippolyta to the life. "Drat the girl! This is absolutely typical—just typical!"

Roche chose a non-committal grunt as a reply. From their vantage point he could see the road twisting down into the valley, and there was plainly no sign of *Mossad* on it.

But he ought to pretend he'd been looking at something. "I was looking at these vines, coming up through the stubble . . ."

"Oh . . . yes!" Lexy's face was slightly flushed, and the dirty mark had enlarged itself. She looked as though she'd just got out of bed. "Tragedy, isn't it—corn instead of wine! But typical Peyrony avarice, we think . . . though she says she can't get the labour—all her boys have *gone off*—" she transmuted the words from BBC English into the aristocratic *gawn orf* "—gawn orf to the army, to get themselves killed in Algeria, she says. But we think it's the price of corn—I say, darling . . . you're as white as a sheet!"

Roche was about to say that it must be something he'd eaten, but realised just in time that he would thereby be condemning the Lexy Special for what it surely was.

"You must have caught a touch of the sun, darling," said Lexy solicitously.

"Yes, I think I must have done," agreed Roche, who had never caught a touch of the sun in his life. "Mad dogs and Englishmen, and all that . . ." Maybe he had, though: a little sun and a lot of terror, and a Lexy Special: that was surely enough to turn the strongest stomach.

"Well, then—it doesn't matter about Steffy bedding down with her mysterious boyfriend for extra time! You can't possibly go to the orgy like this, David—" Lexy's solicitude was positively enthusiastic "—Jilly can go on her own, and I'll stay and mop your fevered brow," she beamed at him.

"Ah . . . no—no, I must go," said Roche quickly. Whatever Lexy had in mind—ministering genuinely, or even something much more attractive, he had to go to the orgy. In another life the opportunity would have been irresistible, but this life left no room for self-indulgence. "I have to go. And I'm okay now, anyway."

Lexy appeared crest-fallen. "But, David darling . . . it'll be so *boring*—if you're feeling a bit fragile . . . I mean, David—David Audley—spouting endlessly on—on barbarians and things . . . on history, and Arabs, and Russians, and . . . and on whatever comes into his head . . . and they'll all get drunker and drunker . . . and I shall go to sleep, and my mouth will fall open and I shall *snore* horribly—and Jilly and Steffy will become even more intelligent . . . and then you'll never speak to me again, and I shall be *desolate!*"

Lexy had cooked her own goose. In that other life . . . but this life belonged to David Audley, and especially David Audley drunk and talkative—that was a particular Audley he needed for his collection, and perhaps even the final one he required to complete the set. Even if he'd been half-dead he couldn't have missed such a chance.

"Lexy, I'm sorry. But I've got to sleep somewhere eventually, remember. And I am okay now, really." He grinned at her. "I don't want to be a bother, either."

"Oh—phooey!" She rejected the grin. "The trouble with nice men is, they always have to be noble and unselfish and brave, damn it!"

"I'm not being any of those. I'm only being logical." And the trouble with women, thought Roche, was that (all except Julie) they were none of those things. "Besides which, Jilly said Madame Peyrony wouldn't like me to hang around you three ladies."

"Huh! That's just where you're wrong! We've just had a message from the old witch about you—La Goutard's already been on the phone and La Peyrony is desperate to meet the young English colonel—"

"I'm not a colonel, for God's sake! I'm only a captain—"

"Well, she made you a colonel, so you jolly well have to stay promoted while you're here . . . And I made you a paratroop colonel too, with a chestful of medals—"

"But—"

"But nothing! Those two old witches have both got nephews serving with the *paras* in Algeria, under some colonel or other who appears to be a cross between Napoleon and Joan of Arc, the way they talk about him . . . so she's promoted you and I've—what's the word Father uses?—seconded?—I've given you a parachute, anyway," she shrugged, utterly unabashed. "So you'll have to jump now, when you meet La Peyrony."

Roche regarded her reproachfully. "You didn't have to make me a paratroop colonel—that's overdoing it a bit."

"Not at all! 'Never tell a little fib if you have to lie', Father always says.

'Tell a whopper and make a proper job of it'—that's what he says." Lexy brushed at her hair, and then turned the gesture into a vague, unrepentant wave. "You're lucky I didn't make you a general—French *para* generals jump with their men, Etienne says."

"Etienne?"

"A friend of David's—Etienne d'Auberon—or d'Auberon-Something-Something, terribly aristocratic . . . I mean, not like me, but *really* aristocratic, like from St. Louis and the Crusades, and all that . . ." Lexy turned the vague wave into an even vaguer sweep, as though 'all that' included the ownership of everything in sight, with the appropriate feudal rights and privileges. "A *French* friend of David's," she added unnecessarily. "Anyway, you'll probably meet him tonight, if you're set on going to the Tower. He often turns up . . . mostly to argue with David about the Hundred Years' War, so far as I can make out . . ." she trailed off, apparently losing the thread of her own butterfly monologue.

Etienne d'Auberon-*Something-Something?* That would be another name for Genghis Khan, when he could get Jilly to decode the 'Something-Something' part of the Frenchman's name anyway, thought Roche grimly. Because, as of now, everyone connected with the Tower was under suspicion of being an enemy until proved otherwise, even Frenchmen. It was their country, after all.

Meanwhile mild interest was in order. "Lives round here, does he, this Etienne?"

"He does *now*. I mean, he always did, after a fashion, in the family château—like Mummy and Daddy retire to freeze in the Cotswolds from time to time . . . But he used to live in Paris, in a fearfully smart flat near the Bois, when he was working for the Government there . . . Only then he had this absolutely frightful row over something—Algeria, I expect . . . they're always having rows over Algeria—but it was one of those awful rows the French have, all about honour and France, and things like that—honestly, you wouldn't credit it! I mean, can you imagine Jilly rowing about *honour*? Or Cousin Roland pitching into *his* Minister about England? But *they* do—the French—honour and France, and probably Liberty, Equality and whatever the other one is . . . *Fraternity*, that's it! Fraternity my eye! According to David . . . 'Tienne was all set for fraternal pistols at dawn in the Bois over whatever it was—and *they* were all set to put him up against the wall for a firing squad!" She shook her head in disbelief at her own story, cornflower-blue eyes wide. "Which is ridiculous, isn't it—because, I mean, Cousin Roland didn't exactly *celebrate* over that ghastly Suez business last year, he got so stroppy in the end that they had to pack him off to Scotland to let off steam shooting grouse to get it out of his system . . . But with 'Tienne, it was like they were about to put him in the Tower of London under close arrest."

Etienne d'Auberon *Something-Something* was becoming very interesting indeed. But if the scandal had reached such serious proportions, even allowing for Lexy's weakness for hyperbole, why hadn't he heard of it? thought Roche.

"It was all hushed up in the end, of course." The blue eyes narrowed knowingly. "David Audley says de Gaulle spiked their guns somehow, but Jilly thinks it was because 'Tienne knew too much, and they were scared he'd spill the beans about whatever it was . . . I mean, if it was as awful as *that*, then there must have been an awful lot of beans to spill, wouldn't you think, David?"

"Mmm . . ." agreed Roche cautiously.

"But you must have heard about it, darling, surely?" The vague blue eyes blinked at him.

That was what was beginning to disturb him. Because if Etienne d'Auberon had been involved in a big Government scandal and he hadn't picked up a whisper of it—and Philippe Roux hadn't dropped the slightest hint of it—even the fact that d'Auberon's name rang no bells could mean that he was a well-covered backroom boy . . . then the scandal had been very efficiently hushed for once. And that meant it was *big*—

"I'm just a simple soldier, Lady Alexandra." And, for that matter, how *simple* was she? For, while her style and vocabulary were debutante, since when did debutantes chatter knowledgeable asides on Suez and Algeria and de Gaulle? Or was all that *simply* what had rubbed off from Audley and Jilly and Cousin Roland?

He had to know. "What makes you think I've heard about it?"

"I didn't darling—Jilly did. Just before I came up here she said I ought to tell you about 'Tienne, anyway . . . because he might turn up at the orgy. He does sometimes." She shrugged. "And you move in those sort of circles."

"What sort of circles?" So it was a Jilly after-thought!

"Oh—hush-hush ones. You know!"

But that joke had gone far enough. "I told you—I'm just a simple soldier."

"Simple my eye! Simple soldiers don't make friends with our Jilly . . . and they don't make phone-calls either. They make passes at me, is what they do. I'm an expert on simple soldiers, darling—and you don't fit the pattern, believe me!"

Roche realised that he was on a hiding to nothing on Lady Alexandra's own ground so long as he tried to play the game his own way. Jilly had given him better advice than she could imagine, but so far he'd made too little use of it.

"Tell me more about this fellow d'Auberon then—if I'm not simple," he challenged her directly.

"Why d'you want to know about him?" Now she couldn't help being suspicious.

"Because I'm not simple. I like to know all about the opposition before I make *my* pass, Lady Alexandra."

"Oh . . ." She was vastly relieved by his frankness. "So that's the way the wind blows! And I've been stupid again, haven't I!"

"A bit. But tell me, anyway."

"There's nothing to tell. He's much too honourable—and high-powered—for me . . . He's just an acquaintance of David Audley's, that's all—high-powered, like David . . . and also weird . . . also like David—"

"Weird?"

"Funny."

"Funny?"

"I don't mean funny ha-ha . . . but sort of . . . contradictory." She nodded into the valley. "Like, he's mad about rugger—he's gone all the way to Cahors today to talk about rugger with these Frenchmen who are also bonkers about the silly game." She looked at Roche suddenly, and he realised that she'd shifted from the Frenchman to Audley. "And that's pretty weird, isn't it—the way these Frenchmen in the south play rugger—I never knew that until I met David Audley."

"Indeed?" He shrugged. "But I don't quite see how that's . . . contradictory. Lots of people play rugger."

"Ah!" She pointed at him quickly. "But you don't play rugger, do you? Hockey's your game, you said?"

"Yes. But—"

"But you know about it. And you know about cricket and soccer and tennis—who's good, and who's playing who, and all that sort of thing . . . I know, because I've got all these cousins—Roland's got a rowing blue, and Jimmie played for the Occasionals, and Jake had a county cricket trial last year—"

The Perownes come up like mushrooms . . . positively hordes of cousins—

"—I *hate* sport, personally," continued Lexy vehemently. "It's boring, and they all get drunk and sing dirty songs. And all I get to do is cut sandwiches and serve tea. But I know what they're like—it's all *balls*—"

Roche fought to hold in position whatever expression was on his face.

"—balls, balls, *balls*—just so long as they can kick them, or hit them, or throw them—big ones, little ones, white ones, red ones, all shapes and sizes . . . it doesn't matter which is their special sport—if they're mad about one sport, they *know* about the others, what's what, and who's who . . . the British do, anyway . . . Roland does, and Jimmie and Jake—and you too, David—" she drew a quick breath "—*but David Audley doesn't!*"

He couldn't maintain his look of polite interest any longer. Incredulity and incomprehension had to take over.

She observed his discomfort. "You haven't the faintest idea what I'm getting at, have you, darling?"

"Not a lot—no," admitted Roche.

She nodded. "I'm not surprised. It takes one to spot one."

"One—what?"

She laughed. "You know, when Mike was up at Oxford he played everything. I mean, when he was at Harvard, before that, he played football—American football, where they all dress up in the most extraordinary way and do even more extraordinary things to each other . . . But when he came to England, he played English games—rugger and cricket, and suchlike, and if you give him the chance he'll talk about them non-stop. All about deep square legs, and kicking for touch . . . it's *ghastly* to hear the way he goes on—it's so *boring*. But they're all like that, I tell you—all except David Audley."

A surfeit of sporting cousins had clearly scarred Lady Alexandra for life.

"I'm still not with you, Lexy."

"No? Well, you just watch David Audley's face when anyone else talks about sport. He gets that glazed look of his."

Lexy herself usually had a slightly glazed look, as though she didn't quite understand what was happening to her, or what had just happened. But also she had already put on record that 'it takes one to spot one', whatever that meant.

"Darling—he *hates* sport, just like me—that's what I think. Even rugger, which is the only game he plays—I honestly think he's bored with that too . . . and as for all the rest . . . he simply doesn't care to know anything about them. It's all a great big façade."

"Clubbable?"
"Yes and no . . . And I rather think I mean 'no'—"
And then Stocker had gone off at a tangent, without trying to answer what he didn't understand, into the equally unsatisfactory labyrinth of Audley's finances.

"Anyway—" Lexy grabbed the word with special emphasis, as if she was using it to haul herself away from her own private experience *"—anyway,* that's David all over: he just never quite fits . . . like, he absolutely hates the army, but he's terribly proud of the Wesdragons—the regiment, Father's regiment . . . and he hates the jolly old Establishment even more—that's the only time he swears, when he talks about them—but when Davey— Davey Stein—when Davey pitches into the British Empire, because of Palestine, and all that, David gives him both barrels and waves the flag like my Great-Aunt Maggie, who was in Amritsar when they shot all those Indians, and still swears by General What's-his-name who gave the order to open fire—it's positively hilarious . . . and yet, at the same time, he likes the Arabs—And then, to top it off, he thinks the Israelis are really rather super, the way they give everyone the two-finger sign—including all Mother's State Department friends in Washington. Oh—and he likes the Egyptians—he's terribly unfashionable there—"

"And the Russians?" The sixty-four thousand dollar question.

"Oh . . . they're the New Barbarians, darling—just inside tanks instead of on innumerable little shaggy ponies. You'll hear all about them tonight, I shouldn't wonder," Lexy waved away the whole might of the Red Army with a slender and very dirty hand. She stopped abruptly as she focussed on her own hand. "My God! just look at me . . . I'm absolutely filthy again—I don't know where it comes from, but I seem to attract dirt!" She lifted her face towards him. "Is my face dirty, David?"

Roche pretended to examine her features critically. All that was needed was soap and water, for under the clumsily-applied make-up and the soot from the boiler was a complexion not far short of Steffy's.

"Well?"

"A bit of touching up maybe," he said diplomatically.

Lexy examined her hands again. "God! Just look at the time!" She stared round in sudden panic. "It's even starting to get dark—and I've been blethering on—and Jilly's supper's still in the oven! We must get back, David."

Roche didn't want the blethering to stop. "But Steffy—"

"Damn Steffy!" She turned away, down the hillside.

"And you were just getting interesting—"

"About David Audley?" She flung the name over her shoulder as he plunged after her. "Don't waste your time trying to understand David—nobody does! It'd take a lifetime, and I'm certainly not volunteering for the job—" Her voice faded as she drew away from him. "I don't have a lifetime to spare, anyway—"

And neither did poor bloody Roche, thought Roche.

Depending on how much lifetime he had left, of course . . .

X

"WE'RE NOT GOING to wait for Steffy," announced Lady Alexandra. "I'll just get my bag, and then David can escort us through the Wild Wood by the short-cut. With him along we shalln't have to worry about those swarthy rapists."

Roche frowned at her. "What rapists?"

"No rapists," said Jilly. "Honestly, Lexy—you're the limit!"

"Well, they could be rapists for all you know."

"Rapees, more like, if you have anything to do with them!" Jilly turned with a shake of her head from Lexy to Roche. "There are these gypsy-types we've spotted in the wood—"

"Saw them again yesterday, too—skulking up behind the old dovecote, down towards David's place," said Lexy firmly. "And I've seen them further afield, too."

"They won't be the same ones," snapped Jilly.

"They were the same ones. It was when Steffy and I were collecting the bread. I saw them." Lexy didn't budge.

"And they were following you?"

"That I can't say, they were stationary at the time. But they were the same ones, because they've got an old motor-bike and a couple of battered old pop-pop mopeds they swan around on."

Jilly sighed. "Well, they're a bit slow, getting down to the job then! We've each been on our own here often enough!"

"They're casing the joint," said Lexy airily. "I think we ought to tell La Peyrony—or, better still, David Audley. He'll sort them out!"

"I've no doubt he would! And you're the sort of person who gets innocent youths lynched during the sorting process." Jilly turned to Roche again. "They look about sixteen years of age, and they're about half Lexy's size put together—and a quarter of David Audley's—and a hundredth as dangerous. And they're probably from down south, just looking for casual work and living rough meanwhile, poor kids."

Another thing about Jilly, thought Roche, was that she didn't scare easily. Although she hardly came up to Lady Alexandra's shoulder, it wasn't Jilly who needed protection, it was Lexy.

But it was also Lexy for whom he was supposed to be making a play, although he had not done much with his opportunities so far, he remembered.

He looked around the area of the cottage with a suitably protective air. The steep-pitched dark-grey slate roof of the Peyrony mansion could be seen through the trees to its left, but otherwise it was enclosed by thick woods on either side of the roadway. As a holiday-house it had a Perrault fairy-tale look, with its browny-pink pantiles and tiny windows set in dormers and thick stone walls. But as a refuge for three pretty girls in a foreign country, with strange young males in the woods roundabout, it had its disadvantages: other than the Peyrony place, there didn't seem to be another house in sight.

"You are rather isolated, aren't you?" he said gently, trying not to take sides too obviously.

"Oh no, David darling," said Lexy lightly. "We're within easy screaming distance of Madame Peyrony, who is not a day older than seventy . . . and old Angélique . . . and there's Gaston, who undoubtedly remembers Waterloo, if not the battle of Agincourt—"

"Gaston's as tough as an old boot, and as strong as an ox," protested Jilly.

"Gaston?" queried Roche.

"La Peyrony's wrinkled retainer—old Angélique's antique brother," explained Lexy sweetly.

"Younger brother," corrected Jilly. "He's Madame's handyman-gardener—"

"Younger . . . meaning he was a hero of Verdun, or somewhere, in the First World War, darling."

"That's right! And with a chestful of medals—David Audley says he was the finest trench-mortar-man in the whole French Army—*and* the Cross of the Liberation too." Jilly turned to Roche. "Back in 1944 he sat on the ridge above Brivay and held up a German column for six hours with his mortar, David says."

"Yes. And he's still got his private arsenal up in the stable, above his bedroom," Lexy mocked her friend. "But now he's got a gammy leg and he's rather short of breath with his asthma, and you have to shout at him to make him hear . . . But there's always little Gaston, his grandson—or maybe great grandson—little Gaston can always let him know when we start screaming. So we've got nothing to worry about . . . . Not that I really care, anyway. What's a fate worse than death between friends?"

"They're just boys, Lexy—"

"Okay—so they're just boys! Innocent little nut-brown boys!" Lexy shrugged. "At least let David here escort us while we've got him. Just let me get my bag, and we'll go."

"No," said Jilly.

"Why not? I don't see why we should kick our heels until Steffy deigns to put in an appearance, for heaven's sake! Just because she's gone out on the tiles again—"

"It's not Steffy." Jilly shook her head in despair. "You've clean forgotten why I sent you to go and get your new David already, haven't you? It's because Madame has summoned him to her boudoir, that's why." Jilly switched apologetically to Roche. "And I'm afraid you must go, David—if only to improve our image with her, to lend us a touch of respectability, let's say—and she will give you a drink, too."

Roche didn't have to pretend to look unwilling. He didn't want to waste any more time before getting to 'The Tower', where the action must be; and he didn't want to jump through any hoops for another version of Madame Goutard, anyway; and he certainly didn't want another drink, of any description.

"I'm afraid you must go," repeated Jilly.

"Well, I'm jolly well not going!" exclaimed Lexy. "Not even to improve my image, darn it!"

"And just as well, *Lady* Alexandra," said Jilly severely. "What you're going to do is to go to the bathroom and improve your image there. You look like something out of the black-and-white minstrel show pulled backwards through a hedge."

"Oh God! Do I?" Lexy put her hand to her face, and then to her hair, and then studied the hand with dismay.

"David . . ." For the umpteenth time Jilly returned to Roche. ". . . she's an old woman, and she's lonely . . . and Lexy and La Goutard have sold you to her as the English d'Artagnan between them . . . . It would be a kindness just to have one drink with her—just one drink. She loves Englishmen, because of the war; and she's still trying to love them, even after Suez, and the way we seem to have let down her nephew in Algeria. So it really would be a kindness."

Put like that it was an order. "Because of the war?"

Jilly nodded. "She was on an escape line. It was Limoges–Brive–la-Gaillarde–Toulouse when things were going well. But it was Limoges–Château Peyrony–Toulouse when things became difficult. She may be an old witch, but she's an old witch who can wear the MBE alongside her husband's Croix-de-Guerre."

Put like that it wasn't an order, it was an honour.

"Besides which, David—David Audley—won't be back from Cahors yet, so there's no hurry," said Jilly. "And even if Steffy's not back we still don't need to take the short-cut through the woods, over the top of the ridge. We can use your car—and we've got to use your car anyway, to shift your gear to the Tower if you're going to pitch your tent there."

Put like that it was simple common-sense, apart from the honour and Jilly's insistence.

"Silly me!" muttered Lexy. "The gear—of course! And my face!" And fled into the cottage.

Jilly led the way through the trees to a doorway in a wall. Then she halted and turned back to him.

"Apart from which, David, I did have a male caller while you were rolling in the hay with Lexy. But not one of her teenage would-be rapists—in fact, he was looking for you."

"For me?"

"Little fat Frenchman named Galles." Jilly watched him. "He has a garage on the Les Eyzies road over the river—petrol and repairs and hire cars. He says he knows you."

Roche returned the stare. "You know him?"

"Uh-huh. Or rather, Lexy knows him—she has a natural affinity for anyone who can help her to get filthy, particularly car mechanics. They met under the bonnet of David Audley's car, to be precise."

A circumstantial coincidence, to be precise. "How did Audley light on him? There must be garages closer to here than Les Eyzies?"

Jilly smiled. "David dear, there's nothing close to here—the Tower's our next-door neighbour, and that's over half a mile by the short-cut . . . But no, David Audley didn't light on him—he's one of Madame Peyrony's special friends, ex-Resistance. He was in charge of the transport system from Limoges to Cahors, she was in charge of the midway safe house, that's all. And ever since then he's serviced her car and kept the generator going for the electric light, and because they're both almost as antique as La Peyrony herself—the car and the generator—he's a fairly regular visitor . . . Satisfied?"

Not satisfied, but it would have to do. "What did he want?"

"He'll tell you himself. I told him you'd be back soon, and he said he'd be in the stables at the back of the house, where the car lives. If he isn't, then you're to phone him *toute de suite*—there's a phone in the house, amazingly enough." She paused. "You'll note that I'm not asking any questions."

Roche nodded, trying to smile back. "You don't want to know—very sensible!"

" 'What you don't know can't hurt you'." She stopped smiling. "I just wish I could believe that."

"Have you a reason for not believing it?"

She considered him in silence for a moment. "I've never had anything to do with . . . your side of the business before, David."

"My side of the business is pretty dull most of the time. Probably duller than yours, Jilly." It was a pity that the truth sounded so unconvincing.

"I hope this is one of the duller times, then."

"I see no reason why it shouldn't be." The thought of Meriel Aspasia Stephanides *(active, inform Central Records movements priority urgent)* made that a black lie, as Ada Clarke would say. But it sounded no more unconvincing than the truth. "If I could tell you what London wants me to do I think you'd be . . . reassured, let's say." More truth. "You might even be rather amused." Half-truth, anyway.

"I can look after my own amusement." She didn't smile. "It's just that . . . Lexy was right—we are rather isolated here. And there's more than one way of being raped." Another moment's pause in which she took him apart piece by piece. "I wouldn't like anything to happen to Steffy and Lexy . . . and Madame Peyrony and Gaston—and little Gaston."

He'd been wrong, she *was* scared. Or, he hadn't been wrong at all, and she didn't scare easily, she was brave—brave as Julie had been, not scared for herself, but worried to death about other people.

(Julie, Julie—if only you hadn't been so scared—so worried to death, literally worried to your death! If only you had waited, to let things work themselves out . . . then I wouldn't be here—it would be some other poor damn Roche; it might even be Oliver St.John Latimer if there was no Roche to hand—and you wouldn't be there, wherever you are, with bones of coral and pearls for eyes . . .)

Roche smiled. "Once I've seen Raymond Galles, I can be at the Tower pretty soon after that—and then you won't have to worry. I shall be David Audley's problem then!"

She gazed at him sadly. "I shall still worry."

"For heaven's sake—why? I'll be off your hands—and Lexy's!"

"I shall be worried for you."

"Why for me?"

She drew a long breath. "Very well. Because you're frightened."

Roche felt his grin sicken. It was his own fault for pushing so hard, but he couldn't let the truth lie there in the open between them, unaccounted for.

133

"Of course I'm frightened. I have an important job to do, and I'm frightened of failing. I don't want to be the oldest captain in the British Army."

She half-closed her eyes. "I didn't ask why." When the eyes opened fully they were expressionless. "Let's go and see this man Galles. And after that I'll take you to Madame. And then we'll drive to the Tower."

Roche followed her along a winding path through the trees. In the half-light the house ahead seemed bigger and gloomier than it had done when he had first glimpsed it as they'd approached the cottage, but perhaps that was only because he felt smaller and his own mood was even more sombre. He felt that Jilly's instinct to get shot of him, to get her small part of the operation over and to extricate herself and her friends from him, was sound and reasonable. It was only a pity, and it disturbed him, that since Steffy was one of those friends she might not find the process of extrication so easy.

And, as for himself, and what was more disturbing still . . . he had done so much, and learnt so much, and yet he hadn't even started. He hadn't even clapped eyes on David Longsdon Audley.

There was a collection of smaller buildings, mostly single-storey, at the back of the house. As Jilly led the way through an archway in the tallest of them they resolved themselves into a courtyard of stables and gabled hay-lofts and what must have been a coach-house in the days of the horse. The great double-doors of the coach-house stood wide-open and yellow light streamed out of them, illuminating the herring-bone design of the brick-paved yard.

Jilly pointed towards the light. "I'll wait here," she said.

In the opening, half-concealed by one of the doors, stood a tiny corrugated Citroen, bearing the legend *Raymond Galles et Fils* in flowery white on faded Royal Navy Mediterranean grey, and *Garagiste—Location de Voitures*, with an indecipherable Les Eyzies-de-Tayrac telephone number beneath it, alongside *Route D773*. Roche had just started to squint at the telephone number to confirm that it was the same as that which Galles had given him that morning, when his eye was pulled away by the glitter of yellow light on gleaming silver to his right, further inside the coach-house.

Huge in the centre of the open space—dominating it, even though he was simultaneously aware that it was flanked by a great black coach with brass lamps at its ears—was an enormous car.

Raymond Galles appeared suddenly on the far side of the car—the distant side, rather—next to a miniature searchlight fixed handy for the driver to manipulate to dazzle anyone outside the beams of the two almost full-size searchlights which sprouted from the sweeping front mudguards.

Galles grinned at Roche, and the grin was repeated in his reflection in the deep polish of the maroon-coloured cellulose of the bonnet. Viewed along the line of the bonnet he appeared to be a long way off, and there wasn't a speck of dust on the gleaming expanse of metal between him and Roche, though the cobwebs trailed from the naked electric bulb above him and festooned the carriage behind him.

"Ah—M'sieur Roche!" Galles bobbed his head and disappeared again, to reappear eventually at the far—furthest—end of the car ahead of him, still grinning hugely.

"And well-met, beside my beauty!" Galles touched the bonnet of the car lightly, and then instantly produced a snow-white rag from his back pocket to erase the touch. "Beside your namesake, one might say!"

"My namesake?" Roche goggled from Galles to the Beauty, and back to Galles again.

"You do not know? But *Roche* is a good French name—and yet also a common one, I grant you . . . But she—*she* is not common, you will grant me that, eh?"

Roche blinked at him, and then edged sideways to get a sight on the curious chromium-plated (or silver-plated?) object on the top of the radiator. It looked a bit like the iceberg that had ripped open the *Titanic*, in size as well as shape, with an ornate 'D' imprinted on it for some unfathomable reason by the collision.

"It's not a . . . Daimler—" that was obviously a stupid guess, though! ". . . or a Delage, maybe?" he hazarded.

"Delarge—*pouf!* Daimler—*phuttt!*" Raymond Galles lifted his right forearm, with two fingers extended on its hand, and struck the crook of the arm a rabbit-punch with his left hand. "Rolls-Royce!"

It clearly wasn't a Rolls-Royce, from that gesture of ultimate contempt as well as the absence of the Rolls-Royce emblem, apart from the iceberg 'D'.

Roche wasn't willing to try again. And Galles was bursting to tell him, anyway.

"A Delaroche—a Delaroche *Royale!*" said Galles triumphantly.

And Roche wasn't going to say 'Never heard of it', either.

Galles very nearly touched the Delaroche again, but thought better of it at the last moment.

"Only three Royales were made. The first was for King Zog of Albania, as a gift from an American mining company—that was destroyed by Italian bombers in 1939." Galles' face twisted with the memory of the bomb-bursts. "The second was fragmented by German bombers in 1940—in the factory, while a minor modification was in progress—it was the property of the Prince de Coutrai . . ." the twist suggested this time that Galles held the Prince personally responsible for hazarding his *Royale* unnecessarily in the face of the enemy ". . . I salvaged the remains myself, and transported them to this very place, together with the pilot of a Blenheim bomber—a flight-lieutenant of the Royal New Zealand Air Force by the name of Robinson, who is now a librarian in the city of Auckland." He nodded at Roche. "I remember that because he was my first allied aviator—it was in 1941—and the first to set foot in the Château Peyrony. Flight-Lieutenant *Ashiballe* Robinson—"

Ashiballe?

"*Arrrchee* for short—"

Archibald!

"And *here*—my beauty—" once more the almost-touch, but not quite "—is the third and last and *only* Delaroche Royale in the whole world." The little Frenchman beamed at Roche. "And that is a good omen for us both, m'sieur—a French *Dela*roche greets an English Roche, eh?"

Oh—*shit*, thought Roche. Time was ticking away, and he still had to submit to Madame Peyrony, and here he was, snarled up with a monstrous vintage French car and its enthusiastic *garagiste* and *locateur des voitures*, for Christ's sake!

But he smiled nevertheless. "She's a beauty, m'sieur." Pause—one-two-three! "But you have an urgent message for me, I believe?"

"But yes . . ." Galles peered past him. "Mademoiselle?"

"Waiting for me out in the yard."

"Ah! It was permitted that I make contact with you through her, you understand?" Galles's expression became serious, as if to reassure him that he had not approached Jilly casually, and Roche instantly regretted his impatience. Rather than scorn the little man's enthusiasm for the big car, which was in itself possibly no more than a cover for being here now, he ought to remember that Galles had been fighting Nazis—real fascists—when he himself had been working for his grammar school entrance.

"Of course, M'sieur Galles."

"Very well, m'sieur. You are to telephone Paris as soon as conveniently possible."

"There's a phone in the house, I believe—"

"More urgently, there is an American whom you are likely to meet, by name Bradford—"

"Mike Bradford. He's staying with Audley, yes?" Roche produced a polite frown. "A writer of some sort?"

"You've met him already?"

"No, just heard about him. He's a writer?"

"Of some sort—yes, m'sieur. And, it is thought, an agent of some sort also, of the American CIA."

Roche deepened the frown. "What the devil is a CIA man doing here? He can't be interested in Audley, surely?"

Galles shrugged. "If we are interested in Audley . . .?"

"No." Roche shook his head. But perhaps now was the time to start playing both ends against the middle. "There's also an Israeli staying with him, an old RAF pilot—Stein. Do you know anything about him?"

"No, m'sieur. He was not mentioned. Only Bradford."

So the British didn't know about Meriel Stephanides. If they were on to Bradford, they would not have missed her if they'd known about her, now that they'd finally got round to warning him about the opposition. But there was nothing particularly surprising about their not knowing something that the Comrades knew only too well, he reflected sadly; and, to be fair, the Comrades hadn't performed so well either, having 'lost' Steffy until he'd given them her location, and never having properly 'found' Bradford's Category 'A' status.

But Galles was frowning at him, as though there was something he was in two minds about saying.

"Yes, m'sieur?" he pushed the Frenchman gently.

"I don't know . . ." Galles shook his head ". . . but there is one that I have—how shall I say it?—not reservations, not suspicions about . . . but . . . a feeling from the old times."

"About Stein—the Israeli?" Roche pushed harder, and deliberately in the wrong direction. He realised that he wanted the Frenchman to say *d'Auberon something-something*, to save him from having to do so.

"No, m'sieur. I refer to the beautiful one, that Milady—Mademoiselle Lexy—speaks of as 'Steffee'."

"Meriel Stephanides?"

Galles nodded. "Mademoiselle Stephanides—yes. But I have no reason . . . except that there is this feeling from the old times, in the war, when no reason was often good reason."

Roche nodded back at him. "I understand." And bully for you, Raymond Galles! "You know she's a Cypriot? Or Anglo–Cypriot, anyway?"

"Ah! And you have troubles in Cyprus—as we have in Algeria?"

Roche nodded again. "And Israeli intelligence is very strong there . . . You may be right—I'll see what Paris thinks about her . . ." He gave Galles his own version of the in-two-minds frown.

"Yes, m'sieur?" The Frenchman picked up the signal.

"I have a name for you also—and also with no reason. A French name."

"M'sieur?"

Here I go then! "Etienne?"

"Etienne?"

"He's a friend of Audley's, and he comes from an old local family—a distinguished family—"

Galles's eyes widened.

"—and he left the government service recently, I gather. Do you know of such a person?" Roche concentrated his soul into an expression of honest curiosity.

"But yes, m'sieur! The Vicomte Etienne!"

"The Vicomte?"

"Of the Château du Cingle d'Enfer—above the river, on the bend."

Well, at least that made the identification certain: Lexy simply hadn't been able to twist her Anglo-Saxon tongue round Etienne d'Auberon du Cingle d'Enfer, and had reduced him in typical Lexy-fashion to 'Tienne!

"What d'you know about him?"

Conflicting loyalties strove with each other in Raymond Galles's face, his sixteen-year commitment to the British against what might well be a more ancient identification with the Languedoc, which was older than either England or France, whose armies had each arrived here as foreign occupiers in their day.

"What d'you know of him?" repeated Roche patiently.

Galles shrugged. "He was with the General during the war—he passed through here once, in the spring of '44 . . ." he ran out of steam prematurely at that point in the history of the Lord of Hell's River Bend, so far as Roche could translate *Something-Something.*

"He was in the Bureau Central de Renseignements—or the Organisation Civile?" prompted Roche.

Galles spread his hands. "I do not know of such things—he was with the General, that I know. But I was going to say . . . he was very young then. And after the war he was of the Quai d'Orsay in Paris for many years, and seldom here."

"But now he's back?"

Galles nodded. "Now he is back, yes."

So the older loyalty was the stronger. Or, if that was merely a romantic historical illusion, perhaps Galles was only a *garagiste* and car-hirer now, and knew no better. But either way he would have to depend on London now, and Thompson in Paris before that.

He grinned and shrugged at the Frenchman. With all the trouble and strife poor France had had since the end of the war—with the falling franc and Indo–China, and now Algeria, and most recently Suez and the impotence of the West during the Hungarian rising against the Russians . . . not to mention the endless succession of governments, each as short-lived as it was feeble . . . no one could find much comfort in the Fourth Republic, and a one-time follower of the ageing General de Gaulle would be more disillusioned than most.

"He's probably just pissed-off with politics altogether," he confided. "And I can't say I blame him . . . Mollet or Bourges-Maunoury—Eden or Macmillan . . . they're all the same!"

The addition of British prime ministers to French ones appeared to do the trick: the shrug-and-grin came back to him, only more eloquently, as only a true Frenchman could package such a mixture of regret and resignation.

Nevertheless, in view of Galles's equivocal attitude, an over-sudden loss of interest in d'Auberon might be unwise.

"Still, you'd better check up on him, I suppose—why he's here, what he's doing, and so on. Let me know if you turn up anything of interest." He raised his hand in farewell, and then checked himself as though an afterthought had struck him. "Presumably Madame Peyrony knows about him?"

Galles gave him a guarded look. "That is very likely," he agreed. "She knows a great many things."

"The young ladies seem scared of her—" As Roche spoke Galles turned without warning and began to polish an imaginary blemish on the gleaming bonnet of the car.

"What's she like, Madame Peyrony?" persisted Roche.

Galles went on polishing for a few seconds. When he looked up at Roche again his eyes were still on guard, but the ghost of a smile had relaxed his mouth. "She is a great lady, M'sieur Roche. And my advice to you is . . . if you should decide to lie to her about anything, lie very carefully."

Roche left him to his polishing.

XI

IF IT WAS gloomy under the trees which overshadowed the Château Peyrony on all sides, it was positively sepulchral inside the house: what little evening light the leaves permitted to approach it was further checked by the heavy drapery at the windows; and the single electric bulb in the chandelier high above Roche's head, inadequately fed by Raymond Galles's ancient generator, did little more than illuminate the crystal droplets around it.

"Christ!" murmured Roche under his breath.

"Yes," whispered Jilly, who could hear him because she was standing very close to him. "Decor by Charles Addams, Lexy says. With additional advice from Boris Karloff. And it's not much different in broad daylight, either."

"I was thinking of Dickens." He could smell her perfume, but beyond it smells of dust and unopened rooms. By comparison, The Old House at Steeple Horley had smelt fresh and had been full of light and excitement.

"Dickens?" She felt for his hand.

"Miss Havisham's house." He squeezed her cold fingers.

"With me as Jean Simmons and you as John Mills, you mean?" She squeezed back. "But you're too tall for him . . . we'll have to recast with Stewart Grainger as Pip—okay?"

Her juvenile film-going must date from the same period as his own. "If there's a choice I'd prefer to be James Mason," he hissed down at her.

She shook her head. "Sorry—no resemblance . . . apart from the miscasting."

Somewhere in the bowels of the house a door closed.

"David Audley's got an old house, Lexy says," whispered Jilly. "Full of ghosts, she says it is. Like this one."

It was on the tip of Roche's tongue to agree, with the only difference being that the most likely ghost in The Old House would be wearing smartly-pressed battle-dress. It also rather suprised him that Lexy, of all people, had picked up such vibrations.

But neither of those thoughts would do. "This isn't a very old house, not really . . ." He screwed up his eyes in an attempt to penetrate the gloom ". . . Second Empire, at a guess. The furniture looks like Second Empire—"

"Sssh!" Her fingers tightened, and then let go.

The crone-in-waiting, well camouflaged in her shapeless black dress, reappeared on the landing halfway up the staircase ahead of them, like one of the Château Peyrony's resident spectres.

But, ghost or not, she was beckoning them now.

Their destination, as soon as they'd reached the main landing at the head of the stairs, was clearly marked by the bright strip of light under the door in front of them, even before the duty ghost tapped on it.

"Entrez."

At least the voice was thoroughly unghostlike, with only the slightest quaver of age beneath its feminine strength.

Roche followed Jilly Baker out of the gloom into the light.

The first thing he saw, other than a general impression of a room full of things which only its size prevented from seeming cluttered, was the fire burning in a grate, set in a white marble fireplace surmounted by the inevitable ormolu clock and a huge portrait of what looked like the Empress Eugénie.

"My dear Gillian—" the voice, with its strangely softened 'G', orientated him immediately to the speaker "—how good of you to come!"

Unlike Madame Goutard, the shopkeeper's wife, Madame Peyrony had never been a great beauty—the face was too thin, the nose too Roman, even allowing for the depredations of time which had sharpened both. And the eye which settled on Roche, too, did not appraise him with anything like the once-upon-a-time might-have-been Goutard longing: either he was out of her class, too far below it for consideration, or sex had never figured largely in her calculations of worth and need.

"*English*, Madame? Je crois . . . ici on parle français, n'est-ce pas?" The confidence had come back into Jilly's voice, and into her face.

"One speaks French to those who need to have French spoken to them, my dear—like the incorrigible Alexandra, who has a good ear, but no mind . . . and that young man, David Audley, who has too much mind, but no ear." Her eyes, which had been darting back and forwards from Roche to Jilly, finally settled on Roche. "But there are those who do not need such instruction, so I gather . . . . Introduce me, *G*illian, my dear."

There was something wrong with her English. It was idiomatically perfect, but there was something he couldn't pin down in her pronunciation that wasn't right. And yet, even after years of listening to Englishmen murder the French language, he couldn't make out just where Madame Peyrony was wounding the English one.

"Pardonnez-moi, Madame—I mean . . ." Gillian looked at Roche desperately. "Madame—Captain David Roche, of Supreme Headquarters NATO, attached OEECD liaison, Allied Forces Central Europe, Fontainebleau."

Roche almost smiled, almost wanted to hug her for trying to do her best for him with that mouthful. It was unfortunate that Lexy had already spoilt it, that was all.

"Captain?" The demotion unsettled her momentarily.

"Madame," Roche willed himself forward to take the yellow hand, which was as thin-skinned as the carpet under his feet was thin, equally time-worn. "The incorrigible Lady Alexandra somewhat anticipated my promotion to higher rank, I believe."

She smiled at him then, showing small ivory-white teeth quite unlike Madame Goutard's yellow fangs; and the smile was what he wanted, because what he wanted was what she knew about the Lord of the Devil's River Bend, and betraying Lexy was a small price to pay for that.

"But a *para* nevertheless? Is that the English?" The smile mixed hope with doubt now. "We never had a . . . a parachute soldier through here during the war, so I am unfamiliar with the correct word."

Those two old witches have both got nephews with the paras in Algeria, remembered Roche.

Well—he would give her what she wanted, a *para* or a horse-marine, or a Bengal lancer if she wanted it.

"Paratrooper, Madame." He didn't dare look at Jilly, he just hoped she wouldn't give him away, that she would let him *lie carefully!* And there was Lexy's father's advice on that subject, even on that same lie: *Tell a whopper and make a proper job of it!* "3rd Battalion, Parachute Regiment."

That was a big enough one, anyway: the 3rd had dropped at Suez last year, with Massu's 2ième RPC.

She looked at him proudly. "My nephew is a *para*, Captain Roche—at this moment in Algiers."

"With Massu?" Roche didn't have to pretend to be impressed: the word from Suez had been that Massu and his men had been impressive.

"With Massu, yes." She inclined her head slightly. "And Bigeard." Then she shifted her gaze to Jilly. "And now you may leave us, Gillian my dear."

Jilly blinked at her. "Madame?"

"Sit down, Captain Roche," commanded Madame Peyrony, pointing to the chair opposite her own, beside the fire.

"But Madame—" began Jilly huskily. "Madame—"

Madame Peyrony transfixed her with a look. "*I* do not need a chaperone, at my age . . . *You* are going to the Tower tonight—is that not correct?"

The orgy!

"Yes, but—" Jilly tried to look at Roche.

"Very well!" The Orgy in the Tower didn't appear to worry Madame Peyrony in the least. "Go and superintend Alexandra's *toilette*, then. Somebody must do it—and the Jewess will not—so it must be you. So . . .

141

allez-vous en, my dear, and don't argue the toss with me."

Roche did a double-take. He had just been watching Jilly's resistance crumble when *don't argue the toss* was incongruously delivered in a strange nasal tone only a moment after he had puzzled out the *Jewess*—the Jewess was Meriel Stephanides, of course—it had to be . . . and the nuance of anti-semitism (never far away in this class—shades of Captain Dreyfus!) was really no surprise at all. But *don't argue the toss*—?

"Off you go, then!" Madame Peyrony gestured imperiously to dismiss the super-intelligent female ornament of the British Embassy in Paris.

The super-intelligent ornament went like a lamb, without a second glance at the *ersatz* paratrooper from Fontainebleau, who sat down like another lamb as he had been told to do.

"Now, Captain Roche—"

Captain Roche was a little bit too hot already after having been too cold, Captain Roche decided.

"—what exactly is it that you are doing here?"

Much too hot—

"Doing, Madame?" Hotter still. "I'm on leave—"

"On leave, naturally. But why here?"

Hot, to be precise, under the collar: she shouldn't be asking a simple question like that—accusingly, as though she didn't expect the first answer to be truthful, thereby ruling out any conventional response about the beauty of the countryside and the attraction of foie gras and truffles. So all he was left with was Thompson's bloody *bastides*—

"I'm by way of being a student of medieval history, Madame." God! It sounded thin, and how he wished it was Thompson himself who had to spread it! "You have some very fine *bastides* round here—Beaumont and Monpazier and Domme, for example."

The only thing to say for the *bastides* was they were so unlikely that she might accept them . . .

"In fact, I was only looking at the church in Neuville this afternoon, with Lady Alexandra—" He paused as something changed in her expression.

"There is wine on the table beside you, Captain. Please pour yourself a glass. Nothing for me, thank you."

The decanter weighed a ton and the long-stemmed glasses were as fragile as eggshells.

He turned back to her finally, after having made heavy weather of pouring, like a peasant unused to such artefacts.

The wine was golden-yellow, and much too sweet for him.

She sat back in her chair, folding her hands on her lap. "Is it Alexandra, then?"

"Madame?"

"If it had been *G*illian she would not have let me send her away." It was almost as though she was talking to herself. "And you are not a mouse— *paras* are not mice . . . and it will not be the Jewess."

"I beg your pardon, Madame Peyrony?" It was well enough to relegate the *bastides* to the nearest wastepaper basket, where they belonged, but the repetition of *jewess* was beginning to set his teeth on edge.

"The question is, if it is Alexandra, is it with her father's knowledge? The man, David Audley—he would be a mistake, but she is aware of that . . . but at least he would be suitable."

He was just about to say 'What the hell are you talking about?' suitably bowdlerised for the occasion, when he remembered Raymond Galles's advice: he knew exactly what she was talking about, and that would be a stupid lie.

The realisation of how close he had been to such stupidity cooled him down. The age in which she lived had long passed, but she lived in it still. Also, Madame Goutard would have described to her the sheep's eyes Lexy had made at him after the episode in the shop.

Actually, marriage to Lexy wouldn't be so bad, once he had become accustomed to her cooking. Marriage to Jilly would be even better, and certainly more stimulating . . . but with a senior peer of the House of Lords for a father-in-law, and an American heiress for a mother-in-law . . . Champeney-Perowne multiplied by Vanderhorn divided by Roche might still produce a sum total big enough to protect him from the simple addition of all his enemies. It was only a pity that such prospects were altogether Utopian.

But, more immediately, Madame Peyrony's technique of thinking aloud was an interesting one.

"And I'm not suitable, Madame?" His brain shifted into the right gear. "A *para*, but not suitable?"

"I did not say that, Captain."

"But you implied that." It was like crossing swords.

"And you did not answer my question."

"It was . . . an insulting question." And he would win, because he had more at stake. "If you will permit me to say so." But as yet he wasn't sure *how* he was going to win, that was all.

She took stock of him. The lightweight suit was right (expensive, but not too expensive; a little rumpled, but he was on leave); and the tie was only his old hockey club's, but it looked like something better; and the haircut was safely French military, Fontainebleau '57. And she already knew that he spoke Parisian French, and an Englishman who didn't speak the French of Stratford-atte-Bowe couldn't be all bad, especially an English *para*.

"You are not married, that is certain," she pronounced that judgement with an air of finality, because that was her technique. And although he didn't know how she had arrived at it he knew instinctively that the answer to his question, *how to win?* lay within reach.

"No, I'm not married." It was a risk, but not a very great risk—certainly not a very great risk for a *para* accustomed to risks. And, finally, instinct also made him want to talk, and for once not lie while talking.

"I was engaged once, unofficially, Madame. But never married— definitely *not* married, Madame."

She didn't interrupt. Wise woman!

"She was an American girl. I met her during the Korean War, Madame— while I was in Japan, after I'd been posted out of Korea."

Cultural shock: Japan is beautiful, and the people are kind and ordinary . . . just ordinary people, no better and no worse, in spite of the true stories of Changi and the Siamese railway, and Imphal and Kohima—

"She was very beautiful, Madame. Beautiful like . . . the Jewess. And intelligent—like *G*illian . . . and slim like her, too. And as full of life as Lady Alexandra." Perhaps all that was a bit too good to be true, after six years of looking back through rose-tinted spectacles—maybe not so beautiful, and not so intelligent and not so full of life. Maybe nervous at times, and highly-strung, and full of doubt about America, and where it was going, and what it was doing in the name of Liberty and 'We hold these truths to be self-evident' and 'the government of the people, by the people, for the people'. But Julie still—Julie *always*—

'In War it is as it is in Love . . . Whether she be good or bad, one gives one's best once, to one only—'

True! So Madame Peyrony had nothing to worry about—though this was not quite yet the moment to tell her so.

"She killed herself." There was no way of making it other than brutal: it *was* brutal. "She told me once, the way to go was to swim out—there was a current on the bay where we used to swim, if you went far enough out in the evening it would carry you out to sea, the fishermen said—and swim and swim and swim, until it didn't matter any more, until the sea and the sky joined. And that's what she did. *Tout simplement!*"

He'd only met Madame Peyrony five minutes before, and never before had he told that to anyone, because there was no one to tell who didn't have someone else to tell it to.

But Madame had no one to tell it to, only the resident ghosts, who couldn't tell it to anyone else, so it was all right to tell it to her.

And, besides, now was the time to tell it anyway, even if she did pass it on. Because now he was breaking faith with Julie—and because now, in a few days' time anyway, it wouldn't matter either way! *Tout simplement!*

"Why?"

He hardly heard the question, it was asked so softly. But he had intended to answer it anyway.

"It was a bad time. The bomb . . . MacArthur . . . Senator McCarthy— Senator McCarthy most of all—the senate sub-committee investigation . . . Julie's step-father worked for the government, and he'd subscribed to all sorts of causes, from the Spanish Civil War onwards . . . And she adored him—he was a great chap, a nice man—"

Julie's Harry, who knew all about England, as no other American he had ever met knew about the country, from his service there in the war—even

144

knew about the railways there, the very lines over which his own father had driven his engine—the old London North-Eastern—

"You've got a great chance in England, boy, to make real Socialism work—to show the Russians how to do it, so they can get it right . . . they're trying to, and they'll get the hang of it if you can show them the way—"

He was relieved Harry hadn't seen Suez. But he was even more glad he'd missed the East German riots and Poland, and above all the Hungarian massacres; they would have done the job just as surely as McCarthy had done, perhaps even more cruelly—

"He committed suicide. He shot himself with this German pistol he brought back from the war. He wrote a letter—"

Dearest Julie—

"—he wrote her a letter, explaining why."

She waited until she was sure he wasn't going on. He wanted her to ask the question.

"And because of that—because of her step-father—?"

"Also because of me. She wrote me a letter also—"

My own David—

"Because of you?"

"She'd decided I ought to be a teacher. But I was in the Army then . . . she got it all mixed up—she thought, if they found out about her, and then about Harry . . . with the way Senator McCarthy was hunting down people with the wrong connections . . . she had this crazy idea that they'd throw me out of the Army, and then they wouldn't let me teach after that. She said I'd be tagged as a 'subversive'—it's funny, really."

"Funny?"

"Harry wouldn't have made that mistake. He would have known that it wouldn't have made any difference to my becoming a teacher. They don't work that way in England, he would have known. They couldn't have cared less—particularly in the sort of school I wanted to teach in . . . not even if I'd been Stalin's stepson-in-law—or Krushchev's . . . and McCarthy never carried any weight in England—Harry would have known all that. But Julie didn't, that's all."

She stared at him. "And that is . . . funny?" She was questioning the word, not the fact.

"Ironic, is what I mean, Madame."

"Ah!" she nodded. " 'A funny sort of cobber' means 'a strange one', not a humorist. And 'funny business' is not comedy, but the exact opposite—I remember." Her wrinkled eyelids closed momentarily.

'Cobber' was purest Australian; and, more than that, she pronounced the word with an authentic Aussie twang. And yet there was no Aussie in her 'funny business', it was drawled in what might almost have been American.

She was staring at him again. "And the army too? They would not have cared?"

Roche shrugged. "I was only a National Service officer at the time—a

145

conscript. I was due to be demobbed—demobilised—pretty soon, anyway. It might have worried them a bit, in some ways. But it wouldn't have worried me, anyway."

She frowned suddenly.

"That surprises you, Madame?"

"You did not teach . . . in this school of yours?" She nodded, still frowning. "You remained in the army . . . Yes, that surprises me."

Roche relaxed. They had prepared him for this one long ago, if his connection with Julie had ever surfaced. It was another in the long succession of ironies that he had never needed their carefully rehearsed explanation until now, for a purpose and an interrogation very different from the one they had envisaged.

"In what way, Madame?" But it would do, just the same, their explanation.

"After such a tragedy . . . such a mockery . . . you must have been a very young man—" the hint of a sad smile crossed her mouth "—you are not an old man even now . . . I would have expected bitterness, if not anger, Captain."

Roche constructed his own frown carefully, as Raymond Galles had advised him to do. "Against whom Madame?"

"Against those in power. Against the . . . the brass-hats? The hats of brass, is it?"

Again the strange—funny-strange—pronunciation: it might almost be broad Yorkshire this time.

"The Establishment?"

"The Establishment? That is new to me . . . But—the Establishment—yes, that has the right sound and the right meaning," she nodded, mimicking him. "The . . . *Establishment*—yes!"

She echoed him again exactly. And that, of course, was what she was doing, thought Roche, the mists clearing from his mind. Once upon a time many Allied escapers had passed through this house, and some of them must have stayed for days, until the coast was clear, since it was an emergency hide-out for the times when the normal route was compromised. Australians, Americans, Yorkshiremen—they had all come and gone, leaving nothing behind them but memories and the echoes of their dialects in the vocabulary of this elderly French lady, who had an ear for the music of language!

"Oh . . . the I see—" He felt himself warming to her, with her so beautifully and carefully enunciated mongrel English and all the courageous stories behind it which would never be told, of bomber crews from Lancasters and Flying Fortresses, from Bradford and Brisbane and Boise, Idaho. But there was a cold layer beneath the warm one: if she could hear and remember so much, could she hear and distinguish the untruth also—Raymond Galles had warned him that her ear was razor sharp? "Yes—angry, certainly Madame."

That was the very truth, he was safe there: first the paralysing shock of grief and despair . . . then—*then* anger and bitterness both, which he had been too cowardly to turn into outright rebellion, which had been in a fair way to turn into the lethargic boredom of serving out his time as a messenger-boy in Japan, hauling brief-cases of decoded intercepts from American to British headquarters in a humiliating one-way traffic—

How he had hated the Americans then . . . hated the Americans, and hated the British by simple extension, the servile allies of the hated Americans, who had killed his Julie—his American—and now received the scraps from their master's table, carried in the brief-case chained to his wrist, the very ball-and-chain of servitude!

—until that evening, that never-to-be-forgotten evening, along the very beach from which Julie had swum out . . . along which they had walked so many times, to which he had returned . . . *all you have to do is swim out until the current takes you, and cherishes you—*

"—anger, certainly, Madame." Pain. "Anger—yes." Nod.
"Yet you remained in the Army?"
Smile, bitterly but knowingly. "But anger against whom?"

Against whom?
He had felt, even beyond anger and bitterness and grief—he had felt impotence!
He could have ripped open the brief-case, and scattered its contents along the way, or made a bonfire of it. But they had copies of it, and other officers to carry it—the uselessness of the gesture, as well as his own cowardice, had baffled him, even though the thought of going back to teach in England without Julie had filled him with despair.
And then, out of the soft blue of the Japanese evening, had come the offer of revenge, unexpected and unlooked for—revenge, yet at the same time a keeping-faith with Julie and Harry, and a keeping-faith with his own idealism—

Or had it really been idealism?
It was hard to think back now, to remember what he had really thought—*how* he had really thought, and why he had thought as he had done: it was like trying to capture the thoughts of a stranger, to re-capture his own thoughts from time past.
Anger and bitterness and grief and impotence and . . .
And boredom?
Perhaps if the war had flared up again . . . but it was clear at British headquarters, even to the errand-boys, that the Americans and the Chinese had both had enough of Korea—
Perhaps if Julie . . . but without Julie the idea of going back to do what they had planned to do together, always *together*—

147

Instead, there had been nothing but anger and bitterness and grief and impotence, and boredom and cowardice and irresolution and uncertainty, and maybe plain foolishness too, and maybe also idealism—but at the time he had only recognised the first four of them, and the last one . . . But they had been enough, all of them together, to open the wound through which the parasite had entered his blood-stream, to take him over—*Christ! Was that how it had really been?*

"Anger against whom, Captain?" Madame Peyrony prompted him gently, watching him with an intentness entirely devoid of gentleness.

The contrast between the voice and the expression was disconcerting, even almost frightening: that intense stare, half-veiled but not concealed by the wrinkled eyelids, was better suited to Genghis Khan's eyes, or Clinton's, than to those of an old lady in her boudoir—better suited to a small room without windows than to a boudoir.

Anger against whom? He must *lie well* now, and better than well, his own instinct more than Raymond Galles shouted at him: the past he must remember must be the version which the Comrades had so carefully created for him, not the newer and heretical interpretation which had directed his actions over the past few days.

He sighed. "I had a friend once, Madame . . . a brother officer in Tokyo . . . he was knocked over and killed by a police car." Pause. "The police car was badly driven." Pause again. "But it was pursuing a bank robber nevertheless."

She continued to stare at him, giving nothing away.

"I suppose I was angry with the police driver . . . even though the road was slippery at the time, I was angry. But not for long." Final pause, longer than the others. "Without the Communists, Madame . . . or without the Russians, if you prefer . . . Joseph McCarthy would have been just another stupid politician."

There had been a lot more, to be used as required, according to the depth of the interrogation. The six-year-old lines came back to Roche with mocking clarity, even to the small amendments he had decided to make on his own account (no patriotic young Englishman would have referred to 'Soviet expansionism' in a month of Sundays when he meant simply 'Russian aggression'. . .).

But this was not the time and place, and not the interrogator, for a lot more. The lie they had given him would stick here, or not at all, Roche judged.

Madame Peyrony subsided slowly into her chair, becoming somehow smaller and more ancient as she did so. "I will have a little wine now, Captain, if you please."

Perhaps it was not the lie which had stuck, but the truth itself. Because somewhere along the years, and particularly since the bloodbath in Hungary last year, he had realised that the lie was the truth indeed—that the

148

false reasons *they* had given him to give to the British ought always to have been his own true reasons for fighting *them*—that he had deluded himself, and been deluded; and that, worse still, that Julie and Harry had in some sense been deluded too, and had played an innocent part in deluding him.

But he had to pour the wine.

"And for yourself, Captain."

His hand shook. How incredibly sure the Comrades must have been of him, to feed him the truth to use, confident that he would accept it as untruth!

"I'm all right, thank you, Madame." He watched her sip the Monbazillac.

She inclined her head. "Very well . . . so I will apologise to you, young man—of course . . . But not unreservedly."

"Not . . . unreservedly?" He was glad she was forcing him to forget the humiliation of his previous thoughts.

She nodded. "You have set one of my fears at rest. You must understand that I have certain responsibilities so far as Alexandra is concerned. Alexandra is—shall we say—vulnerable?"

Roche smiled. "Or susceptible?"

"Vulnerable, Captain. To be fair to you, since I am apologising for this, I will tell you that last year she formed a liaison with a young man—not such as yourself, but a foreigner, Captain."

That was rather hard on Lexy's CIA boyfriend, thought Roche. And doubly hard, since the CIA man was technically not a foreigner so far as Lexy was concerned, as well as being very much like Captain Roche in another way.

"Altogether not suitable, in fact?" he said mischievously. "Unlike me?"

She sipped her wine.

"But then . . . I'm not in the least interested in Alexandra, of course," added Roche.

She set the glass down carefully. "Just so, Captain. But then what is it that interests you? And I beg you not to tell me anything more about *bastides* . . . I am certain that you know all that there is to know about them. But I am equally convinced that you are not in the least interested in them." She paused momentarily. "Are you acquainted with 'bum steers', Captain?" This time the pause was even briefer. "I presume you are, so you will understand me when I say that I believe you are endeavouring to sell such an animal to me, and I am not about to purchase it."

Roche managed to close his mouth, but decided that he had better not question this animal's precise pedigree.

"I said that you had . . . allayed—that is the word—*allayed* . . . one of my fears. I suppose that an old woman, and a stranger also, might be flattered that you have told me so much . . . so much of such a very personal nature . . . in order to reassure me as to Alexandra's safety. But not this old woman, Captain." Madame Peyrony paused yet again, this time for effect. "For now this old woman has another fear, which you have *not* allayed. And

149

I will tell you why, in order to spare us both the waste of time which *bastides*, and whatever else you have ready, might otherwise . . . otherwise . . ." she searched for the appropriate English word, but in vain.

" 'Occasion'?" Roche discovered that his mouth was dry from lack of use.

" 'Occasion'?" She filed the verb away for checking, but without accepting it into her vocabulary, as though it might be another 'bum steer'. "Very well . . . so you have given me your confidence, which I do not believe a man such as you gives easily, and least of all after you have been insulted to your face . . . and by 'an old witch', which is Alexandra's favoured word for me, yes?"

But Roche was back to tight-lipped silence. If she knew that then she probably knew the maker's tag on his underpants, and she certainly knew too much for comfort.

But how? And, just as important—or more important—*why?*

"So . . . there will be a reason for that, because no young man from Fontainebleau, who is interested in *bastides*, but not in Alexandra, wastes his time with 'an old witch'—to tell her that he is a *para* . . . and also in some sort maybe a policeman too—"

She cut off there, at 'policeman', quite deliberately, to let him react. But of course she had known that all along, probably even without the scattered groundbait of Fontainebleau and what he had deliberately told her.

"Policeman, Madame?" If she wanted him to react then he would do so. But he kept denial out of his voice.

"Of a particular type. Does it surprise you that an old witch should know about policemen?"

No, it didn't surprise him—not this old witch . . . of all old witches. If she had run escaping aircrew through her backyard, the men who had left their vernacular in her vocabulary, and lived to tell the tale, then she would know about policemen indeed; and not just the village gendarme, who was probably in her pocket, but other more particular and deadly types, from Darnand's original Vichy bully-boys and their *Milice française* successors to the professionals of the Abwehr and the Gestapo, who had decimated the resistance movement between them.

So—no lies now, except life-and-death ones. Because if she had passed herself off to all those in-some-sort policemen as an innocent old lady, then an innocent old lady she most certainly wasn't.

"No, Madame. It doesn't surprise me."

She stared at him in silence for a moment. "But naturally," she said drily. "I am . . . like the *bastides* of course."

"Madame?"

"You have done your homework on me."

Well . . . here was a necessary lie, if not a life-and-death one: she would surely find the truth of the combined incompetence of the British and the Russians unflattering, if not unbelievable.

"Not quite like the *bastides*, Madame." Roche decided to outflank the lie with a compliment. "Your defences are in better order."

She accepted the statement with the ghost of a smile, but in silence. She wanted more than that.

"But I would be fascinated to know . . ." he let himself trail off deliberately. "That is to say, I've never thought that I looked like a policeman—of any type." He gave her a wry smile, as boyish as he could make it, backing his instinct that if she had a weakness it might be for a young ex-*para*, albeit an English ex-*para* and an *in-some-sort* policeman, who could take defeat like a gentleman, with good grace.

Again, the moment's stare in silence. "On the face of it you don't, Captain. But also you remind me of someone, and in part it is because I see him in you, I think." The ghost-smile remained, but now it haunted a sad memory. "I think also . . . perhaps I should not tell you."

"Tell me." Roche knew, with self-revealing eagerness, that if she told him this then she would withhold nothing. "Please."

"He was an enemy." She weakened.

"A Frenchman?"

"No. A German, I think."

"You . . . think?"

"He claimed to be a Surf Efrican. Perhaps he was, though he was not the Surf Efrican whose identity discs he had."

Roche frowned. "A Surf—?"

"From Trekkersburg in the province of Natal. Pete—Pi-et—Prinsloo was his name. Or not his name."

South African! Her impeccable ear had picked up the original sound, and had retained it across the years.

"He was very young and very brave—to do what he was doing needed courage, even though he was our enemy. And handsome . . ." Her eyes glazed for an instant, then focussed sharply on Roche. "You understand, Captain, that we ran an escape route through this place during the war?"

Roche nodded wordlessly.

"Of course—you know!" She nodded back. "But what you do not know is how a good escape route works—not as a continuous road, but a series of independent links which do not touch each other, so that if one link is broken the others are still safe. And . . . and so the way to destroy the route is not to break it, but to introduce one of your men into it, to pass along it from link to link until the last one—and then . . ." She blinked at Roche. "But perhaps you know all this?"

Roche said nothing.

"No matter. We were on our guard against such men—we had our methods too. And we could not afford to have any mercy on them, for the sake of our own lives as well as our work." She gazed at Roche sadly. "But he was beautiful, was Pi-et. He helped me cut—" she frowned "—no, *prune* is the word—prune the roses in the garden, by the wall near the stables where the sun shines all the afternoon. And that is where he lies now, Captain—under the roses in the sunshine, whoever he is—whoever he was—under my beautiful roses. Which is a good place for a brave man, do you not think—even an enemy?"

Roche's backbone was made of ice. The Château Peyrony, with its garden planted so, was no place for double agents.

"You are shocked?" Madame Peyrony shook her head slowly. "I should not have told you, do you see?"

He licked his lips. "Only—" the word came out as a croak "—only because I remind you of him, Madame. I wouldn't like you to think that I'm brave enough to qualify for your rose garden—I'm much too frightened for that honour."

For an instant he was afraid that his nervousness had made him too flippant, but then she smiled—not a ghost-smile, but a genuine old-witch-smile of pleasure edged with a touch of malice.

"He was frightened also, Captain—courage without fear is a counterfeit *louis d'or* made of lead, with heads on both sides. That is how you are both alike: you are both hunters who are also hunted, I think. That is what I see in you."

God! thought Roche—after what Jilly had said that was more than disquieting, it was positively macabre! If she could see his fear in his face—if both of them could see it, or smell it, or somehow sense it with some sixth sense—then what had Genghis Khan and Clinton seen?

The malice became triumphant, and then abruptly vanished, leaving only a pure smile. "But do not despair, Captain—you are the true hunter, the honourable hunter, not like my late husband and his friends with their shotguns in the forest—you are the original hunter."

The original hunter? For once her strange but impeccable English must have deserted her, decided Roche.

She observed his confusion. "You are going to the Tower tonight, to the orgy?"

The original hunter's confusion only became greater.

"To stay with David Audley?"

The original hunter managed to nod to that.

"Good. So there you will meet another Jew—Professor Stein of Cambridge University—"

The nuance of contempt in her voice snapped the hunter's confusion. "Colonel Stein, you mean, Madame?"

"*Colonel* Stein?"

"Late of the Israeli Air Force." Roche heard his own voice sharpen with outrage. "And late of the Royal Air Force, DFC—Distinguished Flying Cross, Madame. Professor *Colonel* Stein—yes?" He wasn't going to put up with that any longer, and she wouldn't help him if she despised him.

Her lips compressed into a thin line, puckering the wrinkled skin round her mouth with lines of displeasure. "He is a friend of yours?"

He gave her the wry-boyish-English-gentleman's smile, as near as he could resurrect it, instinct encouraging him to stake all he had left on it. "I shalln't know that until I've met him. Maybe he is—maybe he isn't." He shrugged. "Does he know about original hunters, this . . . Colonel Professor Stein?"

The frown disappeared, and the displeasure too. She gazed at him sardonically. "As a matter of fact, he does. He is an authority on them."

The penny dropped inside Roche's memory. Stein was an expert on paleolithic art and this region was famous for its prehistoric remains. "Ah—the cave painters."

She shook her head. "The cave painters were not hunters, they were priests—their pictures were hunting-magic, to help the hunters."

"Indeed?" Roche was mightily relieved to be out of recent history and safely in prehistory.

"So I am told." The old-witch malice flashed. "Obviously you are not an expert in such matters, but only in *bastides*?"

"Among other things." He bowed. "But you see me as an ancient hunter, nevertheless?"

"Ancient—of course! How foolish of me, Captain!"

"Original will do. It's the 'true and honourable' I don't quite understand, Madame."

"It is simple. The hunters of today in these parts kill small game with big guns—my late husband's gun room is still full of them. But ten thousand, twenty thousand years ago in these same parts . . . along this ridge and in the valleys below . . . they hunted big game with spears tipped with flint—and the lions and tigers hunted them at the same time."

Yes, thought Roche grimly, *and being human, or nearly, they probably hunted each other too! Though, being poor savages, they only killed each other for the pot, not to keep the red flag flying or the world safe for democracy . . .*

"I see." But she was still playing with him, and she had been doing that for long enough. "So I am the hunter and the hunted. And you have concluded that simply by looking at me?"

"And listening to you, Captain. It seems to me that so far we have both been agreeably open with each other, up to a point. From which we may further conclude that we each want something from the other, would you not say?"

The old—witch! But what could she possibly want?

"Fair enough, Madame." And what had he to offer? "I won't . . . how shall we say? . . . trifle with Lady Alexandra's affections?"

" 'Trifle'?" She savoured the word. "You think you could?"

"I don't see why not. They'd be worth trifling with."

"You would do better with Gillian."

"She wouldn't have me."

She nodded. "Yes—she's a clever child. But you are not here for that."

"How do you know that?"

"Because I have been expecting you. Or someone like you."

"What? Someone . . . like *me*?"

"Of course. This is my territory, Captain—my ridge, my valleys, my villages. Since a child—my territory . . . child, young girl, young woman, wife, mother, old woman—old witch, as Alexandra would say. So the spells here are *my* spells, not yours—not David Audley's, not the Jewess's, not any stranger's, but *mine*. You are a hunter, Captain, but now you are hunting in *my* territory. You are not the first of your kind, remember?"

Roche remembered the rose garden, and the young German.

"But I do not know everything any more—there was a time when I did, but times change—"

And on whose side was Madame Peyrony, for God's sake?

"—yet I still feel the pulse—I know when there is something there in the dark which should not be there, that something is loose out there." She pointed towards the window.

The light in the room turned the late evening outside into inky blackness. But that 'something loose' was nothing so innocent as any sabre-toothed tiger or cave bear out of the original hunter's deepest memory: it was the modern horror of man stalking man, the unknown enemy which Wimpy would have identified as *negotium perambulans in tenebris*—something wicked, to make the thumbs prick . . . something hunting out of human conviction, not out of honest hunger . . .

Christ! If he continued along this road he would reduce himself to a quivering jelly of fear, out of pure imagination! There were only men and women out there, like himself; and Madame Peyrony was only a frightened old woman, by herself in a frightening old house in the dark; and she was only on *her* side, and he was only on *his* side; and all each of them wanted to do was to survive, and not go into the dark.

He wanted to ask her how she knew all this, but there wasn't time, and probably she wouldn't tell him, and it didn't matter because he believed her anyway, because what she had said fitted in with what he already knew.

Much more to the point, she had something to give him—she would know things about Audley and all the rest of them, but most of all about Etienne d'Auberon du Cingle d'Enfer, about whom neither the British nor the Russians appeared to know. For now he had something to offer her in return, to bargain with, and he only had to make the offer, that was all.

"Very well, Madame—I will hunt the thing for you—right?"

She had expected him to say that. "And in return, Captain?"

"In return, you will make hunting-magic for me. You will make pictures for me."

XII

NEITHER OF THE girls objected very strongly when Roche told them that he was going to Neuville to make his phone call.

"You could have phoned from the château, you know," said Jilly, demurring more for form's sake than from genuine irritation, judging by the kindness of her tone. "La Peyrony lets us phone."

"But she also listens in on the extension," said Lexy. "I distinctly heard the click when she did it last time—I jolly nearly asked her if she minded me speaking English on her line, just to let her know I was on to her. But then I thought 'what the hell', and I got my own back by referring to her throughout as 'that old witch' . . . no, I don't blame you one bit, David darling. The only thing is, we're late already and it's a quarter of an hour there if you step on the gas, and quarter of an hour back, so we'll be even later still—"

"Since when did you ever worry about being late?" murmured Jilly. "You'll be late for your wedding, always supposing you get the day right."

"Chance would be a fine thing—if I should be so lucky!" Lexy tossed her head, and then grinned at Roche. "But she's right—and Steffy's still absent without leave, so we can always blame her . . . and it'll give *them* time to get tanked up and good-tempered before we arrive—so what the hell!"

"It'll also give *you* time to bone up on Galla Placidia and the hairy Visigoths, Lexy dear," said Jilly, rummaging among a pile of books on the chair beside her. "A bit of last minute swotting among the footnotes in the back is what you need—I bet you haven't read them."

"Oh—*eff* Galla-*bloody*-Placidia!" exclaimed Lexy.

"That's undoubtedly what they did—or King Ataulf certainly did—but there's no need to put it so crudely—" Jilly continued to rummage "—*ah!* Here we are!"

"But I'm on holiday!" protested Lexy. "And I have a broken heart to mend!"

"Broken fiddlesticks! You have a job to do, and I intend to see that you do it—*here!*" Jilly tossed a book at Lexy.

Lexy made a clumsy attempt to catch the book, succeeding only in deflecting it onwards across the room to strike Roche painfully on the shin. "Oops! Sorry, David!"

Roche bent down to retrieve the book, which had become separated from its dust-jacket. As he reassembled the two his eye was caught by the jacket's design, which was dominated by the face and bare shoulders of a beautiful woman who appeared to be wearing only jewellery, and by two men, one heavily-bearded and blond and the other dark-haired and clean-shaven. All three were drawn in a mosaic background in which the title of the book itself was picked out in purple and gold—*Princess in the Sunset* by *Antonia Palfrey*. The whole effect was striking and yet somehow vulgar, oddly contrasting with the blurred photo of the bespectacled Miss Palfrey on the back flap.

The book itself had fallen open at its first page—

"I, Sidonius Simplicius, Bishop of Ephesus and sometime secretary of the most illustrious lady, Galla Placidia—"

It was not Roche's kind of book, but it reminded him strangely of other scattered novels he had picked up from the ground, on the track leading to The Old House, which fitted David Audley's tastes no better than his own.

And there was another narrow strip of stiff paper that had also come adrift, which had fitted round the dustjacket: *TENTH IMPRESSION: 250,000 COPIES SOLD!* " *'Gone With The Wind' restaged in Imperial Rome"—Daily Express.*

If it was not his kind of book he was clearly in the minority, thought Roche as he put the pieces together and handed them to Lexy.

"Thanks, David." Her arm sagged as she took the book from him. "Six hundred bloody pages!"

"Just the chapter notes at the back, dear," said Jilly sweetly.

"But nobody reads *them.*"

"They're the only thing in the book worth reading."

"But—"

Roche left them to it.

To his surprise, Roche found himself talking to Thompson within a minute of establishing his credentials with the duty man.

"You took your time," said Thompson accusingly, as though he also had an orgy scheduled, for which he was now late thanks to Roche.

"This isn't a metropolis—it's one of your sodding *bastides,*" Roche snapped back. "I had to find a phone."

"You received the word about Bradford, the American?"

"Yes." If they were beginning to run scared in Paris, as he was already running in the back-of-beyond in Neuville, then it was time to accelerate them. "What about Stephanides?"

"Who's he?"

"She. Cypriot–Jewish. There's a he in London—her father. I was just wondering if he and she might not be Mossad, that's all."

"What?" The cat was now among the pigeons.

"And Stein." Roche threw in a fox for good measure. "He's a reserve colonel in the Israeli Air Force—ex-RAF photographic reconnaissance. Do you know about him?"

"Stein? Stephanides? Hold on there!"

"I can't wait long. I'm due at an orgy, old boy."

"What?" Collapse of *bastide*-fancier. "*Wait!*"

It would have been invigorating, this speedy revenge, if it had not been so frightening, this discovery of their incompetence. It was a basic truth that none of them were omniscient, certainly not the British, but not the Russians and not the Americans either. But basic and inevitable truths didn't protect the men in the field, the Poor Bloody Infantry of all three services who had to get up out of their slit-trenches in the hope that at this precise point there were no mines and machine-gunners ahead of them.

Mutter-mutter-mutter. There was someone else there, and not the duty officer, just as there had been when he had phoned the other side.

Roche looked at his watch. "Oh—for Christ's sake, take your fingers out and get on with it!" he murmured into the muttering instrument.

"Roche?" the instrument squawked back at him instantly.

Who? Not the *bastide*-fancier—

"Sir?" he answered uneasily.

"Now . . . not to panic, Roche—" the new voice sounded almost kindly, almost reassuring, and was all the more unreassuring for that. "Are you listening?"

"You bet I'm listening." The new voice hadn't identified itself, it took it for granted that he could do that. But the distortion of the line confused Roche. "And I'm not panicking, I'm only terrified half out of my wits, that's all."

"Good, good—that's fine!" The line crackled an obscene chuckle at him, the owner of the voice mistaking his mixture of trembling fear and bitterness for British stiff upper-lip understatement of courage.

Oh—*shit!* thought Roche, despairing of being able to communicate the truth. "I'm listening."

"Fine. It's simply that the order of battle is changed a little. Have you talked to Audley yet?"

"I haven't even met him yet, for God's sake!"

"Don't worry—"

"I'm due to meet him as soon as I get off this phone."

"Good, good. And how do you rate your chances with him?"

Good, good—fine, fine—don't worry! The very imbecility of the reassurance sobered Roche. He could see, across the angle of the square, a French family at an outside corner table in the restaurant which had one star in the Michelin: the father was studying the menu calmly, dutifully watched by his wife and two impeccably-behaved children. Everything was right and well-ordered in their world in which the vital decision was *confit d'oie chaud* or *confit de dinde mayonnaise*, and their lives would go on untroubled regardless of his own agonies.

"I know one hell of a lot more about him than there is in the file."

"For example?"

The French father handed the menu to his wife and took up the wine list.

Well, as Lexy would say, *what the hell!* "He's the illegitimate son of a schoolmaster named Willis, who probably screwed his mother at a commem ball at Oxford in the twenties," he said brutally. "Will that do for a start?"

"Willis the Godfather?" inquired the voice politely. "Does he know?" Pause. "Audley, I mean."

The father closed the wine list. That decision was not within his wife's competence.

"They all knew in the end. I suppose he was the last to find out. But I don't think anyone ever told him, actually."

Another pause. "So what?"

"They've been screwing each other since, in their own different ways." That wasn't fair so far as Wimpy was concerned: Wimpy had been suffering in too-late silence ever since; and Mr Nigel had died too early for Master David to achieve anything except the purely intellectual satisfaction of restoring what his official father had neglected.

"And knowing that will help you?" The voice, which was more likely Stocker's than Clinton's, was cheerfully sceptical.

"Well, at least it accounts for him being such a bastard." But then again, it wouldn't be too difficult to cherish The Old House for itself, so perhaps he was also being unfair to Audley. Except that the man's deliberate neglect of Wimpy over recent years, which might have been dismissed as unthinking youthful carelessness in anyone else, fitted the first image better: Mrs Clarke's lively, affectionate little boy had changed over the years into nothing if not a careful and calculating man, so it seemed.

"And that helps?" The Stocker-voice persisted, blandly devaluing his progress and rousing Roche's own contrariness.

"For Christ's sake, Major—let the dog see the bloody rabbit before you start whistling at it! I told you, I haven't even met the man yet!"

The Frenchman was ordering his dinner now, and from the way he was placing the order, with precise gestures of the hand and the fingers, he was accompanying it with instructions about the cooking too.

Sheer envy roused Roche to further contrariness. "Don't you want him now, Major?"

"Of course we do." Stocker didn't deny the identification of rank. "But things have moved on a bit since you were briefed, and we're running short on time. So we've got to look to the next phase of the operation."

Ah! At last, the poor damn dog was about to be shown the wolf hiding in the thicket behind the rabbit!

"What next phase?" asked Roche obediently.

"We have a job for Audley to do down there. You didn't think recruiting him was the end of it, did you?"

The wine waiter was hovering over the Frenchman.

"Roche—"

"Yes, sir." Roche had no more precious time to waste. He had to show that the dog could bite back. "This second phase—would it have anything to do with a Frenchman named d'Auberon?"

158

"What?"

"D'Auberon. D-apostrophe-A–U–B–"

"D'Auberon—yes," Stocker crackled the line. "What do you know about d'Auberon?"

Roche wondered whether it would not have been safer to have let Stocker say his piece first rather than to have tried to impress the Major with his cleverness. Because that 'D'Auberon—yes' had only been an acknowledgement, not a confirmation, and if Madame Peyrony and Lexy were wrong . . .

"I said 'What d'you know about d'Auberon?' " repeated Stocker. "Well?"

The trouble was, he knew absolutely nothing about d'Auberon beyond Madame Peyrony's praise and Lexy's prattle. Until a few hours before, he'd never heard of the man.

"I know he's here, for one thing," he played for time, blessing the miles of telephone wire separating him from Stocker-in-the-flesh. The fact that d'Auberon *was* here, not half-a-dozen miles from Audley—and from all the rest of them, and not least himself—was all he really did know for sure. But try as he would, he still couldn't even place the man's name, never mind which particular Algerian row had sparked his resignation. The hijacking of Ben Bella from the Moroccan air liner on General Beaufre's order had caused a flurry of such resignations, but the date didn't quite fit. The oil discoveries or the building of the Morice Line were much better bets—

"Come on, man!" snapped Stocker. "What else d'you know?"

Not *how* but *what*, thought Roche. "Well, naturally I know what he was doing, Major," he said dismissively, as though to state the obvious.

"But you weren't in Paris then, Roche."

Wasn't I? The months flashed before Roche's eyes. Except for the odd weekend—except for the long, boring communications course and his long leave which had together caused him to miss the whole ghastly excitement of the Suez crisis—

God! It wasn't Algeria at all—*it was Suez!*

"But I made up for lost time when I got back, naturally."

"Those meetings had nothing to do with your work, Roche."

What meetings?

"No, they didn't, I agree. And of course I don't know everything that went on in them . . . I only know what I heard."

What meetings, for Christ's sake?

"You never reported what you heard," said Stocker accusingly. "Why not?"

What meetings had gone on during Suez? He'd been out of circulation for the best part of three months, sweating and fretting on the communications and instructional courses, and then on leave. There would have been dozens of meetings, political and military, during that last desperate revival of the moribund *Entente Cordiale*, attended by all the ghosts of 1914 and 1939 as well as everyone from Eden and Mollet downwards! But they had all been dust and ashes by the time he had returned—ashes still hot with recriminations against perfidious Albion which he hadn't dared to rake over.

"Why not?" Stocker snapped the question at him again.

The quick answer to that was 'It had nothing to do with my work, like you said, Major', but the thought of Suez cautioned Roche against facetious answers. That wound was too raw, and too much pride and too many reputations had been lost over it, for that sort of reply.

"It was just gossip, sir—bazaar gossip . . . after-dinner coffee stuff. I didn't rate it."

"Gossip be damned! I should have thought any suggestion of a leak from the RIP sub-committee was worth reporting, gossip or not."

Lord God! thought Roche, thunderstruck. *The RIP sub-committee! Sir Eustace Avery's own sub-committee!*

"Well?" Stocker poked the question down the line fiercely.

"Sir?" But what was the question? And, whatever the question was, how was he going to answer it?

RIP.

"Well?"

Requiescat in pace.

Roche swallowed. "Yes, sir. It was . . . in retrospect . . . it was an error of judgement, I admit. But it was just gossip."

Rest in peace—

"Of course it was an error. I don't mean that." Stocker clearly wasn't going to let him rest in peace. "What do you know about it, is what I mean—what d'you know about it?"

Roche's flesh crawled. That was the precise question Jean-Paul had asked him when he'd finally got back to Paris last December, just before Christmas, when it was all over—

"What do you know about it?"

"The what?"

"The RIP sub-committee."

"What's that? I've never heard of it."

"Then start hearing about it. Whatever you hear, we want to know. Start earning your keep, Captain Roche—"

He hated Christmas, not because of the memory of Christmas Past, or even of the bleak image of Christmas-to-come, but because of his annual thought of Christmas-might-have-been—all the Julie-Christmasses that would never be, which made the food stick in his throat and the drinks taste of wormwood at the parties.

But this time it was *earn your keep, Captain Roche—*

"RIP, old boy? 'Rest in Peace'—*Requiescat-in-bloody-pace* for evermore." But Bill Ballance knew, because he always did know.

"I don't mean that, Bill. I mean—"

"I know what you mean. But that's what I mean too—dead and buried, never to rise again, more's the pity! Our unknown top secret warriors . . . your glass is empty, old boy. Fill it up and we'll drink to them . . . That's the spirit! So now—to our unknown warriors—the men who got the right answer to the wrong question—RIP!"

"RIP, Bill? I can't toast a set of fucking initials."

"No? But they *were* fucking good, David—bloody incredible, when you think about 'em . . . everyone else was getting their sums wrong, and they were absolutely spot on right down the line—alpha double-plus . . . bloody miracle!"

"RIP, Bill?"

" 'Russian Intentions and Policy', for short. And if they'd only put 'em on to the Americans instead of the Russians, we wouldn't be drowning our sorrows here alone tonight like lepers . . . have you heard the story about Eden?"

"Which story?"

"When the telegram from Krushchev arrived. I was here in Paris . . . I suppose poor old Mollet got the same message, more or less, but he was cool as a cucumber too—of course he'd got the same intelligence report as Eden had, so it's not to be wondered at, is it!"

"What telegram, Bill?"

"The one in which Kruschchev said if we attacked Egypt he'd bomb us all back to the stone age—that was when the *second* wave of our chaps was just landing, and the jolly old Fleet Air Arm was clobbering the Gyppo defences to hell . . . and when Ike got the news in Washington he wet his pants—or went off to church and prayed, or played a round of golf, according to which version you believe—"

"Bill—"

"—but *Eden* . . . he just read the telegram once, and tore it in two, and went off muttering 'nonsense' to have his mug of Horlicks without turning a hair, same as Mollet—only he wouldn't have drunk Horlicks—don't you see?"

"No, I don't see at all—"

"*Requiescat*—or *requiescant*, to be exact . . . or should it be *requiescaverunt?* My Latin's a bit shaky nowadays . . . But no matter—the point is that everyone gives the two of them, Eden and Mollet, the credit for getting *that* right at least, even if they got everything else wrong—that the Russians were just bluffing . . . Of course the Russians were bloody well bluffing, with a few million angry Hungarians, and half the Hungarian army, shooting at them, so they wouldn't have cared less if we'd tarred and feathered Nasser and run him out of Suez on a rail, for all they could do about it except make loud threatening noises . . . but the point, dear boy, is that Eden and Mollet knew that for a fact, because the jolly old Joint Anglo–French Russian Intentions and Policy Intelligence Sub-Committee had told them so—that they could Rest in Peace so far as the Russians were concerned. Which is what I've been saying all along—and which is really the whole tragedy, old boy, because what Eden really *needed* to know was not what the Russians would do, but what the Americans would do—our friends and allies—not Mr K., but John Foster Dulles and Dwight D. Eisenhower, eh?"

"Oh—ah—"

"*Oh-ah* indeed! Though maybe the RIP chaps might not have worked out what Ike was going to do, since Ike probably didn't know himself, so it might not have done us any good to have an inside man in the White House, like we did in the Kremlin—"

"An inside man?"

"Stands to reason. You don't get one hundred per cent certainty by studying your navel and trusting to luck—you only get it when someone gives you the answers in the back of the book. RIP—*quod erat demonstrandum*, dear boy. And I think the French had him, because we certainly didn't—and don't, more's the pity. But I'd like to have been a fly on the wall when they met, all the same!"

"Who was 'they'?"

"Lord knows! None of our people here, that's for sure . . . I thought you might have been one of them, young David—you weren't in circulation at the time, and you're a bit of a dark horse, writing all those non-event reports of yours all the time, to no possible purpose . . . . They came and they went, and but for one of 'em—that stuffed shirt Avery—Useless Eustace—I've no idea . . . . But it was the French who produced the information, Avery just took the credit. And we shall not look upon their like again, I fear—because the French will never speak up again, after what we've done to them, and I can't say that I blame them. Have another drink—to your next report on the incidence of scurvy in the French Mediterranean Fleet, say—?"

RIP.

He had known that Jean-Paul would already have all that, even before he passed it on, and that he would not earn his keep with Bill Ballance's carefully indiscreet ramblings, just as he knew that it would be dangerous to push Bill further, beyond Bill's suspicion that his Christmas drinking might be the subject of an internal security check by the dark horse. But that had been the last whisper he had been able to overhear about the near-legendary Joint Anglo–French Russian Intentions and Policy Sub-Committee, from Bill or anyone else. So he had never had a useful name to give to Jean-Paul, either British or French, let alone Russian.

But now he had a name.

"I heard d'Auberon mentioned in connection with it." He needed more time to think, but there was no time. "I'd never heard of him—he isn't an Army man." Stocker shouldn't expect him to place Quai d'Orsay names. "Until I got down here I didn't know he'd resigned."

162

But what the hell did Sir Eustace want with information about meetings which he had jointly chaired, for God's sake?

"Where did you get all this?"

"Sir?" Playing stupid was easy, once the role was accepted.

"Who told you about RIP—and d'Auberon?"

"Bill Ballance told me about RIP, sir." Betrayal, always providing it wasn't himself he was betraying, was even easier than stupidity, and Bill didn't give a damn, anyway. "And one of the girls down here told me about d'Auberon's resignation—she knows him socially—Lady Alexandra Champeney-Perowne." That bit of truth could do no harm, but he would keep Madame Peyrony up his sleeve. "She met him through Audley, I think . . . Anyway, with what she said and what I already knew, all I had to do was put two and two together."

He watched the Frenchman tuck into his *potage*. Whether or not Stocker was enjoying his *omelette Roche* equally, with its tiny truffle-specks of truth, could not be deduced from the silence at the other end of the line. But it might be as well not to let him test its quality too long in case he caught the flavour of lies in it too.

"I'm running out of time, sir. I was supposed to meet Audley five minutes ago."

"Yes." Stocker came to life instantly. "So you don't actually know what d'Auberon's got, then?"

D'Auberon had got something.

But of course d'Auberon had got something. If he had quit his job in anger and disgrace with top secrets merely locked up in his head he would never have got out of Paris alive, let alone been allowed to settle comfortably in the Dordogne: the SDECE's Bureau 24 would have seen to that, if 'Colonel Lamy' hadn't simply farmed out the job to the West German contract assassin who was working his way through the foreign arms dealers at the moment . . .

It didn't matter—what mattered was what was obvious: Jilly's guess that d'Auberon had 'beans' to spill had been right, but she hadn't taken the guess to its logical conclusion . . . which was that those beans had to be in a can somewhere safe, rigged to spill in the event of d'Auberon's untimely demise. It was so obvious that Stocker hadn't bothered to add that two-and-two for Roche's benefit.

"No, sir." But now other twos-and-twos presented themselves in a natural progression, following that obvious one, plus what Bill Ballance had said at Christmas: it would be the name of the inside man—it must be that, nothing else fitted so well, nothing was more likely to arouse such greed. That name would be worth almost any risk.

Any new department, starting out secure but in the cold, needed something hot to get things moving; and Avery of all people would have desired to get his hands on d'Auberon's can of beans, because Avery of all people would know its value—it had already turned him into *Sir Eustace* when his colleagues were being demoted or passed over or bowler-hatted. If he could lay his hands on the one intelligence source that was accurate and secure *and came from the very top in the Kremlin*, then he could write his own ticket in both London and Paris—the poor bloody French wouldn't have any choice, knowing that the perfidious British would shop them otherwise.

"Now, listen here, Roche—"

Roche could feel his heart thump in his chest, not with fear and simple arithmetic but with the multiplication of excitement at last: *not Avery—not Sir-bloody-Eustace—but he himself—poor-bloody-Roche—could write his ticket with that name anywhere in the world, from Washington to Moscow and back—*

". . . this is why we have to get Audley . . ."

Audley! He had forgotten Audley!

". . . because we have good reason to believe that he can supply us with the d'Auberon material."

Audley!

". . . we had originally intended for you to bring him back to us first, and then to take it off him as a bonus . . ."

The red flare cooled instantly into icy determination, all Roche's anger chilled into bitterness by Stocker's crude lie. Perhaps they did want Audley, he seemed a natural candidate, sure enough; but what he had was what they really wanted, he was just the bonus. And Roche himself had originally been cast as the recruiter, not to be trusted with the important work and not to be given the full credit and the proper reward.

". . . but now we can't wait, Roche."

They couldn't wait because they hadn't bargained on the arrival of the Americans, let alone the Israelis, on the scene ahead of them—probably ahead of them because Mossad and the CIA had also heard of Audley's peculiar virtue, and had moved more quickly to exploit it.

"You understand?"

He was expected to understand about the Israelis and the Americans. What he didn't understand was why they were still so confident he could achieve all this. But Stocker would surely tell him that before long; and, more than that, any minute now he'd be offering back-up, with this sort of opposition.

"Yes, sir," said Roche.

"I'll get down to you as soon as I can. Not tomorrow . . . I have things to do up here . . . but maybe the day after. Galles will look after you, anyway."

That wasn't the answer he'd been expecting—Stocker the day after tomorrow . . . and what use was Galles? He wasn't even sure that the Frenchman was still trustworthy, never mind capable.

But Clinton had said he had been very carefully chosen, and oddly enough that was easier to believe now than it had ever been before: quite simply, d'Auberon's 'material' was too important to be allowed to slip through their hands if there was the slightest chance of getting it—it was worth risking someone *good* in fact.

"There's just one thing, sir." There was no way now that he could ask those questions and get a useful answer. But there was another question which could be answered. "You said you've got 'good reason' to rely on Audley—that he can obtain d'Auberon's . . . material. How d'you know that?"

Stocker was silent for a moment. "Mmm . . . 'how'—I'm sorry, Roche, the 'how' is off limits to you. All you need to know is that he's our man. But if you want to know *why* he is, I can give you that—because I was about to give it to you anyway."

The fine distinctions of the answer seemed almost indistinguishable to Roche.

"Can't you guess, man?" Stocker teased him. "I should have thought it was obvious enough, in all conscience."

Obvious enough?

All the emphasis was on Audley, not d'Auberon. It had been Audley, Audley, Audley . . . and then not d'Auberon, but 'd'Auberon's material'—Audley, Audley, Audley—and d'Auberon's material—and 'good reason', and 'he can get it', and 'he's our man', and in the end *certainty?*

"He's got it already—is that it?" The question had answered itself before he had whispered it into the mouthpiece: it would never have been enough for d'Auberon to hide away his can of beans in some safe deposit to which he had access, because Bureau 24 had ways of making people give such things up—ways the Gestapo had taught the French, plus all the refinements of cruelty Indo–China and Algeria had added. So the can would have to be at one remove from the owner, out of his hands and to be handed over only under certain controlled conditions of safety, back to him and no one else. That was what he, Roche, would do in the same dangerous position—nothing else would combine self-preservation with security.

"Bravo!" exclaimed Stocker.

But the catch was, thought Roche bleakly, *you needed a friend you could trust, willing to shoulder the risk for you.*

"So now you know," said Stocker encouragingly.

Now he knew.

He knew that d'Auberon had such a friend, and that it was his job to engineer the betrayal of that friendship to save his own skin.

"Yes," he agreed. "It's not going to be easy."

It wasn't going to be easy, even though Sir Eustace Avery had chosen better than he knew—had chosen a real expert on betrayal, with a more urgent incentive than mere promotion to spur him on.

"I'll think of a way though," he murmured.

That was, Genghis Khan would think of a way, he thought grimly.

SKIRMISHING:

The Orgy in the Tower

XIII

"BARBARIANS," SAID AUDLEY, perching himself on the stool.

"But Steffy's not here yet," said Lexy. "We can't start without her. And what about 'Tienne?"

"Lexy doesn't want to start at all," murmured Jilly. "She's playing for time."

"Lexy's just saying that Steffy isn't here," said Lexy. "But if Jilly doesn't shut up Lexy will say something nasty."

"Etienne won't be coming. But I agree Steffy isn't here," said Audley. "So our guest will take her place." He raised his glass towards Roche. "You are hereby summoned to this orgy, Captain Roche. Your attendance is requested and required, no longer as a mere onlooker, but as a participant, with all the rights and privileges and duties appertaining thereto. *Ave*, Roche!"

Until that moment Roche had been in two minds about the soft light diffused by the paraffin lamp on the low table between them, for it veiled his expression no less than everyone else's. But now he wished that he could distinguish more of Audley than the man's voice and words revealed to him.

"Now come on, David—fair's fair." Stein stirred lazily on his nest of cushions beside the wine-rack. "He may not want to be summoned. He may prefer to on-look."

"Or he may just think we're crazy." Bradford's contribution came from behind the bottles on the table; all Roche could see was his dark head shake agreement.

"And he could be right there," said Lexy. "Some orgy!"

"He doesn't have to play, surely?" said Stein.

"You can't turn him out into the night if he doesn't." The American's dark curls shook again. "The laws of hospitality forbid it—we took him in on your behalf."

But it wasn't the laws of hospitality which mattered here, in this weird place, thought Roche: it was *play*—he doesn't have to *play*—which was the operative word—Jilly had said as much—

"He may want . . . he may prefer . . . he may *think*." Audley ranged his glass from one to the other, the lamp reflecting twin points of light like bright animal-eyes in his spectacles and throwing a huge shadow on the wall behind him. "He may even be right. But he will play, nevertheless."

"Why?" snapped Lexy. "Why should he?"

"Because I say so. And I am in the chair tonight. So I make the rules."

"You just have to argue with him—you have to debate the subject, whatever it is."

"What subject?"

"Whatever it is. We take it in turns, and he picks our brains. With Davey—David Stein—it was paleolithic art, with Mike Bradford it was the Great American Novel, and what Hollywood does to it . . . and with me it was the aftermath of the Korean War."

"It all sounds a bit juvenile."

"So it does—yes, you're right . . . a bit juvenile . . . It is."

"And they put up with it—Stein and . . . the American—what's his name?"

"Mike Bradford? Yes, they do. I think they quite enjoy it, to be honest. You see, they're the same really—they all missed out on that—the juvenile bit. What they call now 'the teenage', don't they?"

"Missed out? How?"

"It's just a theory of mine. They grew up in the war, or just before—and as a result they missed out on something we had. Something we took for granted."

"What was that?"

"I don't know, quite . . . They grew up too quickly, perhaps. Or they had to grow up, rather. Because they were at war when they should have been at college."

"But they all came through."

"That's right. Maybe they felt guilty about that—maybe they're too serious—or too frivolous—because of that . . . I told you—I don't know. All I know—all I think—is that you shouldn't be surprised that they don't behave quite normally, because they don't know how to. Because they don't have the same rules as we do, that's all."

"What rules do they have, then?"

"Don't ask me—I don't know! 'Give us back our teenage', perhaps. Only we can't—and they know it. It's just my theory. But . . ."

"But what?"

"Well . . . we were sitting in the Tower the first evening, the six of us, and . . . we'd been drinking . . . and I said, 'we'd better get back, otherwise La Peyrony will think we're engaged in an orgy', or something like that. And David said—David Audley said—'That's a jolly good idea'. And I said I'd be damned if I was going to hand over my body to the three of them, just to spite La Peyrony . . ."

"Yes?"

"And then he said—I'll never forget what he said, because suddenly he was dead serious, and he didn't say what I expected him to say—he said 'Damn your body, Jilly—it's a perfectly good body, but I prefer Lexy's, it's more pneumatic and more my size, as well as being more available—but bodies are two-a-penny these days, and have been ever since '39 . . . it's your mind I want to get into—if you can open that to me you can hold a penny tight between your knees for as long as you like!' And . . . so that's how it all started, anyway."

170

"Is that agreed and understood?" said Audley. "That I am in the chair tonight?"

"In the chair?" Jilly echoed him inquiringly, mock-innocently. "But if you fall out of the chair are you still in it, David?"

That might be an explanation of the slight slur in Audley's voice, for all that the grammar and the syntax were still clear enough. But Roche had never heard that voice before, and so could not judge the degree of slur against previous experience, even if the rugger players of Cahors were as alcoholically inclined as their English counterparts.

"In—or on—or out—or off . . . or under or beside . . . I am still *in* it tonight, until cock-crow or the wine runs out, whichever comes first," said Audley defiantly. "And I say that he's summoned—and he plays. Right?"

Still he didn't look at Roche, and still Roche couldn't decide whether or not the faint slur was public-school-and-army-drawl or a sign that the speaker was loaded over the Plimsoll line. But it didn't matter, because Roche would play now whatever the game was—because now he had the chance of playing for what he needed to win the real game.

"He plays!" He lifted his glass towards Audley. *"Moriturus te saluto!"*

"And a classicist too, by God! Bravo!" Audley's teeth also caught the lamplight. "Fill the man's glass again, Lexy . . . The wine of Cahors, Roche—they sent Cahors wine to Rome in classical times, did you know that?"

"I'm not a classicist. Just a soldier."

"Huh!" murmured Lexy, tipping the bottle inexpertly.

"But not merely a soldier—if I heard a-right?" Audley cocked his head.

"I told you . . . he's a sort of historian," said Lexy vaguely. *"Bastides* and things . . ."

"So you did!" Audley wasn't letting go. "University?"

"Manchester," said Roche.

"A good school of history," Audley nodded patronisingly.

"I'm afraid barbarians are a bit out of my line, though." Roche swallowed his pride. "Not my specialist field."

"That's what they all say." The Israeli spoke across the table to the American. " 'Not my field'. He's a historian right enough!"

"It all depends on what you mean by 'barbarians', as Professor Joad would have said," interposed Jilly. "We have to define our terms first."

"Latin—*barbarus, barbari*—a stranger, a foreigner . . . anyone not a Roman or a Greek." The Israeli's voice carried an edge of bitterness. " 'Jews need not apply', even though they lived in cities before Rome and Athens were villages of mud huts."

"Oh, come now—that's a bit hard on the Romans," said Audley. "Roman citizenship spread wider than the mud hut circuit. The Jews were just . . . difficult, let's say."

"I hear tell they still are," said Bradford from the floor.

Stein swept a glance over them, the light catching the surprising gold of

171

his hair—the crazy contrast of the blond Jew and the dark, swarthy American, whose identities Roche had immediately confused, struck him again.

"Yes?" inquired Audley politely, yet insultingly.

It was a game, Roche reminded himself. At the moment they were playing to bait each other with their opening moves.

"I'd say you've got a lot to learn," said Stein mildly. "We haven't half started yet."

"Yeah . . ." The American's dark head nodded. "I also hear tell you're in with the French on the nuclear testing site at Reggane in the Sahara, so you don't need to labour the point."

"I agree all this is *barbarous*," said Jilly. "But I don't see how it connects with *barbarians*."

"Quite right, dear." Audley bowed in Jilly's direction. "We have digressed—and just as Stein very properly related the *barbari* to Hillard and Botting!"

"Hillard and who?" The American reached for one of the bottles on the table.

"*Botting*, Bradford, *Botting*. Or maybe North and Hillard. Or A. H. Davis, MA, of revered memory. And if you were in receipt of their royalties—if you could write *that* sort of best-seller you'd be living high on the hog in Monte Carlo, swilling Château Latour with a bevy of starlets."

"What? Botting? North . . . ? What have they written?"

"Oh, *sanctissima simplicitas*—you are a rude barbarian if ever there was one, Bradford! Tell him, Stein."

The target had switched from the Israeli to the American, thought Roche: that was the way they worked, not all for one and one for all, but all in turn against each.

"A. H. Davis!" murmured Stein. "There was a man for you—a great author!"

"Who published him? What does he write?" Bradford rose to the bait, transformed by the mention of royalties from a cool American into an envious author.

Stein ignored him, looking round the shadowy audience in the Tower at everyone else and settling finally on Roche himself. "You know A. H. Davis forecast it all—1914 and 1939? He was unbeatable on the Germans: 'They regard it feeble and stupid to get by the sweat of their brow what they can take by spilling their blood'! How's that, eh?"

"It was Tacitus who said that, actually," Audley disagreed. "In his *Germania*."

"But Davis quoted him deliberately. And that's what history is all about—putting it all together," said Stein passionately. "By God! Do you remember that ratty little friend of yours at school, selling us all the classics after Hitler marched into Czechoslovakia? Williams—Williamson? He was always quoting A. H. Davis at us!"

"For God's sake, one of you tell me—who's Botting?" said Bradford irritably.

"He was a schoolmaster," snapped Audley, turning towards the American. "They all wrote Latin text-books—Latin and Greek—*Latin Prose Composition* and *Greek Unseens* and *Graduated Latin Selections*."

"Best-sellers?"

"Too bloody right! My Hillard and Botting was the fifteenth impression of the seventh edition, dated 1930. Can you beat that with any of your novels, old boy?" said Audley nastily.

Jilly gave another of her characteristic attention-drawing sniffs. "Or can you, David?"

"Yes—well, that wouldn't be difficult." Audley took the jibe well. "There simply isn't much popular enthusiasm for medieval history these days."

Roche decided to be interested. "That's what you're working on now?"

Audley nodded. "That's why I'm here."

"Here?"

"Yes. I'm putting the final touches to the sequel to my worst-selling book on the defeat of the Arabs by the Byzantines in the 8th century. This one is set at the other end of the Mediterranean. Here, in fact—early Carolingian France."

Roche ran his early French history through his memory at break-neck speed; this, after all, was one of the reasons why he was here, and he had to justify Sir Eustace Avery's confidence.

"Charles Martel?" That was a safe name to remember.

"That's right." Audley seemed pleased, but not surprised any more. "Battle of Tours—732. It always astonishes me to think that the Arabs got to within a hundred miles of Paris. And if it hadn't been for Charles Martel their next stop might have been the English Channel."

"They qualify as barbarians—the Arabs?" inquired Stein.

"The Arabs?" Audley sounded shocked.

"His prejudices are showing," murmured Bradford.

Audley coughed primly. "The Arabs in Spain used mostly Berber infantry—and in France—and the Berbers were *rather* barbarous. In fact, they really only went to Spain in the first place to pick up women and loot for their Berbers. And one thing led to another."

"Franco used them in Spain too," said Bradford. "They were still barbarous."

"The French are finding that out in Algeria at the moment," said Roche.

"Yes, things don't change, do they?" Audley nodded. "But, of course, the Arabs had it easy in Spain. The Visigoths hadn't quite succeeded in making a go of it there—nearly, but not quite . . . And they'd persecuted the Jews there—"

"Just another bunch of Krauts on the loose—things don't change, you're damn right!" said Stein bitterly.

"The Visigoths!" exclaimed Lexy with a start.

Everyone turned towards the region of deepest shadow in which she had concealed herself.

"Lexy, honey—you're awake!" said Bradford. "The Visigoths?"

"I haven't been asleep."

"Of course not. But what about the Visigoths, Lex?"

"Nothing." She tried to shrink back into the darkness. "Don't mind me."

"But we do mind you, Lady Alexandra," said Audley. "You mustn't hide your light under a bushel—you're supposed to be the chief questioner tonight. You drew the short straw last time—remember?"

"And obviously she knows about the Visigoths," said Bradford. "Are they barbarians, Lex honey?"

"Maybe she thinks they're rugger players," murmured Stein. "Wasn't that your old team, Audley—the Visigoths?"

"Yeah, and they *were* barbarians," nodded the American. "When they played there was blood everywhere."

"We haven't even defined what a barbarian is yet," cut in Jilly sharply, moving to Lexy's rescue. "All we've had is Hillard and Botting, and Charles Martel, and David's darling Arabs-who-aren't-barbarians." She sniffed. "A fine chairman you are, David Audley! You couldn't chair a cup of tea across a vicarage parlour!"

"And which barbarians, that is the question?" said Stein. "Come on, David—Audley—which barbarians are you going to tell us about? Julius Caesar's ones—which I take it will include your own woad-covered ancestors?"

"Boadicea's Ancient Brits, you mean?" inquired the American. "Like the statue near Big Ben, by the Thames—the chariot with the scythes on its wheels?"

Jilly leaned forward. "But I didn't think that was your period, David—I thought you were strictly medieval?"

Audley nodded. "So I am."

"So—"

Audley held up his hand. "So listen, my children, and you shall hear what you shall hear!"

"And know neither Doubt nor Fear?" murmured Roche.

"Ah!" Audley stared at him, and rocked dangerously on the three-legged stool, the huge shadow dancing on the wall behind him. "*You* know then! 'I am born out of my due time'—remember? 'Five hundred years ago . . . five hundred years hence . . . I should have been such a counsellor to kings as the world has never dreamed of'." He tapped his head. " 'Tis all here . . . but it hath no play in this black age'—remember? *Puck of Pook's Hill*?"

"De Aquila?" Roche was almost certain of the reference, and it was interesting to him that Audley identified himself with the cunning old blackguard. For either by accident or design Kipling had drawn a classic blueprint for the successful spymaster there, using a judicious mixture of force, blackmail, threats and torture to turn an enemy agent. It was an irony that he himself had identified with de Aquila's victim, the faithless Fulke, envying him his chance of changing to the winning side with honour and profit.

Audley nodded back, the lamplight glinting in his spectacles. " 'The Old Dog' himself. Good man, Roche!"

"Kipling lives again," murmured Bradford.

Audley drew himself up on the stool. "All right then—you barbarians, I'll give you barbarians . . . barbarians all the way from the Rhine and the Danube into the Sea of Grass in the east, to the Volga—Angles, Saxons, Franks, Lombards, Thuringians, Burgundians . . . Alemanni and Marcomanni . . . Quadi and Rugians and Gepids and Vandals and Goths—Visigoths and Ostrogoths—"

"As far as the Volga?" Bradford emphasised the name disbelievingly.

"That's right. Stalingrad wasn't the first time the Germans were there. The Romans turned them away from the west, so they went east."

" 'Lebensraum', it's called." Stein nodded. "An old German custom."

"But then they came back." As ever, Jilly had her facts neatly cut-and-dried. "Third century AD? Fourth century?"

"Fourth'll do. Say . . . sixteen hundred years ago . . . give or take a few decades." Audley smiled. "Sixteen centuries ago we could all have been sitting here, nice and cosy, drinking our wine—the good wine of Cahors—" he lifted his glass "—drinking our wine, and listening to . . . Lady Alexandra's titbits of scandal from the City, and Stein's news from Alexandria . . . and Jilly would be trying to convert us all to Christianity, probably—" the glass moved from one to the other of them "—and Roche . . . now what would Captain Roche be doing here, among us fat civilians?" The lamplight caught the blood-red of the wine. "On leave from the frontier, maybe? From the heather and the bare hills where the wolves howl and the clouds play like cavalry charging? What price Britannia, Captain? Will the frontier hold next time?"

The American saved Roche with a grunt. "Huh! So where does a god-damn Yankee figure at the Court of King David?"

Jilly chuckled. "You don't, Mike—you're an anachronism."

"A who?" asked Lexy.

"A Visigoth, honey," said Bradford.

"And that's exactly right," said Audley quickly. "The hirsute Bradford doesn't fit in our Roman orgy—not sixteen hundred years ago. But if we make him a Visigoth and move on another hundred years . . . then he's here, by God!"

"The frontier didn't hold," said Jilly.

"You didn't do your goddamn job, Captain," said Bradford accusingly. "You let the Krauts in!"

He had to play—

"We didn't have enough men. It was the government's fault—" he spread

175

his hands "—you expected us to hold the line all the way from the Black Sea to the Irish Channel—"

"Excuses, excuses! You had a job to do, and you didn't do it, soldier!"

Jilly leaned forward towards Audley. "But I thought it was the Huns that were the cause of it all, not the Germans? I mean, they pushed the Germans westwards again, and the Germans were just shunted into the Roman Empire, running away from them?"

Lexy sat up. "I thought the Huns *were* the Germans?"

"Oh, for God's sake, Lexy!" Jilly turned on her irritably. "You've read the book—don't you remember? *Germans*—big and blond and hairy; *Huns*—short and dark and ugly."

"I read somewhere that if you were downwind of the Huns, you could smell them at twenty miles," said Stein. "Is that true? Or was it the Mongols?"

"Much the same article," said Audley. "But twenty-five miles, not twenty, if there were enough of them."

"Anyway, *they* forced the Germans back to the west," said Jilly firmly.

"If they smelt that bad I don't goddamn wonder," said Bradford.

"Well, the book didn't say they were different," complained Lexy. "They were just nastier, that's all."

"What book?" inquired Stein. "You haven't been actually reading a history book, have you, Alexandra?"

"*No!*" snapped Jilly irritably. "*Not* a history book—a historical *novel*, that's all."

"Well, it's like a darned history book, anyway," said Lexy. "It's got footnotes at the back, saying that it all really happened—all about this Roman princess, and how the Visigoths carried her off, after they sacked Rome, and how she had to marry the king's brother . . . At- —*At*-something—"

"Ataulf." Audley sounded surprised. "Brother of Theodoric the Great?"

"That's him—Atwulf—" Lexy plunged on breathlessly "— and because of her he decided to save the Roman Empire instead of destroying it—"

"That's a large assumption," said Audley.

"Well, *she* said so."

"She?"

"This princess—Galla Placidia, of course. And she ought to know, after having been thoroughly screwed by Atwulf and his elder brother! Only their little son died, and the Romans got her back, and she married this great general, Constantine—"

"Constantius."

"That's the one. And after he died she ruled the whole empire, with the help of her confessor, Simplicius—"

"Who?"

"Simplicius. He's the one who tells the story—who's in bed with who, and who's double-crossing who—"

"Lexy—there's no such person as Simplicius," Audley shook his head. "And Galla Placidia didn't leave any memoirs. You're talking fiction, pure and simple, nothing more."

"Huh!" grunted Bradford, from behind his bottles. "Maybe fiction, maybe not. But not pure and not simple, by God!"

"Eh?" The tone in the American's voice made Audley drop Lexy. "Not . . . ?"

"Not pure—damn right not pure, because the Hays Office threw a fit over it. And sure as hell not simple, because a million bucks isn't simple, old buddy." Bradford shook his head. "In fact, that was one dirty, crafty book, if you ask me. And written by one crafty lady, too."

"What lady? What book?" Audley looked around him.

"Hell, David—are you really telling us you haven't heard of Antonia Palfrey and *Princess in the Sunset*?"

"I don't read historical novels."

Roche was glad of the shadows which masked his reaction to this most palpable and absolute untruth, the evidence of which he had seen scattered on Audley's own driveway. In the litany of the man's defects neither Wimpy nor even Oliver St.John Latimer had included intellectual snobbery, but here it was. And yet, even allowing for the envy of a non-seller for a best-seller, it struck an oddly discordant note.

"You missed out, then," said Bradford. "Because it wasn't at all bad, minus the purple passages about Ataulf pawing Galla Placidia's heaving bosom, and Constantius putting his hand up her toga."

"Oh yes?" Audley spread a disparaging glance over Bradford and Lexy both. "As observed through the keyhole by the Right Reverend Sidonius Simplicius, presumably?"

"The *New York Times* gave it half a page, nearly," said Bradford. " 'Scholarship prostituted' was the theme."

"Scholarship?"

"Apparently." Bradford nodded. "It seems that when Miss Palfrey wasn't groping around below the belt she kept a pretty tight hold on her history . . . . You know, I'm really quite surprised you haven't read it—the *Times* man said it was a cross between *Gone With The Wind* and *I, Claudius* on one side, and *Forever Amber* and *The Decline and Fall of the Roman Empire* on the other, but I think it had Kipling undertones—not just your children's stuff, but the real McCoy short stories, like *Love-o'-Women*—"

"Good God!" exclaimed Audley.

"Oh yes—we Visigoths know our Kipling. And a lot better than most of your civilised Limeys, I'd guess. We haven't got your hang-ups about him, for a start."

"Not mine. I haven't got any hang-ups about Kipling." Audley was on the defensive, and clearly didn't like it. "But you seem to know a great deal about this—what's it called?—*Princess of the Sunset*?"

"*In*, not *of*." The American began to move the bottles again, and then thought better of it and shifted them off the table altogether. "Goddamn empties—we're running out of booze! Let's have some more bottles out of the rack, Lex . . . *In* the sunset—the sunset of the Roman Empire—you're damn right I know about it—the book anyway, if not the sunset. That's why I'm here."

"What d'you mean, Mike?" Jilly passed the corkscrew to Lexy. "I thought you were here to write?"

"Another Great American Novel," murmured Audley. "About how Patton liberated Europe in spite of Monty and me."

"Shut up, David," said Jilly. "Mike?"

"Yes . . . I'm writing—sure. But I also have this little job on the side, for a friend of mine." Bradford grinned at her. "A bit of intelligence work, actually."

Roche forced himself to watch Lexy struggle with the corkscrew.

"Intelligence work?" Stein leaned forward. "For whom?"

Lexy looked up. "Just like David, you mean?"

"Not at all like David!" said Audley.

"Not you, David—*that* David—" she nodded towards Roche, and then addressed herself to the cork again "—how the hell does this thing work?"

"Indeed?" Audley looked at Roche, whose astonishment had graduated to consternation. "Intelligence is your line, is it?"

Roche pointed at the corkscrew. "You screw it the other way, Lexy—clockwise." He shrugged at Audley, and shook his head, and hoped for the best from the shadows. "Nothing so romantic, I'm afraid. Just Signals liaison with NATO—because I speak fluent French."

"He jolly well does, too," agreed Lexy enthusiastically as the cork popped. "He had La Goutard eating out of the palm of his hand—you should have seen it!"

"Oh . . ." Audley sounded disappointed. "Jolly good . . ." He turned back towards the American. "So what's this cloak-and-dagger 'little job' then, Mike? A little something for Washington?"

The American chuckled. "Washington hell! *Hollywood*, I mean—"

"For a film?" cried Lexy. "Mike—you didn't tell us! Are you going to make a film of your book? Gosh! Let me fill your glass—then you can *discover* me. I've always wanted to be discovered—"

"Shut up, Lexy—" Jilly waved her friend down "—it isn't *his* book, it's got something to do with *Princess in the Sunset*. Right, Mike?"

"Dead right, Miss Smartpants."

"Antonia . . . what's-her-name?" Lexy refused to be waved down. "Wow! Come on—tell us, Mike—"

"He's trying to tell us, if you'd only shut up! They're going to make a film of it?"

"Yeah . . . That is, they've bought it . . . . There are these guys I know in the studio—I was over here with one of them in '44 . . . and I've done some script advising for them, and they sent me the *Princess* draft—that's how I know about it—" Bradford nodded to Audley "—there was this historical analysis from a history professor at Harvard, plus all the reviews from the papers, you see."

"A professor from Harvard? Big deal!" Audley's sniff of derision would have done credit to Jilly. "So what did he say?"

"Oh, he said the history was good. Like . . . well, it seems she really was beautiful, this Galla Placidia lady—beautiful and mean, like Scarlett O'Hara and Lucrezia Borgia rolled into one, with her pretty fingers in a lot of pies."

"Yes?" Audley prodded him.

"Well . . . it was one hell of a time, with your barbarians flooding into the West, but the Romans still in there pitching—Theodoric the Gothic king . . . and this guy Constantius, the Roman general, who forced the barbarians to settle down beside the Romans—he was big time as well. And after him there was an even bigger man, with an unpronounceable name—"

"Aëtius," murmured Audley. " 'The last of the Romans'—yes, I think you could call him 'big time', Bradford."

"Right—and all the time the Huns are knocking on the door, ready to destroy everything if the Romans didn't line up with the Goths somehow. And all the while Galla Placidia was playing both ends against the middle—I tell you, it's one hell of a time, and one hell of a story."

"I don't think she was as bad as that," said Lexy. "She had a lot to put up with—the way the Goths—the *Visigoths*—treated her, you know, Mike." She nodded wisely. "Simplicius describes it all."

Bradford laughed. "Yeah—the purple passages!"

"Who is Simplicius? I've never heard of him." Audley rotated on his stool.

"He's the one who tells the story. And 'Simplicius' is a joke-name, because he's a real crafty son-of-a-bitch—he's really the guy who pulls the strings, in fact."

"But not historical, eh?"

"Maybe not. But he comes over like a real person. For my money he's the best thing in the book. He ends up a bishop, but he's really another pagan bastard just using the Christians as his intelligence service."

Jilly held out her glass to be filled. "But . . . where do you come into all this, Mike?" She lifted the glass towards the bottle. "That's enough—I want to stay sober to hear about Mike's 'intelligence' assignment."

"Fill 'em all up, Lexy," ordered Audley. "And then open another bottle."

"Yeah . . . well, Antonia Palfrey is my assignment." Bradford paused for a moment to watch the last of the bottle's contents descend into his glass. "And Miss Antonia Palfrey's small print is my problem."

"In her book, you mean?" said Jilly.

"The purple passages, eh?" Stein chuckled wickedly. "The Hays Office doesn't mind the barbarians murdering and looting, but they're drawing the line at rape?"

"She's just a simple little old spinster lady . . ." Bradford sighed and shook his head at no one in particular.

"They're always the worst ones," said Stein mildly. "They should have known better—your Hollywood friends."

"Damn right!" Bradford looked up suddenly. "Not the book though . . . though they should have read the damn thing more carefully—they should have figured anyone who dreamed up a character like Sidonius Simplicius would be tricky . . . but no, not the book." He grimaced. "Or not really the book."

"What then?" asked Jilly.

"The contract, of course!" Stein sat back.

Bradford nodded wordlessly.

"Oh—bloody good show!" The shadows on the Israeli's face creased into a delighted grin. "The little old spinster lady took the studio lawyers for a ride—did she?"

"It isn't so goddamn funny, Davey."

"I think it's hilarious, old boy!"

"Not with two million bucks riding on it, it isn't!"

"Which *she* gets?"

"If they make the movie she does."

"And if they don't?"

"She's already got half a million."

Stein laughed. "What's she objecting to, Mike?"

The American grunted morosely. "Ostensibly . . . to some minor changes in the plot—"

"You mean, you want to change the history from the way it really happened?" Stein pointed accusingly.

"And she can do that?" Jilly looked from one to the other of them. "I didn't think Hollywood let authors call the tune like that?"

"Especially little old spinster ladies," agreed Stein mockingly. "Little old spinster ladies should know their place."

"They gave her half a million bucks, man," said Bradford.

"Of course! And who cares about the truth? So . . . they dangled another million-and-a-half in front of her, like the philanthropists they are— because they just *love* little old ladies—believing she'd take the money and cry all the way to the bank, and the hell with history and truth!" Stein's voice hardened.

Lexy looked out of the shadow at the Israeli's shoulder, to lean past him to deposit another bottle on the table.

"Oh—come on, Davey darling!" She brushed her cheek against his. "It's not Mike's fault—it's only Hollywood making a film in gorgeous technicolour. Don't take on so!"

Stein melted perceptibly, smiling up at her. "Lexy dear, I write about

180

things fifteen thousand years before Galla Placidia, and I wouldn't change a word just to please someone if I didn't think it was true." He shifted his glance to Audley. "I'm not being awkward—ask David there if you don't believe me, he's the chairman tonight . . . . What does the chair rule on truth?"

Audley looked down his Roman nose at them. "The chair rules that its glass is empty. Fill my glass, Lady Alexandra!"

Bradford raised himself up. "And I say—the truth isn't like that. It's a lot more complicated."

"So what is the truth, Mike?" asked Jilly.

Bradford turned to her. "The truth is, Jilly honey . . . first, there were two studios bidding for *Princess in the Sunset*—and little Miss Simplicitas Palfrey had a smart shyster lawyer from back East playing one off against the other, selling each of them the idea that she was a greedy old bag who'd be a pushover once the contract was signed, and screw the history."

"But she wasn't—she isn't?"

Bradford stared at her for a moment. "Yeah . . . well, maybe so . . . but my guess is she doesn't give a damn about the history, from the letters I've seen. She's just using that clause to get what she wants in another clause where she doesn't have the say-so—where they'd never have let her screw them . . . like, she's ready to have Attila the Hun in the action twenty years before he actually appeared on the scene—thirty years, more like, even—" he looked at Audley "—Attila, huh?"

Audley shrugged. "He crossed the Danube in 440—is that what you want?"

"I mean the great battle—the one that settled the fate of Europe, darn it."

Another shrug. "The Mauriac Plain? Near Troyes—451?" Audley clearly wasn't about to release much of his history just for Hollywood's benefit. "Romans and Visigoths versus Huns?" He made it sound like a rugger match.

"Yeah, that's it."

"I know all about that," said Lexy.

"Indeed?" said Audley. "Tell us?"

"It's all in the book, darling—*Princess in the Sunset*—" Lexy faltered "—remember?"

"I don't read such books—remember?" said Audley cuttingly.

Roche was simultaneously aware of why Audley had been so comprehensively disliked and that he wanted to help Lexy.

"They beat the Huns, didn't they?" He smiled encouragingly at her. "For the first time ever—they beat them?"

"On points," said Audley. "Strictly speaking, it was about 16–15 in tries and penalties, with no goals."

"But they beat them," said Roche, ignoring Audley.

"Oh yes!" Lexy's courage flamed up. "The Roman general—Thingummy-what's-his-name—"

"Aëtius," Roche plucked the name out of recent memory.

"Him, yes—*he* got the Visigoths to help him fight the Huns . . . but it was all set up by Simplicius really, so they'd all kill each other."

"It was a double-cross—or a triple-cross?" said Stein.

"It was a double-cross, that's for sure!" said Bradford. "Only it's Miss Palfrey who's doing the double-crossing. She doesn't give a damn for all this—it's the casting she's after. I think we could put George Washington into it for all she cares—just so she can say who's going to play him . . . . Those are her terms, and she's driving the studio nuts with people they've never heard of!"

"Who's going to play Galla Placidia?" asked Lexy eagerly.

"Huh! You may well ask! At the rate the negotiations are going probably no one."

"Let me guess!" Lexy plumped herself down alongside Roche, smiling up at him happily. "You know, I never expected the Dark Ages to be so interesting! But let's see now . . . Joan Fontaine—no . . . Janet Leigh—no . . . Jean Simmons—maybe . . . Elizabeth Taylor—how about her?"

Audley growled something unintelligible.

"Not for the daughter of Theodosius the Great, Alexandra dear," said Stein quickly, with a seriousness which Roche was now able to identify as purely mischievous, aimed equally at Audley and Bradford. "You need someone more aristocratic—say Deborah Kerr?"

Bradford opened his mouth, but Lexy was too quick for him. "Not sexy enough, darling. You should read the book—Galla Placidia's hot stuff, I tell you! The way she fixes poor old Atwulf—"

"*Ataulf.*" Audley pronounced the name through gritted teeth. "This is monstrous!"

"You're damn right it's monstrous," agreed Bradford bitterly. "Because Lexy's got it plum on target—the studio was trying to line up Liz Taylor, after they'd finished shooting *Raintree County*—"

"Super!" exclaimed Lexy.

"Super hell! Miss Palfrey won't have her at any price. She wants Barbara Jefford, Lex honey."

"Barbara—?" Lexy sat up straight. "Barbara Jefford?"

"Barbara Jefford!" Astonishment replaced mischief in Stein's voice as he too sat up. Then he swung towards Lexy. "Now don't you dare say you haven't heard of her, young Alexandra!"

"Of course I've heard of her. But . . . she's an *actress*—"

"God save us!" Stein raised his hands. " 'She's an actress'!"

"I mean a stage actress—Stratford and the Old Vic, and all that, Davey—"

"And so do I. She's a splendid actress—" Stein switched to Audley

"—you remember her from Stratford, David? Hotspur's Kate? Marvellous!"

"Sure she is—marvellous," Bradford intervened. "I'm not arguing she isn't a great actress—they're all terrific—they're all great . . . but who ever heard of them in Denver or St. Louis, for Christ's sake?"

"Heard of who?"

"Hell, man—Quayle and Badel . . . and Griffiths—"

"*Hugh* Griffiths?" Stein beamed. "But this is gorgeous, my dear fellow— Anthony Quayle and Alan Badel *and* Hugh Griffiths—she wants them in the film of her book, Antonia Palfrey does?" He paused for half a second. "And—don't tell me—Michael Redgrave?"

Bradford's mouth opened. "Who told you that?"

"Ah-hah! All is known to Stein . . ." The Israeli wagged his head at the American, and then stopped suddenly as though an afterthought had struck him. "But what about young Burton? If she's got all the others she has to have him—" the afterthought was transferred to Audley "—Burton above all—right, David?"

Audley frowned. "Burton who?"

"But you *must* remember! He was the fellow you liked so much once you found out he was a rugger-player. Didn't he have a trial for Wales, or something? And you said he'd come down in the world, to play the lead at Stratford?"

"Eh?"

"I don't know what you're talking about either," snapped Bradford. "But you're right about Richard Burton—in fact he's the only one they agree on, Palfrey and the studio. But who told you about *him*—the Palfrey cast list is supposed to be ultra secret—who told you?"

"No one told me." Stein continued to look at Audley. "But David there knows. He's just playing dumb, that's all."

Audley drew himself up stiffly. "I am not playing dumb, damn it! Burton . . . yes, he was an actor from somewhere—but I can't be expected to remember actors' names. I don't go to the theatre."

"You did once. In fact, you did several times—with me—to Stratford . . . in fact . . . *in fact*, I taught you to drive that summer, in that terrible old car of yours—'50, or '51—and we were staying with those girls in that cottage near Banbury . . . and you drove home every night drunk as a lord—damn it, David . . . the Stratford season we went to—" Stein spread his hands and looked around for support "—he had these tickets for the Stratford Shakespeare season, and there were these two girls—and he had this car he couldn't drive, and I was teaching him . . . and we saw the whole season— *Richard II*, with Redgrave as Richard, and both parts of *Henry IV* and *Henry V*, with Burton as Prince Hal—and *The Tempest* with Redgrave as Prospero—and he was also a cracking good Hotspur in *Henry IV*—" he rounded on Audley "—damn it, David . . . you had these matinee tickets, and we were stuck in the middle of this schoolgirl outing, from Benenden or some such place—and Redgrave was massaging his wife's right buttock and left breast like mad on stage, and these little schoolgirls were *ooh*-ing and *aah*-ing at every squeeze in the audience alongside of us—you have to remember that!"

Roche covertly observed the lamplight shadows twitch on Audley's face as the circumstantial tale unfolded around him, and found himself questioning why the big man continued to resist it.

"Yes . . . well—" Audley rocked on his stool as though embarrassed by the return of the memory "—we did see the *Histories* season at Stratford, I grant you. But I don't remember any schoolgirls wetting their pants next to me . . . and I certainly don't see what that's got to do with Bradford's curious obsessions now, either."

"Nor do I," said Bradford.

"But I do." Jilly ignored him. "They were all in the Stratford season—you're right, Davey. I only saw *Richard II* and *The Tempest* . . . but they were all in it—"

"Richard Burton's *yummy*," said Lexy. "I've seen him in something in the West End—and in a film. He'd be scrumptious with Elizabeth Taylor, I should think. And I wouldn't mind him tackling me in a loose scrum!"

"Shut up, Lexy!" admonished Jilly. "Davey—she's cast the film from the Stratford season, is what you're saying—is that it?"

Stein nodded. "That's exactly it. Quayle played Falstaff, and Badel was Pistol . . . Griffiths was Glendower . . . plus Redgrave and Burton and Jefford—coincidence just doesn't stretch so far, it has to be intention."

"She saw the plays, of course," said Jilly. "And she liked what she saw."

"Which is not to be wondered at—it was pure magic, that season," said Stein. "Quite unforgettable!"

"Well—so what's all the fuss about?" Lexy looked around. "I mean, if they're all so marvellous and magic and unforgettable—?" She zeroed in on the American. "Mike?"

Bradford sighed. "Maybe . . . But it doesn't work like that."

"You mean Hollywood doesn't work like that," said Jilly.

"I mean you can't pick names out of a hat," said Bradford heavily. "It's who's available, and who's under contract, and who's box office—and you can't just cast a Hollywood movie straight out of Shakespeare hits from Stratford-upon-Avon, England, no matter how good the cast was—or how wet the schoolgirls' pants were. It's a crazy idea."

"Olivier did it with *Henry V* and *Hamlet*," countered Jilly.

"But they were Shakespeare plays—this is a goddamn epic."

"So why not make it in England?"

"Like *Caesar and Cleopatra*? Honey, you must be joking!" Bradford reached for a bottle.

Stein leaned forward. "But Miss Palfrey isn't joking."

"The hell she isn't!" Bradford refilled his glass. "Just a simple little old spinster lady living in seclusion with the blinds drawn to keep out the sunlight . . ." he drank deeply.

"What's she really like?" asked Jilly.

"Huh! That would be telling!"

"Tell us, Mike," asked Lexy.

"Sure. For five thousand bucks on account, and twenty thousand to come . . . she's a two-timing, double-crossing, obstinate, secretive, avaricious, scheming old hag, who'd make your Madame Peyrony look like Florence Nightingale, Lex honey." Bradford drained his glass. "Or . . . to put it another way . . . I haven't the faintest idea. Okay?"

"What d'you mean—you haven't the faintest idea?"

"And where does five thousand dollars—or twenty thousand—come in?" asked Stein. "It's what they're paying you? For what?"

"Twenty thousand doesn't come in, the way it's looking—" Bradford nodded at Audley "—unless David there can pull the rabbit out of the hat." The nod was converted into a slow shake of the head. "Because you're my last hope, old buddy."

"Then you've got no hope, *old buddy*." Audley looked down his nose at his friend. "It's not my field, the so-called 'historical' novel."

"Archie Forbes said you could."

"Archie Forbes at Cambridge?" said Jilly suddenly. "*That* Archie Forbes, d'you mean?"

"Yeah—*that* Archie Forbes—Dr Archibald Forbes of Rylands College—" Bradford gave Audley another nod "—*his* old tutor and drinking buddy."

"My old brigadier and *eminence grise*," said Audley. "Why don't you split your bounty-money with him, for God's sake—and leave me alone!"

"Because he doesn't know—that's why. And you do."

"Know what?" asked Jilly.

"Crap!" exclaimed Bradford. "All you have to do is *think*—"

Roche stirred himself. "Think what? Know what?"

Bradford turned towards him, screwing up his eyes in the darkness. "I took the goddamn book to Forbes at Cambridge—"

"But why?" asked Jilly.

"Because he's an expert on medieval history, honey. They gave me his name in UCLA—they said whoever wrote it is a historian."

"But Antonia Palfrey wrote it, Mike."

Bradford spread his hands. "And who the hell's Antonia Palfrey? It's just a name on a book jacket—a nom-de-plume name, not a real one."

"But there's her picture—"

"Sure. But with no address. And she just turns up at intervals, out of the blue . . . sometimes in London, but mostly in New York . . . and then disappears again before the press can catch her. Or anyone else."

"But her publishers must know where she lives, Mike."

"And her lawyers," said Stein.

185

"Huh! Well . . . if they know, they're not telling me!"

"There are ways of finding out," said Stein.

"Sure there are ways." Bradford pointed at Audley. "He's one way—"

"But why David?" Jilly looked from one to the other.

"Why indeed!" murmured Audley. "Because that vindictive old swine Forbes set him on to me, of course! He hates my guts."

"But you were his favourite pupil, David," said Stein.

"Favourite? That's rich!" Audley rocked on his stool.

"But you were, old boy," said Stein. "When you won the Hebden he even gave a party for you. I was there."

"So you were. And so I *was* . . . so long as I danced to his tune." He nodded at Stein. "I took the Hebden Prize from a chap at King's—Bodger, or Badger, or some such unlikely name—who was the pet student of old Professor Hedley, whom Forbes cordially detested . . . After which I had great plans for myself. And so did Forbes." He rocked again. "Unfortunately . . . unfortunately for *me*, that is . . . the plans did not coincide."

"What plans?"

"Oh—the usual sort of thing," said Audley airily. "After my doctorate, a fellowship. There was one timed just right for me at Rylands, in medieval history. Number Two to Forbes, in fact."

Jilly cocked her head. "But David, if that was Professor Forbes's plan, why didn't you—"

"My dear Jilly, that wasn't *Forbes's* plan—that was *mine*." The lamplight caught Audley's teeth again as he smiled, but for once the shadows seemed to Roche to betray his true expression in a mask of pain. "Bodger—Dr Bodger—got the fellowship."

For a moment no one spoke, then Stein emitted a sympathetic grunt. "And what was Forbes's plan?"

"Oh . . . that was . . . rather different."

"What was it?" Stein persisted. "More wine, Alexandra!"

"An excellent idea!" said Audley heartily. "And then we shall toast all the Forbeses and Bodgers of this world, that they may receive their just reward." He held out his glass to Lexy. "Fill it up, m'lady."

"Not until you've told us Forbes's plan," said Lexy. "You can't leave us with only half a story."

Audley waved his glass. "I only tell that half when I'm drunk, Alexandra Champeney-Perowne."

"But you *are* drunk, David."

"Am I?" Audley looked around for confirmation.

"Sufficiently," said Stein.

Audley shrugged. "Well . . . I suppose it's no great secret."

"What is?"

"I did a few months in Intelligence at the end of the war. Nasty, dirty, unchivalrous work." He nodded. "Absolutely fascinating too."

"Yes?"

186

Another shrug. "Forbes wanted me to go back to it, that's all. He said it was my patriotic duty—he said 'Of those to whom much is given, much is required'. And 'One must always risk one's life, or one's soul, or one's peace—or some little thing'. And, finally, 'Go where glory waits, Audley my boy'. The old, old story, in fact."

"Yes?" Stein's voice had lowered to a whisper.

Another shrug. "I was young. And I was in love with Cambridge—and history . . . And I was also stupid—I thought he was *asking* me, not *ordering* me . . ." Audley shook his head. "And the pay was rotten—and I needed money at the time rather badly, as it happened."

Roche thought of The Old House.

"I reckoned I could do better for myself by following my own plans. So I told him to stuff his patriotism and his secret service where the monkey put the nuts— and I said the same, only more so, to the perfectly ghastly individual they sent to recruit me . . . Which, dear friends, was a mistake—not showing myself a pure-souled, high-minded youth—a fatal error."

"He blocked your fellowship?" said Stein.

"Oh—he did more than that, the lusty old blackbird. He fixed me good and proper—and *permanently*, what's more. And not a stain on his character, either."

"How?"

"How?" The agonised smile came back. "There was this girl turned up—while I was putting the finishing touches to my doctoral thesis . . . absolutely gorgeous—the girl, I mean—the thesis was gorgeous too, even *he* couldn't do anything about that . . . but *she* was nonpareil in beauty and wit—all that a young idiot could desire—Cordelia-Viola-Miranda-Juliet-Portia . . . Or, as she turned out, Goneril-Regan-Lady Macbeth-Mata Hari."

"She was one of his, you mean?" said Stein.

"*No*, I do not *mean*—you underrate the man! Just the opposite, was what my Juliet was!"

"What d'you mean—the opposite?" said Jilly.

"Exactly that, Jilly dear. He'd put the word out—and the KGB picked it up." Audley laughed. "I was just about to propose to her—we were punting on the Backs, all white flannel and silk—only she popped *her* question first." Audley spread his hands. "And we had a row. And she fell into the river—"

"*She* proposed to *you*—?" Lexy sounded thunderstruck.

"She certainly did! She proposed that, since I didn't want to serve the filthy, capitalist, war-mongering fascist beasts, then how about the other side? And, I tell you, Lexy love, the pay's better—a lot better, so it seems. A man could employ a lot of builders and carpenters and plumbers and tilers just for the downpayment."

"Good God!" exclaimed Stein.

"Not so good," said Audley. "Because then he put out the word a second time. Only it was a different word, because my ex-Juliet was a known agent, who took the next plane back to Moscow after her swim in the Cam." He surveyed his audience. "It's what's called 'Guilt by association', you see. It put my name on the red side of the ledger—*Not to be employed in a position of trust* . . . quite unofficially, of course. But with the Cold War hotting up 'quite unofficially' was quite good enough to scupper me."

"But that's awful, David!" said Lexy. "If I tell Daddy about that he'll talk to them for you—he'll sort them out—"

"Don't bother, Lexy love," Audley shook his head.

"But—you could try Oxford, David. Daddy's a fellow of All Souls—sort of honorary, or something—and he meets the Prime Minister there—*he* could get you a fellowship."

"I said *don't bother*," Audley's voice sharpened. "I don't want a bloody fellowship now—at Oxford, or Cambridge, or anywhere else. They can stuff their fellowships."

"But—"

"What I want, Lexy love, is the one thing your daddy can't give me. And not even Macmillan can give me either, if he's doing his job right—that's the whole delicious irony of the thing, really."

"What is?" said Stein.

"Irony?" echoed Jilly.

Audley's eyes travelled across them, settling finally on Roche. "You wouldn't understand—*he* might, but you wouldn't—if what you say about him is right."

"Me?" squeaked Roche, caught unawares.

"It probably isn't right, my dear chap. But if you've got anything to do with intelligence work . . . would you employ me?"

Roche swallowed. "I beg your pardon?"

Audley shook his head. "I beg yours, Captain. I shouldn't have asked the question . . . but if you were—which I'm sure you're not—and you wouldn't admit it if you were, anyway—but if you *were*, you *wouldn't*. That's all." He rocked on the stool. "But don't bother to answer, Captain—it was just a hypothetical statement."

"I don't understand a word you're saying," said Lexy. She looked at Roche. "What's he saying, David?"

Roche understood exactly what Audley was saying, but still couldn't believe what he had heard, because luck didn't come to anyone packaged so neatly, not in a million years.

"David—" began Jilly.

"Don't worry, Captain," said Audley. "Have another drink and forget everything I said."

"No!" snapped Jilly. "David—are you saying that you'd like to go back to intelligence work?"

"That's exactly what he's saying," said Stein. "But *why*, David, for God's

188

sake? The sewage doesn't smell any sweeter these days—if anything it's dirtier, I should think."

"Dirtier for sure, old boy," agreed Audley. "Everything gets grubbier with time, it's a natural process. No more worlds fit for heroes, no more capitalist heavens or socialist utopias."

"And no more British Empire," said Stein. "You wouldn't be playing Kipling's 'Great Game' in the high passes any more—no more Bengal Lancers, old boy. No more glamour."

"There never was any glamour."

"No money either. You said they were stingy before—they'll be even stingier now. You'll spend half your time trying to cook your expenses." Stein shook his head sadly.

"Oh . . . that wouldn't worry him, darling." Lexy surfaced again. "He's positively rolling in the stuff, you know that!"

"Maybe he doesn't like being on the losing side," said Bradford. "Losing isn't his style."

Roche knew he couldn't let that pass—not with what he still had to do. "We're not damn well losing."

Audley shook his head. "Oh—but we are, my dear chap. We're losing very thoroughly and comprehensively—Mike's right." He nodded at the American. "Ever since we won we've been losing. Suez merely broadcast the message: no more 'Rule Britannia', no more Thin Red Line, no more *Civis Britannicus Sum*. The gateway in the wall has been bricked up, and John Foster Dulles has scratched 'Finish' on the plaster. You're just commanding the rearguard, Roche."

Roche scoured his wits for a reply. The trouble was that it was all true, and he was living proof of it, and all he wanted was to be on neither of these two sides, losing or winning—a plague on them both. And a plague on rearguards too, for that matter!

"The rearguard usually gets cut to pieces," said Stein, smiling at him across the table. "It's the place of honour, but the honour's not quite your style either—now, is it?"

"Wrong again!" Audley revolved on his stool. "I told you—if Roche was recruiting, I'd be his man. Like that fellow Burton said—*if it be a sin to covet honour I am the most offending soul alive.*"

"Hogwash!" said Bradford, the embers of his recent anger glowing through the word. "Not you, David. Mischief—maybe. But not honour."

Stein chuckled. "I wouldn't put it as strong as that, Mike. But . . . not honour, I agree."

Audley continued to revolve from side to side, as though he preferred to present a moving target. Yet he didn't seem to be offended by the insults. "Well, maybe I was joking. But it's all academic anyway—thanks to dear Archie . . . So let's get back to my barbarians. I particularly want to tell you about the Vandals, a people for whom I have great sympathy—a people much misunderstood, like myself . . . In fact, when Izzy Collins and I started our rugger club, I wanted to call us the Vandals. But Izzy wouldn't have it—he said we might as well call ourselves the Hooligans, and have done with it. So we settled for the Visigoths in the end, and—"

"No, David!" said Jilly. "We haven't finished with you yet."

Good girl, thought Roche gratefully.

"With me, Jilly love?" Audley stopped rotating.

"That's right," said Lexy. "You still haven't told us why you want to serve Her Majesty again, darling."

"Won't 'Honour' do?" Audley cocked his head at her.

"No," said Stein.

"The Vandals are much more interesting. King Gaiseric is right up your street, Stein—"

"And it isn't the money," said Lexy. "We've established that—it's poor old Mike there who needs the cash, not David—"

"Gaiseric," said Audley. "King of the Vandals—"

"Oh, do shut up, David!" said Lexy. "We're on to something interesting now—really interesting. I've always wanted to know what makes you tick." She rested her elbow on the table, and then her chin on her fist, and gazed at Audley fixedly. "*Not* honour . . . and *not* money . . . and it isn't as if he'd get a pretty uniform to wear, like he used to in Daddy's old regiment . . . so why this sudden rush of patriotism to the head, then? That's what we have to find out."

"Not the power and the glory," said Stein drily.

"No?" Lexy swivelled her chin on her fist. "Why not, Davey?"

"Precious little power. The Russians and the Yanks have all of that between them. The British *are* losers now—he said so himself." Stein folded his arms. "And no glory, because it isn't that sort of game. Not like rugger."

"Not like rugger?"

Stein nodded. "You win in private, but you lose in public when things go wrong. And he doesn't like losing." He grinned wickedly at Audley. "Of course, you could try the KGB again, David. At least you'd have a better chance of winning with them."

"Gosh, no, Davey darling!" exclaimed Lexy. "He wouldn't like them—they wear frightful blue suits, all shapeless and bulgy, with brown shoes. Daddy pointed out two of them to me at a reception we were at. They were awful!"

"Okay . . ." The Israeli shrugged. "Maybe Mike can fix up an introduction to the CIA. They wear better suits . . . Mike?"

Bradford stirred uneasily.

"I knew a lovely boy in the CIA," said Lexy. "At least, I think he was in the CIA."

"I'm told they're always looking for volunteers in England," said Stein. "It's part of the 'special relationship', I suppose."

"He was in something incredibly secret, anyway," said Lexy dreamily. Then she sighed. "But Daddy didn't like him."

"Daddy didn't like his particular idea of the special relationship, you mean," murmured Stein. "Well, Mike?"

"Yeah." Bradford cleared his throat. "I know a couple of guys . . ." He eyed Audley for a moment. "I could give you names and addresses. You just give me Antonia Palfrey's name—real name—in return. And her address, huh?"

"Oh, Mike!" Lexy rounded on the American. "Why must you keep harping on Antonia Palfrey? He's told you he doesn't know her."

"And I've told him I don't believe him."

"But *why*? Not just because of what . . . of what Professor Archie Whatnot says, Mike?"

Bradford shook his head. "Forbes just pointed me at the facts."

"What facts?"

"Honey . . ." Bradford continued to stare at Audley ". . . that goddamn woman is an expert in a very small field. UCLA says so, and Forbes says so, and I *know* so—because I've checked the field out. And there's no one fills the bill, just no one."

"So what?"

"So . . . so maybe she isn't an expert. Maybe she's gotten herself a tame expert—someone who knows the difference between an Ostrogoth and a Visigoth and a Vandal, all about 5th century Christians and heretics and pagans. And also someone who knows about fighting, the way Miss Antonia Palfrey seems to know about it—"

"That doesn't follow, Mike," said Jilly quickly. "Stephen Crane in *The Red Badge of Courage*—"

"*Crap*! She's picked somebody's brains, honey. Somebody who knows about being scared and about . . . *barbarians*." Bradford paused. "You know anyone here fills that bill, huh?"

Roche watched Audley, aware that everyone was doing the same.

"Fills the bill?" Audley sighted the American down his nose. "Dr Bodger, of Rylands College, Cambridge, fills the bill, for a start, old boy."

"More crap. Bodger never fired a shot in his life, old buddy. He worked for the Ministry of Information. He had rheumatic fever when he was a kid. I told you—I've checked out the field. He was never even called up for military service." Bradford shook his head again. "Also, he doesn't commute to Zurich regularly."

"Zurich?" Lexy looked from Audley to Bradford.

"*He* does. And that's where the elusive Miss Palfrey lives." Bradford pointed at Audley.

Audley tossed his head. "This is ridiculous. I've been to Zurich once or twice in the last three months, I have an account there. It isn't a crime yet, for God's sake!"

Stein chuckled. "No flies on our David!"

"*Flies* is right—" Bradford sat up "—flies is *exactly* right. Eh, David?"

Audley grimaced at him. "What d'you mean? F-f-flies?"

"That's what I mean: 'f-f-flies'." Bradford pounced on him. " 'F-f-flies'. Big ones, little ones—fat ones, black ones, green shiny ones—squashy ones—*flies*, David—"

"Don't be disgusting, Bradford!" Audley hunched his shoulders.

Lexy tossed the hair from her face. "Now you're being beastly, Mike—"

"Not at all, honey—"

"You are so! We all know David hates flies, he's told us so. But so do I and so do you—" she gave Audley a quick, sympathetic glance, and then carried on to the Israeli "—and when we talked about them . . . Davey there said there were more flies in that desert of his—"

"Sinai." Stein nodded. "Sinai is the fly capital of the world."

"For Christ's sake!" said Audley.

Bradford nodded at Roche. "There you are, Captain. We don't like 'f-f-flies'—but *he's* obsessive about them!"

Roche observed Audley's face contort, though whether with disgust or anger the shadows didn't tell.

"So . . . just get the book, and I'll prove my point," went on Bradford. "Lexy—?"

"What point?" asked Jilly.

"What book?" Lexy blinked. "Book—?"

Bradford gestured dismissively. "It doesn't matter—you can take my word for it, I can give you chapter and page—*chapters* and *pages*, rather—it's all there to be seen . . . *and* heard—they buzz around from battlefield to battlefield to annoy Simplicius, and from corpse to corpse on the battlefield. On one page she has a whole paragraph about the Devil being 'lord of the flies', and how each fly is a black soul from Hell sent to plague the faithful—"

"Flies!" Lexy buried a hand into her tangled hair. "Of course—yes, you're absolutely right, Mike—and the flies in the food at the wedding banquet, when she's forced to marry Atwulf—Galla Placidia—"

"Ataulf—" Audley corrected her automatically.

"So you *have* read the book, David!"

"I have *not* read the book." Audley closed his eyes. "I do not *want* to read the book—I *will not* read the book. I know perfectly well what happened during the period without having to read any semi-pornographic historical novel."

"I'll bet you do," said Bradford. "Flies included."

Audley opened his eyes. "I . . . happen to have particularly unpleasant memories about . . . flies." He pronounced the word carefully. "Wartime memories, not historical ones. I'd prefer not to remember them, if it's all the same to you, Bradford."

"You remembered them for Antonia Palfrey."

"Shut up, Mike," said Jilly.

"The hell I will!" Bradford's voice was obstinate. "If you think I—"

"*However . . .*" Audley's own voice was obstinate too, and louder ". . . however . . . I will tell you one thing you want to know, if it'll make you feel better."

"Oh, goody-goody!" exclaimed Lexy. "He's going to tell us something that'll make us feel better!"

Audley's mouth twisted. "It won't make *you* feel better. It's all about barbarians—"

"Oh—*merde!*" Lexy's shoulders slumped.

"But it does answer your question, nevertheless—"

"What question?" Lexy cocked her head. "How—"

"Sssh, dear!" Jilly hushed her. "He's about to tell us how he ticks. Go on, David."

"Barbarians make him tick?" Lexy blundered on. "Oh—come on, David—"

"*Lexy*—" Jilly's tone became dangerous.

"Okay! Okay!" Lexy raised her hands. "Barbarians make you tick, David—anything you say!"

Audley stared at her. "They did—yes. After the war . . . during the war for that matter . . . they say war's a great leveller, and so it is. It levelled Aachen—Charlemagne's Aix-la-Chapelle . . . and Cologne . . . *Colonia Agrippina* . . . all in a good cause, of course—I levelled one little Norman church myself, with a few well-placed shots at a discreet distance—there was this brave bugger with a *panzerfaust* in it, who'd just incinerated a friend of mine in the tank ahead of me . . . good causes don't come any better than that."

"David—" began Lexy.

He was drunk, thought Roche. But not totally drunk, because there still wasn't a word out of place, and not stupid drunk either. He simply hadn't liked the drift of Bradford's interrogation—the piling up of circumstantial evidence against him, piece by piece—and was seeking instead to divert it with the one thing he had to give them which might intrigue them more.

"Go on, David," said Jilly.

"Where was I?" Audley blinked owlishly.

"You were demolishing Germany," said Stein.

"In a good cause," said Lexy. "And it had something to do with barbarians."

"Ah . . . of course, *they* crossed the Rhine from East to West—the Franks, and then the Vandals and all the rest . . . but *we* crossed it from West to East, as the Romans did, complete with hostile Germans on the other side." Audley nodded at Stein. "And I remember thinking . . . 'This time we'll get it right, the conquest of Germany—we won't fluff it, like the Romans did'. But, of course, it didn't work out like that, with the Russians—I was escorting one of the 'T' Force groups ferreting out German

193

technological secrets, and we ran into them doing the same thing straight off, and I knew then what sort of brave new world we were heading for." He paused. "Nine months of fighting Nazis . . . and others . . . and eighteen months of fighting Russians . . . and others—that was my war. Uncomfortable, but highly educational, you might say." Another pause. "Then I went up to Cambridge, into the tender care of Professor Archibald Forbes—" he raised his glass, only to find that it was empty; and then that the bottles on the table, tested one after another, were also empty, and focussed finally upon Lexy "—another bottle, pot-girl!"

"Don't you think you've had enough, David?" said Jilly.

"Huh!" Audley grunted derisively. "My dear Gillian, I haven't started to drink yet—not by rugger club standards, anyway."

Lexy drew another bottle from the rack.

"Make it two—or three, seeing as how the night is yet young . . . Stein—Bradford—Captain Roche . . . fill your glasses! Let us drink to our dead youth—you remember your Kipling, Roche? Parnesius and Pertinax on the Great Wall, with the barbarians on the warpath?"

Roche held out his glass obediently.

Audley grinned back at him. "A libation is what we should make—" he looked around, his glance finally settling on the potted plant at his elbow "—just a drop for my lost opportunities, then—" he inclined his glass carefully "—but not too much! Roche?"

Roche leaned forward to bury his own glass among the leaves. "And for mine too!" He tipped as much of his wine as he dared into the heart of the plant.

"Good man!" Audley beamed at him. "Stein—Bradford?"

"I don't sacrifice," said Stein.

"And I don't waste good wine," said Bradford.

Audley shrugged. "Well . . . that's your funeral. I mocked the gods once, and I was punished for my *hubris*—appropriately punished, too."

"What *hubris*, David?" asked Jilly.

"I thought I knew better," said Audley. "I turned Forbes down when he offered me the real world, and chose the other Dark Ages instead. I thought I was uniquely well-placed to interpret them—I thought I had an insight denied to lesser mortals after my wartime education."

"Why the Dark Ages?" asked Jilly.

"Because that was the other time when the world changed, love—the other barbarian age—from the fall of the Roman Empire to when the Arabs were three days' march from Paris, or thereabouts. After which nothing was ever the same again—I found it fascinating." Audley shook his head. "What a time to live in—*fascinating*—"

"Ugh!" Lexy shivered. "Sidonius Simplicius didn't think it was fascinating—he thought it was dreadful! Like the beginning of the end of the world, he said."

"So it was—of *his* world." Audley grinned at her. "But, don't you see, that's what makes it so interesting—the world turned upside down and history speeded up. What an age to live in!"

"You're just like Sidonius Simplicius," said Lexy. "He decided in the end that it was interesting, once he'd worked out how to play both ends against the middle. Then he said it was all the will of God, anyway. But he hadn't been raped in the process, of course."

"Indeed?" Audley half shrugged. "But . . . well, that's what I thought, at all events, *mes amis*: I really believed that I could lose myself in the past, in the old dark ages, using my understanding of the uncomfortable present as the key to it all . . ." his expression twisted ". . . from the comfort of a senior common room at Cambridge, naturally—that goes without saying."

The man's bitterness went without saying also, thought Roche. He was eaten up with it, beneath his self-mockery.

"But you didn't get a fellowship," said Bradford brutally.

Audley bowed to him over his glass, which was empty again. "Hubris, my dear fellow. And it was a rather juvenile theory, anyway."

"Oh, come on, David! You haven't done too badly," Lexy's natural instinct, once she had realised the concealed wound, was to apply soothing ointment to it.

"Yes," Stein nodded. "And, come to that, you could probably get a fellowship somewhere now, if you wanted to. That book of yours was well reviewed in the *TLS*—the Byzantine one . . . Maybe not Oxbridge, but one of the newer places. Or the States—"

Audley winced. "I don't want a bloody fellowship in one of the newer places—or the States . . . *or* Oxbridge, damn it."

"Yeah—of course! You told us. You want your old job back." Bradford twisted the blade. "Maybe you should go crawling back to Forbes, and ask for forgiveness."

"Mike!" admonished Jilly. "Lay off!"

The American shrugged unrepentantly. "Tit for tat, honey. Just being helpful."

"Helpful!" Jilly gestured impatiently. "But why, David? You still haven't explained *why*."

"Haven't I?" Audley blinked at her. "I thought I had."

"You haven't, darling," said Lexy. "Not a word. But—"

"Sssh!" Jilly waved her down too. "Go on, David."

Audley shifted on his stool uneasily, as though unwilling to strip his seventh veil at the last.

Stein chuckled darkly behind his glass. "The great David doesn't want to admit the truth."

"What truth?"

"He's bored, Jilly dear—plain, old-fashioned bored . . . Bored and lonely—lonely and bored!" The Israeli nodded to himself, and then to Audley. "And it's a dangerous combination, that—in a man like you, my friend. It makes you ripe for any mischief, any wickedness in this wicked

195

world." He looked around at the rest of them. "Such men are dangerous, believe me. We would do well to leave him alone—to leave now, before it is too late . . . or he will drag us down with him into some fatal adventure of his."

"Bored?" Lexy echoed the word incredulously. "But he can't be bored—with all he's got . . . And he can't be lonely—he's got us, Davey."

"My dear—we're merely the ingredients of his boredom. Boredom isn't just not having anything to do. It's not being able to do what you *want* to do. If you can't do that, then everything else is weary, stale, flat and unprofitable—believe me, I know."

"How do you know, Davey?" asked Jilly.

"Because it's an infection, Jilly dear—a parasite in the blood that never leaves you once it's there. It can lie dormant for a few years, but it's there waiting for you to weaken. I know because I've got it too, you see—maybe not David's particular bug, but my own special bug."

"What bug, Davey?" asked Lexy.

"None of your business, Lady Alexandra," said Stein.

"He likes to fly planes," said Bradford. "A common bug."

"If you say so," Stein shrugged. "But I'm not complaining."

Audley laughed. "You've got nothing to complain about. You get your jollies from the poor damned Egyptians at regular intervals. All I get to do is write books. And they're no substitute for the real thing, I've discovered."

Lexy sat up once more, this time almost as though pricked. "Simplicius!" she exclaimed.

"I beg your pardon, Lexy love?"

"You're Simplicius—you really are! Sidonius Simplicius to the life, darling—sort of in reverse."

"Lexy love—"

"No, you *are*—it's quite weird, darling!" Lexy turned to Jilly "You've read the book, Jilly—you tell him, he'll believe you!"

"Tell him what?"

"You remember! How he's always on about wanting to write a book about that boring old saint who was martyred by some emperor or other—Saint Somebody-or-other of Somewhere—"

"Saint Vinicius of Capua? The one Diocletian parboiled?"

"That's him! And he's always saying—Simplicius is always saying—that Vinicius lived in much more interesting times . . ." Lexy spread her gaze round them ". . . but of course he never does write the book, because he's far too busy running the whole show from behind Galla Placidia's skirts, which is much more interesting."

Jilly nodded. "You're quite right. That's the whole point of the book—'What the Lord God, our Emperor, and Jesus Christ, his Caesar, purpose for Their servants'—that's right."

"Huh! Audley grunted derisively. "This fellow Simplicius sounds . . . doctrinally unsound!"

196

"I don't know about that, darling—all your heresies and things are beyond me. But what he's saying is that taking part in the real world *now* is the only proper job for a real man. Right, Jilly?" Lexy turned from Jilly to Bradford. "You've read the book, Mike—isn't that so?"

"Yeah. He sure as hell didn't regard life as a spectator sport. He wanted to run with the ball."

"That's exactly what I mean." Lexy turned back to Audley. "And you want to run with the ball too, David—and get your head down in the scrum, and do all those other beastly things you get so worked up about. So you're Simplicius, don't you see, darling?"

Roche saw.

And, suddenly, in seeing, saw more than that.

Saw Lexy, enchanting Lexy, half embarrassed at the sound of her own voice, the lamplight catching the slight sheen of perspiration on her face—

Saw Jilly . . . and on Jilly's plain little features it was the sheen of intelligence which animated that face into something close to beauty—

Saw the handsome blond Israeli, the compulsive pilot; and the dark angry American . . . both his adversaries—

But saw Audley most of all, and at last.

"Here's Steffy!" Lexy held up her hand, listening. "I can hear her on the steps outside."

"And about time too!" said Audley irritably. "I just wish she'd regulate her love life more thoughtfully—" he cut off suddenly, frowning at the scrape of hobnails on stone, which was followed by a thunderous knocking. "But that's not our Steffy, by God!"

Jilly peered at her wrist-watch. "It's past midnight, David."

"So what? We argued until three last time over Stein's esoteric prehistoric gobbledegook, and Madame didn't turn a hair."

"She thinks there's safety in numbers," said Lexy, smiling up at Roche. "She believes we wouldn't call it 'an orgy' if it really was one."

The knock was repeated, even more heavily, and they looked at each other like guilty children, each waiting for the others to move.

"Well, someone bloody answer it," snapped Audley. "I'm too far away."

"Yeah. Well, someone's got to," said Bradford. "Otherwise she'll think we really are screwing around."

The knock was repeated a third time.

"All right, then," Stein stood up. "Muggins does it."

Roche craned his neck round Lexy to get a better view, but the angle was awkward and the light confusing.

"Gaston?" Stein injected a masterly mixture of ninety per cent innocent inquiry and ten per cent surprise, as any man with two girls but a clear conscience might employ after midnight. "It's old Gaston," he called unnecessarily over his shoulder.

"Old Gaston?" Audley's equally unnecessary repetition substituted a rather forced heartiness for Stein's tenth of surprise. "Well—don't stand there, man! Ask him in! Get another glass, Lady Alexandra."

But Old Gaston did not seem disposed to be drawn into the Tower. Rather, he drew the Israeli out into the darkness beyond with an urgent, indecipherable mutter of words.

"What's he want, for God's sake?" Audley called through the doorway, at Stein's back. "Stein?"

Mutter-mutter-mutter. Stein took no notice of the question.

"Gaston's Madame Peyrony's odd-job man," said Audley across the table to Roche. "He stokes the boiler, and does the repairs, and digs the garden, and that sort of thing."

Digs the garden sent a shiver down Roche's spine. If Old Gaston dug Madame Peyrony's garden from way back, then he had planted more than roses in it, for sure.

"Stein!" Audley's voice had lost its heartiness. "What does he want?" There was a touch of bluster about it now, and under that uneasiness. "Stein?"

The Israeli turned round suddenly just beyond the doorway, but then stood there for a moment in silence, without moving.

"Well?" snapped Audley.

Stein straightened up—until he did so Roche didn't realise that his shoulders had slumped—and came back into the light.

"Well?" said Audley again.

Stein looked at Jilly. "Get your wrap, dear. We've got to go."

"What's happened?" asked Lexy.

"There's been an accident."

"Steffy?" Lexy stood up quickly. "To Steffy?"

Jilly had risen just as quickly, pulling her wrap from the back of her chair on to her shoulders.

"Not you, Lady Alexandra," said Stein. "Jilly will do."

Lexy had started to move, but now she stopped. "What sort of accident?"

She knew, of course. They all knew, thought Roche—they knew without the fractional pause before Stein gave up trying to edit the answer.

"She's dead, Lexy," said the Israeli.

XIV

ROCHE'S TRAVELLING CLOCK woke him to order before dawn, into blind man's darkness inside the Tower.

Against all the odds of alcohol and exhaustion, and the too-few hours the night's events had left him, he became fully aware of all the co-ordinates of his mind and body long before the tiny bell mechanism had exhausted itself beneath the folds of his shirt, with which he had deliberately muted it.

He had to get up and get on with the job. Thinking about Steffy—knowing just so much, and nothing at all—only brought back the sour taste of nightmares which he shouldn't remember, like the taste of last night's alcohol.

He fumbled for his torch under the camp-bed; found the torch, and found the matches on the table beside him; put down the torch and struck a match to light the candle Audley had left for him—the flaring match and the sputtering candle-flame illuminated the tower room around him, sending thousands of shadows everywhere creeping into their holes, in the great rack of bottles—the bottles winking and blinking at him.

Before he could think more about it, he forced himself out of his sleeping bag and set his bare feet on the floor. And he saw, as he did so, the slim red gold-embossed book which he had pulled out of his hold-all, with his torch and his little alarm clock—which he had tried to read for a few moments in that same candlelight so few hours before, wanting to sleep and needing to sleep, but fearing to do so . . . Wimpy's gift, Kipling's *Puck of Pook's Hill* . . . and thought of the old Roman general on the Great Wall, with his world falling in ruins around him, listening each morning to his sword and saying to himself 'And *this* day is allowed Rutilianus to live' . . .

He drew his shirt over his head, and hauled his trousers on to his legs; and pulled on his socks and pushed his feet into his shoes, and tied up the laces; and, just as automatically, picked up the torch and acquiesced in the Plan of Action he had formulated the half-night before, as he had assembled the camp-bed and unstrapped the sleeping-bag.

The very automation of these simple actions carried him beyond the getting-up which had been no more than the reverse of lying-down. What the Tower had once been, before Audley had worked on it, he still wasn't sure: it was the size of a great dovecote or a small defensive *donjon* . . . but there was nothing now in it to indicate which it had been, if it had been either of those, only the new wooden floor beneath his feet and the new wooden ceiling twelve feet above his head, with the smell of the fresh timber faint in his nostrils.

He flashed the torch-beam around him. Well . . . maybe it had been both those things in its time: in the bad old days Aquitaine had been famous for its petty barons, who had all needed their castles, and this Quercy region of it had also been celebrated for its dovecotes and pigeon-lofts, over which the avaricious peasants had litigated endlessly to establish their rights to the valuable bird-droppings. On balance, judging from the thickness of the wall in which the doorway was set rather than from the total lack of windows in the room, he was inclined to guess *castle bastion* originally, even though he had seen nothing outside very clearly in the yellow beam of the Volkswagen's headlights to support that theory; most of his attention had been caught by the little cottage in the trees just below, which the lights had transformed into another Perrault fairy-tale house, with its dormer windows and pantile roof.

Not that it mattered either way—whether this was the last remnant of the Beast's castle or Beauty's father's pigeon-loft; what mattered now was that it was Audley's tower, remodelled for his purposes—for his argumentative orgies down below and . . . according to Jilly, for his writing work-room above, up *that* ladder and beyond *that* trap-door.

Of course, the odds were long against there being the sort of final evidence he required for certainty up there, waiting to be found, especially if Audley had so little suspicion of Captain Roche that he was happy to let him bed down in the Tower . . .

He raised the trap-door cautiously, until he felt it lodge against something.

Books everywhere . . . books and learned-looking periodicals—a stack of *English Historical Reviews*, and another of the *Transactions of the Royal Historical Society* beside it, right under his nose, just above floor level—books and periodicals and mounds of type-written papers covered the floor of the work-room. Either Audley hadn't got round to having bookshelves made, or the round walls of the Tower had defeated his carpenter.

It *had* been a defensive tower, not a dovecote, that was for sure: on one compass-bearing the archer's embrasure had been opened up into a full-size window, and Audley had had his work-desk built there, to give him light for his work, but the three surviving arrow slits gave the original game away. Only that wasn't the game he was playing now . . .

He found, and quite quickly from the filed papers and the card-index system, that the man's researches fell neatly into the two parts he had expected—so neatly, so eloquently, that an inner glow of self-satisfaction began to warm away his early morning self-doubting.

Really, it was quite perfect . . . the contrast between the magisterial—almost ponderous—scholarship on Charles Martel and his 8th century Franks and their Arab–Berber adversaries in Western Europe, and the very different notes on King Gaiseric and his 5th century Vandals, who had popped up in the central Mediterranean like the wrath of God two hundred years before the Arabs.

Except for the identical hand-writing, which was curiously childish and unformed, and the passion for logical and meticulously recorded detail, it might almost have been the work of two different men: the painstaking and respectable Dr Jekyll-Audley, who never strayed outside the facts, and the Mr Hyde-Audley, who slavered over Vandal atrocities in North Africa, with scandalous conjectures about their sexual habits . . . and was plainly and unashamedly committed to the Vandal Cause, where Jekyll-Audley maintained a lofty impartiality appropriate to the author of *The Influence of Islamic Doctrines on Iconoclasm in the 8th Century*.

But, at the same time, there were distinctive and tell-tale similarities which betrayed the consubstantiation of the two Audleys. Both were fascinated by religion (though, typically, Hyde-Audley inclined towards the Vandals' Arian heresy), and they shared an equal obsession for military detail, Jekyll-Audley's notes on Frankish and Arab weaponry and tactics being equalled by Hyde-Audley's on the development of King Gaiseric's navy—

Hyde-*Palfrey*-Audley—

With a start, Roche realised suddenly that he was no longer reading by the light of his torch: while he had been burrowing into the papers and the index, drawn ever deeper into them by his study of the two Audleys, the dawn had crept up on him out of the dark to fill the window right in front of him. Below him the morning mist had already started to fall away from the ridge. It still filled the whole valley, blanking out everything to within fifty yards of the tower, with the shapes of small junipers and scrub oaks indistinct on its nearest margin.

He replaced everything very carefully into the semi-confusion in which he had found it, the topmost file, *Town plans of Hippo Regius, Carthage, Leptis Magna, Ostia Antica, Rome—c.500*, slightly askew. A trained man would know it had all been picked over, and there were innumerable precautionary traps Audley could have set to betray such tampering at a glance if he was of a mind to be suspicious. But it didn't really matter now, because now and at last Audley himself was next on the agenda, and after that he would take it for granted that Captain Roche had pried around his work-room during the night.

He looked round the room one last time, more out of habit than necessity after that last thought. If he had still been working for one side or the other, for Genghis Khan or Sir Eustace Avery, perhaps Audley wouldn't have been next—perhaps the burden of responsibility would have driven him to consult with at least one of them first . . . and not Genghis Khan, because by now he would already be on the way to their rendezvous. But *now* he was working for himself, and instinct ordered him to keep one jump ahead of both of them.

His eye came round, past the open trapdoor and the arrow-slit embrasures, over the piles of books and the card-index boxes which he had just closed, to the work-table with its files—*Town plans of Hippo Regius, Carthage*—to the window on the world of junipers-and-scrub-oaks-in-the-mist—

The juniper tree moved!

Or . . . it didn't move—it couldn't move—but it widened first on one side, then on the other, as David Audley passed in front of it, striding across the rough pasture. Even as Roche watched, the mist started to swallow him.

Now? Roche thought. *Why not now?* And then thought simplified into action.

The morning chill hit his cheeks, then filled his mouth and throat and lungs as he drew it in. It surprised him that it could be so cold, where he had seen huge yellow butterflies and hovering humming-bird hawk moths busy with the buddleia outside Lexy's cottage in the late afternoon of yesterday. But—*now*, while instinct and morning courage were in alliance—*now* he had no time for butterflies and buddleias and hawk moths—

At this level, cheated of the bird's-eye view from the tower window, he was no longer sure which juniper tree was the right one, on which to orientate himself.

"Audley!" he raised his voice into the silence of the morning.

The stillness closed back quickly on the sound, damping it down without an echo, like a pebble thrown into mud on the edge of a pond, sending out no ripples beyond its fall.

Roche drew in his breath to try again.

"Hullo there!" The answering words came faintly to him, more distant and at a much more acute angle as though Audley had zig-zagged back on himself, against the fall of the ridge. "Hullo!"

"My dear fellow!" Audley loomed up ahead of him out of the mist as he brushed through the fringe of scrub oaks. "You're up early!"

He watched Roche advance the last few steps. "Couldn't you sleep?" He shook his head at his own question. "Of course, it wasn't a night for untroubled sleep after . . . what happened, I agree—a *bad* night for everyone, I'm afraid. Worse for us, but bad enough for you too." He shook his head again. "Steffy . . ." he sighed, and steadied his scrutiny of Roche. "But you didn't know her, of course."

"I did meet her—briefly." Roche didn't want to talk about Meriel Stephanides. "Just briefly, down by the river, with Lady Alexandra and Miss Baker yesterday . . ."

"You did?" Audley nodded politely, without the least interest in the information. "What a waste . . . what a damn waste—that's all I can think of, you know."

"Yes." He had to turn the conversation from Steffy. "You didn't sleep either, then?"

"Me? Oh . . . I'm always up early." Audley started to move again, waving downhill into the mist. "First job of the day is to collect the bread and croissants for breakfast. Old Fauvet's boy leaves it in a box down by the road at the bottom—I save him the journey and get my morning exercise while my house-guests are lapped in swinish slumber." He shrugged. "No point in changing the routine."

"No." *Now.* "About last night . . ."

"Last night?" Audley frowned at him sideways. "What about last night?"

Roche searched for a moment for his opening gambit, and found Lexy offering it to him, generous as ever. "Do you remember what Lady Alexandra said—about me." He kept in step with Audley. "Well, she was . . . right."

"She often is. She's a clever little girl . . . or clever big girl, I should say . . . in her own peculiar way," agreed Audley unconcernedly.

"You remember what she said?"

Audley grimaced at him. "Yes . . . well, to be honest, *no*. I have this bad habit of not always listening to what Lexy says, you see."

There was no help for it, he had to bite the bullet. "I work for British Intelligence, Dr Audley."

Audley continued walking, not looking at him, almost as though he hadn't heard. But he had heard.

"Yes," he said finally, this time almost as though merely agreeing with a statement of the obvious. "You have the stretched look of some of the field men I once knew . . . or maybe *over*-stretched, from being too long in the field—*some foreign field, that is forever England*. That's what stretched them."

Roche shivered involuntarily at such a deliberate foot-fall on his grave, but before he could react to it Audley turned towards him.

"My dear fellow! Forgive me—I shouldn't have said that, to you of all people!" He raised his hand to forestall a reply. "And when I should be grateful, too! Quite unpardonable!"

"Grateful?" Roche stumbled on a tussock, almost measuring his length.

"That's right." Audley caught his arm to steady him. "Aren't you about to tell me that you'll put in a good word for me up above, with your controller—or whatever they call them now? That I'm ready and willing? That I've seen the error of my ways? That they won't ever again have recourse to Section Nine—or Section Ten, or whatever it is today?"

"Section Nine?" managed Roche.

"Or whatever. It was Section Nine in the 1914 *Manual of Military Law* I inherited. Of course, they never actually threw it at me, not in '46 . . . but it was an awful thing I did—they must have felt like M'Turk did in *Stalky*, when Colonel Dabney's keeper took a shot at the vixen: 'It's the ruin of good feelin' among neighbours—it's worse than murder'. And quite right too, they were, that's the pity of it."

Somehow the opening Roche had expected seemed to be eluding him. "But I don't see what was so terrible, about refusing in the way you did—"

"You don't? Then you damn well ought to!" Audley had no mercy on himself. "It was the moment of truth, and I fluffed it. It's . . . it's like the specimen charge in the back of the *Manual*, for Section Nine: *The accused, Captain D. L. Audley*—name, rank, number and regiment . . . how do the words go?—*is charged with, when on active service, disobeying a lawful order given personally to him by his superior officer in the execution of his office*—I think I've left out something about 'disobeying in such a manner as to show a wilful defiance of authority' . . ."

"But you didn't disobey anyone—you refused to come back in, that's all," interrupted Roche quickly.

"I refused in '51." Audley raised a finger. "I disobeyed in a wilfully defiant manner in '46 . . . *when personally ordered to take up his rifle and fall in did not do so, saying 'You may do what you please, I will soldier no more'*—and that's exactly what I told them . . . *I'll soldier no more!*" Audley threw him another of his characteristic half-bitter, half-mocking smiles. "For them—the unpardonable crime. So don't waste your time with me, old boy," concluded Audley. "I'm out. And that's that."

"No," said Roche. "You're quite wrong."

Audley looked at him again, sidelong, one eyebrow raised, which seemed to split his expression into two, half of it curious to know why he was wrong, the other half contemptuous of that possibility.

"They want you back," said Roche. "That's why I'm here."

The raised eyebrow dropped back into position, but otherwise the man's face suddenly became blank, as though shutters had been lowered behind his eyes.

"They want you back," repeated Roche.

Audley took two or three more paces, and then stopped so abruptly that Roche's own stride carried him on down the hillside for two more, and he had to check himself and swing round.

"Oh yes?" said Audley, and his voice was as blank as his expression.

"Third time lucky." Roche was reminded of what Oliver St.John Latimer had said about Audley; and then it occurred to him that although he had been thinking of the man in Jekyll-and-Hyde terms, perhaps only now was he witnessing the true Hyde metamorphosis.

"Oh yes?" Audley looked through him.

Latimer was right, yet he mustn't let that daunt him. It was the Hyde-Audley he wanted, not the Jekyll-Audley or the self-pitying show-off from last night.

But he couldn't afford to jolly the Hyde-Audley—that had been an error. He must take the whip to the Hyde-Audley.

"Does the name Avery mean anything to you?"

"Avery?"

"Sir Eustace Avery."

Audley shook his head. "Never heard of him."

"Clinton, then?"

Audley studied him for a long moment, then he relaxed his mouth into some sort of smile. Stage Two with Audley would be when he realised that to show no expression at all might be identified as a sign of weakness, and although he couldn't control his eyes he could do something with his lips.

"Colonel-Frederick-Clinton." Audley worked on his face to give it back to Jekyll. As with Genghis Khan, that name wasn't just ringing one bell, but a tocsin strong enough to shake the bell-tower. "Yes, I remember him. He was one of the organ-grinders . . . and I was one of the monkeys. I remember him—yes." Audley nodded. "I remember him . . . rather well."

"Good. Now—"

"You are one of his monkeys, is that it?"

This wouldn't do at all, to have Audley remembering the dark past when he should be rejoicing in the happy present and the exciting future.

"There's a new department being formed, Audley. I'm here to offer you a place in it. A *senior* place. In fact—"

"*You* . . . are saying that *he* . . . wants *me* . . . *back*?"

"Sir Eustace Avery—"

"Bugger Sir Eustace-bloody-Avery! *Clinton* wants me back?"

It had been a mistake to let the big man get above him on the hillside; with the extra couple of inches he had on the level he towered over Roche now.

Roche set his teeth. "I told you. There's a new department starting up—"

"Bugger the new department too! You asked me if I remembered Colonel Frederick Clinton—Colonel Frederick *J*. Clinton—J for Joseph—Joseph of the coat-of-many-colours, that's what I remember. So . . . why does *he* want *me*?"

The trouble with that, thought Roche, was that it was a very fair question.

"He scares you, does he?" He recalled Genghis Khan's sarcasm.

"Yes. He does." Audley brushed the gambit aside.

"You've changed your tune since last night. If I recollect correctly—"

"No! I haven't moved an inch. Last night Mahomet wanted to go to the mountain. But now the mountain has come to Mahomet. And Mahomet mistrusts miracles, Captain Roche—that's all."

Roche lost his last doubts about David Audley, and about Clinton and Avery at the same time. Last night had made it a little too easy, like another miracle—which he also ought to have mistrusted. But Clinton had known, even in knowing that Audley was wide-open for recruitment, that it wouldn't be so easy.

"Or, shall we say . . ." Audley started, and then trailed off ". . . shall we say that I'm beginning to put things together? Things . . . and people?"

Now that he thought about it, Roche understood that Audley was running exactly true to form, and that any other reaction would have been out of character. So what he would expect in return was the authentic crack of Clinton's whip. Nothing else would do.

"We want the papers d'Auberon gave you for safe-keeping, naturally."

"Of course!" Audley's smile acknowledged. "And that's my dowry, isn't it? I sell you 'Tienne—my old friend 'Tienne—you know all about him, *naturally*!"

Roche nodded. The truth was that he didn't know enough about any of them for safety, but there was no time left for the normal precautions, only for half-truth and bluff. "Naturally."

"You know he saved my bacon?" Audley came back to him from miles away. "You know . . . I was stuck in the middle of France in '44—and wet behind the ears, and hotter than a chestnut in a charcoal brazier . . . But

'Tienne helped to get me out, *via* the good Madame Peyrony and her private army. Only I suppose you know all about that too, of course . . . God only knows how, but it's the sort of thing Colonel Frederick J. Clinton would know, *naturally*."

Roche said nothing. They were far off the script now, with the news that Audley owed d'Auberon this old debt of honour. And yet, even if Clinton hadn't known about it, it was a reasonable deduction that Audley had to owe the man something, to be entrusted with that life insurance.

Audley was frowning at him. "Only Clinton reckons I'd sell him out for a nice cosy job, organ-grinding . . ." he watched Roche narrowly for a moment, and then smiled—"A nicely-calculated temptation . . . but unfortunately an academic exercise now."

The big man's sudden brightness struck a chill in Roche. "What d'you mean?"

"What do I mean!" Audley beamed at him. "I mean, my dear fellow, that for once Colonel Frederick J. Clinton has miscalculated. It's very sad really—here he is . . . or here you are . . . offering me marriage—re-marriage—with the old firm, and my past crimes forgotten . . . and maybe it is just possible that I might have sold dear old 'Tienne down the river in the process—who knows?" The smile became icy. "But I must refuse—that's what I mean, Roche. Because I haven't got what you want."

"You haven't got it?"

"That's right. Twenty-four hours ago we just might have done business. But not now. You're a day too late, old boy."

Roche swallowed. "You've given it back?"

"Right again. The trip to Cahors yesterday wasn't to chat up my rugger-playing Frog pals, it was to open my safe deposit there. 'Tienne dropped the word yesterday morning, before you arrived on the scene. And I dropped everything and got it, and gave it back to him last night before I came back to the Tower. That's why I was late . . ." the hands spread eloquently again ". . . we had a jar or two for old times' sake. And that's why I was half-stoned when we first made our acquaintance—I usually manage to stay more or less sober until sundown." He paused. "The funny thing is . . . we don't actually like each other. In fact . . . we hate each other as only an Englishman can hate a good Frenchman. He has elevated ideas of honour, and the ancestors to go with it . . . whereas I like to think that I'm a pragmatic sort of bastard, you know."

Bastard was right. The truth cut deep inside Audley, to confuse the Kipling-bred ideals.

"I can give you some idea of the contents, if that's what you want," said Audley lightly. "Free of charge, of course."

"You've read it?" Roche was beyond astonishment.

"My dear chap—I may be a good Samaritan, but I hope I'm not a complete idiot! Besides which, when 'Tienne took me in back in '44 he picked my brains something horrid to make sure I wasn't doing *la belle*

France down, so fair's fair . . . And, also besides which . . . if I'm required by old times' sake to sit on a bomb I like to know what sort of bomb it is . . . So I took a quick peek at it."

Roche could only stare at him.

"The end part was still cyphered, or it may have been a report of some kind in a sort of appendix, I don't know. But the main body was a transcript—in French of course—of a series of meetings in the Kremlin . . . only it was all pretty much ancient history from last summer and autumn. Mostly Hungary, plus Suez."

The key material of the RIP sub-committee exactly, in short.

"What I'd guess . . ." Audley pursed his lips ". . . is that the French have got one of the special advisers in their pocket—one of the experts they wheel in—probably an Eastern European specialist by the look of it. Quite a smart fellow, too."

"Yes?" said Roche huskily.

"Well, I didn't read the stuff carefully once I'd established it was private Franco–Russian history." Audley waved a hand. "And in retrospect it wasn't all that explosive . . . It was just that the Russians were shit-scared of what was happening in Eastern Europe then, and particularly Hungary, and they reckoned the West knew all about it . . . In fact, they reckoned we were stirring it in order to give ourselves a free hand in Egypt, and there wasn't a damn thing they could do about it. Hungary was so important to them that they more or less decided just to make loud noises about anything we did in the Middle East, but nothing more than that. In short, Nasser could take his chances, but if we moved one tank towards Hungary the balloon would go up . . . Oh, and a fellow called Andropov was usually chairman."

"Yuri Andropov?" *Christ!*

"Just Andropov. They didn't run to christian names. Who's he?"

"He was their Hungarian ambassador. Top brass KGB." *One of my bosses.* "He probably organised the Hungarian business."

"Sounds like the chap. Anyway, that's about the sum of what I was able to read, if it's any help to you . . . Which I assume it isn't, because the Frogs must have passed a good deal of it on to your people by way of encourage-ment. And it's all ancient history now, as I say—" he stopped suddenly. "Except . . . there's always the identity of their Moscow man, of course."

"The satellite specialist?"

"That was my guess. It could be one of several people, but it wouldn't be too difficult to track him down—just a matter of textual analysis and elimination . . . Is he what you're after? Or the encyphered stuff?" Audley eyed him speculatively. "But you'd need the full text, either way, and that's obviously what you want, judging by that sick look."

"Does d'Auberon know you looked at what he gave you?"

"I shouldn't wonder. He merely put me on my honour not to get it photocopied, that's all . . . the transcripts and the encyphered stuff—you want 'em both, so one probably complements the other . . ." Audley was thinking aloud.

"You didn't get it photocopied, by any chance?"

"Are you trying to be offensive? I told you—I owe the man my skin." All the same, Audley spoke mildly, as though he was only giving Roche half his attention while the other half was engaged in more important matters.

"So what's your position now?" Roche persisted.

"My position?"

"Would you be willing to help me try and get it?"

Audley stared at him vaguely. "That's what I'm thinking about at this precise moment."

"You mean . . . you would?"

"Oh yes. Now that I've given it back, and fulfilled my bargain, I don't owe the blighter anything. And I'd still like to be an organ-grinder, you know . . ." He focussed on Roche. "How long have you known I had the d'Auberon stuff?"

"Why d'you want to know?"

"Not long?" Audley crushed the counter-question aside. "Only a few days?"

"I'd guess . . . not very long," admitted Roche. "If you mean how long has Clinton known . . . But why d'you want to know?"

"Timing . . . it's the timing. You popped the question to me at the first opportunity—now, even before breakfast. So Clinton must be pushing you like hell, to go ahead. Am I right?"

Roche nodded. It was almost time to tell Audley about Meriel Stephanides, and the question mark beside Bradford's name. But he might as well see how far Audley could get unaided.

"Timing?" he prodded Audley gently.

"That's right: you were damn quick *but you were still too late, Roche.* Which means that my old friend 'Tienne knew the cat was out of the bag, and he didn't trust me to resist temptation any more. And that's only the beginning of it, by God! Don't you see, man?"

Roche forbore to let slip that in his opinion it was d'Auberon's placing of the documents in Audley's care in the first place which was surprising, not his hasty recovery of them at the first sign of danger. And yet it seemed that the Frenchman had judged his Englishman just about right in the end.

"Or are you holding out on me?" Audley gave him a sharp look.

"Holding out?"

"Who else knows about d'Auberon—and me? My God—if the British know, and d'Auberon's got the wind up, then half the world probably knows!" Mr Hyde was back again.

"What's the matter?" The Hyde-look alarmed Roche.

"Steffy," snapped Audley.

Roche manned his defences. "I don't know."

"Don't know if it was an accident? Who was she working for? The Israelis?"

"Yes. And Bradford is with the CIA, we think."

"Are you suggesting that Mike had her run off the road last night?"

"I'm not suggesting anything. I don't even know that it wasn't an accident!" Roche snapped back.

"You know far too little for my peace of mind. If Steffy worked for the Israelis—"

"She did. No 'if'."

"All right. Let's put it together then. Steffy worked for Mossad, and she showed up ten days ago. Mike may be cloak-and-dagger for the CIA as well as Hollywood, and he arrived a week before she did. And you finally made it *trop tard* yesterday." Audley's voice became grimmer with each arrival. "So what about the Komitet Gosudarstvennoi Bezopasnosti?"

Audley's Russian accent was worse than his French, but there was nothing wrong with his logic, thought Roche equally grimly.

"What about them?"

"Running little girls off the road is more their style, or it used to be in my young days. If the Yankees didn't do it—and I can't see them getting violent over the d'Auberon papers, which don't involve their security . . . and your lot didn't do it, because the same applies . . . and the French themselves didn't *need* to do it, because they would have simply run her out of the country as an undesirable . . . and the Israelis wouldn't want to cause the French trouble anyway. And that just leaves the KGB, who also happen to have the best reason of all for wanting the papers, to find out who was telling tales out of school . . . So what about *them*, then?"

Roche was uneasily aware that this was one question to which he had the exact answer, but one which he still could make no sense of.

"You're not about to tell me once again that you don't know?" Audley mistook his unease for embarrassment.

"We haven't spotted them if they are here." Unbelievable was more like it: with the way the Comrades had French security sewn up it was unbelievable that they hadn't known about d'Auberon long ago. And yet, if Genghis Khan wasn't playing some other, much deeper game, he had no choice but to believe the unbelievable.

"Well, if they aren't it's a bloody miracle," said Audley. "And if it is a miracle it isn't going to last much longer, because if they've got Steffy on their books they'll be likely to want to know why she ran out of road. And then they'll start picking up names . . . and *then* this place will become extremely unhealthy . . ." Audley's eyes unfocussed as the probabilities unfolded ". . . in fact, I'm damn glad I'm not safe-keeping 'Tienne's wretched insurance policy any more—it's about to transmogrify into his death certificate, I shouldn't wonder." The eyes focussed on Roche again. "In fact, since I can no longer work my passage back into the old firm . . . and I have no wish to be caught in your cross-fire . . . I think I'm just about

209

to remember some pressing business a long way from here, Roche."

He started moving downhill once more, without another word.

"No—wait!" Roche swivelled to follow him. "Where are you going, Audley—"

"To get the bread, of course." The words were thrown back at him over Audley's shoulder. "Breakfast first—then a prudent retreat, old boy."

"But you can't go—just like that!" Roche started after him, accelerating desperately to overtake him.

"You just watch me. I think I'll get Bradford to take me to see Holly-wood. That should be far enough."

Everything seemed to have crumbled into ruins just when it had all seemed in his grasp, thought Roche wildly: Audley was quite wrong, but there was no way that he could tell him so.

Or was he wrong?

The mist had almost swallowed up Audley. Above him, but far beyond, the crest of the ridge on the other side of the valley rose up out of the misty sea, the trees on it standing out sharply against the deepening blue of the sky. It was going to be a fine, hot day—a fine, hot, cloudless, utterly disastrous day.

Audley's figure hadn't disappeared yet. Just when it was losing defini-tion altogether it had firmed up again—

Audley was coming back!

Roche watched the big man stumping uphill towards him, a ghostly figure regaining the substance of life with every step, even at last to the expression on his face.

It was a curious face, he thought: the big nose, which looked as if it had been broken more than once in rough scrimmages on the rugger field, divided a boxer's chin from the high forehead. And yet it was the mouth and the eyes, with their manic changes, which dominated these permanent hereditary features—the same features he had seen in the picture on the staircase in The Old House.

The mouth smiled at him. "Our deal is still on, is it?"

Roche nodded.

"If I show you how to get the papers . . . I'm back in?"

Roche nodded again.

"With seniority? I have your word on it?"

"Yes." Roche could just about manage that word.

"Jolly good! Because I've just had second thoughts."

"Second thoughts?"

"Yes. I don't know about Avery—*Sir* Eustace—but Clinton was always a man of his word. So I accept." Audley nodded. "I'm afraid you'll have to do the work—I insist you don't mention my name, in fact . . . that might well turn him against you. But I'll tell you what to say. Okay?"

It wasn't an occasion for caution. "Okay."

"Okay. So we have our deal: if we succeed I'm in, if we fail I shall work for

210

Mike Bradford, who will undoubtedly pay me better. Heads—I win . . . tails—I don't lose. That's the sort of deal I like, old boy."

Arrogant, selfish, ruthless and cunning, Latimer had said, among other defects. But that would be Avery's problem in the future, if there was one.

"So what's your plan, Audley?" Clinton and Avery were both welcome to this bastard, thought Roche.

"My plan? All you have to do is to make him an offer he can't refuse." The smile was pure Hyde now. "If the KGB isn't here yet it soon will be, and that's our lever. If he gives the stuff to us, we'll let them know we've got it—and we'll get the French off his back. That won't be difficult. And if he won't play, we'll feed him to the KGB."

The bastard! "Straight blackmail, you mean?"

"Blackmail?" Mr Hyde continued to smile. "My dear chap, we're saving his life for him!"

BATTLE:

No plan survives reality

XV

ROCHE ARRIVED AT the southern gateway of Neuville exactly on time.

Below him, the old military road along which help or trouble had marched to Neuville from Cahors ran away into the farmland, empty except for two children playing in the dust with a dog and a ball. The first flush of morning had passed, and the sun was rising fast into its cloudless sky. God was in His heaven, and Jilly Baker was at Les Eyzies, or Le Bugue, or wherever the formalities of death had to be transacted, with Davey Stein along for moral support; and Lexy was still in her bath, for all the good bathing would do her; and Audley was packing, ready for whichever master he would be serving tomorrow, in London or Hollywood, and grunting instructions for the maintenance of the cottage to Bradford, who was staying on to continue his quest (or not, as the case might be, according to which of those masters Audley finally served . . .).

There was positively nothing he could see to make him nervous, and the children's voices grew fainter as their ball drew them away into the country, so he sauntered from one side of the gateway to the other, recalling the cold summer wind on the garage forecourt in Sussex, opposite Genghis Khan's church.

The van arrived five minutes later, drawing in close beside the left-hand bastion of the gateway.

Still remembering Sussex, Roche watched it half-hopefully, half-fearfully, out of the corner of his eye, only to have his half-hopes swiftly dashed as its occupants unloaded boxes of fresh peaches from the rear, each carrying an armful through the gateway into the town, with no more than the typical glance at him which the working peasant reserved for the idle foreign tourist, of boredom lightly iced with envy.

Five more minutes dragged by, then the two men returned to exchange empty boxes for fresh ones. Roche's half-fears began to strengthen at their inconvenient presence, which must surely account for the delay in Genghis Khan's appearance. At the best of times the moment of contact was charged with doubt and uncertainty, but here in the open, with miles of countryside below him and a hundred upper-storey windows watching him over the old wall, the dangers were multiplied.

He turned away from them to scan the street again, aware of a prickle of sweat under his shirt which was not caused by the sun's warmth on his back. But this time, as he moved to give them a wider berth, the elder of the two peasants detoured to pass round him, his face half-obscured by the peach-boxes.

"The van," half the mouth whispered.

Beneath the three-quarter rolled-up canvas flap at the back, the interior of the van looked hot and dark, and still full of peach-boxes. Several wasps were already buzzing above the lowered tail-board, attracted by the scent of the peaches and working up their courage to leave the safety of the sun-light.

"Look away—don't look in here," said Genghis Khan's voice out of the boxes and the darkness. "Look towards the country."

Roche looked away quickly, down the Cahors road and over the children, to the fields which the medieval Neuvillians had once tilled when they had been frontier farmers.

"If you can hear me, don't nod—just say so. You understand?"

Roche almost nodded. Every night they had returned to the security of their walls, those old farmers, like the earliest colonists of the Americas. That was how *bastides* worked.

"Yes," he addressed the fields. He hadn't realised until now how delib-erately the place had been sited; but, of course, Alphonse de Poitiers had taken the high ground for his new town, like any good commander.

"From time to time, walk away, as though you are still waiting for someone . . . And if you see anything you don't like, walk away and don't come back. You understand?"

Again Roche very nearly nodded. It was an unnatural way of conversing, almost like talking to an incubus within him, which was whispering inside his head.

"Yes." With an effort of will he drove out the dark thought, to join Alphonse de Poitiers. "I understand."

"Then listen. We know now where Audley's money comes from—"

"So do I. He wrote *Princess in the Sunset*," interrupted Roche quickly. Another advantage was that the memory of that face was less daunting than the actual sight of it: he had to envisage Genghis Khan as he was now—imprisoned in sweaty peach-sweet darkness, with wasps buzzing around his ears, not as the descendant of the Mongols and the out-rider of the next race of conquerors.

"He told you?"

"No." Better to think of the man in there as a Hun than a Mongol: Audley's Aëtius, the Last of the Romans, and his half-civilised Visigothic allies had beaten *them* not far from here fifteen hundred years back. So it could be done—it wasn't impossible if he kept his head.

"What?" The sound of a slight movement inside the van, above the wasp-buzz, encouraged Roche.

"I said 'no'—he didn't tell me. He doesn't want anyone to know he's Antonia Palfrey. It wouldn't do his image as a serious historian any good . . . among the serious historians." Roche smiled at the fields of Neuville as he thought of what Dr Bodger would make of Antonia Audley. In any last resort there was a weapon to hand there.

But not a weapon to use against Genghis Khan. "What's more, he's writing another novel—he's writing two books, actually: there's a novel about the Vandals in the 5th century, which I think he's finished . . . and there's a history of the Arab invasion of these parts in the 8th century. Which is why he's here now—" the weapon he needed for Genghis Khan fitted snugly into his hand "—all of which I think Colonel Clinton and Sir Eustace Avery already know . . . among other things," he lowered his voice deliberately, to make it more difficult for Genghis Khan to hear, for tactical reasons as well as pure sadism.

"What? Clinton *knows*?" The surprise in the muffled voice was balm to Roche's soul. The thing was working—Genghis Khan could be tweaked into a human reaction, he wasn't invincible: Aëtius, when he saw the sun shimmer on the lance-points of the Gothic army coming to his aid must have felt like this!

"He didn't want to make it too easy for me. It's a test for me—" Caution quickly counter-balanced confidence: it was Steffy about whom he needed to know, not the source of Audley's wealth "—at least, it was until things started going wrong, anyway."

"Too easy?" To Roche's disappointment, Genghis Khan shrugged aside *things going wrong.* "Why too easy?"

"Audley wants to come back, he only had to be asked in the right way. I think Clinton knew that—that was never the real thing they were after." He weakened slightly, remembering Genghis Khan's interpretation of the assignment. "You were right there."

"You are sure about Audley?" Genghis Khan also brushed off the olive branch.

"Of course I'm sure." Nothing less than certainty would do for Genghis Khan, even if nothing would ever be certain about David Audley.

Only wasp-buzzing came from the darkness and peach-boxes. It was high time to walk away, and make like a tourist waiting for his girl-friend, but he couldn't leave it at that now, he had to qualify it somehow.

"That's my reading of him, anyway. I'd need much more time to tie it up—and professional advice. But we haven't got any more time," he snapped.

"But you are prepared to stake your life on it?"

So that was what he was doing: *One must always risk one's life, or one's soul, or one's peace—or some little thing!*

"I know he's bloody bored, and that's a fact!" said Roche bitterly, from the heart.

"Bored?" The incubus-voice relaxed. "Ah, yes! Bored. . ."

Roche sensed that he had to keep the initiative. "But what I want to know is . . . what happened to Meriel Stephanides," he snapped at the *bastide*-fields.

"Where is she now?" There was a harsh edge to Genghis Khan's voice. "Have you lost track of her?"

He didn't know about Steffy! The realisation jolted Roche that the Comrades were as criminally incompetent as the British.

"She's dead, damn it!" He needed time to think, and there was one very simple and overdue way of taking it.

He moved away from the van, towards the bastion on the far side of the arched gateway. The street was still empty, and the dog had got the children's ball at last, with which it was joyfully baiting them as they screamed at him to give it back.

Just an accident after all? Or if not an accident, and not the Comrades . . . *then who*?

The sun blinded him for a moment, and he felt another long trickle of sweat run down his back again under his shirt . . .

And if Genghis Khan didn't know, then how much else didn't he know? And how much were events pushing *him*, as Roche himself felt pushed by them, to make assumptions, and to act, and to take risks which would normally be rated as unacceptable?

"Are you there?" Genghis Khan's voice was back to normal. "How did she die?"

A wasp zoomed out of the darkness, gorged on peach-juice and flying somewhat erratically. "Her car ran off the road last night—" Roche ducked to avoid the wasp "—she broke her neck, apparently."

"Were there any witnesses?"

That wasn't the right question. "No."

"What do the police say?"

That wasn't the right question either. "They're not confiding in me. They told Miss Baker it was an accident. The car went off the road and she broke her neck. That's all I know."

"Good! And you haven't reported to Clinton yet?"

The drift of the wrong questions was plain enough. What Genghis Khan wanted was time, not his trusted man's opinions.

"No, not yet. I haven't reported to anyone yet—except you." He shaded his eyes against the glare, and looked intently at nothing. He had given himself a breathing space, but it had been Genghis Khan who had used it to better purpose.

He scrunched away from the van again, glancing over his shoulder at imaginary strangers.

If Genghis Khan knew who had killed Steffy then the Comrades must know about d'Auberon. It was still inexplicable that they hadn't known long ago, but they must know *now*, and that was why Genghis Khan was here in person.

He reached the far side of the gateway. The children had disappeared, presumably in pursuit of the dog, and there was still nothing else in sight.

He turned round. The immediate question was . . . did the Comrades rate the d'Auberon papers as more important than placing Captain Roche in Sir Eustace Avery's new group? If they did, then Captain Roche would be well-advised to cash in the chips he already possessed, in the hope that they might be enough to buy him safety with the British.

He eyed the van speculatively. Whatever happened to the d'Auberon papers, he could bring Audley in, that was no problem; but then, because Audley wanted to come back, that would hardly count in his favour in any reckoning. Genghis Khan, on the other hand, might be worth quite a lot; and even Jean-Paul, betrayed to the British, could be traded off to the French in exchange for a bit of badly-needed goodwill.

Yet, viewed dispassionately, even together they hardly outweighed half a dozen years' high treason—or insufficiently to ensure that Avery and Clinton wouldn't condemn him to the certain death of remaining in post in Paris as their treble traitor, untrusted and expendable.

In fact, as things stood, if he couldn't deliver those damned d'Auberon papers to the British, then he might be even more well-advised to remain a loyal Comrade, at least for the time being, until another opportunity presented itself . . .

True or false? It only took an instant to test the possibility, and feel it crumble. Over the last few days he had committed himself in his heart too far and too absolutely to turn around again. And he could never go back to where he'd started because the wasting disease within him was very close now to the point where it would become plainly visible to everyone. Already Jilly and Madame Peyrony had both sensed something wrong, and—

He was aware suddenly that something had cut through the concentration of his fear, just when it was shaking his knees.

It wasn't a sound, it was a movement: it was the van beside him rocking on its springs as its balance changed. And then, following almost instantaneously on the movement, it was also a sound—

Genghis Khan was swearing—explosively, and in Russian—or maybe it was in Polish, or in some black language unknown to civilised man, or in no language at all, except that it was also in the universal language of pain.

Genghis Khan had been stung!

The van steadied and the oaths carried no echo: five seconds or less encompassed the whole disturbance inside it.

But the earth had turned in those five seconds, shrinking the van back from the Joseph Stalin tank it had been in Roche's imagination to just a van again, rather battered and rusty, with worn tyres which left only smooth tracks in the dust; and, in the reduction of the van, the man within it had been diminished also to human proportions.

"Are you okay in there?" Roche inquired.

Grunt.

Roche hoped devoutly that the sting had been on the tip of Genghis

Khan's index finger, where the concentration of nerves would ensure the greatest discomfort. And at the same time he wished the stinging wasp its escape in the darkness, and a safe flight home.

"The point is, things have changed rather, down here, since I last spoke to you." He listened to his own voice critically, and was satisfied with it. "Also . . . I'm beginning to get the impression that you haven't been as helpful as you said you'd be. It's bad enough to be put through the hoop by Sir Eustace Avery and Colonel Clinton, but at least they hinted they were testing me. I did think you were on my side."

Still no reply. But he had burnt his boats now, and that gave him bloody-mindedness, if not confidence.

"You told me about Miss Stephanides. And about Bradford and Stein. But you somehow omitted to tell me about Etienne d'Auberon. Or have you never heard of him?"

"Don't be clever with me, Roche. It doesn't suit you."

A few moments earlier that would have stopped him in his tracks. And maybe it wasn't bloody-mindedness any more than it was real confidence— maybe it was the nerveless desperation which lay on the other side of cowardice, long after courage had been exhausted.

"It may not suit me. But you're sitting snug in there—" *he mustn't laugh at his own joke* "—and I'm out here in the open. And if I'm not clever I'm going to end up in the Tower of London—or somewhere less picturesque. And that suits me even less."

"What do you know about d'Auberon?" This time there was no delay.

"I know what Sir Eustace Avery wants me to know." Roche fished unashamedly for more information. "Do you still want me to go ahead?"

Genghis Khan digested the question in silence, while Roche observed the two children and the dog reappear in the distance.

"Do you still want me to go ahead?" Roche sharpened his voice to emphasise the question. If Genghis Khan had any lingering doubts about his loyalty, that ought to put them finally at rest: it was exactly the sort of question a loyal Comrade should ask, offering a willingness to fail the British, and lose his chances of promotion, on the Comrades' behalf.

"Avery and Clinton expect the man Audley to obtain one of the copies d'Auberon took . . . of certain documents—that is correct?" Once again Genghis Khan bypassed half a dozen of the questions Roche had expected.

"That's right." So the Comrades *did* know all about d'Auberon—but were considerably less well-informed about Audley!

"What makes them so sure that he can do this for them?" It was slightly disconcerting to hear genuine uncertainty in the man's voice.

"Yes . . . well, there's a bit of a problem there." But at least the questions were coming in the right sequence this time. "It was going to be easy, they thought—"

"Easy?"

"So they thought. But maybe it wouldn't have been so easy, at that."

"How—easy?" Genghis Khan brushed aside Roche's doubts. "What was he going to do?"

"He was just going to get them out of his bank—or wherever they were—and hand them over."

"*Audley?*"

"That's right. In return for letting him back into the service—with promotion backdated, and all that . . . That was what they were banking on all along, of course . . . But I'm inclined to think it wouldn't have been quite as straightforward as that—"

"*Audley* had one of the copies?" Genghis Khan was still struggling with information which plainly astonished him.

Well—so much the better! An astonished Genghis Khan was almost as vulnerable as a wasp-stung one.

"You didn't know that? He owed d'Auberon a big favour, from back in '44, during the war—d'Auberon saved his life apparently, and this was the repayment . . . And that's why it might have been difficult, getting him to sell the man out to the British. I think it could have been done . . . strictly in d'Auberon's best interest, you know, now that the cat's out of the bag." It struck Roche as ironic that the arguments he might have used on Audley were almost identical with those Audley was proposing for d'Auberon. "It might have worked." It might have worked with Audley, anyway; but the very fact Audley wanted him to do the dirty work with d'Auberon, with no mention of *his* part in the plan, cast further doubt on it now. "You didn't know Audley had a copy, then?"

He listened to his own words, and they were still exactly the right mixture of arrogance and obsequiousness.

"What has he done with the documents?" It was to Genghis Khan's credit that his voice was back in neutral so quickly.

"He's given them back—d'Auberon asked for them. That's what I've been trying to tell you. I don't think I was intended to be in on the d'Auberon part of the operation—I suspect they were going to get Audley to London, and then pop the question to him there. But someone's been talking, and the British had to accelerate things . . . and I was here, on the spot . . . But they were still just a few hours too late, as it turned out. That's my reading of what's happened—especially after Meriel Stephanides ran out of road."

At once, and quite naturally, the question he had left behind appeared in front of him again, like an open goal-mouth rewarded to him by attacking play. "Which reminds me . . . you never did get round to filling me in on that little matter, did you? Or do I have to settle for a tragic accident?"

The children were back on the road again, chasing the dog, which still had the ball clenched between its jaws.

"Well?" In this changed situation the man's silence emboldened him to press his advantage. "I can't stand here forever like a spare prick, old boy. Either brief me or de-brief me, or let me go and try my luck with Clinton's

221

man—he'll be a damned sight more forthcoming than you are, I hope."

The dog dropped the ball between its paws and taunted the children noisily. At least it was enjoying the game more than the man in the van.

"He-gave-it-back?" Genghis Khan spaced the words with doubt.

"D'Auberon asked for it back. So he gave it back." Roche shrugged at the children. "What's so surprising about that?"

"You're sure he had it?" Doubt still nagged at Genghis Khan. "He wasn't bluffing?"

"Why the hell should he be bluffing?" Roche decided to become irritable. "Clinton's man said he had it—that was what they were banking on, I told you. And he certainly knew all about it, because he'd looked at it—"

"He'd looked at it?"

"Oh—come on!" He let the irritation flare into anger. "This is Audley we're talking about—not a bloody Sunday School teacher! Do you seriously think a nosey bastard like Audley could resist looking at it? Of course he bloody-well did!" Roche was no longer frightened: Genghis Khan stung into any sort of emotion was thereby further diminished. "That *is* the point—what sort of man Audley is . . . that's what Avery and Clinton set me to find out, because everything else was plain sailing, they thought— they thought he wanted to come back, and they were right . . . and they knew he had the d'Auberon papers, even though they didn't know time was running out on them . . . But they also knew from past experience that Audley's a difficult and contradictory bastard, and if they sent down some-one stupid to make the contact—like the time before—then he just might get bloody-minded again, out of sheer perversity . . ."

There were children's cries in one ear, and only the wasps' endless buzzing in the other.

"He's a Jekyll-and-Hyde character, that's why. It was Dr Jekyll who took the papers, because he owed d'Auberon a debt he had to repay, as a matter of honour . . . and it was Mr Hyde who looked at them, to protect himself— and to see how valuable they were."

"What did he make of them?" Genghis Khan slashed the question at him instantly.

"He thought they were ancient history. But I think Clinton was right—he would have done a deal with us. Mr Hyde would have out-voted Dr Jekyll." It occurred to Roche belatedly that Genghis Khan might not know Jekyll and Hyde from Laurel and Hardy; he was probably an illiterate sod.

"Yes. Clinton . . . Clinton . . ." Genghis Khan was speaking to himself, nodding to himself in the darkness in there, whispering the name of the man whom he saw as his real adversary.

"That's right," Roche encouraged him. "Audley was the key—Clinton knew that." If Genghis Khan fancied he understood Clinton, his own stock-in-trade was understanding Audley, and he must press that advantage to the full. "Maybe he still is the key."

"What do you mean? If he no longer has the documents—?"

222

"Yes . . . But without them I'm never going to get on to the Eighth Floor, alongside Clinton. Turning in Audley won't be enough by itself—I'd guess that Sir Eustace Avery has set his heart on getting those papers, and he's not the man to reward failure. Nor is Clinton." This was a language Genghis Khan understood only too well, not least because his own superiors spoke it even more implacably; and in another moment, after Roche had hooked them both together, he would understand it even better.

"So?" Genghis Khan accepted the cold logic so far.

"So this is where I need your help, old boy. And rather quickly, I suspect. Because if I can get my hands on d'Auberon's little nest egg, then we win hands down—I can make a copy of them for you *and* I get my promotion to where you want me to be. But if I can't, then I'm pretty damn sure someone else soon will. And then we shall *both* be in trouble, I think—eh?"

He was aware, as he delivered the final threat, which was barbed to lodge irremovably in Genghis Khan's soul, that he was raising his voice against all the competing noises—the dog (which had at last lost the ball), and the children, and the wasps, and the awakening town itself.

"Audley's got a plan, you see," said Roche. "Only I don't think it will work. What I need to know is whether *you* can maybe make it work."

"Audley has a plan? What plan?"

Roche drew a breath. "Oh . . . just a simple little mixture of bluff and bribery. He's a ruthless bastard, Audley is: now Dr Jekyll has paid his debt, Mr Hyde is in charge."

"Go on."

Roche decided to try again. "Just who *did* kill Miss Stephanides, by the way?"

The dog and the children had gone again. Only the wasps, his friends and allies, buzzed on regardless.

"I do not know for sure. I can guess, but I do not know, David."

The 'David' surprised Roche. "Then guess for me."

"No. There is no time for guessing. It will be attended to—be satisfied with that. *Go on.*"

Roche was past arguing. Also, there was a horrible thought rising inside him, like a bloated corpse which had freed itself from the weight of his illusions about the British: *it was only Steffy's death which gave substance to Audley's bluff, and if the Comrades weren't responsible for that, could it be that Clinton—?*

"Go on, David."

If it was so, then he was really midway between the frying pan and the fire, both equally unforgiving.

"*Go on—*"

"I like it," said Genghis Khan finally. "It has the mark of the man himself about it—the man you have described, and the man we are beginning to know also."

"What?" Then Roche remembered that Genghis Khan's first offer had related to the identity of Antonia Palfrey. And, in any case, it was foolish to assume that the Comrades had been idle while he had been so busy: they had been digging discreetly but deeply in their own way into both d'Auberon and Audley these last forty-eight hours, that was certain.

"Using us as the threat, to save his friend—and using you to make the offer—"

"He said d'Auberon would deny it, if I mentioned him—"

"He doesn't want to take any risks, of course! If he has nothing to lose, so much the better. And if you fail, he has lost nothing. His good name as an honourable man will be safe. I like it!"

"But can it work?" Roche forced himself not to look at the van.

"He's clever—he could cause us trouble in time. But he will cause the British trouble too, while he lasts—they do not like cleverness."

Roche was astonished by the clear drift of what Genghis Khan was saying. "You think it *will* work?"

"On the contrary . . . it will most certainly *not* work. There is not the slightest chance that d'Auberon will consider giving anything to the British."

"Why not?" Roche found himself taking the devil's advocate's position against his own judgement. "If d'Auberon thinks that everyone has found out about him, then he hasn't got anything to bargain with—he *must* get rid of it to someone strong enough to protect him."

"That would be prudent—yes," Genghis Khan agreed. "So he provided for that possibility—naturally. But not for the benefit of any foreign power. He is, after all, a Frenchman—perhaps he dislikes us more than the British, but that is only a matter of degree. And you are forgetting why he resigned, also."

"Over Algeria, you mean?" Roche recalled Madame Peyrony's version of the d'Auberon scandal.

He realised that he had answered his own question: a man who quit the service for patriotic reasons would hardly be likely to hand over its secrets to another country. So Audley had totally—and rather strangely—miscalculated there. And yet, at the same time, d'Auberon himself had acted out of character in entrusting his insurance policy to the Englishman to pass on to some third and safely French party.

"Politically, he is a Gaulliste," said Genghis Khan. "If it were not for his 'sense of honour'—whatever that is—he would have already revealed the documents to his Gaulliste friends, regardless of his safety. And if anything should happen to him, in any event, it is the Gaullistes who will get the documents now. But that is of no importance."

"No importance?"

"That is one reason why it won't work," said Genghis Khan. "Because he's had his sealed copies lodged all along with two senior Gaulliste deputies, men we wouldn't dare touch. Not even if we wanted to."

224

"You *knew*—" Roche steadied his voice "—about them?"

"We've known from the beginning—about *them*." Genghis paused. "But not about Audley. It would appear that d'Auberon took an extra precaution there."

"You knew?" Roche struggled with the contradiction.

"But all is not lost, even though your so-clever Dr Audley has contrived to get almost everything wrong . . . Even, I think, there is much to gain now," said Genghis Khan.

At least the relative importance of the d'Auberon papers compared with his own future career had been established, thought Roche. But somehow that was no longer so reassuring.

"And he did get one thing right, in a way. He is relying on us to do his work for him, and we mustn't let him down. But we shall have to act very quickly."

"How—" Roche stumbled over the word, jostled from behind by a new mob of doubts and fears.

"How are we going to help him? Why—we shall give him *our* copy of the d'Auberon documents, David."

XVI

LEXY RAISED THE top third of herself up off the towel on her elbows and gazed at Roche pensively, cradling her face in her hands.

"Yes?" Lexy almost totally uncovered was somehow less disturbing than the accidental and unplanned vistas she was accustomed to present when fully clothed, he thought.

"It's all right, David—I'm not about to try and buy your thoughts again for another penny. It isn't a day for buying other people's thoughts."

A sympathetic half-smile was all he could manage. It wasn't a day for smiles either. "Mine aren't worth a penny, Lexy."

"I bet they're more interesting than mine! I have such dull, ordinary thoughts, that's the trouble. That's what David Audley says . . . and what makes it worse is that he's right, the wretch!"

"Huh!" The irony made play-acting unnecessary. "I'll bet you . . . more than a penny . . . that he can be stupid too, you know."

"Yes—but at least he'll be *cleverly* stupid—'too clever by half', that's what Davey and Mike say. And that's better than being *plain* stupid."

She wasn't stupid at all, thought Roche. Even, she made it a day for a full smile, in spite of everything. "Let's say I'm thinking about you—and you couldn't be *plain* anything, even if you tried to be—" he caught his tongue too late as her face fell "—what's the matter?"

225

"Now that's a bloody-*David*-bloody-*Audley*-thought! Not good for nothing—just good for bloody-*screwing*!" She burnt him up with a scowl. "So you can keep your thoughts, bloody-*David*-bloody-*Captain Roche*—I wouldn't buy one of them if you paid me!"

Before he could reply, she had slumped herself back on the towel, presenting only pink shoulders and tangled half-dried blonde thatch in an uncompromising rejection.

Roche stared at her for a moment, and then gave up. He hadn't intended to offend her, but he had also screwed his own chances nevertheless. But then he had never had any luck, and that was the story of his life.

He frowned past her at the river, where the sun caught the ripples on the same stretch of broken water in which he had sported with all three of them yesterday—Lexy and Jilly and Steffy—when the world was young.

He could never do that again, never with Steffy and never with the same water, they had gone down to the sea together.

When it came to *screwing*, nobody had ever screwed anyone more thoroughly than the Comrades had screwed the British and the French, by Christ!

Hypnotised by the rippling light on the water, he put together the d'Auberon papers at last—

It wasn't just that the Comrades had known about d'Auberon and his precious documents all along, and hadn't worried about them at all—about the alleged traitor in their midst, who had fed back to Paris every thought the Kremlin had had, through Hungary and Suez, and every word of it nothing but the truth, checkable and double-checkable from every other Anglo–French intelligence source.

Of course they hadn't been worried! Not about *that*.

What they *had* been worried about, regardless of the British and the French . . . was the truth of those reports about the undercurrents of dissent which had been swelling ever more fiercely in their Eastern European colonies—through East Germany, still disaffected from the Berlin riots, through Poland, where patriotism and religion were inextinguishable, to Hungary, which had been primed to explode any minute by the irreversible tide of hatred even among good Comrades of the appalling Rakosi regime.

And not the men in the Kremlin alone, by God! Even dear old Bill Ballance—red-nosed, superannuated, indiscreet, but always well-informed—even Bill had been worried—

"Have another drink—to your next report on the incidence of scurvy in the French Mediterranean Fleet, say? The Froggies may hate us now—and the Yanks may distrust us even more than before—and the rest of the world may despise us for being a third-rate bunch of paper-hangers . . . but I can play Dr Pangloss to your Candide, young David, for this is still the best of all possible worlds, and I feared very much that it wasn't going to be—I was very worried that it wouldn't be!"

"What d'you mean, Bill?"

"I mean, young David, that we are alive and drinking, and not taking part in the Third World War—Leibnitz was right, and Voltaire was wrong. So I shall retire and teach metaphysico-theologo-cosmolo-nigology in my old age, like Pangloss. Because, for our sins, we have been delivered from war and pestilence and famine—but chiefly war."

"War?"

"Ah—but of course you've been away, on that smart course of yours—so you missed all the fun. Suez saved us, young David—Suez and Hungary together! So it was all for the best in this best-of-all-possible-worlds."

"How, for God's sake, Bill?"

"Why, very simply, dear boy. If there hadn't been any Suez—if Hungary had blown up when everything was sweetness and light between us and the Americans—us and the French and the Americans . . . with what those CIA fellows were up to in Budapest—Christ! It could have been Poland in '39 again! . . . . Instead of which we took our chance at Suez, and offended the Yanks . . . and left the Russians a free hand in Hungary, thank God! But it was much too close for comfort, the Third World War. Much too close!"

"Over Hungary, Bill? Not over Suez?"

"Who'd want to die for Suez? Not the Russians. But they would have fought us over Hungary, no question—it's the one thing they're bound to fight over, to hold that frontier of theirs in the West, come hell or high water—that's why I was so bloody worried, young David. Because I've done my share, and I want to see old age and come safe home. And now at least I'll see peace in my time—"

Yet even shrewd old Bill had only seen the half of it, through the rose-tinted spectacles of a grateful survivor.

He had seen it all as a marvellous slice of luck—the Joint Russian Intentions and Policy sub-committee feeding back the vital and authentic information which had nerved the British and the French to chance their arm in Egypt in the certain knowledge that the Russians would only bark, and not bite, because of what was happening in Eastern Europe . . . which, in turn, was happening precisely at the time of an American presidential election.

But it hadn't been a slice of luck at all, it had been stage-managed from start to finish.

Because, turned round, it was Suez and the collapse of the Western alliance—however temporarily—which had been perfectly timed for the Russians, giving them the free hand they needed to bring the East Europeans to heel . . .

Even, now he thought about the final bungling efforts of Rakosi to suppress dissent . . . even *that* could have been stage-managed to coincide with Suez—turning the inevitable explosion into a controlled blast.

They'd all been set up—the British and the French and the Americans . . . and the poor bloody Hungarians, who had been shot down in the streets by the thousand, most of all!

"David . . ."

"Yes?" He didn't raise his head to look at her this time, because the thing was still continuing inside his brain, like a film which refused to end after the denouement.

"I'm sorry, David. I shot off my big mouth again."

That wasn't the end of it: he was part of it now—part of the continuation of the screwing process.

No wonder Genghis Khan was so pleased, and so determined to help Captain Roche to do his duty: he wouldn't only be placing the said Captain Roche—Major Roche to be—right inside Sir Eustace Avery's operation as a trusted officer who had proved his worth, *he would also be planting a source of deliberately-leaked information at the highest level, an unimpeachable source as proved and trusted as the new Major himself!*

The possibilities were endless—and irresistible—

"David . . ."

Damn the girl! Just as he was getting into his stride!

He raised his head and looked at her, and melted again immediately. And after all, he could afford to melt, for he had it all now, with the crowning opportunity of making a deal with the British which they couldn't resist either.

"Lexy?"

At least . . . he had it all if Genghis Khan and Audley now did their different jobs right. That thought brought him down to earth again with a bump.

"You're angry with me. I can see it in your face. But I don't blame you—I shot my stupid mouth off." She stared at him contritely. "I told you I was stupid."

"I'm not angry." That wasn't what she'd seen in his face: it was the face of treachery-in-doubt that she'd seen, poor kid. "And you're not stupid." And anyway . . . there was no reason why both men shouldn't do their jobs right: they each had sufficient incentive, by God!

"You looked black as thunder."

"I was thinking dark thoughts, that's why. But not about you." Once again, she relaxed his over-stretched nerves. And, in preparation for what was to come, they needed relaxing. "I couldn't think dark thoughts about you."

"What sort of thoughts—damn! I'm doing it again, aren't I!"

"Doing what?" He surrendered to the game.

"Sowing ideas. And I usually reap—or rape, as David Audley says—where I sow. But I'm tired of reaping and raping, even though I can't seem to stop sowing. So don't let's bother with thoughts, David darling."

"No bother. Sad, maybe . . . but no bother—my thoughts about you."

"Sad?"

"Unattainable, let's say." Because he had just been thinking of Bill Ballance, who had left half his right hand by the roadside between Nijmegen and Arnhem in '44, the war came to his rescue. "Speaking as a soldier . . . a bridge too far—or several bridges, possibly."

"Me? Unattainable?" Her eyes widened.

Her humility irritated him. It hadn't been the loss of Julie which had brought him to this pass—he could have lost her in any one of a hundred ways, and still not been vulnerable to the Comrades' offer after her death . . . . It was the *waste* of Julie which had been unforgivable—it was for that he had wasted his own life in an empty and foolish protest.

A ball splashed into the water, a yard from where he lay, where a sluggish back-current from the fierce flow in the centre caught it, turning it slowly.

A small boy, thin and brown as an Indian, tripped across the stones on small feet which made light of discomfort, to retrieve it.

The boy picked up the ball and looked shyly at Roche.

"Pardon, m'sieur!"

Roche nodded dismissively.

"M'sieur—là-bas—" the boy spoke breathlessly, nodding towards the trees on the bank beyond the expanse of stones on the flood-plain of the river and trying to keep his voice down to an urgent whisper at the same time "—M'sieur Galles vous attend!"

Roche stared back at him for a moment, observing that he held the ball one-handed now to keep whatever coin Galles had given him safe.

He nodded again, but solemnly this time, to keep the great secret between them intact, so that the coin would be fairly earned.

The boy looked back at him for another moment, huge-eyed with surprise that he hadn't immediately followed the direction of the nod, and then scampered away across the stones.

Roche looked at his watch on the towel beside him, and then slid it back on to his wrist. It was later than he had imagined, and he was glad of that because time had dragged on him, ticking away too slowly to H-Hour. Training and racial memory from a thousand battles in which he had never fought had prepared him for action at dawn, but never for combat over an early evening drink. But in the end God disposed the minute of the hour, and for the purposes of this great battle Genghis Khan was God, with Audley and Raymond Galles attending to the details in all innocence.

But he had to do it right: custom decreed that, and with Lexy there, almost at arm's-length, custom and inclination both—and even something more than that, maybe even Audley's Kipling-bred, self-denying honour.

He looked at his watch again, and still didn't look at the trees on the bank—he didn't need to look at them, he knew Galles was there waiting for him—but looked instead at Lexy.

The unattainable *Lady Alexandra Mary Henrietta Champeney-Perowne*, pink-and-blonde in her unsuitable scarlet bikini: she had heard what the little boy had said to him in that childish treble whisper, which mocked the secrecy he had been trying to achieve for half-a-crown in francs. Probably she had already looked where the boy had nodded, and she wasn't stupid, no matter what she said.

She didn't know—couldn't know the tenth of it, never mind the half of it. But it didn't matter now, whatever she guessed, or didn't guess, because he had nothing to lose now, anyway.

The last thought armoured him against any reaction she could have against what he was about to say, because he was at last truly angry with her.

He raised himself up on the towel.

"I've got to go—I've got work to do. You go back to the Tower—don't worry about my car, I'll collect it later—you go back and tell Audley I'm getting what he wants, and he's to wait for me there. Do you understand?"

"Yes, David." She sat up to match him, hair every-which-way, and busting-out-all-over-like-June, and cornered by realities she couldn't possibly comprehend; but neither subservient, nor concerned to vex him with silly questions about anything—least of all about herself.

"Your trouble, Lady Alexandra, is that you're selling yourself *cheap*, to clever bastards like Audley—and cheapskates like me. What you want to do is to sell yourself *dear*, to someone who understands your true value, damn it—if you want to be dear to anyone, then force the price up . . . be as expensive as you really are, Lady Alexandra!"

He turned from her, grabbed his clothes and headed for the gap in the trees, beyond the parked cars, towards which the little boy had nodded.

There was no one there, but he saw the little grey corrugated Citroen parked just off the track further down, near the main road, yet half-hidden by bushes.

So Galles was at pains not to advertise himself more than necessary now. But perhaps that was understandable, after what had happened to Miss Stephanides last night.

He looked at his watch again, trying to judge minutes against distances. As usual on such occasions, time was behaving erratically: it had gone slowly at first, and then it had speeded up while Lexy had taken his mind off it. But it was still too early for his final contact with Genghis Khan, and that was what mattered. Unless and until he could be sure that the man had superimposed his own plan on Audley's, he had to take things easily.

So . . . trousers first, and then socks and shoes . . . because a man without trousers couldn't face the world, and a man without shoes couldn't run away from it.

Then shirt and tie: shirt to make him respectable, tie to add formality, because a man in a Royal Signals tie was ready for anything and anywhere, even Le Château du Cingle d'Enfer.

He slung his coat over his shoulder, feeling the comforting weight of passport and wallet (a man with those could run faster and further), tucked his *bastide*-book and notes under his arm, and advanced in Full Service Marching Order towards the Citroen.

The engine was already running.

He bent down to the window. "What's all the hurry?"

Galles scowled at him. "Get in the car, m'sieur."

The little Citroen eased forward slowly, protesting at the potholes on the track, laboured up the incline on to the road, and then slammed him back in the seat as it accelerated away.

"What's all the hurry?" repeated Roche.

"No hurry, m'sieur." Galles had his foot down on the floor. "M'sieur Audley wishes me to say that he has telephoned M'sieur d'Auberon, and that M'sieur d'Auberon awaits your visit with the keenest interest, at 6.30 if that is convenient."

"Are we being followed?" inquired Roche, even though the question was superfluous, since Galles was already staring fixedly into the wing mirror.

"M'sieur Roche—" Galles continued to study the mirror "—I have been followed ever since I picked you up at the station yesterday. And I should guess that you have also been followed. Have you not noticed?"

"By whom?" Roche ignored the question of his own inadequacy.

"I do not know. To my shame, I failed to remark upon the coincidences until this morning. It . . . has been a long time, since the old days, m'sieur. I am not as suspicious as I once was."

Shit! thought Roche. It could hardly be the Comrades, or Genghis Khan would have told him so. Therefore it had to be . . . whoever had attended to Miss Stephanides . . . and that was frightening, even though Genghis Khan had promised to attend to them himself.

"A motor-cyclist, I think," said Galles. "Though I cannot see him at this moment."

Shit again! thought Roche. There were altogether too many faint motorcycle noises in his memory, from the last twenty-four hours back.

"Lose him, then," he commanded. This sort of thing, beyond a little checking before he made a carefully prepared contact, was out of his routine experience. He had never been a bloody cloak-and-dagger man.

"M'sieur . . . one does not lose a motor-cyclist—he has too many advantages. One *kills* motor-cyclists—nothing else will serve."

"Kills?"

"But yes! I killed one once—by accident, of course, you understand . . . on the blind corner before La Roque, it was . . . I braked to avoid a child who had run into the road—my cousin's little niece, it was—and there was a cement-lorry broken down on the other side of the road at that exact moment—the child ran out from behind it . . . so there was nowhere the motor-cyclist could go—he was travelling too fast, of course—and nothing anyone could do. It was a tragic accident, with no one to blame except the victim himself, poor fellow."

"Yes?"

Galles shrugged. "Well . . . it will take me at least twenty-four hours to find another niece, and another cement-lorry, if that is what you want, M'sieur Roche."

Roche reviewed the situation. A single follower was there to follow and observe. And Genghis Khan himself had required him to lay on an observer for what he had in mind, whatever it was—a reliable observer. So one more trained observer couldn't do too much harm.

"We'll go on—and let him follow." Long-forgotten OCTU training supported him: orders must always be given confidently, to encourage the other ranks' ill-founded belief that the officers know what is going on. "But I need a telephone at 6.15—I must report in before I see d'Auberon."

Galles gave him a searching look, as though to suggest that, however rusty and far-removed from tragic accidents he might be, he was too old a hand to cherish ill-founded beliefs.

"Go on, man!" He tried to meet the look arrogantly. "But just don't drive like a maniac any more. This is important, and I don't want to be part of any tragic accidents."

The look continued to search him. "Like that which befell Mademoiselle Meriel last night?"

The poor sod was as much in the dark about Steffy as everyone else, thought Roche. The years of peace since 'the old days' had not prepared him for a new generation of violence.

He shook his head. "I don't know about that. You think it wasn't an accident?"

"The Police say that it was. But I do not think so."

"Neither do I."

"Very well." Galles gave him another five seconds'-worth of doubt, and then reached under the dashboard. "M'sieur Audley sent this too, to introduce you to M'sieur d'Auberon."

Choses et Gens de la Dordogne et ses Pays, by Etienne d'Auberon

It was a rather slim, typically French rough-cut volume, rather dog-eared but unmarked by ownership—at a guess, Audley's own copy, because Audley would never bother to put his name in any book of his, it would be beneath his dignity.

He looked up *Le Château du Cingle d'Enfer* immediately in the index—

"*. . . high above the bend of the river, with the fertile river-plain on either side to supply it, which successive generations of d'Auberons terrorised to enable them to keep up the state of great barons . . .*"

"A motor-cyclist," said Galles. "Or perhaps a motor-cyclist and an *auto-cycliste*—I think we have maybe united two separate tails into one now, m'sieur."

Roche looked up, and couldn't identify his surroundings.

"Where are we?" he demanded.

"Just coming into Laussel-Beynac. You wished for a telephone, and I have a cousin here—"

"A public telephone," said Roche quickly, moving to minimise unacceptable risks. "That's the regulation."

Overhanging trees gave place to overhanging houses clinging to a steep hillside in the middle of nowhere.

"Over there," said Galles, pointing.

The telephone was beyond another 1914–18 Poilu, unsuitably overcoated and weighed down with equipment on the top of a marble plinth, standing guard aggressively on behalf of the men of Laussel-Beynac who had not come back from the Marne and the Aisne and the Somme to the Dordogne. He was, so far as Roche could recall, the same soldier who had presided over Neuville's dead *enfants*.

He tripped the switch in his memory to activate the number Genghis Khan had given him, from among the peach-boxes.

"David. For Johnnie." It seemed very strange indeed to think of Genghis Khan so innocently.

"Johnnie. For David—"

It wasn't Genghis Khan's voice, or any other voice that he could place. But it was *Johnnie for David* nevertheless.

He listened, and replaced the receiver without bothering to acknowledge, just letting *ersatz*-Johnnie cut him off.

Never again, Johnnie for David. That was the last time ever!

And now one other call—but at least *Johnnie for David* gave him strength for that—

"Hullo? Roche here."

He held on, studying the stained copper-green-and-grey soldier, forever *Mort pour la Patrie*. No one was going to remember Captain Roche that way, by God!

"Roche?"

It was Thompson, and that made it easier. If God wasn't an Englishman or a Frenchman at least He wasn't anti-Roche!

"Listen—you tell Stocker—"

"Hold on, old boy! You should have checked in this morning, you know! He's off-net at the moment, but he'll be back any time now. So call back in half an hour, and you'll get him, eh?" Thompson sounded a tiny bit rattled.

"I was busy this morning—and I can't wait now. Tell him I'm going in, to get what he wants—tell him that. Right?"

The *bastide*-fancier gobbled impotently for another rattled moment, and then took a grip of himself. "Do you want any back-up . . . for whatever it is?"

"Can you get back-up to Laussel-Beynac in five minutes?" Roche looked at his watch, almost happily.

"Where?"

"It doesn't matter. Our man down here is with me. Just tell the Major that. And I may not be able to call him again until tomorrow—you tell him that as well—" *By tomorrow I'll be long gone to ground, with a leaf or two taken out of d'Auberon's book too* "—right?"

"If you say so, old boy. But you sound a bit over-confident to me—"

"*Shit!*" Roche wasn't sure whether he'd put down the phone before or after he'd pronounced his last farewell to Thompson, but it no longer mattered.

He retrieved *Choses et Gens de la Dordogne et ses Pays* from the passenger's seat, and nodded encouragingly to Galles.

"It's okay. I'm cleared to go ahead. How far is it?"

"Three kilometres only." Galles glanced uneasily at his wing mirror. "Did they have any ideas about our followers?"

"Are they still there?" It would be as well to reassure the little Frenchman, even with lies, so that he could concentrate on seeing what he was required to see.

"I cannot see them. But they are there."

Not that what Galles saw, or didn't see, really mattered any longer either . . . But it would be better to go through with Genghis Khan's plan to the letter, just in case.

"I don't think we need worry too much about them." The memory of their meeting in Madame Peyrony's coach-house came to his rescue. "It's most likely the Americans keeping an eye on us, it seems. They won't try anything rough."

"No?" Galles sounded something less than disarmed by the forecast, possibly because of some wartime recollection of OSS roughness. "I hope you're right, m'sieur. But just in case . . . if what you are doing is so important . . ."

Roche watched him swivel to rummage in a large metal tool-box wedged behind him amongst a collection of jacks and crowbars and towing-ropes, finally to produce a sacking bundle secured with greasy twine.

"Good God, man!" He watched in horror as Galles produced an enormous military revolver and a tiny automatic pistol from the sacking. "We don't need those—we're not going to storm the château!"

"Here—" Galles offered him the little automatic, ignoring his reaction "—I will keep the man-stopper, you can put this in your pocket. It's only a Ruby—my cousin René brought it back from Spain in '38—it will do no one any harm, but it may make them think twice."

"Good God—*no!*" exclaimed Roche, hypnotised by the weapons. "We're not into that sort of thing!" He knew he had to make allowances for the vast arsenal of weaponry which defeat and occupation, not to mention well-supplied resistance, had distributed throughout France, but the casual appearance of small arms from a middle-aged mechanic's tool-box, from among the wrenches and screwdrivers, shook him nevertheless.

"Eh bien! So you suit yourself, m'sieur." Galles shrugged. "But I choose rather to be safe than sorry."

He closed the sacking loosely over the weapons and placed the bundle at his feet. "So now . . . just what exactly is it that you wish me to do, eh?"

"Drive to the château—" Roche swallowed nervously, then took hold of himself "—and drop me off in the parking area in front of the main gate . . . do you know it?"

"Yes, m'sieur. The new parking area which M'sieur d'Auberon has had prepared for the tourists—there is building work in progress still on the gate-house—"

"That's right." Galles' information tallied with Genghis Khan's. "You wait for me there. That's all you have to do, *mon vieux*."

"It is . . . a pick-up?"

That was a perfect question, better even than he could have imagined. "Yes. And we are picking up dynamite, I can tell you."

Galles touched the sacking with his toe. "Then we will make your pick-up, m'sieur—never fear!"

Roche used up the last three kilometres inside *Choses et Gens*.

Most obligingly (though no doubt by design, now that he intended to convert Le Château du Cingle d'Enfer into a tourist-trap, milking foreigners where his *hobereaux* ancestors had once composed the peasants out of their money), Etienne d'Auberon had included a plan of the château.

"*. . . the outer courtyard, reached by way of a ruined gate-house of formidable proportions, leads the visitor to a second and more attractive gateway, built in the Renaissance style, bearing the family motto 'Solum perfectum me attrahit' intertwined among delicate devices . . .*"

So he had two gateways to pass—

"*. . . the interior of the château, soon to be opened to the public for the first time, comprises a succession of noble rooms, furnished with the everyday objects of life in the XVI, XVII and XVIII centuries, including priceless tapestries, furniture and family portraits . . .*"

Either the château had somehow escaped the excesses of the French Revolution, or the present owner was lying through his teeth! But here, once again, was illustrated that unrivalled ability of the French to triumph over adversity . . . and he could only hope that his own diluted French blood would do the same for him.

"We are close, m'sieur."

Roche craned his neck to take in the view. They had left the last houses of Laussel-Beynac behind among the trees, and had twisted and turned in a series of hairpin bends to rise above a great *cingle* of the river, to bring into view the towers of the château ahead.

The last turn opened up the new parking area, bulldozed out from the hillside on the peasants' side of a great dry moat which had been cut across the limestone headland on which the castle itself had been built to command the river valley.

The medieval defences of the castle lay directly ahead, wreathed in scaffolding, with a lorry in the foreground from which men were even now unloading bags of cement, and with the delicate conical towers of the Renaissance château he had glimpsed earlier rising in the background.

He was oddly reminded of The Old House, which was so absolutely different and so English, but which was the same for all that: possession of these *things*—Le Château du Cingle d'Enfer and The Old House at Steeple Horley—could twist some men out of true self-interest, just as any abstract ideas could delude others, like himself and Genghis Khan, who had no such *things* of their own, into other follies.

The distant sound of a motor-cycle, somewhere behind him in the trees on the twists and turns, recalled him to reality.

He picked up *Choses et Gens* and his own *bastide* nonsense, and walked round the Citroen to the driver's window.

"Just you keep your eye on that gateway. When I come out of there I don't want to hang about admiring the view—you understand?"

He didn't wait for Galles to acknowledge the instruction, but launched himself straightway towards the first gate.

"The visitor will observe the gun-ports, pierced low in the gateway by Jean d'Auberon, who died with Robert de Montal at the battle of Pavia in 1525 . . ."

He observed the gun-ports.

And he also observed the cement-bag carriers, who took no more note of him than the peach-box carriers outside Neuville.

Under the shadow of the archway ahead—*"rebuilt by Etienne III d'Auberon, who led the best shots in France in the hunt for the last wolf of the Dordogne, in 1774"*—there was a pile of cement bags, laid away safe from any August rain, as Genghis Khan's man had said they would be.

He paused halfway down, out of sight of everyone, as though to adjust the tightness of one shoelace, and picked up the brief-case planted between the bags.

It was dusty with a fine powder of cement, and the key was in the lock. He turned the key and put it into his trouser pocket, dusted down the case with his hand, as he straightened up, and stepped out briskly into the light of the inner courtyard beyond.

It was only a matter of ten seconds, but he had it now—*King, Cawdor, Glamis, all*—he could turn round and run now!

He continued on towards the 'Solum perfectum me attrahit' doorway, tucking the d'Auberon book and the *bastide* material more comfortably under his arm. A thing done right was a thing done well, Mrs Clarke had said.

There was a heavy bronze dolphin knocker on the great door. He looked back across the courtyard and saw that the cement carriers were back on their job.

A small grill clicked open in the door, startling him.

"Captain David Roche—for M'sieur d'Auberon." He projected the pass-word into the grill, slightly off-put by the pink scalp which was all he could see through it. "M'sieur Audley has telephoned, I think?"

Heavy bolts echoed on the inside. Getting into the château, with all its ancient treasures and its more lethal post-Suez *objets d'art*, was not just for casual callers.

There were three steps forward, and then two steps down, over white Carennac marble into the hall, while the great door crashed shut behind him.

". . . and its greatest architectural beauty is the splendid Renaissance stair-case, which comprises a superb transition between the spiral and the stair in flights, as at Montal . . ."

"If M'sieur le Capitaine will come this way?" The little bald man who had peered up at him through the grill, grey-coated and black-trousered, indi-cated a door to his left.

Roche regretted desperately that he had come so far, but he was trapped now beyond all thought of retreat.

". . . a succession of noble rooms . . ."

Here he was in one of them, complete with tapestries on one side, and a breath-taking view beyond the river on the other!

"M'sieur d'Auberon will attend you here shortly, M'sieur le Capitaine." The second door closed behind him.

Door—enormous windows, with five-mile views across the river—vast carved fireplace . . . and an immense faded tapestry picturing heavily-armed Renaissance Romans martyring naked Christians in ingenious ways . . .

But he hadn't come to admire d'Auberon's treasures. There was a huge oak table in the centre of the room, on heavily carved legs. He walked towards it quickly, first dumping the *bastide* notes and *Choses et Gens* on top, then tucking the brief-case down out of the way behind one of the legs, feeling for all the world like Stauffenberg planting his bomb under the table in the Fuehrer's bunker.

Only, unlike Stauffenberg, the moment he'd abandoned the brief-case he wanted to pick it up again. The thought of letting it out of his grasp even for a second left him desolate, clenching the empty hand which had relin-quished it into a tight fist in a reflex against temptation.

He felt the temptation grow. It wasn't really necessary at all, this

237

charade—he was still obeying Genghis Khan when the man's orders no longer mattered—when nothing mattered except the possession of that brief-case—

A sound outside the room straightened him up just as his hand started to unclench.

"Captain Roche?"

Roche turned slowly towards the sound.

"Captain Roche—what a pleasure! You are David Audley's friend? Or, more accurately, Miss Baker's friend?"

He hadn't consciously tried to imagine what Etienne d'Auberon would be like, beyond vague instinctive images founded on what Lexy and Madame Peyrony had let slip, crossed with his own experience of superior Quai d'Orsay types.

"M'sieur d'Auberon." He mouthed some sort of reply, letting the Frenchman come towards him while moving only slightly himself so as to mask the brief-case more effectively.

"And staying with him, in the Tower? While on leave from Paris, he said?" D'Auberon's handshake was firm and dry, and neither too strong nor too weak, like the man himself. Roche found himself recalling another of Bill Ballance's *obiter dicta*, on the Anglo–French love-hate complex: *'the best Frenchman is the one you can admire as an enemy if you can't have him as a friend'*.

But meanwhile he had replied again, one half of his brain working automatically to make the necessary conversation along lines already planned while the other half tried to betray him.

"Ah, yes—our *bastides*. And there is nothing recent written on them in English? You are lucky David Audley hasn't thought of that. He is a most able historian . . . but then his interests are strictly Merovingian, aren't they?"

Far beneath the surface of the words Roche sensed the truth of what he already knew, that d'Auberon and Audley admired each other in enmity, not as friends.

He replied once more, and saw d'Auberon smile, and the smile hurt him. For *d'Auberon* was another name in the list of his betrayals, as surely as if there had been a bomb in that brief-case. And if there was another thing that was sure, it was that this man would never be in the business of betraying anyone—Audley had been wrong even to imagine it as a possibility, and Genghis Khan had been right to reject the idea. He didn't know how he knew it, but he knew it.

More pleasantries and agonised conversation. And then d'Auberon's eye fell on *Choses et Gens*.

"I see you have my little book. *Not* a great work, I'm afraid—it bears the stamp of too many official reports, without style . . . it is just another pile of facts, without interpretation." D'Auberon gestured round the room, and towards the window. "All this is beautiful . . . but what does it mean?"

The pretentiousness of the question surprised Roche: it seemed out of the man's character. But at last it broke the spell, enabling him to unite the two parts of his brain. What did it matter, what happened to a stranger, compared with what happened to him?

"I thought it was fascinating—how one of your ancestors led the king's huntsman to kill 'the Beast of Gevaudan' . . . and about the château itself, of course."

"Would you like to see the house? And then a glass of something?"

The predictable responses hardened Roche's heart finally. He looked at his watch guiltily, to confirm that enough minutes had elapsed to run d'Auberon out of time. "That's very kind of you . . . but—most unfortunately—I am required to be back at the Tower. I merely wished to make myself known to you . . . if perhaps you could provide me with some introductions—particularly in Monpazier and Villeréal . . . there's no hurry—" the words tumbled out as he scooped up the book and the *bastide* papers, blocking off d'Auberon's view of the table leg "—another time, perhaps?"

His bad manners creased a tiny frown on to d'Auberon's forehead. "Another time—of course, Captain."

It was a little more difficult to force the Frenchman into leading the way out, so that he could still mask the case, but he managed it with a mixture of English clumsiness and lack of *savoir faire*, and the genuine nervousness and reluctance he felt in abandoning the most precious object on earth.

In the end d'Auberon positively strode ahead, out into the entrance hall, irritated by his gaucheness, and Roche's last view of the room was agonisingly rewarded with the sight of the thing poking out from under the table like a sore thumb.

The little bald door-keeper was hovering in attendance at the entrance.

"I will see m'sieur out, Martin," said d'Auberon brusquely.

Roche hurried after him into the courtyard. "The trouble is, you see . . . my car broke down by the river, where I was bathing with Lady Alexandra—" (another strike against d'Auberon was that he hadn't zeroed in on Lexy, as any sensible man should have done, and as her father and Madame Peyrony might well have intended; or was that a strike *for* him, damn it?) "—so I had to get a lift here . . . and that's why I'm so late, you see—"

"A lift?" D'Auberon was halfway across the courtyard already, eager to get rid of Captain Roche from the premises.

"With Lady Alexandra's garage man. He's waiting for me, to take me back to the Tower," said Roche breathlessly.

D'Auberon stopped alongside the pile of cement bags. "What?"

"I had to get a lift here." Roche feigned embarrassment. "*Oh—damn!*"

"What?" The vehemence of Roche's *damn* caught d'Auberon's attention. "What's the matter?"

"I'm an idiot!" Roche turned embarrassment to apology. "I've left my

brief-case behind—with all my other stuff in—I put it down somewhere—"
he looked around him helplessly, and finally back towards the door of the
château "—it was by the table, I think—"

D'Auberon regarded him with a suggestion of weariness, which was then
overtaken by good-mannered tolerance as Roche grimaced apologetically
at him.

"I'm so sorry." The words put the matter beyond argument.

"It is no matter. I will go and get it." D'Auberon shrugged and turned on
his heel.

Roche's legs, still programmed by Genghis Khan, carried him on past the
cement bags, into the light beyond the arched tunnel of the gate-house. The
lorry had gone, and the parking area was empty except for the little grey
Citroen. He could see Raymond Galles' face turned towards him.

He felt almost played out, but in the last minute of the game, when the
team which was going to win was the one which forced itself to play harder.
Facing Galles, he raised his hand across his stomach and damped down the
man's expectations with a palm-down signal.

The light had lost its brightness, which he had first seen this morning
dissipating the mist on the road from Neuville to Cahors. It was like the field
where he had been sick the evening before, just in advance of Lexy's arrival.
Now he felt sick again—sick with all the different prospects ahead of him, in
which Lexy could never take part.

But really there were only two prospects; either d'Auberon would come
back, or he wouldn't.

When he did—he had to think only of that—*when* he did, all that
remained was to drive back to Audley, and fob him off with success . . . and
that would win him another day, at the least—maybe more, since both sides
trusted him, and when he didn't surface each would worry first about what
the other one might have done to him, and by the time either of them started
to smell a rat he'd be long gone to ground, and ready to deal for his
survival—

Long gone, Julie—

And *long gone, Lexy—*

And *long gone*, all the rest of them—the man on the beach in Japan and
all his successors down to Genghis Khan; and the man in the British
Embassy in Tokyo, and all his successors down to Sir Eustace Avery and
Colonel Clinton; and David Audley and Etienne d'Auberon—and the hell
with all of them!

No more self-pity, just self-interest and the future—no longer the past or
the might-have-been, no more deluding himself with silly ideas—there was
no more time for any of that—

In the stillness he heard the door under *Solum perfectum me attrahit* close
again behind him in the distance, through the arched gate-house and the
courtyard.

Raymond Galles, and whoever else was there to witness the transaction, was still watching him. And the only thing that worried him was the faintest suggestion of doubt which had been in d'Auberon's eyes as he turned away.

"Here you are, Captain Roche—one brief-case!"

Roche's left hand, feeling in his pocket among his loose change, closed over the key. It was the same case, and there hadn't been time for anyone to pick the lock, even if anyone had had reason to pick it.

His right hand took the case for Galles to see. He had entered the château without it, but now he was leaving with it—*and d'Auberon had given it to him*.

The thing was done—and if anyone else was watching, it could only be Genghis Khan's man who had witnessed it, he decided. And that would just give him even more time.

"Just one thing—"

Another thing? He looked at d'Auberon questioningly, the case weighing down his arm to his side, but there was something else weighing down his mind at the same time.

"Why did you really come to see me, Captain Roche?"

"I beg your pardon?" He heard the lack of conviction in his own voice.

"It's simply that . . . I've never seen a man more nervous than you, Captain—underneath the polite civilities, that is." D'Auberon smiled— half-smiled—at him. "But of course you don't have to tell me . . . though you make me nervous too, because now I come to think of it, there is one man you remind me of: he despatched me into the Chausse Mejean in '43, to work with the Bir Hakim maquis when things were bad—and that only makes me more nervous."

"Why?" He knew what the other thing was: it had been there in the back of his mind ever since the plan had taken shape.

"Why? Well . . . I think he thought the Germans were waiting for me. And so they were . . . but the drop went wrong—there was low cloud and we never saw the dropping zone, so I jumped almost blind, and broke my ankle five miles away, falling through a pigsty roof outside Brassac. A fortunate disaster . . . but he didn't know that when I jumped, you see."

Roche hardly heard him. He was trapped by his own knowledge of what the Comrades must do next.

Up until now they had had no incentive to do anything about Etienne d'Auberon, with his secret already safely in their possession; if anything, he was more useful to them alive than dead. But now . . . it was always possible that sooner or later the British would get round to checking Captain Roche's story, just to be on the safe side, in spite of Galles' eye-witness account of the transfer. Then it would be his word against d'Auberon's, but even if they took his word there would always be a niggling doubt—and there would be no place for any niggling doubts in Sir Eustace Avery's operations.

"What is your work in Paris, Captain?" D'Auberon weakened enough to

241

ask directly the question which must have been uppermost in his mind from the start.

Simply, they couldn't afford to leave the Frenchman alive now. They wouldn't do it today or tomorrow—they'd allow just enough time to allow Roche to win his spurs, but not a minute more—maybe the day after tomorrow, trusting that the French themselves would handle the problem of the other two copies. But they would do it.

"I shouldn't be here." He felt strangely relieved to hear his own voice. "I shouldn't be here . . . but we owe you."

"You owe me?" D'Auberon seemed puzzled.

"Audley does, anyway." He'd promised not to mention Audley's role in this, but he hadn't promised anything else. "From the war."

"Mon Dieu! He doesn't still remember that, does he!" D'Auberon reacted as Audley had predicted he would do at the mention of his name.

"It doesn't matter. The fact is, the Russians know what you've got. So you'd best go to ground somewhere safe—at once."

"The Russians?" With the thirty-foot walls of his home behind him d'Auberon didn't appear scared.

But there was one sure way of changing that. "The KGB."

To his chagrin, he watched d'Auberon's face relax. "The KGB? My dear Captain Roche—the Russians are the least of my worries! There might be some people who could misunderstand the situation . . . owing to the nature of my work when I resigned . . . but not the Russians—not *them*, of all people, Captain."

Roche was already beginning to regret his idiotic moment of altruism. If the KGB didn't frighten the man, then nothing would.

D'Auberon was almost smiling. "Obviously, you've never read my report—obviously!"

His report? But if that was the encyphered part of the papers weighing him down now . . . then the Comrades would have broken it long since, with all the advanced Enigma machines they captured in '45.

"But you came to warn me—and on your own initiative?" The suggestion of amusement was suddenly tempered by an even more humiliating cast of gratitude. "So . . . my people haven't ever told the British—in spite of everything?" In turn, gratitude became tempered by anger. "Even in spite of my resignation?"

Roche held his tongue.

"Oh yes, Captain—that was also part of it. It was mostly Algeria, but it was also the matter of my report, which should not have been withheld from your people in the circumstances—not in *any* circumstances, in honour—no matter that your Government had so shamefully withdrawn from the Egyptian operation—so *shamefully!*" He shook his head at Roche, the very incarnation of Bill Ballance's 'best Frenchman' sorrowing over a once-honourable enemy's declension into the role of dishonourable ally.

Roche wondered nervously about what Raymond Galles would be mak-

242

ing of this exchange, even while not knowing what to make of it himself.

"So . . . it is still a matter of honour. But you have changed the rules now, Captain—because now it is *I* who owe *you*. And if the Russians know everything, then it is only right that the British should know everything also, I think."

This was going to be something Genghis Khan hadn't told him, thought Roche. But then no bugger had told him *everything*, but mostly as little as possible. It was this old-fashioned Frenchman's weird sense of personal honour—and his own equally inexplicable rush-of-blood-to-the-head—which was going to blow the gaff.

"You see, Captain, I handled all the special material from Moscow last year, from spring to late autumn—it came through the diplomatic bag, it was judged too important for any other method—and also too important to pass directly to the British. Commandant Roux and I made a digest of it for them."

Good old Philippe! So that settled one outstanding problem very simply: Philippe had been the stage-manager.

"Then I was promoted, to take charge of our plans for the fortification of the Tunisian frontier, as a reward for my good work . . ."

It had been promotion all round for the RIP beneficiaries of the 'special material' from Moscow, naturally—Eustace Avery and Etienne d'Auberon both!

"But then I started to think about it—all that had happened, and how it had gone wrong for us."

That was where Avery and d'Auberon had parted company, thought Roche grimly: Avery had capitalised on his *good work*, and d'Auberon had started to think about it. And now, one step ahead of the Frenchman's debt repayment, he knew what was coming.

"I managed to draw the file out—nobody had any reason to question that, as I'd written most of it myself."

Philippe Roux had been slow off the mark there.

"The truth is, Captain, we were 'taken for a ride', as the Americans say. Everything we got from Moscow was correct—it was genuine top-level material—but it was deliberately given to us to direct our policies in a particular direction, and we never questioned it. And, as a result, we gave the Russians a free hand in Central Europe . . . and ruined ourselves into the bargain. *That* was the report I wrote—you understand?"

Roche understood—he even understood more than d'Auberon was actually telling him. "So what happened then?"

The Frenchman shrugged. "It was not welcomed, I regret to say . . . And then there were other troubles, related to my new job."

I'll bet there were! thought Roche. Philippe—good old Philippe!—couldn't abolish the report once it had been written, but he would have made up for lost time in every other way, by God! Etienne d'Auberon was much too smart to be allowed to prosper: short of killing him, which would have made too many people suspicious at the time, he had to be discredited.

He didn't want to hear any more—*he wanted to get away from here, and think about what he knew now, which he hadn't known before*—

"There's no need to tell your people all that, though." D'Auberon looked at him a little uncertainly, as though the enormity of what he had let slip for honour's sake was beginning to come home to him. "Get them to analyse all the transcripts of the joint discussions—we gave them a lot of what we got. If someone really good does that, then he should be able to reach the same conclusions as I did."

It had been a mistake to let the man live that first time, whatever the risk, thought Roche. Beyond all doubt now, the Comrades wouldn't make the same mistake twice. But there was no way of explaining it to him.

"I still think the KGB's interested in you," he compromised, paying as much of his new debt as he dared. "And you never know what they're up to."

D'Auberon shook his head. "What I know, Captain . . . they know that already—better than either of us, I fear."

Roche felt the woods at his back. In a couple of days' time d'Auberon would come out here to admire the progress of the restoration of his 'ruined gatehouse of formidable proportions', and some sharp-eyed, telescopic-sighted hireling would put an end to that illusion. But there was nothing more he could say to prevent it, without saying too much for his own good.

"If you think so." He turned away, wanting to reach the Citroen, yet still aware of the weight of guilt in the brief-case.

A thought surfaced, as his hand touched the door handle, turning him round to face his brother-under-the-skin for the last time—they were both just as foolish really—nothing could be more foolish than the pair of them, but he couldn't let it go at that.

"Meriel Stephanides was killed in a car crash last night," he threw the news across the widening distance between them. "But it wasn't an accident—she was working for the Israelis."

D'Auberon could bloody well make what he liked out of that.

XVII

HE FELT THE shakes coming on just as they were passing the overburdened poilu on the war memorial in the square at Laussel-Beynac, so to give his hands something to do, he made a great production of producing the key and unlocking the brief-case on his knees.

"Well . . . let's see what we've got, then!" He riffled through the thick file of official French and the thinner folder of encyphered gibberish.

244

"That's it!" He relocked the case. "I didn't think he'd give it to us, but he did!"

Once he started to negotiate with the British, then they would take Galles to pieces bit by bit to reconstruct every detail of this journey, back over every word he'd said. But it didn't really matter now what they thought. Getting away was all that mattered—Genghis Khan's clever scheme had become as irrelevant as Avery's original intention. He no longer needed either of them—he was free of them both at last. All he had to do was think straight.

"Go back to the river," he ordered Galles. "I want to pick up my car."

His hands were steadier now, clasping the brief-case to his chest.

All he had to do was think straight—

Item: If d'Auberon did go to ground, after that last flurry of half-truth, then that would do no harm—it would only give him more time;

Item: If he didn't go to ground, and the Comrades did what he was pretty damn sure they would do, then so much the better—it would give him all the time in the world!

(In retrospect, he still didn't know why he'd warned d'Auberon to start running, when he didn't need to do it, and it had been against his better judgement, and he didn't owe the man a damn thing; and yet—which was even more baffling—he didn't regret doing it . . .)

But—*item*—why was Genghis Khan so delighted—not merely resigned, but delighted—to surrender all this to Sir Eustace Avery?

Just to get Roche in position?

Shit! The question answered itself as soon as it was asked! Of course getting Roche inside was important. But it was knowing the nature of the gift—and knowing the nature of Sir Eustace Avery, that 'great survivor'— that had delighted Genghis Khan.

The Comrades weren't giving up anything important, after all, because d'Auberon's report had effectively destroyed the value of the Moscow source for ever—because they could never be sure that word of it hadn't been leaked to the British.

Indeed, *maybe it had* . . . maybe *that* was why Sir Eustace was so desperate to get his hands on it as his own special possession?

Because it was still vitally important to *him*, of all people, as the proof that in reality the Russians had made a monkey of him—and that he'd made a monkey of the Prime Minister in turn, and got a knighthood for it as a reward!

Not even a 'great survivor' could survive that, if it got into hostile hands first. But in his own hands, with time to think and plan and shift responsibility . . . that was something else . . .

Maybe he was doing the man an injustice. But it didn't matter, because his reaction would be the same, either way, given his will to survive—*and that was what Genghis Khan was counting on, to give him the edge on the head of the whole Avery operation, with Roche at the heart of it to monitor progress.*

It wasn't bad—it was good.

Even, it was better than good—it was getting better and better and better, right up to the very best he could have imagined: with this he could make his own terms, and write his own ticket—with a little care, and a little time, and only a little more luck, nothing could stop him.

(It had been a mistake to warn d'Auberon, and he regretted it now. But he would make no more such mistakes.)

In fact, the only thing that could stop him was if Raymond Galles ran out of road.

"Steady on—you're driving like a maniac." He realised that his body, as well as his thoughts, had been rolling madly from side to side.

"We're still being followed. I don't like being followed." The time spent outside the château had evidently frayed the little Frenchman's nerves.

Roche peered around him. "This isn't the way we came. How close are we to the river?"

"We aren't going back to the river."

"But I want to pick up my car, damn it."

"We're not going back there . . . all alone there . . . if what you've got is so important. I am to look after you, and that is what I'm doing."

"What the hell d'you mean?"

"I mean, m'sieur, that it was unwise of you to receive that thing which you are holding . . . to receive it with such pleasure . . . in the open, for all to see." Galles twisted the wheel savagely. "Because . . . if that is what you have been waiting for, then perhaps . . . that is what *they* are waiting for . . . I think."

That made uncomfortable logic, because he still didn't know for sure who *they* were, or why they had been waiting, even though Genghis Khan had promised to attend to *them*.

"So what are you doing?"

"I am taking you back to the Tower, where there are other people—first. . . . You will be safe there . . . and also, in that little car of yours you would never be able to get away from anyone, if it came to that."

More irrefutable logic. "And then?"

"And then, when it is dark, I will bring you the other car, which I have ready for you. Then you will have the necessary petrol and performance, if that is what you require."

Roche estimated his capabilities as a getaway driver. "But you said no one loses a motor-cyclist—"

"Also by then *I* shall have made certain preparations . . . . You may rest assured that you will not be followed far. And there will be a man with you, to guide you wherever you wish to go . . . And there will be no *motor-cyclists*." Galles pronounced the last word through his teeth. "I may be getting old—and I have been careless, to my shame . . . but this is still my patch, m'sieur."

Was his *patch*? For once Roche's vocabulary faltered. Country—piece of land—playing-field—home-ground—stamping ground—*killing-ground—burial plot—*?

Madame Peyrony had said almost the same thing. But whatever the word meant, it meant the same thing: that strangers came into it at their peril, and that these strangers now were in line to discover something about *les choses et gens de la Dordogne et ses pays* which would never figure in any guidebook.

"He is hanging back now—I haven't lost him, but we are getting close to the Tower, so he thinks he knows where we are going," murmured Galles, steadied by the prospect of vengeance. "Around the next corner I will accelerate, and then I will stop quickly and you will get out quickly, and drop down out of sight even more quickly . . . and then I will be gone, and he will not be quite sure whether we have not been perhaps a little clever, to deceive him, one way or the other. Because he knows now that I know he is behind me."

"He knows?"

"Oh yes—I have played this game before, I told you—he knows! It is like the old days . . . so we will play a small trick on him from those days: when he turns the corner and sees neither you nor this vehicle by the roadside it is possible that he may think we have decided to make a run for it after all, eh?"

Now he sounded almost as though he was beginning to enjoy himself, thought Roche resentfully, more irritated than frightened by the unexpected requirement to take part in such cloak-and-dagger activity just when everything had at last begun to seem straightforward.

But so long as he needed the man it would be as well to humour his hankering after the excitement of the old days.

"Very well."

"Good!" Galles dropped a gear unhurriedly as the little Citroen began to labour up the final incline on to the shoulder of the ridge. The view opened up at Roche's elbow, across the valley to the other side, which he had first glimpsed this morning in Audley's company; then the distant ridge opposite had risen out of the dawn mist and now it was sinking into evening blueness, with the first lights twinkling on it. It would be dark in less than an hour.

Galles turned the wheel slowly. "Be ready!"

The engine surged with a sudden burst of power just as Roche caught sight of the Tower ahead, standing alone in the open, slightly downhill to his left. It looked dark and untenanted under its conical hat of black tiles—perhaps Audley was waiting for him in the cottage—?

"Brace yourself—" the Frenchman held the wheel tightly with both hands "—I will return in one hour—or not more than two—bonne chance, m'sieur—*now*!"

Roche had one hand on the door handle, with the other still clasping the brief-case to his chest, as Galles stood on his brakes. The truck's tyres slithered on the loose gravel at the side of the narrow road, and a tree sprouting out of a tangled blackberry bush flashed past his face.

The urgency of the whole procedure, rather than the idea behind it, threw him out of the vehicle. While he was still straightening up, before he could turn to slam the door, he heard it snap shut behind him—his last impression had been of Galles reaching across after him—and the truck was moving again. He stopped thinking about it instantly, and concentrated only on making himself scarce in a few yards of ground which he had seen only once before in daylight, and never studied with that aim in view.

But Galles had known it well enough, and had allowed for that: the Tower was fifty yards away down the track, and the cottage itself another fifty or more, both in the open and too far off to be worth a second glance. But the blackberry tangle was thick and in full leaf.

Three strides forward and two—three—sideways carried him away and down from sight of the road, into the long grass behind it, in automatic obedience to instructions.

He held his breath, and for a moment heard the blood pounding in his ears . . . and then exhaled slowly . . . and heard only the already distant sound of the Citroen's engine fading into the trees down the road, halfway to the Château Peyrony already.

There was no other sound—no other sound within miles, by the absence of sound—least of all a bloody motor-cycle making up for lost time!

Roche counted off his heart-beats, through another minute, while regaining his breath. During the minute a sound did register . . . of a dog barking far away, angry at something—something which was most likely a grey *garagiste* Citroen being driven too fast, with imaginary motor-cyclists in hot pursuit.

He sat up behind the blackberry bush, feeling more angry with himself than with Galles—if they'd given him a superannuated old fool, living in the past on memories of outsmarting the Gestapo and the Milice, then what else could he expect? He could only hope that Audley and his cronies hadn't witnessed the whole charade.

Still no sound. He rose to his feet and brushed himself down irritably, observing that he had scuffed the knees of his clean slacks with grass stains.

Not a whisper of sound. The road was clear, and the woods on the other side of it dark and empty with that peculiar evening stillness which always presaged the awakening of the night-hunting creatures.

He sighed, and picked up the brief-case. Because of the Frenchman's imagination he had another hour to kill—and an unnecessary hour too, in Audley's awkward company . . . and Audley, being Audley, would surely want to have a look inside the case!

Well . . . he could kill that idea stone-dead by pulling rank—captain now, but major-to-be—because as yet Audley had no rank, he was still just a bloody civilian, nothing more.

He smiled to himself as he set off down the track. Not major-to-be, but major-never-to-be, thank God!

Also, the cottage was as dark as the Tower, even though Audley's ugly black Morris Cowley was parked outside it. With just a bit of luck, the man would be busy making his farewells to Madame Peyrony and the girls down the road, and he wouldn't have to bother with him at all. He would leave him high and dry, in the middle of another great British intelligence disaster—that would be good training for him, if it didn't put him off altogether—

The sound of the motor-cycle engine shattered his rosy dream into fragments.

It swung him round in disbelief, like a hand on his shoulder, and the dream-fragments flew together again into nightmare as he saw men behind him on the road, which had been empty a few seconds before—

The disbelief and the nightmare became real instantaneously as the sight-line between them met, and they saw that he had seen them.

He was right alongside the Tower, where the stone steps leading up to the door met the track, and the door itself—the heavy oak door—stood invitingly ajar, offering him protection as nothing else did, beyond any second thought.

His feet took off, every muscle and sinew springing them so that he hit the door with his shoulder to burst it inwards as though it had been closed against it—

The door crashed back into darkness—not quite darkness, but yellow light—faces and people and yellow light and darkness, which registered for an instant, utterly confused, and then exploded into a chaos of ear-splitting noise—and he was falling into the chaos, with something soft under him—

—yellow light flared up, screaming at him—and the thing under him was no longer soft, it was insanely alive, with its sharp nails raking his face across forehead and cheek, and nails then turning into fingers grabbing at his throat—

—the light and the noises meant nothing any more—the fingers were digging into him, sickening him with unexpected pain—

—he swept them aside—they were feeble, compared with his pain—and caught his own fingers into hair, twining them in it as he smashed the thing now in his hands on to the floor again and again—again and again and again—until there was a different feel about it, and the pain had gone from his neck, and what was under him was soft and boneless again—

Words came into his head, through his own shuddering breath—

"The bolts—bolt the door!" The hoarse cry was cut off by a tremendous *crash* just behind him somewhere.

249

"I've done it!" Another voice—a boy's voice, shrill with fear, answered.

"Get away from it, Jilly—get away from it!"

The light wasn't light—it was orange fire flaring up from the floor, from the ruin of a lamp—fire and acrid smoke swirling up, lighting and obscuring at the same time.

Another *crash* behind him—

"Get away from the door!" The voice lifted. "Now!"

Another *crash*. Then a pause, and a sharp *crack-crack-crack*—

"Yes, David . . ."

The name roused Roche. "What?"

"Roche?"

Roche's scattered senses came back to him. "Audley?"

"Mike?" The vague presence behind the voice and the smoke and flame rose up into the semblance of a man crunching something broken under his feet. "Mike?"

"God damn—*aw, shit*—God damn—" the voice trailed off into a mixture of exasperation and anguish, unintelligibly.

"Lexy?"

Roche looked down at what lay beneath him, in sudden horror.

The flames illuminated a strange dark face, open-mouthed, eyes open but rolled back, with his fingers still entwined in the long black hair.

"Lexy?" said Audley again.

Another *crash* at the door—

"Don't worry about that—it'll take more than muscle to move it . . ." Audley's voice levelled ". . . and bullets."

Crack-crack-crack—the three paper-bags exploded again, the last one metallically, as though soft steel had splayed out against hard iron.

Roche pulled his hands away in horror from the thing he was still holding, the hair dragging at his fingers before it released them.

"You better do something about that goddamn lamp—or we'll choke if we don't burn," said the American thickly.

"Put the carpet on it," ordered Audley. "I'll get my torch—put the carpet on it, Mike!"

"Put the fucking carpet on it yourself—" the American's voice cracked. "—I'm hit—I'm hit, God damn it!"

"You're hit?"

"Christ, man! He squeezed off half his magazine—where the hell d'you think it went?" The voice came back, this time with the anger momentarily blotting out the pain. "Jesus Christ!"

"Roche!" Audley dismissed his friend from the reckoning.

But Roche was already moving—as much to get away from the thing underneath him: if he smothered the flames then he would smother the sight of that also.

The centre of the room was a shambles— the whole room was a shambles, with the human beings in it thrown to the wall by the sudden explosion of

250

fire and violence. But he could see, by the flames themselves, that the lamp had fallen off the carpet on to the floorboards, spreading fire around it.

It felt like an expensive carpet, but he ripped it up all the same and flopped it down on the fire, stamping fiercely on it to smother the flames.

Darkness enveloped him at once—the shattered bowl he could hear and feel under his feet must have been almost empty of paraffin to give up so easily. Then a beam of light blinded him. *Typical Audley—not to fill the lamp—*

Then the light left him, swinging round the room to pick out the American first.

He was backed up against the wine rack, sitting on the floor, covered with blood—

No, *covered with wine*, which had cascaded down on him from the smashed bottles behind him—his hair was plastered down with it, and his shirt was soaking with it.

He blinked in the beam, and lifted a hand still clutching an automatic pistol to shield his eyes. "Did I get the son-of-a-bitch? But I think he's broken my fucking arm—" the shielding pistol-holding hand moved across his body to touch his shoulder "—Christ! So he has!"

The torch swung back to Roche. "You took the other one, Roche—?"

Roche ceased stamping, but found himself beyond any sort of answer. If it was *the other one* he'd *taken*—he didn't know where, or why, or who even—then there was no answer to give—

The torch left him again, answered by his silence.

"Jilly?"

"Yes, David." Jilly was leaning against the wall, by the door.

"Get Mike up the stairs—see what you can see outside, between you—but keep down and be careful. Okay?"

Roche cancelled out the lack of paraffin in the lamp: the big man was thinking for all of them, in an attempt to salvage something out of chaos.

"Okay, Jilly?" repeated Audley, projecting encouragement at the girl.

She stared into the torch beam. "Lexy, David—"

"I know. But you go with Mike, there's a good girl. Roche and I will see to Lexy."

Lexy?

Roche cast around in the darkness helplessly. There was the faintest light coming down the stairway from above, where the trap-door must be open. But it was only enough to indicate a pattern of the stairs where the wine rack ran up the wall beside its uppermost treads.

Lexy—

"Go on, Jilly." The voice and the torch both directed her from the door across the shambles, to where Mike Bradford was already raising himself up to meet her, with a mixture of grunts and curses.

Roche started to feel his way off the carpet, vaguely orientating himself into the quarter of the compass Audley had left dark.

"Wait!" Audley hissed at him, while still directing the ill-matched couple up the lower half of the staircase, until they could see their way for themselves.

"All right, Roche." The torch at last into the forbidden quarter, on the edge of a glistening pool of wine.

Lady Alexandra had chosen a simple white dress in which to welcome back Captain Roche from his so-important duties. But it wasn't all-white any more.

Nor would Lady Alexandra ever again be the flawless English rose, matching those in her father's garden: an unaimed bullet or a flying splinter of glass had scored her cheek to the bone, masking half her face with blood.

"Oh God—Jesus Christ—what have I done?" whispered Roche, lifting her up into his arms. "What have I done?"

"You haven't done anything, man!" snapped Audley from above him. "Or not that wouldn't have been worse if you hadn't done anything—put her down—you're only making her bleed worse!"

The shortened beam had dropped from the face to the spreading patch of blood below her shoulder, which oozed freshly as Roche stared at it.

"Here—press that against it—*hard*—" Audley dropped a large silk hand-kerchief directly on to the mess "—I'll be back in a moment—press it down hard, man!"

The torch beam shifted again, more on Roche than the girl, so that he looked up involuntarily into the light even as he pressed the handkerchief into a ball over the wound. Audley had wedged the thing into an empty space in the rack, just at his eye-level.

"Audley? Where the hell have you gone?" The torch blinded him again, but as he opened his mouth to protest he felt the girl squirm under his hand.

"*Ouch!* Mind what you're doing—you're *hurting* me!" Her voice was surprisingly strong. "David! *David*?"

He couldn't reach the torch to free himself from its beam. "It's all right, Lexy darling—just lie still."

"Then stop hurting me! . . . Golly! You *do* look a mess! What on earth have you been doing to yourself?" Doubt weakened the voice. "Your face is all bloody—!"

Roche was aware that his face was smarting. "I scratched myself on a bramble-bush—*Lie still*."

"No you didn't!" Doubt shifted to urgent certainty. "They came in—the men from the woods—I said they would! And they wanted you—they wanted something you'd got, I think . . . and they made us wait. There were two of them, David—where are they?"

He could hear Audley's feet on the staircase. "It's all right, Lexy. Just lie still, Lexy darling."

"No—it isn't all right—" Her voice weakened "—there were two of them—and they wanted it, whatever it is . . ."

Roche remembered the brief-case. It was out there somewhere, in the shambles alongside the man whose head he had hammered into a pulp.

"She's conscious, is she?" Audley recovered his torch. "Good."

But then he moved away into the smoky darkness, knocking clumsily on obstacles and crunching on debris.

"What are you doing?" cried Roche.

"I'm scavenging for weapons." The light searched the wreckage. "All we've got is Mike's gun, but there are two here somewhere . . . and the man you clobbered still has a full magazine . . . which is more than Mike has . . . *Ah!*"

He would see the brief-case.

"Now for the other one," murmured Audley. "Got it!"

"What the hell's happening?" said Roche.

"Yes . . . you may well ask!" Audley picked his way back. "It would seem . . . that we made a rather serious error of judgement somewhere along the line . . . a most regrettable error . . ." He knelt down beside Roche. "How is she?"

Roche looked down. Above the mask of blood her eyes were closed again, but he could feel her chest rising and falling under the pressure of the sodden handkerchief.

"Was there an exit wound? I don't think there was . . ." Audley stuffed a huge pistol into his waistband alongside a smaller one, and felt gingerly under the girl. "No . . . fortunately it was your man who had the cannon, and you were just too quick for him . . . but unfortunately we don't really know the angle of entry, and that's what matters . . . Still, the Perownes all have constitutions like cart-horses—they bleed a lot, but they're notoriously difficult to kill off."

Roche stared at him speechlessly for a moment. "Damn you, Audley!"

Audley returned the stare. "Damn me if you like—but don't go soft on me, that's all. There are too many *fellagha* out there for that, and—"

"*Fellagha?*"

"That's right. Didn't you look at the man whose brains you beat out? There's a whole bloody *faoudj* of Algerian FLN out there—and they're not planning to go away empty-handed . . . I take it that you did get the thing from d'Auberon?"

"But—" Roche's brain whirled "—but it's got nothing to do with them!"

"You try telling them that! I did—when they came in to wait for you—and I got a clout across the face for my trouble." Audley touched his cheek.

"But *why*, for Christ's sake?"

"For Christ's sake—not for Allah's sake—d'Auberon was working on the Morice Line plans when he resigned. And with the Israelis here, sniffing around him—man, they've put two and two together and made five, that's what they've done—"

There might be some other people who could misunderstand the situation—the scales fell from Roche's eyes at last.

A most regrettable error of judgement—there had indeed been that, and it had been his own as well as Audley's . . . and Genghis Khan's too—or maybe Genghis Khan had more likely realised exactly who had killed Steffy, but had reckoned on the Comrades' ability to rein in the Algerians—and had also misjudged that situation.

"But we can't piss around with politics—we haven't the time," said Audley harshly. "An hour from now—or less if they've already got the stuff to hand—they'll blow in that door with a bit of *plastique*. And then it's just routine house-clearing—a grenade first, then they'll be in down here . . . and then they'll fire through the floor up above with automatic pistols. It isn't difficult, house-clearing . . . I've seen it done, believe me . . . and half these *fellagha* have been trained in the French Army to do it, what's more. All they need is darkness, and they'll have that soon."

In an hour from now Raymond Galles would come back.

Or maybe two hours—and Galles wouldn't be expecting a pitched battle . . . Roche felt hope extinguish within him.

"Give them the bloody brief-case, then." The words tumbled out, but they were the right words. The girl in his arms was worth more than the brief-case.

"No." Audley's rejection was uncompromising.

Roche's mouth dried up. "It isn't worth fighting for."

"It's worth fighting for."

Roche moved his arm slightly beneath Lexy's shoulders. If he stood any chance of jumping Audley he'd have to put her down first, and he wanted to do that as gently as possible.

But the movement betrayed him. Audley lifted the larger of the two pistols from his waistband quickly.

"Don't be silly, Roche."

It seemed to Roche that he had been silly all his life, and it was a bitter pain inside him that now at last, when he had stopped being silly, he had fluffed the transformation.

But there was still one last chance to make amends.

"It isn't worth anything." It was like the old soldiers said: no plan, however clever, survived its first encounter with real life. "I've worked for the Russians for years, Audley—ever since Korea. D'Auberon didn't give me his papers—*they did*. They know all about them . . . they ran the whole thing from start to finish. They've only given them to me now because it suits them. Do you understand?"

It was simpler than he had imagined.

"God bless my soul!" At another time, in another world, Audley's astonishment would have been comical. But now it was merely inconvenient.

"So you let me take it out. I can talk to them—I can tell them who I am . . . why I'm here. Right?"

The black hole of the pistol wavered, then steadied. "It won't do, Roche—I'm sorry, but it won't do!"

"Why not?"

"Because they won't believe you—that's why. Because you're a European—because we've killed two of their comrades . . . It won't even do if they believe you're KGB, because they don't trust the Russians either. What have the Russians ever done for them? At the best, they'll reckon we've given them something to delay them, while they look at it—and they'll take you apart to make sure. And they're good at that . . . they've had plenty of practice, right from Roman times."

All that was the truth—he knew it from his own knowledge, from the last report he had submitted—

French and Algerian FLN perceptions of Russian involvement and policies, with regard to the present situation in Algeria—his own work was arguing against him!

But not quite—

"Well—at least it'll delay them. And Raymond Galles is coming back here sometime—in the next hour or two. At least it's a chance, Audley."

The black hole was still unwavering. "Why?"

"Why what?"

"Why should I believe you—if you're a traitor?" The pistol jerked. "You could be delaying me now—"

"I'm not a traitor any more—I've done with that!" Roche felt the pulse of life under his hand. But that wouldn't do for Audley, even if it was true: Audley needed something he could recognise. "I don't belong to either side now—I choose for myself, and I say *I'll soldier no more*, and to hell with both sides—and all the other sides too!"

He looked into the pistol and the light, caring beyond calculation at last, finally free of everything which had bound him.

"All right." Audley's voice sounded strange. "But my way, not yours. Because whatever we do they won't leave us alive, even if we did give it to them."

"Your way?"

"There's a trap-door by the wall there—it's where the table is overturned. It leads down to a sort of cellar . . . the peasants who lived here years ago kept their chickens down there—there's a little hatch in the wall . . . it lets out into a ditch—not much of a ditch, but there are a few bushes there, and some nettles . . . You squeeze out there, and keep down flat, and keep going . . . If they have got a man covering the back he'll be in the trees away to your right, but he won't be looking for anyone, because he can't know about the chicken-door . . . Also, we'll be attracting their attention in the front—when you're ready to go we'll try to parley with them from up above. And if they think we're fool enough to trust them, that'll tempt them to delay, maybe."

"Parley?"

"That's right. They can't leave us alive, but if they can get in without making too much noise . . . and my French is bad enough to confuse them

255

. . . You go out there—a hundred yards down the ditch should be far enough—and then run like hell to Madame Peyrony's—get the police."

Roche's spirits lifted. "Yes—"

"But there's something else, then—" Audley offered him the pistol "—take it . . . and you'll need the torch too . . . just shift the table in front of me, and I'll take Lexy—that'll maybe give us some protection, if the worst comes to the worst . . . the something else is that you've got to come back, Roche."

"What?"

"To distract them. Because we'll be running out of time by then . . . So you come back as close as you can, and make a noise—flash the torch, fire the gun, shout 'A moi, la Légion!'—whatever you like, just so you distract them. You've got to win us *time*, man!"

With a terrible bleak self-knowledge, Roche knew that he wasn't quite done with treachery. Maybe here, with Lexy in his arms, and no choice . . . but not out there, in safety.

"Why don't you go?" He didn't want to put himself to the test. "You know the way."

The torch and the pistol were both thrust at him. "Don't argue—a hundred yards' crawl, and then turn left—and run like hell . . . you can't miss it, as the Irishman said." Audley paused. "Besides which, I can't get through the chicken-door—I'm too big. I was going to send you anyway, if you must know." Then he grunted half-derisively. "Don't argue, man—it's the only chance we've got. Go on—be a soldier this one more time, and we'll call it quits."

Under the trap door there was an undulating earth floor, dry and dusty . . . or maybe it was a thick layer of chaff and ancient chicken-droppings from the powdery texture of it, and the mixture of feathers in it, even though the smell had long gone.

He ploughed through the stuff, inches deep, towards the crude little door, following tracks already furrowed before him.

Could he really squeeze through that?

The detritus had been scooped away from it, to reveal its full size, and the rusty iron hinges had been oiled, but it still looked more like a chicken-door than a Roche-door.

He lifted up the latch, and then dowsed the torch before he eased it open, his hands trembling.

His head ached and the sweat poured down his face. He was long past thinking clearly, and nothing mattered any more: *this wasn't how it was meant to be, but this was how it was—*

He reached above him, at full stretch, and rapped the butt of the pistol on the flooring. Then he eased the door wide.

Cold air wafted around him, cooling the sweat on his face. He could just make out the stalks of weeds and vegetation ahead, black against paler blue.

Then he heard someone shouting, far away but insistently: Audley was drawing their attention to the front, as he had promised to do. So it was now or never.

He squeezed himself into the aperture, parting the weeds ahead of him as carefully and silently as he could with his hands, feeling his shoulders first compress, and then scrape, on the rough stone.

As his hips came through, and he knew that he was out and free, he held his breath. The shouting continued in the distance, only marginally louder than the beating of his own heart.

Through the weeds, and in between the thicker stems of some kind of bush . . . and then the shallow ditch opened up before him, half filled with coarse grass.

He wouldn't be able to stop that grass moving, yet it might not show above the top of the ditch, and the light was bad now—but was it bad enough?

Anyway, the man covering the back shouldn't be watching the ditch— they'd hardly have looked over the Tower expecting this sort of siege—

Siege? He examined the ditch again, and saw that although shallow it was wide—even wide enough to be the remains of a defensive moat round some petty *hobereau's* fortified manor, of which the Tower itself was the last relic. And the wideness encouraged him to make himself believe that it was deeper than it seemed.

He crawled—and crawled as he had been taught to crawl at OCTU, with the fear of Staff Sergeants above him.

And at last stood up, *and ran—*

He had not the slightest idea where he was at first, but Audley had said turn left, and somehow the geography of the ridge came to him as he ran—it curved into a re-entrant, such as the army map-reading experts loved—until there at last, black-towered among the treetops, was the Château Peyrony.

The gloomy woods didn't frighten him now, he was too breathless to be frightened, but the door wouldn't let him in.

He banged on it—hammered on it, starting up echoes which the house had never heard before, and went on hammering.

"M'sieur!" The old crone was outraged even before she saw his appearance. "*M'sieur—*"

He pushed past her, taking the stairs two at a time, scattering the house-ghosts headlong.

The light was glowing under the door, exactly where he remembered it—there was no need to knock—*she was expecting him—and not only because of the noise he had made, coming to her now—she had known all along that death was loose in her country—*

"Madame—"

She didn't move, she didn't turn a hair and she didn't interrupt him as he spoke, until—

"Gaston! Put that thing down—*at once!*"

Roche turned into the twin mouths of a shotgun, with his own pistol hanging uselessly at his side. The old man was breathing heavily—and, for God's sake, the old woman had something in her hand too, just behind him!

Madame Peyrony stood up. "Angélique: you will telephone the Police and tell them that Algerian terrorists are attacking the Englishman's Tower—they must come this instant. Then, you will telephone M'sieur Galles with the same message. *At once!*"

"Oui, Madame." The old woman didn't turn a hair either—she might just as well have received orders for supper. She simply vanished from the doorway.

In her place, with a scampering slither, a small boy appeared behind Gaston, wide-eyed and tousle-haired.

Roche drew in his breath. It was there, just as he had known it would be—the last treachery of all, deep inside him, where he had always known it would be, waiting for him.

He looked at Madame Peyrony. Nobody could do more, or more efficiently, than she was doing. And no one could blame him for waiting here with her for the distant sound of the police klaxon—he was only one man, and too far away from the Tower to get back there in time. Whatever happened now, there was nothing more that he could do.

"Yes, Captain?"

He could feel her read his mind, through every twist of his fears, right down to the bedrock of cowardice.

"I must go back to the Tower—to . . . divert them," he said thickly. "I promised."

"Of course." She inclined her head graciously. "How many of them are there . . . to be diverted?"

"I don't know." His mouth seemed full of pebbles. "But I must go now—at once."

"But of course." She nodded again. "So you must take the car—that will divert them."

"The car?"

"Petit Gaston—" she threw the command past him "—you will start the car for M'sieur le Capitaine. *At once*—and then attend your grandfather!" She came back to Roche. "It is complicated to start, so I am informed, but the child will do that for you."

Roche was momentarily diverted by the scampering sound behind him, and then by the look on her face.

"You have a weapon." She nodded down at his hand. "So you must do your best—as you promised."

He looked at her speechlessly.

"Off you go then!" Her voice became an order. "And, for your information, Captain . . . I have disliked that car for over twenty years—you understand?"

Roche went—it was as though he was moving in a dream—down the staircase, across the hall—into a darkening world eerily lit by light streaming out of the courtyard on the left of the door, which drew him towards it.

This wasn't how it was meant to be—

The Delaroche Royale was already alive and waiting for him, with huge headlights blazing, but only the faintest *thrumming* of the engine buried deep inside it.

The child swung out of the driver's seat, making way for him.

"How do I make it go?" He looked despairingly at the bank of instruments. "Where's the gear-lever?"

The child came up at his shoulder, standing on the running-board. "There is a switch—*there*—" he pointed "—and then m'sieur presses upon the accelerator pedal—down *there*—and then the brake is off, and she goes—"

Roche snapped the switch and felt for the brake—the monster was already moving—there was no gear lever—*Christ!*

The child dropped away. "*Turn quickly, m'sieur!*" he shrieked at Roche.

The wall on the other side of the courtyard was looming in the blazing light—Roche twisted the wheel in panic—his foot had hardly touched the accelerator pedal—the gateway of the courtyard came to meet him—*but too fast, and it was far too narrow—*

Something crashed ahead of him—scraped hideously alongside him—and then was lost behind. A whole wood of trees, sharply picked out in ranks by the searchlights, sprang into view on either side of the car: it was a steep drive, by the angle of the car—but not by the way the monster breasted it, without effort.

Turn left, along the ridge—he had done something wrong, so that the engine was roaring at him now, angry at his stupidity—

And he was going too fast, even though he didn't know why—the slightest touch on the accelerator made the monster go mad—and he had to turn off, down the Tower drive, the moment the trees thinned—and they were thinning already—*Christ!*

And—*Christ!*—there were figures dancing in the road—scattering left and right—

The last temptation was the worst of all, because it was the least expected: *he could put his foot down and drive for ever, and nothing this side of Hell could catch him!*

But he swung the wheel to the left with all his might instinctively, and jammed his foot down on the brake without consciously weighing up the temptation—*apt to make rash decisions under pressure* would have to do as an epitaph.

The monster tried to turn in a civilised fashion, but its weight and the laws of motion were against it: it slithered, and the wheels locked, and it lost control of itself, as Roche himself had already done. Trees—a tree—and bushes, and black space—and finally the Tower itself whirled in front of him, like a newsreel. Then it crashed sideways into something solid, half throwing him out of the soft body-fitting seat.

The engine stalled, but the lights still searched out every detail of the Tower—every small unevenness and shadow, everything pale bright yellow or black—and the cottage way past it, trailing creeper and blank windows, and a man throwing himself down out of the door—

He rolled down sideways as the window starred and cracked and burst in on him, even as the noise of the automatic weapon caught up with the sound of the shattering windscreen.

Everything went dark around him—inky black, pitch dark, after the brightness. He fumbled for the pistol, which he remembered out of the past—he had put it on the seat, ready to hand, as he had entered the car—

It wasn't there—he felt around for it—it wasn't there—*it wasn't anywhere*, and it was too late to go on searching for it.

The door on the driver's side had already burst open with the impact, so that his legs were sticking out of it; he pushed himself in the same direction, holding on to the wheel to enable him still to keep his balance as his feet felt the ground. But then standing upright no longer seemed sensible: *hit the ground* was what the Staff Sergeant always shouted—

He dropped flat, willing the earth to open up. But it was hard as rock under him.

Silence.

He lifted his head cautiously. It wasn't really night, he realised—not now that the bright light had been extinguished: it was almost night—there was a thick quilt of cloud high above him, illuminated by the moon far above the quilt . . . but he could still see too much, and could be seen too easily if he moved away from the shadow of the car.

The sudden sound of breaking glass broke the stillness. Then a sharper *crack*—the crack of a pistol—fixed the sound ahead and above: Audley had fired out of the high arrow-slit in the Tower, smashing the window first like the cowboys in the films.

Silence settled down again.

"You bastards down there!" An American voice rang thin but clear from above. "You just keep your goddamn heads down—okay?"

Bradford was buying time—and he was buying it in the belief that the crash or the burst of fire which had blacked out the lights had finished off Roche's rescue attempt, and Roche himself with it.

As a diversion, he had started well, but he had screwed everything up after that—as usual, Roche summed himself up. Madame Peyrony would expect better of him than that. And Lexy too—if the Perownes died hard, *then what about the Roches?*

Out here in the open he was lost anyway. As soon as one of the *fellagha* snaked up close enough . . . it was only pure accident that one of them hadn't spotted him already . . . and it was only a matter of time before his time ran out on him. He had nothing to lose any more—he had had it all, but he had thrown it away, and for no reason that made sense now.

Silence.

But *not* silence: he could hear sounds building up all around him. They were moving in on him at last, and it was too late for heroics.

He pulled himself upright against the wing of the Delaroche. He ought to do something, but he couldn't think of anything to do. *It seemed a silly way to die*, was all he could think.

"Oh . . . *shit!*" he said angrily to himself, but also to the world at large.

The spurt of flame registered in the ten-thousandth of the second before the impact of the bullet slammed him against the car.

A great light flowered in the sky above him—unearthly, as he expected it to be—but in a point of incandescence which reflected up to the clouds as well as down on the woods and the Tower and the car.

He stared at the light, somehow puzzled by it, and yet at the same time recognising it from out of the distant past.

A thunderclap burst vivid orange-red on the edge of the wood twenty yards away, silhouetting the man who had shot him as it exploded—the impact of the sound hit him like a second bullet, pressing him back on the car a second time.

Pain and understanding came together, as a second mortar-bomb exploded to his left, on the far side of the road. With disembodied interest he remembered that a good mortar-man would have half-a-dozen bombs in the air before the first one hit the ground, and the best mortar-man in the French Army could probably do even better than that, even allowing for three-score-years-and-ten and only Little Gaston to help him—

As the third bomb landed a mixture of weakness and delayed instinct slid him down flat alongside the car. Its great bulk was comforting, and the darkness beneath it enticed him to try to roll under it. But for some reason his body at first refused to follow the idea.

And when it did, he fell into a great black hole with no bottom.

EPILOGUE:

Soldier no more

OVER THE LENGTH of days, once the light ceased to hurt his eyes, Roche became obsessed with the ceilings above him.

The first had a complex tracery of shadows, the design of which he could never quite unravel as it floated above him; then there were dark bars which made him think of prisons, giving him terrible nightmares interspersed with faces, mixed up with a succession of confusing events. But after that there were several happy days, when a ceiling with interesting cracks and stains appeared above him, which he transformed into the islands and continents of a new world to be circumnavigated on voyages of discovery, with the far-off sounds of creaking masts and rigging, and the changes of watch in his ears to mark the passage of time.

Finally they pricked his arm to cancel consciousness, and he awoke to birdsong, and the knowledge of good and evil, and a plain white ceiling without shadow or blemish; and shortly after that he was allowed to look around, and then to sit up and see walls, and tree-tops through the window; and he was back in England again with a nurse to prove it, soft-voiced but business-like, plumping his pillows.

In fact, it was a very nice room, dazzling and well-furnished and airy. What he didn't like about it, which was different from the French rooms, was its absolute silence except for the bird-song, with none of the French bumps and bangs and distant traffic noises which he remembered in retrospect; from all which he deduced that they had him tucked away in one of their secret places; which didn't surprise him, now that he had failed to die on them, but also didn't reassure him.

And, having deduced that, he concluded then that there was really no point in asking anything of his nurse, or of the basilisk sister who superintended her; and the doctors themselves were of course even more out of the question, whatever the question was. So he retreated into the wasteland within himself, knowing that he wasn't going anywhere, and that they would come when they were ready, which would be when he was ready, and there wasn't anything he could do about it.

Only it was Audley who came; and, more surprisingly, he came alone, towards the end of an Indian summer's afternoon.

"Are you all right?" Audley mistook his surprise for weakness, by the inflexion he gave to the routine inquiry.

"I'm fine," said Roche. It occurred to him out of habit that he could spin out the game by pretending not to be fine, but he quickly dismissed the notion as ridiculous. He had nothing with which to play games any more, besides which there were things he wanted to know very badly which Audley of all people might actually tell him.

Or, at least, there was one askable thing, which protruded out of the oily surface of both his daydreams and his nightmares.

"How's Lady Alexandra?"

"Disgustingly healthy." Audley still smiled that lop-sided smile, but there was something different about him nevertheless: part of it was greater self-assurance, in so far as that was possible, yet there was also something hesitant, which was new. But that might be because he wasn't used to sick-rooms; or it might just be in the confused eye of the beholder.

"Really?" He dropped the irrelevant thought to concentrate on the important one. "Honestly?"

"Really—honestly." Audley pulled up the chair. "I told you—the Perownes are practically indestructible by conventional means—they're all built like Tiger tanks. In fact, she's even making the most out of her scar, Lexy is . . . she tells all and sundry that she got it duelling at Heidelberg. *In fact* . . . I've got a letter from her for you somewhere—" but he made no move to produce the letter "—are you sure you're okay? The dragon-lady out there said I mustn't be too long . . ."

So the letter had to be earned, and the game had to be played even here, after the final whistle.

"Honestly . . . I'm fine." Roche jibbed at the prospect, but he wanted the letter. "Sister says . . . 'we' have been very ill, but 'we' are on the mend. It's just that . . . 'we' expected someone . . . different." Roche opted for the truth, for want of anything better.

Audley regarded him doubtfully. "Ah . . . well, *we* have a special dispensation from above—a bit of the old influence-in-high-places, old boy. There will be somebody along to de-brief you formally in due course, naturally. But not yet."

"De-brief me?" Roche wasn't surprised by Audley-with-influence-in-high-places. But he knew that self-confessed traitors weren't de-briefed, they were interrogated.

"Uh-huh." Audley fielded his doubts confidently. "Originally they were going to lock you up, and throw away the key. And they're not exactly well-disposed to you even now . . . naturally. But things have changed." He made a Caliban-face. "You'll have to resign your commission—and sign a lots of bits of paper . . . And you'll have to come clean on everything—eh?"

For five seconds Roche was beyond astonishment, then for a moment he was in nowhere. And after that he recognised the familiar features of the wasteland, which were cratered like any battlefield, and full of slimy things which he'd already imagined.

Audley's face was scrubbed of emotion now. "You *are* prepared to come clean?"

"To betray everyone, you mean?" Roche could smell himself, washed and re-bandaged that morning, in preparation for this.

The scrubbed face changed to one of unconcealed interest. "You really did mean it, did you—back in the Tower? Nobody's side?"

That was something Roche was still working on, to be adjusted according to circumstances. But it had happened by degrees, and irregularly, and also irrationally; and he wasn't at all sure that he could sustain it against the unexpected clemency which Audley appeared to be offering him.

But mercifully Audley didn't wait for him to resolve his dilemma. "Yes . . . well, as it happens, you don't have to worry too much about *them* . . . because by now they'll have run a mile in all directions—back to their Moscow *dachas* if they're lucky, I shouldn't wonder!"

Jean-Paul and Genghis Khan—

And Philippe? *God!* Philippe out of range of Paris didn't bear thinking about—that was greater punishment than Burgess and Maclean had had to bear, in swopping London for Moscow.

Audley nodded. "Yes . . . You see, Mike Bradford and I were a bit naughty really—we decided to re-write a bit of the script on our own account, after things went . . . not quite according to plan, you understand . . ."

Things? But there had been so many *things*. "Things?"

"Mike did the actual work. Because he had the best contacts—and also the CIA had seconded him to me, with a free hand, so it was no skin off his nose . . . But Fred Clinton agreed afterwards that it had its merits—putting it out that you'd worked for us all along, ever since Japan—sort of *double-double, toil-and-trouble*—and we had to do it quickly, to make it stick, for the maximum effect—do you see?"

Roche saw—or half-saw, with the fleeting image of every Comrade he had ever known, or ever half-known, running for cover as the disinformation about him spread—not just Jean-Paul and Genghis Khan and Philippe—*Christ!*

Again, Audley read his expression. "That's right! Nothing like it since father drank the baby's milk, and made the baby suck a large Scotch—blood and confusion everywhere! *And*, what's more, your erstwhile employers will be having the most awful doubts about all their other doubles—from Cambridge and Oxford onwards . . . . If you were a ringer, then what about *them*, eh?"

Roche saw again, and saw more. Because if the Comrades had noticed that he had become increasingly twitchy, this would now only confirm their retrospective belief that he'd been setting them up for the final *coup*—which only Gaston's last mortar-bomb had dislocated, as well as peppering him with bits of metal.

"Right?" Audley continued to misread him. "Besides which, we also told

Fred Clinton that you were dying. Which, to be honest, we thought you were when we pulled you out from under that extraordinary machine."

Roche lay back against his pillows, grateful for their support.

"And the virtue of that, from your point of view, is not only that *they* won't pursue you—because although they're rather down on traitors, they're curiously old-fashioned about patriots—but also Clinton himself will have to let you go now . . . In fact, he'll probably have to give you a medal and a pension, to make it all stick. But that's cheap at the price, with what he's got—you and the d'Auberon papers!"

Clinton?

You and the d'Auberon papers? Roche exercised the names weakly, trying to place them in the right order.

"The d'Auberon papers?"

"Them most of all. They were the whole point of the sodding operation—and you did a grand job of getting them! So it all came out right in the end, in spite of the unpleasantness at the Tower . . . which was all Clinton's fault, anyway—he was so bloody busy planting his rumours, it never occurred to him that the Algerians and the Israelis would pick up the wrong signals, and get stuck into poor old Etienne! But all's well that ends well, anyway."

Roche recalled Latimer's assessment of Audley. "But not for Miss Stephanides."

"Ah . . ." Audley screwed up his expression ". . . now that was jolly strange, you know."

"Jolly strange?"

"Yes. The eighth deadly sin—in that French film about the seven deadly sins—remember?"

Roche set his teeth. "No."

"Suspicion—you must remember? To see sin where there is none? One of our occupational diseases too. We had the report a week ago—it really was a genuine accident. The poor girl always did drive too fast, and something important in that old car of hers broke." Audley waved his hand vaguely. "Besides which, some wretched Algerian the French interrogated said he thought you'd done it, and that was why they'd zeroed in on you—seeing you collect the brief-case merely clinched what they'd suspected was going to happen after that. Only they were convinced it was the Morice Line blueprint, of course."

"What did the French do?"

"They weren't frightfully amused. But by the time it dawned on them that there was something not quite kosher going on I'd swopped your *bastide* notes for the real stuff. And d'Auberon then insisted that he hadn't broken his agreement with them . . . which was nothing less than the truth, after all. So all they were left with was a terrorist outrage against innocent tourists and a lot of nasty suspicions. The only real trouble we had was getting you out . . . they did rather want to take you to pieces to see what really made you tick. Or *who* made you tick. But your SHAPE status gave us the edge there in the end."

A hideous suspicion had been spreading inside Roche, much nastier than anything French security could have imagined. "You knew . . . about me?"

"Oh yes—Clinton did. From way back."

"From way back?" The steadiness of his voice surprised him.

"From Japan onwards—it was the company you kept, you see. That's why you never got any decent jobs . . . only the ones where we were already compromised—or when we wanted something passed on . . . In fact, in a way, getting the d'Auberon stuff was the first really important job you were ever given. Clinton had to have it, but he knew Etienne would never give it up—not to us. But he also knew there had to be a copy snugged away in the KGB files in Paris. The trick was to get you to winkle it out—from them or d'Auberon, it didn't really matter which. But he reckoned you could do it—he's a lot like King Gaiseric of the Vandals, really . . . and in more ways than one, too." Audley smiled. "Sitting there, waiting for the winds to carry his fleet to the country that God desired to ruin, I mean. Only, like King Gaiseric, Fred Clinton was pretty damn sure which way the wind ought to blow, that's all."

It wasn't as bad as he'd expected, it was much worse. But he had to blank out the pain before it became unendurable in order to press his questions while Audley was willing to answer them. "I was set up—from the start?"

Audley nodded. "Very comprehensively. And he had all sorts of other things going to back you up—rumours dropped, bits of information available . . . people briefed to say the right things—"

The pain *was* unendurable. "People?"

"All sorts of people, yes—"

"Who?"

"Stocker . . . people you've never met . . . me, latterly." Audley shrugged. "Lots of people."

"Major Ballance?" The thought of Bill despising him was horrible, yet not the unkindest cut because it was Bill's job to screw the enemy. But he couldn't bring himself to the worst straight away.

"I think he had the general task of looking after you—yes." Audley seemed unaware of the damage he was doing.

Roche's chest itched under the bandages, with the wounds of every single mortar-bomb fragment registering individually.

He gritted his teeth. "Major . . . Mr Willis?"

Audley frowned. "I think . . . I think he was just ordered to answer your questions. But—"

"Jilly?" The itch was graduating to discomfort.

"No. She had her instructions, that's all. Only, about old Wimpy—"

"Colonel Stein?" Roche didn't much care about the Israeli, and Bradford must be career-CIA and didn't matter. But he still couldn't work himself to *her*. "Where was he?"

269

"At the Tower?" Audley shrugged again. "He was away somewhere taking his prehistoric pictures." He shook his head. "Davey's got nothing to do with intelligence—never has had, never will have. Davey takes pictures and flies planes. He's just a very nice man, and a good friend of mine."

The discomfort became physical pain, joining the agony inside his head as he came to her at last. "Lady Alexandra?"

"Lexy?" Audley looked at him incredulously. "Oh, come on, man! Lexy couldn't keep a secret—or obey an instruction—if her life depended on it! And you were an *ultra* secret—Clinton couldn't take chances on you, for God's sake!"

The pain abated just when it was beginning to blur his vision. *Lexy didn't know*—

"Besides which, Fred didn't dare give you everything on a plate. The whole aim was to let you come to your own conclusions, to work things out for yourself—to get at the truth in your own way—"

"The truth?"

"Ninety per cent of it, yes! All the best lies are made up of truth—that's what makes them stick—nothing else will do . . . So almost everything you were given was *true* . . . as well as almost everything you were allowed to find out—" Audley leaned forward, his face twisted into a curious expression, half sly and half shy "—the risk was that you'd see clear through to the other side. And that's why you had to be hindered as well as helped—right?"

"Hindered?" Roche was sweating with relief about Lexy.

"*Side-tracked* is better. That's why they gave you *me* to get your teeth into, don't you see?"

With an effort, Roche shook himself free of her. "You?"

"Uh-huh. You see, Fred Clinton has these tame psychologists he sets great store by . . . and they said, after they'd had a bloody good look at you, that you had to be given something to divert your attention—like 'give him an interesting tree to study, and he won't see the wood itself', roughly. And I was the tree." Audley's eyes narrowed. "So was I really interesting?"

"Interesting?" Roche lay back, and played for time. Audley had never really accounted for his presence here, ahead of the professional debriefers. Nor, for that matter, was there any professional reason why he should pile up indiscretion on indiscretion like this . . . But, with Audley, there always had to be a reason.

"Just idle curiosity." Audley patted his pockets, as though looking for a cigarette or his pipe. But he didn't smoke.

"I'm sorry?" Roche plucked at the coverlet with his hand, trying to win another minute.

"I'm wondering if the head-shrinkers were right, that's all, Roche." He didn't smoke, and he was too casual, so the pocket-patting was to remind Roche about a certain letter.

"It's not really very important," said Audley. "I merely wondered what you'd dug up—if it was interesting."

So there it was. And of all the things that were not important, this was genuinely unimportant. But everyone had an Achilles-heel, even Audley . . . and even though he'd challenged the world by hanging a picture of it on the wall of his home for all to see, as though it didn't matter.

"I didn't have enough time to put you together," said Roche carefully. All the best lies were mostly truth, after all.

"No?" Audley only just failed to conceal his relief. "Well, that was part of the strategy, of course. Clinton wanted to keep your people a bit off-balance all the time. That's why we stirred Mike Bradford into the pot."

Roche nodded. He could see now where he was safe. "And all that stuff about Antonia Palfrey? But that wasn't all moonshine, was it?"

"Well . . ." Audley bridled. "Not quite all. Bradford's Hollywood people do want to dig her out—that's all above board and checkable."

"And Antonia Palfrey?" Roche could feel the ground firm under him: a lot of valuable effort, both his own and that of the Comrades, had been devoted to Miss Palfrey. "She's checkable too?"

Audley grimaced happily.

"So you really did write *Princess in the Sunset*?" Roche pretended to be not quite absolutely certain.

The grimace completed itself as Audley nodded. "But that's not for public consumption, Roche. Because after the publication of *The Winds of God* next spring Antonia Palfrey is going to fade away gracefully . . . but permanently. Is that understood?" Audley simulated grimness.

"I'm not really in a position to argue, am I?" Roche led him on.

"Not really." But Audley still hadn't got what he wanted. "But what else did you discover—that was interesting?"

They had come to it finally, thought Roche. "I discovered that your legal guardian—your *former* legal guardian . . . Willis—Wimpy? . . . that he can talk the hind leg off a donkey—that's what I discovered." He sighed. "But I couldn't understand much of what he was saying."

"No?"

"No." He shrugged painfully. If it meant so much to Audley, then the less said the better—as Wimpy himself would have put it! "I never did come close to realising that you were already working for Sir Eustace Avery, if that's what you want to know."

All the best lies were still mostly truth. And even the Comrades, with all their resources, had failed abysmally there, so he had no reason to feel ashamed.

"For *Avery*? Good God, man—I've never worked for him!" Audley relaxed into derision. "You were sent to recruit me—don't you remember?"

"What?" But he couldn't have been further deceived, surely?

"Are you all right?" Audley half rose from his chair. "Your dragon-lady nurse said I mustn't stay too long—?"

"No! Don't go . . ." Lies and truth swirled inextricably before him. "I think I'm just beginning to feel totally humiliated."

Audley perched himself on the edge of the chair. "But . . . my dear chap—you don't need to feel that. It wasn't your fault—the odds were stacked against you. Actually, you did rather well, all things considered."

"I mean . . . I don't even understand what you're talking about any more." Roche looked down, and saw his hand shake on the coverlet.

"And *I* mean you don't need to be humiliated. I've never worked for Avery."

There was no more time now than there had ever been to sort things out—lies from truth, doubt from certainty. "But you did work for the British?"

"Up to '46. But then I had this big row, like I told you. And you couldn't possibly know that I put things together differently after Cambridge—that was when I went to Clinton and asked to be taken back—"

Taken back?

Taken back?

"—he was the only one I knew. And Archie Forbes sent me . . . But Clinton wouldn't have me—not then. He said the bad times were coming, and the service was compromised . . . 'let me tuck you away for a rainy day' was how he put it, for when he needed me, when the time was ripe . . . So he and Archie laid everything on after that—how I should refuse them in public, and how they'd stick the Russians on to me, to make matters worse, so they'd be sure I was fed up with both sides after what had happened in '46 . . . So I became a sort of 'sleeper-in-reverse'—that's how Archie put it . . . on a private feudal arrangement between them and me, with nothing in writing—*they* spread the word, and *I* went to ground, to wait the bugle-call. Do you see?"

Roche saw, but still didn't see.

"The trouble was, I needed money," said Audley. "In fact, I needed it rather badly at the time, for my house as well as my expensive Cambridge tastes . . . Only they wouldn't give me the Cambridge fellowship I wanted—Clinton said it wouldn't pay well enough, but I rather suspect they thought that once I'd got it I'd never come back into Intelligence . . . So he had this American friend of his—ex-OSS—who was a literary agent, and who owed him a favour from '45 . . . and I'd written this joke novel, just for fun, about Galla Placidia. So Mickey Tempest made me take out the jokes, and tighten up the dirty bits—and then he sold it for a bomb . . . . It was a bit embarrassing, what he did with it, but it did solve my cash-flow problems."

This time Audley wasn't pretending. And—*Lord God!*—he didn't have to pretend, either: what had happened was something unfair, which neither Clinton nor the Comrades could have allowed for—the perfect cover of a runaway best-seller! That must surely have disconcerted Clinton almost as much as it had deceived the Comrades, to loosen his grip on Audley . . .

272

"I must admit I've enjoyed all the money," said Audley simply. "Because I've done all the things I ever wanted to do . . . to my home, and all that . . ." He shied away from what *all that* implied, which Roche wasn't meant to know. "But I haven't enjoyed trying to avoid being that damned woman Mickey thought up—she's someone I'm really going to enjoy killing off, you know." He twisted a smile of pure mischief at Roche. "But not until *The Winds of God* are blowing in the bookshops next spring . . . because the more independent I am from Colonel F. J. Clinton, the more I shall like it, to be honest."

Audley being *honest* was something beyond Roche's imagination. But he could remember how he had relished his brief freedom from Genghis Khan, and the sense of no longer depending on anyone else, and that gave him a hint of what Audley's bank balance could do for another *soldier-no-more*.

And Clinton wouldn't like that much. And Clinton, Clinton, *Clinton* was what it all came back to with Audley—not *d'Auberon*, or even *Avery* . . .

"Clinton?"

Another chilly smile. "Now you're beginning to put it all together the right way! It was foxy Fred who picked up the whisper about d'Auberon's inconvenient report from his German friends in Gehlen in the spring— because they really *do* have a man in Moscow . . . or they *did* have, because they must have pulled him out after they leaked the Stalin denunciation before the Twentieth Congress to the Americans . . . So Fred had the details, but what he needed was the real thing, because he had to have tangible proof—"

"Why?"

"My dear fellow! Avery was just getting the job he wanted—the job he deserved—with him as Number Two Dogsbody . . . which was what he *didn't* want. But Avery was *king* after Suez, and Fred couldn't screw him without d'Auberon's report—and d'Auberon wouldn't give it to him . . . and that was when he remembered *me*—and *you*!"

Clinton, Clinton—*Clinton!*

"I was just finishing *The Winds*—and my real book, on Charles Martel— down near Carcassone. And that's where I got the call at last, after six fat years—to go and settle on the Dordogne and renew my old wartime anti-pathy with Etienne, when we were supposed to be on the same side, more or less . . . by which time I was so bloody fed up with fucking around, if he'd asked me to escalade the Château du Cingle d'Enfer single-handed I'd have tried it . . . Instead of which I chatted up Madame Peyrony again, and bought the Tower for twice what it's worth—not on expenses, either—"

Truth.

And lies and lies and *lies*—

"You never did have a copy of d'Auberon's report?" Audley had already told him that twice over, but he wanted to hear him say it aloud just once.

"Christ! D'you think Etienne would have given it to *me*, of all people? That'd be the day!" The question hurt Audley. "I didn't even want you to *talk* to him—I thought that was where it would all go wrong . . . But Fred Clinton reckoned the KGB would be so mad-keen to plant the stuff on Eustace Avery that they wouldn't risk involving Etienne—not if they could get you promoted at the same time . . . What he said was that they were bound to take the risk, for the profit, so we could take the risk too, and then Avery's goose would be cooked." The accuracy of Clinton's forecast seemed to hurt him as much as the original question. "So he was right—and I was wrong—okay?"

Avery's goose.

Clinton had known all along that the d'Auberon papers were useless—except for the damage they would do to Avery. But Avery himself hadn't known that—any more than he'd known that Audley was already Clinton's man . . . 'on a private feudal arrangement'!

"So what's happened to Avery?"

"He resigned four days ago," said Audley.

All along Clinton had been gunning for Avery, and the Comrades had supplied him with the ammunition he needed.

"Full of honours, and with several succulent jobs on well-paid boards in the City," continued Audley. "But just in time, before they sacked the bugger . . . What did you expect?"

Roche tried hard to look wiser than he was. But of course it wouldn't be a bullet-behind-the-ear for Sir Eustace Avery, whatever it might be for Genghis Khan. It was Captain Roche who had had all the luck, even though he still didn't quite know why.

"So we're under new management now: *F. J. Clinton, sole proprietor*—and *Sir Frederick* in the next New Year's Honours, if I'm any judge of the government's well-placed gratitude for hushing things up."

A lot could happen between the Queen's birthday and the New Year—Bill Ballance always used to say that.

"Which, to do him justice—and the government justice—is fair enough. Because he'll be a damn good *sole proprietor*, not like Useless Eustace . . . And also because the bloody Russians need taking down a peg—which you of all people ought to understand, Major Roche—eh?"

Roche thought of the Comrades as Russians—not for the first time, but more clearly: *Russians*, not *Comrades* . . . not with their union of socialist republics, but with their groaning colonies stretching from Hungary to the deserts of Asia and the Himalayas, where Kipling had played his game once upon a time, and Audley had learnt Kipling's rules.

And he also recalled Genghis Khan's confidence, at the prospect of fooling the stupid British again: as much as anything—as much as F. J. Clinton's clever plans—that over-confidence had confounded the Russians.

"You do, don't you?" Audley read his expression. "They've done so bloody well of late that they're chancing their arm too far for comfort—that's what Clinton relied on. But some of the things they've been doing have been positively dangerous, and that was my best argument for not

274

using you to play games with them—better that we should call a halt, and shut them up for a bit, so we can both catch our breath. Better to clear the board and start again from scratch."

That put the record straight, but it hurt nevertheless. "And that's why I'm getting off the hook, is it?"

"With a medal—and a disability pension, *Major?*" Audley's lip curled. "Free and clear? Don't be ungrateful, *Major!*"

The *Major* twisted in the wound, and so did *free and clear*: he might become the former, but even if he found a place to teach *être* and *avoir*, and the kings and queens of England, he would never free himself from what he had been.

"But not just that." Audley stared at him for a moment, and then rose from the chair and moved towards the window.

Roche waited, watching Audley peer outwards and downwards at the lawns and flower-beds which he had never seen, which lay below the tree-scape he could see from his bed.

"Madame Peyrony sends her regards to you . . . Her regards, but no apologies for the mortar-barrage . . . I rather think she takes the view that if the Choosers of the Slain didn't have your name, then it's no business of hers. She's seen a lot of men die in her time, has Madame . . ."

That was the truth, and maybe more so than Audley imagined.

"But she thinks well of you . . . Whereas I don't think I can go so far as that." Something below him seemed to have caught Audley's attention, from the way he craned his neck to observe it. "In my book a traitor is a traitor."

The broad back-row-of-the-scrum rugger-playing back gave away nothing.

"On the other hand a debt is also a debt."

Roche experienced a curious déjà-vu feeling, but this time from inside the van, with his own wasps buzzing him.

"Because you did come back to us, at the Tower . . . and I didn't think you would . . ."

He could feel the cobweb-touch of wasps on his hand, where it lay on the coverlet like an old man's, with the veins raised on it.

"If I could have squeezed out through that damned hole, then I would have . . . But I couldn't, so I didn't have any choice . . . But you had a choice," said Audley to the garden.

Roche realised that Audley was talking about a debt of his own, not something Major Roche had left unpaid behind him.

"Also you warned d'Auberon. And I know that because I phoned him later that night, to tell him to lie low . . . But you'd already warned him. And you didn't have to do that either . . ."

Roche felt light-headed. "But you don't like d'Auberon—"

"No . . . Or, more accurately, we don't like each other—there's too much history between us, ancient as well as modern . . . And he's a most intractably honourable man, and he thinks I'm not . . . Perhaps he's right, too." The immense shoulders flexed under their width of expensive broadcloth. "Though, oddly enough, if he'd given me those wretched papers of his I'd never have turned them over to Fred Clinton—not in a thousand years . . ."

A thousand years?

It is knightly to keep faith—even after a thousand years!

Roche understood at last what he had never really believed until now. And more than that—that Genghis Khan had been right, and Wimpy had been right too: that Clinton was recruiting trouble—that where he had acted from some irrational urge which he still didn't understand, this man's code of conduct was already chiselled in stone, for better or worse, regardless of intelligent self-interest.

And d'Auberon too?

So the French and Clinton—and the British—had both got their bad bargains, to screw up the commonsense order of things . . . the French already, and the British in due course, as Genghis Khan had forecast—

But he was getting his benefit *now*, against the odds, because of it. And that was the only thing that mattered *now*, never mind a thousand years!

Audley swung round. "You probably don't understand a word I'm saying. But it's of no consequence, it's purely a private matter between me and myself."

He looked at Roche, and dismissed him, and started past the foot of the bed, but then halted with his hand on the door-knob, and turned back.

"The trouble with you, Roche, is . . . you've always been a victim—at least, right from the time that clever little Russian bitch fixed you up in Japan—and we've got a picture of her, large as life, in Dzerzhinsky Street three months after she drowned herself—Clinton has, anyway."

Beyond pain there was nothing. It wasn't very different from falling under a Delaroche Royale: *nothing* couldn't hurt—

"But you weren't a victim that evening—you were all your own man. So if anyone comes to you now, and tries to change that, I've given you more than enough to put them down—*right*?"

Nothing still couldn't hurt.

Audley almost turned away, into the doorway he had opened for himself, but then slipped his hand into his pocket before he could complete the turn.

"Don't let the buggers get you down, eh?" He flipped a letter on to the bed, beside Roche's hand.

Before he summoned up the strength to touch the letter, Roche saw that someone had already opened it for him. But that was to be expected.

It was funny about Julie: once it had been said out loud it was as though he had always known it, but had merely hidden it from himself as he had tried to hide so many other things. So the words had no echo: they were said and done with, leaving nothing more to say that he didn't already know.

276

My own dearest David—

There was a nice breathless Lexy-sound about her proposals for their future, even though she'd got him all wrong. But then so had Audley—and so had everyone.

Also . . . it did rather look as though he was about to become a victim again.

But this time round that didn't seem such an unhappy fate.